WYNTER ECLIPSE
STORM BLOODLINE SAGA

EMMY R. BENNETT

Dream Script Media LLC

14751 N. Kelsey St. Ste. 105 PMB 186

Monroe, WA 98272

ISBN: (pbk) 978-1-950501-19-9

ISBN: (Ebook) 978-1-950501-20-5

Visit website: erbennettbooks.com

HUMAN
AUTHORED
Authors Guild
6343273

WYNTER'S THOUGHTS

I feel a storm coming. It's close. Every detail is slowly falling into place, but I am overlooking something. Something big, and I can't quite put my finger on it. Cory is missing. Dragon-scale is missing. Eleena and Aunt Fran have vanished. And my mother used to whisper in my ear from time to time. Where is she? They're all quiet. Yes, it definitely feels like the silence before a storm.

I

SHIFT CHANGE

"I told you not to shoot, Rory! Now look what you got us into?" The dragon's swooshing wings are loud, and smoke still trails from its massive muzzle. Rory and I are in the grips of one talon while Redmae is in the other.

"So, sue me!" Rory wriggles to be free.

"Stop struggling before you kill us both!" The wind rushes through my hair and feathers against my face. I look over at Redmae in the other dragon claw. *"Hey, can you still hear my thoughts?"*

"Yes." I sense Redmae's frustration.

"Where do you suppose this beast is taking us?"

"To his nest, high in the clouds of course." If thoughts had tones, hers are quite clear. She is not at all pleased with our situation. *"I bet we're close to the Crimson Moors."*

The ruby red sky illuminates behind the cumulous clouds as lightning flashes behind them. A sign that a storm is on the rise. Thunder resonates forward after a second lightning flash bursts through the clouds. *"How can you be sure?"*

"It's just a feeling."

A volcano in the distance spews lava down the slopes and molten rock spits through the fissures. It's a similar view of Dragonscale Island but this isn't that place. It's much darker—more ominous. Looking down, charred trees and a desolate ground covered in ash brings me to think Redmae is correct and we're near the Crimson Moors. *The irony* of being hauled off across an endless bottom ravine in the grips of a dragon's talons isn't what I had in mind when I told Rory and Redmae to run.

Redmae disrupts my study of the lands below. *"Was this part of your master plan, Wynter?"*

"You mean being dragged away to be eaten by a dark dragon? Sure, why not... Don't be ridiculous, Red."

The dragon grunts. *"Relax, I'm not hungry.*

"Huh?" I look over at Redmae, confused. *"Did you hear that?"*

She growls. *"Yeah. Who are you? We demand to know how you're able to invade our thoughts."*

Rory continues struggling. "If I could just get my hands free!"

"In due time I shall tell you my secrets, but for now, I'd like to keep you guessing."

My left brow instinctively raises as if it has a mind of its own. *"Oh you're a spicy kind of sauce aren't you, beast.*

"Aw, did I get under your skin?" Our captor soars higher, with a rumbling chuckle that permeates our thoughts.

The laughter gets under my flesh, and an uncontrollable response kicks in. My muscles burn. First, it's itchy then the hairs on my arms prickle. Scales form slowly, a clear warning that I'm about to transform. *I'm not supposed to shift.* If I don't reach my medicine soon to curb this impulse, it could mean we all die. I won't be able to catch either Rory or Redmae from falling to their deaths.

Scales on my forearms continue growing, creeping up my

arms to my elbows. The feeling that my bones are about to twist and break into wings has me bursting into a scream.

"Is everything alright?" the beast asks.

"Why do you care?" I bite back, as I try to push the pain away.

"Wynter, take your meds before you shift and kill us all," Redmae says.

"Ya think? What a great idea, Red." I grunt as the burning pain increases and travels through my veins. *"I can't reach them."*

"Medicine, you say?" the dragon, says.

"Mind your own business, beast!" My anger grows. This monster has my hands locked in tight.

The dragon snorts letting out a blast of smoke. *"I'm not a monster! As you can see. I'm a Dra—"*

"I said shut it!" The rage in me boils, almost to a breaking point. *"Loosen your mangy talons."*

"Again, with the name calling...it's not necessary..." our kidnapper continues to glide higher.

Redmae growls, looking up at the flying beast. *"You heard the lady. Release your grip. She can't reach her medicine bottle. It will keep her from shifting. Unless of course it was your plan all along to drop us to the depths of the abyss below?"*

The dragon snorts.

"You'd be wise to listen to her. I've seen her bite, and it's lethal." I keep a steady breath and look over at Red through the pain.

"Yes, I know. It is said a dire wolf is quite the foe if given the chance. And I am listening. I'll loosen my grip but don't blame me if you end up falling. I won't be able to save you or your friends." The dragon blows more steam through its nostrils while climbing higher through the heavy clouds. *"So... feisty."*

I hear through our telepathic thoughts, another growl

rumble from Redmae's throat. *"And you're taking too long to act."*

The dragon rumbles back. *"Fine."*

The grip loosens. Slipping a hand to my inside pocket I grab the temporary antidotal medication and take a quick swig. Instantaneously the scales on my arms fade and the burning subsides. *"Thank you."*

"Thank me later when we're out of danger." He flies across the vast canal separating one cliffside from the other. Ocean waves crash against the rocks below. Sea birds fly lower near the cliffs signaling concerns to their fellow fowl that danger approaches—us.

"Are you saying you're not the danger?" Redmae grumbles again.

The dragon chuckles.

"Where are you bringing us to?" I tuck the medicine bottle back into my pocket. *"Clearly you have a motive."*

"Aw yes, the presumption that you think I'm bringing you home to dinner. I hardly know you. So, clearly you have the wrong idea. That's like third date status," the dragon answers.

Redmae tries to hide her snorting chuckle.

"Not the answer I was expecting, but okay I'll play. You're not my type!"

"Say it isn't so!" the dragon mocks.

"You still haven't answered my question."

The beast sighs. If that's what that was. It was more like a cough of defeat. *"Somewhere safer than where we are now."*

Rory continues to struggle. "If I can get one hand—"

A loud thunder-like crackle strikes behind us, followed by several roars.

"I was afraid this would happen," the dragon says.

An arrow whizzes between the dragon's hind legs, nearly hitting me. "What the—" I turn around. "Dark dragons!"

Rory turns with me.

"Hang on." The dragon climbs even higher than before. *"We need to get past the clouds and hide in plain sight."*

"You knew they were coming?" I ask.

"I suspected they would, yes."

Rory continues to squirm. "Wynter, I need my hands. If I can reach my arrows, I may be able to shoot back."

I look up at our kidnapper. *"Hey, genius, did you hear her? Rory's a good shot, you know."*

"Yes, I do know. Let me gain some distance first. Hang on to your cookies." He glides upward sharply.

"What do you mean you know?" I squint. Something isn't adding up with this guy. The dragon's abrupt ascension grabs at the pit of my stomach. Bile creeps up my throat.

"Breathe," he says. *"And don't focus on your stomach. That's the secret to avoiding a mess you'll regret."*

We're cut off by a second arrow that bounces off the dragon's scales. Our *lizard friend* roars.

"Dragon! Loosen your grip and let Rory shoot!" I continue to fight the nausea and manage to focus on my inner magic. Fire and ice.

"Fine, but only enough for her to do that. One wrong move and I'll be forced to drop all of you."

I nod. *"Yes, I understood all warnings you've said before."*

The dragon grunts again. *"Now, let me concentrate before we all die."* The beast pushes through the dark crimson clouds to a clearing in the sky and turns around facing the way we just came from. *"A surprise attack is always a bit helpful, don't you think?"*

There's a worried look on Rory's face. "Wynter, what is this creature doing?" The dragon loosens its grip just enough to free her hands. She grabs two arrows from her quiver set.

"Focus, Rory, and get ready." I form a fireball in one palm. "The dragon thinks a surprise attack will end our chase, so get ready to shoot."

Rory takes aim at the cumulous cluster before us. We wait patiently. The silence is daunting. "Where are they?"

"Hold steady, I can hear them. Be on guard," the dragon answers, as though Rory can hear its thoughts.

"Be ready, Rory. They're coming." I ignite my fireball to grow a bit larger.

Trusting my information, Rory takes her cue and aims.

A loud roaring sound comes from behind the clouds in front of us. The dark dragons burst through, followed by a swirl of red, with fire blazing from their mouths.

"Shoot, Rory!" I throw my first fireball at the dark beast, and it does nothing, showering them with flakes of ash.

Rory's arrows make a direct hit with two quick shots. One slams into the rider, knocking him off while the other arrow lands dead center in the heart of the dragon. The beast disintegrates into a cloud of raining dust-like residue. I quickly slam the second dark rider with a fire blast pushing him off his mount and sending him free falling, which distracts the his dragon to go after him.

"It isn't over, there are more coming." Rory takes up two more arrows, nocking both on the bow at the same time. She targets the dragons first, this time with two quick shots, landing a direct hit to the center of both dragons' chests. They diminish into dust leaving the riders free falling to their deaths.

Stunned, I ask, "Rory, the scales are too thick to penetrate past the dragon's shell. How are you doing that?"

She grins and blows on the shaft. "Arryn gave them to me. They're specifically designed to kill a supernatural such as yourself." She winks.

A chill runs up my spine. "Not funny, Rory."

More dark dragons emerge. These ones are enraged, spewing green fire of darkness.

"We need to get out of here. Hang on! This one might make you a little queasier than the last one."

"I don't know if I like the sound of that." I look at Redmae.

She responds with criticism, *"I hope you know what you're doing."* Redmae is powerless to help in her wolf form.

The dragon chuckles and darts upward escalating higher, at higher speed than before. *"Trust me."*

"Hah! They will follow us, ya know."

As expected, the dark dragons pull in behind us at full speed.

"I'm counting on it." Our beast makes a full stop. *"Ready for some fun?"*

"Rory, I think this beast is about to do a nosedive. Get ready." I look above my head, watching the dark dragons speed past us.

"I like how you think, Wynter." The dragon dives at superspeed.

The frustration from the other dark dragons' roars echo through the clouds.

"I don't think we're going to lose them," I say.

"Perhaps not, but if we can get on solid ground maybe we will have a fighting chance. And you could shift." The dragon spins to make us dive faster.

"I think I'm going to be sick." Rory tucks her bow close to her.

My thoughts jumble. *The dragon knows I'm a shifter.*

"Of course I do!"

"I'm not supposed to shift."

"I don't think you have much of a choice. Do you not know how powerful you really are, Wynter?"

"Wait a second, who are you? You say my name as if you know me."

The dragon glides downward more, weaving through the thick clouds. *"Let's just say I'm like you. And leave it at that for now. These are no ordinary riders, and I don't have the time for details. I've seen them once before long ago and the memories were not pleasant."*

The frustrating roars of our enemies are lost within the crimson haze. We've gained a bit of distance.

"What do you mean no ordinary riders?" Redmae asks. *"Are you saying what I think you're saying?"* She looks over at me. Her eyes tell me she's concerned.

"What is it, Red?"

She grunts.

"These are Vothule's lackeys." The dragon turns around once we clear the clouds. *"Get ready for round two. This time I want you to use your ice powers."*

"Wait, how do you know about that?"

"I told you. We're the same, you and me. Now, quickly, they're close. If you don't want to be captured as his prisoners, I suggest you prepare that ice ball now, Wynter." He rears up his body to prepare for battle.

"Wynter, why is this beast turning around?" Rory asks, worried. Her bow and arrow are still in her hands.

Redmae grimaces.

"Wynter?" Rory questions again.

"Rory, just point, and shoot when ready."

"On it." She nocks two arrows on the bowstring for a second time and grins. "Watch and learn, my friend."

"Hah! Two can play this game." I form an ice ball as the dragon suggested. *"May I ask why ice?"*

"Ice or water of any form will burden them. Using fire will just make them angrier."

"Thanks for the tip."

Rory grins. "That's new."

I grin back. "New dark riders and I've been given new ideas on how to deal with them."

We wait for the dark dragons to clear the clouds again. The silence is intense.

Our protective beast roars a blast of blue flames toward our foes, surprising them as the dark dragons come into view.

Rory takes this opportunity and brings her eyes level with the bow. "One." Rory pulls back the string. "Two." It happened so quick that my brain didn't register her first kill shot let alone the second.

"Three!" I blast it with a frosty touch, but instead of the beast being encased in ice, they both blow up, blasting ash into the air. "Wait, a minute...that's not ash."

"Is that snow?" Rory looks at me for confirmation.

The dragon chuckles. *"Now you know why I mentioned the ice blast. Let's just say unfortunate past experiences help later on and leave it at that for now."*

"That's one way to get snow, I guess," Rory says.

"Let's get out of here before more come," the dragon says.

"More? You mean it isn't over?" I ask. I give Rory a worried look.

Her smile fades. "What is it?"

"If you haven't guessed, Wynter, it's never over," Redmae answers sarcastically.

I pierce a glare at Redmae. *"And why is that, Red? What are the two of you not telling us?"* I clear my throat answering Rory, "He said there will be more on the way."

"I'm taking this opportunity to cloak us. Do not cast spells or it will break our protection. The dark dragons seemed to have pulled back."

"Question is why?" Redmae asks.

"I don't know," the dragon answers.

"Wouldn't now be a good time to call Namari? He could get us to safety."

"Wynter, there was a breach at Dragonscale Island. Calling him might put us all in danger," Redmae answers.

The thought of Dad, Geneviève, Blair, and all the others

suddenly has my stomach in knots, again. I look over at Red. *"Do you think everyone is okay?"*

"We can only hope."

Rory glances to the other talon that tightly grips Redmae. "What is she telling you?"

I stiffen at the thought of being a prisoner in Vothule's dungeon. "That a shifter is never safe, Rory."

"And that's another thing, beast... How is it that you know I'm a shifter?"

The dragon grumbles in an amusing tone. *"I told you I have my ways. A dragon doesn't tell all their secrets. What's the fun in that?"*

The sky crackles, once again warning us we're about to have more company, indicating our conversation will be put on hold.

"Remember, no sudden movements. We are safe as long as we are cloaked," the dragon reminds us.

Rory pulls out an arrow.

I lower her hand. "Don't shoot. We're invisible at the moment."

Our dragon drifts closer to the ground where he flies across a ravine and drops us off in a strange area while we wait for the danger to pass. A pinkish haze crosses over us like fog. The trees are a blend of fir and maple with colors of oranges, yellows, and reds blending together like before when we ported into this creepy world.

The dragon releases us.

"How strange. Where are we?" Rory asks.

"The edge of the Crimson Moors," the dragon says.

"The Crimson Moors, apparently." I look a Rory.

"Is that what my sister said?"

"No, the dragon said it. It means we're close to Scarlet Hollow's Veil, too," I say.

"Did your dragon say that too?" Rory asks, sounding annoyed. "How do you know about the Scarlet Hollow Veil?"

"I dreamt it."

A swirl of white smokey fog swooshes in, distracting us, followed by a loud grumble. It's the outline of the dragon that kidnapped us. It sits in an upright position with smoke trailing from its nostrils. Its wings flap a few times, shaking off what looks like soot and ash, leaving behind shimmers of silver reflecting off the scales. *This isn't a dark dragon after all.*

2

THE SECRET IS OUT

Rory prepares her bow, ready to strike.

"Stand down." I put my arm in her line of sight. "I don't think this creature intends to harm us." I tilt my head. "I think they are one of us. I mean, this dragon did save us after all. Dark dragons, the evil ones, are all black with no other color on them. This dragon has silver coming from its scales." I point. "See?"

"Makes no difference, a dragon is a dragon," Rory says. She lifts her bow back to eye level.

"Ah, come on, Rory. After saving your behind, you're still going to shoot me?"

"You know she can't hear you right?" I say aloud.

"What?" she lowers her bow and looks at me, surprised. "So, you really can communicate with this beast?"

I shrug. "I can communicate with this dragon, apparently. Rory, not all dragons are the same. This one just saved our lives. Loosen up."

A whirl of wind forms, making a funnel cloud and we shield our eyes from the kicked-up debris. When the dust settles the dragon shifts, leaving in its place the figure of a man.

I squint. It's hard to see clearly, because wherever we've landed, it's dark, aside from the full moon glowing upon our heads.

The transformed human-like person stands sideways, with their hands facing outward. They flip their palms then pat themselves on the chest and shoulders, appearing stunned that they are no longer in dragon form. Nervous breaths express their concern. There's something familiar about them though. Their hair is platinum, and the shape of their body looks like... The frantic person turns toward us, stunning all of us.

"Cory?" *That's impossible. Cole sent him to Scarlet Hollow.*

"Well, imagine that. He's a dragon shifter after all," Rory says. "Cole's back from the dead."

I should feel shocked but somehow nothing astounds me anymore when it comes to the Storm family. "You know what this means, Rory?"

"That Cory must be a shifter, too," she answers.

"Well, this is a twist," Redmae remarks.

"Tell us, Cole, have you always been a shifter, or did you wait until today to spring this revelation on us?" Rory asks.

"That is a good question, isn't it?" He wrinkles his nose. "Honestly, I had no idea. And I wish I had an answer, but I don't."

"Ha!" Rory scoffs.

"Come on," he teases. "Didn't you like the suspense?"

"You mean you really didn't know?" I ask.

"Not until I rose from the ashes back there where Sarmira appeared," he says. "My question is what triggers the shift? I've never been a dragon before, so why now?"

"I, for one, want to know that answer as well." I look over at Rory. "Any ideas?"

She clears her throat. "Perhaps we can narrow down that your father was a shifter, Cole."

He shrugs. "Actually, I have no clue. Your guess is as good as mine. I'm assuming my brother doesn't know this amazing secret either. And we have never heard from our father. If only I knew who that was, it could possibly shed some light on the mystery."

I look at his watch. "Do you think the demon is gone?"

He looks down at his wrist. "As far as I can tell, yes."

Rory and I hold our stares, waiting for a better answer.

"What?" He tilts his head, looking at us confused.

"Oh, I don't know, Cole, perhaps you could've warned me while we were in the air, fighting off the dark dragons. That would have been a good time to say something," I say.

Anger and distrust show on Rory's pinched face. "You're wearing a watch." She tilts her head to the side.

"The watch Jeff was able to finally put on your wrist that was intended for you, years ago, and Moyer—Sarmira—is out of your head, and now, we're just supposed to trust you? Is that it?" I cross my arms.

"I can't hear *her*, if that's what you mean. The demon is gone. Not sure how, exactly. Doesn't matter whether you believe me or not. What matters is finding my brother." He looks at me. "I mean I assume you, of all people want him found." He pushes past us, walking toward the ledge over-looking the valley.

"Of course I do." I tail after him and pull at his arm. "Hey, Cole."

He flinches back still walking ahead of us.

"Is it so wrong that we question you? I mean I've only known your demon side. How are we to know you're truly back to your old self?"

He turns around, angry. His eyes glow bright blue. "Being burned to ashes might have given a slight clue, don't you think?" He looks over at Rory. "I assure you, if the demon still resided in me, I would have been a dark dragon and charcoaled all of you to a burning crisp back where I rose from ashes, of that, I'm sure."

"Cole?" I try to touch his shoulder.

"It's nothing. What's in the past stays in the past. Can't change it." Cole's lips tighten. "I don't want to talk about it." He changes the subject trying to lighten the mood. "Nice aim back there, Rory. I do have to admit, your bravery is commendable."

"Thanks...I think?"

"Hang on a second. You're not off the hook just yet. Why didn't you tell us you were a dragon shifter?"

"That is a good question, isn't it?" He gives a lopsided smile.

I stare him down, probing for an explanation.

He sighs. "I was going to bring you safely across the ravine and away from danger before revealing the truth." He looks up at the sky. "I wasn't given much time to explain. But hey, my secret is out. Now can we move on?"

"Okay, fair enough," Rory says, "but that doesn't explain why you tried to char us earlier."

He snickers. "Is that what you're so miffed about, Rory? You're still standing, are you not?" He pauses, walking up to her, stopping inches from her nose. "I didn't try and barbeque you. You must have some sort of memory loss in that tiny brain of yours. Didn't you see those prowlers were about to have you for lunch?"

"Insults won't break me, Cole. Why are you so nasty?" I can tell she's nervous, and her heart skips a beat.

Cole pulls away. "You may not believe me, but I needed to sneeze."

"That was a sneeze?" She mocks him by laughing.

"It's true, Rory," I say defending him. "When a dragon turns, especially for the first time, our head gets congested. Like we have a cold, and we want nothing more than to blow out that crud." I grin, looking at my cousin, Cole. "The first time I shifted, I blew a hole clear through the floor in Ashengale Castle."

Rory raises a brow and Cole smiles.

Rory clucks her tongue. "Fine."

Red gives a low grumble. *"Can we get beyond this juvenile banter, please?"*

"I know what you mean, Red. Watching Cole and Rory go at each other is extremely energy draining."

Rory scoffs. "How was I supposed to know you weren't a dragon dragging us off to our deaths at the time?"

I turn around looking behind me. The air is softer than when we arrived. Too quiet in fact. "Speaking of which, can they follow us here?"

"Only time will tell." Cole steps between us and walks a few yards away to the edge of the cliff. He points across the way. "There's a lighthouse across the ocean valley."

I observe with him. The lighthouse looks familiar. "Hang on a second." Cole mentioning the possibility that a person can become a dark dragon, has me going down a deep rabbit hole. "Are you saying that these dark dragons can shift into a different form, too?" My question to Cole has me thinking there is a real clue into the dream I had in respect to where we have landed in reality.

He turns toward me. "Oh, I see you didn't get the memo when you were back on Dragonscale Island learning how to be a dragon shifter."

I scowl at him. "I'm trying to be serious, Cole. Humor me, please."

He huffs. "Demons. They turn into demons. And you're wondering what happens to shifted dark dragons?"

"That was the question, Cole." Rory scowls at him too.

"I want to know if they can take shape into beings other than themselves."

"Oh, I see where you're going with this, Wynter. Can they take the place of someone else like the Trek did with my mother back at Geneviève's Ranch."

"I'm not sure about that, but what I can say is Sarmira has worked centuries to get the dark dragons an exact DNA," Cole answers.

"You mean there are different forms of Shadow Walkers?"

"Yes. She has vampires, werewolves, necromancer witches, and dragons. She hasn't quite mastered the druids yet." He looks over at Rory. "She's working on that."

"And she won't succeed if I have anything to say about it." Rory squints. "Wait a second. I have a question, Cole. How is it that your clothes haven't torn away. You were ashes before turning to a dragon. When I shift to a wolf and back, I find myself using leaves to cover my...um parts..."

He laughs. "No clue. Would you prefer me naked?"

She blushes.

I roll my eyes. "The way Dragonscale explained it, the particles we are wearing before shifting have memory, so, when we shift back to a human form, those particles come back just as they were."

Rory's eyes widen and her jaw slacks. "Huh."

I smile at her confusion. "It's a dragon thing..." I wave my hand in front of her eyes. "Careful, a fly might buzz into your mouth."

She swats my hand away. "Knock it off."

Redmae softly chuckles. *I don't mind being naked.*

"Red! TMI," I say.

"So, where are we?" Rory asks.

"Somewhere on Elleirodal," Cole answers. "I'm not too familiar with this area. Although, I have to say it does resemble Scarlet Hollow, like you said, Wynter."

"You wouldn't happen to remember being here with me

before, would you?" I ask, thinking back to the nightmare I had when I was asleep for nearly a week.

He raises a brow. "No, why?"

"Because you brought us over here like you knew this is where we needed to be."

Cole shrugs. "Something tells me we're supposed to be here... Is that weird?"

"No, not weird in general. I feel it, too. It's just strange that we both feel it at the same time."

He turns to face us. "Can you hear that? Listen closely." He steps closer to the cliff that overlooks the lands below.

"You mean the ocean?" I listen with him. Rory and Redmae step next to me.

"No. It's something else. I mean yes, the crashing waves are soothing, and the gulls are sounding the alarms that we are strangers lurking about, but it's something else," he answers.

"I don't think I am hearing what you are hearing, Cole." I close my eyes and try to find the sounds he's curious about.

"I hear it," Redmae says. *"Sounds like crows in the distance."*

"That's odd Cole would think crows have triggered something within him, don't you think, Redmae?"

"I'll keep a watchful ear for anything concerning."

"We should keep moving and out of the clearing where the nocturnal beings have a clear scope of us." Cole walks ahead down an overgrown path toward a wooded landscape, and we follow.

"Tell me, Cole, do you remember anything while being under the control of Sarmira?" I ask.

He quickly glances at me, then looks away.

"Yes, everything. What do you want to know?"

"Do you know where Cory is?"

He takes his time answering. I can tell it's a sore subject. "House of Bloodbane."

"Then we're close, yes?"

"It's not easy to get to."

"But you know the way?"

"I do." His tone is grim.

"But?"

"Listen, I want to find my brother just as much as you, but the way to him is virtually impossible." He points to the lighthouse across the ocean passage that separates us with smoke escaping the chimney. "I know the witch that lives there. My mother would visit her when I was young."

"And yet I hear hesitation in your voice."

"She's not to be trusted. She will grant you any request you ask, but it comes with a price."

"You say this like you're speaking from experience."

"I am." He breathes deep and slowly exhales. "A request my mother made."

"You mean Blair?"

"Yes. She requested safe passage to Ladorielle. To shield our family from Sarmira."

"That didn't work out well for you..." I observe the birds as they fly across the oceanside cliff.

"Oh, no, it worked. Quite well in fact, until a certain child screamed across the lands waking the Underworld beasts." He stares at me with daggered eyes.

"That's why you hate me so much."

"I don't hate you. I'm not fond of your choices, and I think you're a little naive and hotheaded, but my brother seems to like you and that's good enough for me."

"Says the vampire who wanted to turn me."

He chuckles. "That was the vampire part of me. It burned to ashes. I don't think Sarmira knows I survived..."

"You mean she isn't aware that a vampire with dragon blood can be reborn as a shifter?"

"I don't think so." Cole gives a lopsided smile and

continues to walk toward a trail leading down along the cliff to the woods ahead.

"There must be another way to get Cory back."

"There is another way, but you're not going to like it."

"Try me."

He ignores my persistence. "We should go check out this lighthouse. Watch your step. The trail is this way." He pushes aside some tree branches.

"Cole, stop."

He turns and glares.

"What is the other option?" I ask.

"The only way to reach my brother is if one of us dies."

I shiver in response.

A gust of wind pushes across our bodies nearly knocking Rory over the edge. An ominous, but soothing voice, adds to our conversation, "I can help with that..."

3

THE RAVEN

Redmae holds a stance and growls while Rory quickly pulls to her feet and grabs an arrow.

"Relax, I have no intention of killing you. I merely meant I can help you cross over to Scarlet Hollow." A woman approaches dressed in a black feather cloak that covers a midcalf black linen robe and laced up black leather boots. She holds in her hand a staff taller than herself. Her hair is the same jet black with thick white strands that parts on either side of her head. Her green blue eyes are striking; however, one eye is half shut with a scar lined down her cheek.

"Who are you," I demand.

She smiles. "Most know who I am, and need not to ask, but seeing how you are strangers in our world I can understand why you might wonder." She steps closer. "I am the Oracle of Wisteria Keep."

Cole creases his brows. "I thought Wisteria Keep was a mythical place?"

"Oh, it's quite real indeed. The city has been in hiding for centuries. Luckily, we were able to rebuild after the great war. Thanks to Petra." She turns to me and smiles.

"How do you know Petra?"

"She was my student long ago. And thanks to her we were able to replace the damage to our world. But that is for another time to explain. The winds called to me; thus, I am here before you."

Cole takes a step forward. "So, what shall we call you... Oracle?"

"Ha, funny boy." She's quite entertained by his innocent question. "I'm known as the Eye of the Raven. Some refer to me as The Raven. You can call me just Raven. Although my birth name is something else and well, I quite like this name."

"Okay...Raven... how have you come to help us?" Cole sounds suspicious. "If you're so intuitive then I gather you know why we need to enter Scarlet Hollow." Cole looks back toward the lighthouse overlooking the opposite cliff.

"Ah yes, the Lighthouse of Cliffside Rock. The keeper of the house doesn't take too kindly to strangers." Raven takes her staff and holds herself steady with both hands. "I'd tell you not to go, but then that would prevent you from free will."

"That sounds a little like you're trying to distract us from free will by implying it to us now," I say.

"Perhaps." She smiles. "You do what you will, but if you change your mind..." She raises her hand as though she is about to disappear.

"Wait!" Cole presses forward once more toward her.

She raises a brow. "My boy, make your choice."

"I have one question."

"I think there may be more but go on."

"How do we know what you say is the truth? How do we know if you really can get us safely to Scarlet Hollow?"

"What does your gut say, Cole?"

"That you're not to be trusted.

"Well then I guess that's your answer."

"How does that make any sense?" I ask.

"My thought exactly," Cole adds. "How do you know my name? You speak as if you know each of us."

"I trust you," Rory bursts.

Shock coats my mind. "Rory what are you doing?"

"No, I mean it. I don't fear her nor do I think she means any of us harm." She steps between us. Redmae paws next her.

Raven comes closer and looks deep into Rory's eyes. "Ah, I see now. You're of dire blood."

Rory shies away as though what the woman said was shameful.

"Not to worry, your secret is safe with me. It does, however, explain why I was called."

Cole crosses his arms and firms his lips, staring. "Care to elaborate," he finally asks.

"Your grandmother"—She addresses Rory—"Laveena of Shadow Vine Forest and Wisteria Keep are connected allies for the common good."

"You know our grandmother?" Rory turns to Redmae and rubs the side of her neck.

"Indeed, I do, and I also know about the curse your sister has been burdened." She briefly glances at Redmae.

"Can you cure her?" Rory's excitement raises.

"Possibly, but that will take more research and time." She looks over at Cole. "I can, however, lead you to your brother, Cory, but I must have all of you on board, else the magic will not work."

"We're listening," Cole says, dropping his arms.

She backs away. "Follow me this way and I will show you the rear entrance to the Underworld's Veil called Scarlet Hollow." She turns around, then shifts into a raven. She takes off and flies above our heads. Her loud call prompts us to follow as she flies toward the forest ridgeline.

I run after her, leaving the rest still standing and realize they're not following. "Do you want to find Cory or not? Let's go, guys."

Rory grunts. "I hope you know what you're doing."

"Ha! No! But what is the alternative?" I veer to the lighthouse on the cliff. "A sinister witch or raven shifter? I'm about done with my share of witches at this point. Am I going alone or are you with me?"

Reluctantly, the others follow. We lose sight of The Raven, which has us walking blind in an unfamiliar forest. Cole lights the way with his shining blue eyes. Noises in the woods have us on alert. Each step we take shifts to a crackling echo of snapped twigs and crunch of soft rock beneath our feet. Nothing quiet about walking this trail. Any predator could hear us miles away. Birds above in the trees caw as we attempt to quietly walk the overgrown trail.

"We're lost," Rory says.

"She'll show when she needs to. We're going the right way, I'm sure of it, else she would have appeared." I look down at my necklace. "Besides the compass is glowing pointing us in this direction."

The path leads down a narrow passage that leaves room for one person at a time, forcing us to line up. A few rocks fall as we make our way down the cliffside.

"Don't you find it suspicious that some stranger appears out of nowhere? This could be a trap, ya know." Cole points. "See, a dead end. Where to now, genius."

The trail ends with a large boulder. To the right of us a cliff that leads down to the ocean and to the left a hillside of ferns, trees, and brush. My compass glows bright telling me we're in the right area, yet Cole is right, the path ends here.

The Raven swoops down by our feet. She doesn't shift. She honks aloud a couple times and hops toward the boulder.

A mist pulls in. The air feels refreshing. A red glowing light peeks through the trees along the cliff, and I look to see it's coming from the moon. Its light hits with timing. A blue stone appears to the left of the boulder and glows. The Raven crackles softly and flutters her wings.

"Are we supposed to touch the stone?" Rory asks.

"I don't know." Gently I tap the glowing embedded rock, but it disappears, and my hand goes through the boulder instead. "What in the—" I pull my hand back, and the glowing stone reappears. I look back at the others.

Rory shrugs, shaking her head.

"Wait a minute. It's an invisible gateway." Cole puts his arm through and moves it up and down. "Let's go." He steps completely through and vanishes.

Redmae does the same. *"He's right. This is a tunnel in the side of the cliff. Wynter, come in here. You need to see this."*

Rory goes after Redmae, leaving me the last one to pass through.

The blue stone fades as I touch my way to the other side, except I'm abruptly stopped by a solid boulder. The Raven hops about screeching and fluttering its wings.

"Wynter, are you coming?" Redmae asks.

"Apparently not. The boulder has solidified. I can't get through." I look up to see both moons covered by clouds with no evidence in anything clearing soon.

"You waited too long." The woman appears behind me. She hands me a note. "Give this to Cole. Do not open it. Do not lose it. Once you reach Cory, and only then, are you to give this to him. It is of grave importance."

"I don't understand."

"It is all part of a great plan, my dear." She forces the note into my hand.

The front of the envelope reads *Cole.* I tuck it into my inside pocket. "Raven, I cannot get past the boulder."

She smiles, looks up, the clouds part, and the light from the moon again shines through, allowing the blue stone to light up once again. "You can now." She transforms back into a bird and flies away. Something tells me she had something to do with the weather change.

I push through the boulder before the clouds cover the moons again.

"There you are," Rory says coming by my side. "We were getting worried. Come look at what we found."

Drips of water trickle down the walls and the smell of sulfur assaults my nostrils. The air is dense but the beauty surrounding me makes up for the uncomfortable smells. Crystals in all shapes, sizes and colors protrude through the layers of rock, clay, soil, and petrified elements within the walls of the cave. Light bounces from one prism to another. Rory pulls me to a room filled with gems of all kinds. A workbench filled with tools lay across a table. "It feels like we're trespassing."

"This place is amazing," Cole says.

A little farther in, a large circular room opens up with a clear crystal quartz as high as a ten-story building and as wide around as a rocket, hovers in the center of a bottomless pit. A gold railing circles around the crystal and separates us from reaching over and touching it. Beyond the massive rock more tunnels reveal themselves going in several different directions. "I feel like we're in an underground mining shaft."

"It's giving Grengore Mine vibes," Rory says, "except this is more crystalized."

"Careful, Wynter, there is a huge drop between us and that crystal." Cole looks down. "I'd say at least a mile deep.

"So, are we in Scarlet Hollow?" I ask.

Rory comes and stands next to me along with Redmae. "I don't think so."

"No, it's not Scarlet Hollow," a voice says behind us. "It's the gates of Crystal Cove that leads to Scarlet Hollow."

A woman with long blond hair and emerald eyes, high cheekbones, and fair skin approaches. "I'm Jasmine the gate keeper of this domain. I don't need to ask how you came upon my presence, but I am curious why she brought you here."

Cole bows his head. "We're sorry to intrude my lady, but we were told that we could find our way to Scarlet Hollow through this passageway."

"And why would you ever want to go to such a horrid place?" She eases closer to us. Her robe looks to be made of white linen and a gold rope tied to her waist. Golden tassels hang from her long sleeves.

"My brother Cory. He's trapped."

"Trapped how? Rarely if ever has Scarlet Hollow made a mistake of death. Is he in a coma? That would be the only exception."

Cole seems to be at a loss for words. "Deep sleep perhaps? You see, it's quite a long story of how it came about—"

She interrupts him. "I have all the time in the world." Chairs and a table appear between us, along with a tray of cookies, cakes, and mugs filled to the brim. "Have a seat. I insist." She looks deep into Redmae's eyes. "You look very familiar."

"Oh, I doubt that—" Rory is cut off.

She whips her head to Rory. "Dires. You and this wolf are of dire bloodlines. I see the silver in your eyes and your sisters. However, this wolf is several decades older than you." She notices none of us have taken her offer. "I said sit!"

The force of her words prompts us to do as she demands.

"I'm normally not this forward but I like to get to know

my guests before assuming the worst in them. Right now, all of you are failing miserably."

"Forgive us please," I say. "We didn't mean any harm by coming here."

"Yes, well, I gathered that. I have a spell that detects ill intensions when someone passes through my gate. Had any of you had that, you would have disappeared into the ether."

Rory gulps.

"Like a protection spell." I'm reminded of something similar to the cottage at Storm River Manor. "My mother had a similar protection on her home."

"Really? That is quite intriguing indeed. Is she a light witch or a dark witch?"

Her comment takes me by surprise. "Um, well, I don't really know. She died right after I was born."

"Ah, so her magic faded. Which means, you're a witch!"

"Not a practicing one, I assure you. I know nothing about spells or magic—well witch magic that is."

Jasmine looks at the rest of my friends and sits in a chair, opposite of us and leans back. "You are all such a curious bunch."

A low growl echoes through the crystal caverns.

Rory raises a brow, and we look at Redmae thinking it was her.

"*We have company,*" Redmae says.

4

CRYSTAL PASSAGE

A grey wolf about the size of Redmae with a white stripe down its back comes around the corner on the opposite side of the large quartz. It's black ears and muzzle make it look like the animal is wearing a mask.

"Relax, it's my familiar coming back from scouting the mountain," Jasmine says.

The wolf comes to her side and grumbles. *"It appears we have company."*

"How are you in my head? I thought my telepathy only reached a select few." I look over at Redmae for assurance.

Jasmine smiles. *"As predicted, your ancestral roots run deep I see. I had to be sure."*

My eyes dart to Rory and Cole, wondering if they can hear her too. *"To be sure of what, exactly?"* They seem unalarmed by my sudden shock.

Rory isn't paying any attention as she glances upward admiring the different crystals peeking through the raw stone walls and ceiling. She touches a gem. "Utterly amazing."

Cole squints dubiously at the wolf comparing him to Redmae.

"This is Baine." Jasmine reaches for him and scruffs his neck. *"You will do great things, Wynter. All in due time."* Baine yawns, not seeming the least bit interested in small talk, and slumps down at her feet and shuts his eyes.

Cole points back and forth between the animals. "I'm sorry, am I missing something? Are these dogs related?"

Baine's eyes dart open and growls at such an insult. *"I beg your pardon!"*

Cole step back and holds up his hands. "Oops. It appears I struck a nerve."

"Ya think?" I step between them.

"Of course they're similar. Redmae and Baine are dire wolves. Redmae is magical in her own right, however Baine is a warder, or a familiar. He, too, can change to a human should he choose." Jasmine pulls Baine close to him. "He didn't mean it, my love."

Rory's attention is diverted. "With all due respect, my lady, my sister cannot change at will."

"Oh, I see. Well perhaps we can discover why." Jasmine looks deep into Redmae's eyes from across the way. "Oh my, I do see that there is a problem."

"You can say it, you know. We all know she's cursed," Rory presses.

"Not just any curse. It's a Blood Moon curse."

"Can you cure her?" Rory asks.

"Unfortunately, I cannot. This can only be lifted by an oracle."

All of us look at each other, knowing full well an oracle led us to Jasmine.

Jasmine stands. "My family and I have been living in these crystal caves since losing my sisters years ago. Baine is my eyes and ears to the outside world."

"I'm sorry for your loss," I say.

"Oh, they're very much alive."

"How do you know for sure?" I ask.

"Follow me and I'll show you." She walks toward the giant clear crystal in the middle of the circular room. Bright prisms bounce off the cavern walls in rainbow beams of light.

"This is gorgeous," I say, looking up at the ceiling. A circular window above allows in light.

Jasmine looks up with me. "Indeed, it is. Even during a dark blood moon evening such as tonight, light somehow still escapes and bounces off the clear crystal illuminating the cave. The crystal filters dark magic, turning it to light. Sarmira has been after this hidden gem for centuries. After many failed attempts to free my sisters, I was visited by the Elementals of light. They offered me a proposal I could not refuse."

"Let me guess," Cole interrupts. "To be the keeper of the crystal."

She turns to him. "Why, yes but not in so many words. You see, I'm the last Ashburn light witch." She smiles. "For now..."

Rory gasps. "There are so many stories told about the Ashburn coven. We were told they were wiped out."

"Well, I suppose that might be true if I had been captured, too. Many of my sister witches were imprisoned by Sonjah—a fellow light witch, gone dark. She learned necromancy. Learned how to take their souls. She would, breathe in their essence, gaining their knowledge and power, leaving their soul, and placing it in a jar on a shelf with their bodies placed in coffins. She kept the souls like prized trophies. To this day we do not know where my fellow sisters lie in peace."

"How disgusting," Rory says.

We roam halfway around the crystal and stop. Jasmine waves her hand in front of a wall and a mirror appears. "This is how I know my sisters are still alive. I have seen them through this mirror, roaming about, looking lost. They don't see me, but I see them."

"Hang on a second, I have seen this mirror before. It hangs

in the Hall of Secrets. It has the same shape, and the same silver-pewter metal decorative casing that has a continuous infinity loop design all around the frame."

"Yes. It's one of several mirrors. There are three in this world. It is said there are many others in other worlds. There used to be many more here on Elleirodal, but they've been destroyed. This one is the Mirror of Darkness." She turns around. "This crystal cleanses the mirror, keeping the portal clean of any impurities. I invite you to gaze into the reflection and tell me what you see." She looks at me first.

"Obviously I see me." Through the reflection, I see Cole, Redmae, and Rory, and yet I do not see Jasmine. Startled, I turn quickly. "You're a vampire?"

Her smile widens. "No, thankfully I am not, but I just demonstrated to you what an illusion potion will do."

"Hold on a minute." Cole squints, cupping his mouth in thought. "You mean if this crystal was not here the mirror would—"

"The mirror would darken, and the demons would freely enter this world." Jasmine stiffens. I can tell that she doesn't like to think of that outcome.

"Doesn't seem to keep the darkness from entering through the blood moon phase in the Earth's atmosphere, though," Rory argues.

Jasmine turns to her, confused. "I don't understand how you would know that. Why would you be near Earth's atmosphere? That is one of the most dense and heavy energetic plant in the universe."

"We had a battle at Storm River Manor not too long ago. It's why we're here. My brother, he seems to be trapped between that world and here," Cole explains.

"Only because you killed him," Rory remarks.

I elbow her.

"I did not..." Cole shuts his eyes and takes in a deep breath. "...kill him. Rory likes to exaggerate. We had a little scuffle—"

"Ha! My as—"

I bump her again.

"We were fighting each other in battle—but to be fair I was still possessed by a demon—"

Jasmine raises her brows. "A what?"

"Wait, let me finish. Clearly as you said, if I was truly evil, I would be non-existent right now..." He points toward the entrance from which we came.

She glances at the same entrance. "Fair... go on."

"As I was saying, we were fighting, and my brother dropped his dagger, and I grabbed it before he could. Instantly I stabbed him, knowing full well that" —He looks over at me and Rory —"that he wouldn't die, as he's a vampire—we all know a stake will not kill, only petrify, the body—"

"But..." Jasmine probes.

"But that didn't happen. I too became jailed within my own body. I was also imprisoned within Scarlet Hollow's Veil. And in The Veil, I found my brother. We were able to communicate. Something we hadn't done in years."

"I see." She looks intently at him. "And you think that somehow you can save your brother now?"

"He's alive. I know he's alive. I feel it."

"Quite curious indeed." She cups her chin looking into the mirror, gazing at her reflection that's now visible. "There is something you should know before we go any further." She turns back around. "If I help you, we will need to establish ground rules. And you must abide by them strictly."

We all nod.

"Once you enter Scarlet Hollow you cannot leave the way you came in and you will need tourmaline to enter the dimension."

"Sound's easy enough, we have a druid among us." Cole looks over a Rory.

Jasmine smiles. "It's not that simple." She points. "As I mentioned there are three mirrors. The second one is the Mirror of Souls. That mirror is the portal to freedom; however, it has been hidden from the souls on the other side. It needs to be found in the physical world for the souls to find it in the spiritual world. It would lead you out of Scarlet Hollow but these mirrors have been severed magically. Should you find it, that would be a better outcome than a druid. It's never a hundred percent accurate for a druid porting out of Scarlet Hollow. This dimension drains energy more than any other place. More energy than Earth."

"Great. We all know I'm having issues." Rory rolls her eyes. "Based on the risk assessment chart, I'm dead last in reliability."

"What do you mean?" Jasmine comes closer. "Ah, I see your eyes are a little dim. What are your symptoms?"

Rory looks at everyone else in the room. "It's not a comfortable situation to talk about."

"Humor me, child. This isn't the first time I've seen this sort of thing." She summons a pencil size flashlight and it lands in her palm.

"Ever since I ported Wynter, Cole, and Redmae out from the Hall of Secrets, someone in our party has either died or gotten injured." Rory looks at Cole.

"Clearly I'm alive," he says.

Rory smirks, continuing, "E-ever since I was impaled by the poison arrow on the shores of Geneviève's Ranch, I have had issues."

Jasmine's eyes widen. "My dear, I'd say you have been dealt your share indeed. What was the poison?" She continues to prob at Rory's eyes. "Look to the left." Jasmine flashes a light. "Now to the right."

"Seaspike."

Jasmine pulls from her pocket a tongue depressor doctors use to see the back of peoples' throat. "Open wide and say ahh..."

"I would say it was after that, Rory. Remember when you had the Waxlily at the Lake of No Return? You couldn't port us out of there and we had to call our dragongryphs," I say. "And once you choose a destination, we don't end up there, either. She attempted to port us to Storm Castle, but we landed here on Elleirodal instead."

"Oh my. I can see why you're concerned." Jasmine presses Rory's tongue down and shines a light once more. "Say ahh again, please."

Rory obeys her.

"Stick out your tongue." She clicks off the light. "I was afraid of this." Jasmine takes in a deep breath and firms her lips.

"What?" Rory asks, worried.

"I think you have a developing case of Gate Rot."

"That doesn't sound appealing," Cole says, disgusted. He's about to vomit. "Where's your bathroom?"

Jasmine points. "Down that hall, left of the mirror. Weak stomach, Cole?" She continues, talking to Rory. "It's one hundred percent curable, but your porting abilities will need to take a rest. Not to worry though, I have a solution for this, but first, it sounds like I'm going to need to whip up a batch of lavender oil mist with salt water."

"What will that do?" Rory asks.

"It will halt the infection from spreading. I won't be able to completely cure you until I have a rare key ingredient."

"Let me guess," Rory says. "Waxlily."

"How did you know that?" Jasmine seems surprised.

"Been around that block a few times already." Rory shrugs, looking over at me.

"In the meantime, this should work, though, right? I mean how are we to port out of Scarlet Hollow?"

"Right, Scarlet Hollow. As I mentioned, if you can find the reflection of the Mirror of Souls from the other side you can simply step through. A soul without a body cannot penetrate through, but one of flesh and bones can."

"How are we supposed to find this mirror?" I meet Rory's worried gaze.

"That is the magical question, isn't it?" She roams back to her workshop. "First, we need to make a quick potion to clear up your symptoms, Rory." She opens a drawer and pulls out different utensils.

"And second all of you will need to drink a potion of spirit illusion while in Scarlet Hollow, to avoid the soul reapers from finding you. And there is a time limit of one hour." She looks back at us. "If you do not find Cory before the potion expires, you'll be trapped there indefinitely."

"Unless we find the Mirror of Souls, correct?" I ask.

She nods. "I guess that is one way of looking at it."

"I'm not sure I like the sound of that," Rory says.

"The sound of what?" Cole comes back.

Rory looks at Cole. "We could be trapped in Scarlet Hollow. I think we were better off going to the witch at the lighthouse."

"Ha! Hannah, the Scorned Witch of the Sea. She's a peach." Jasmine grabs a few empty vials from the shelf. "I mean if you want to be contracted to her soul for eternity, be my guest."

"You mean like a soul contract?" Cole asks.

"What do you think, Cole?" Jasmine hums as she works. "Do you think your mother Blair wanted to see her the day she sought freedom from Sarmira?"

"How do you know about that?"

"I told you, I'm a light witch. I have a way of knowing a few things. And I know Sarmira must be stopped. I shall not tell all my secrets today." She brings down her mortar and pestle. "I mean, if you feel uneasy about pursuing your journey, please tell me now before I waste all these ingredients." She turns to face us.

"Cole, she has point. Besides I trust her before I trust the witch on the hill. I mean you said so yourself that she was a tricky sorcerous." I look at Redmae. *"Thoughts? I mean you've been quiet."*

"I'm resting my brain."

I raise my brows. *"Really? That's all you have to say?"*

"Yes, really." She slumps down in the corner and shuts her eyes.

"It can't be all that bad, right?" I look at Jasmine. "Is there a map of the area we might be able to reference this mirror of where your sisters might be?"

"I might have something you can take." She focuses back on the potion making. "I do have one warning, though."

"Which is?" Cole crosses his arms, not a hundred percent on board.

Jasmine tilts her head slightly. "You will not be able to communicate with my sisters Sage or Angelica. They simply will not see you while under this illusion I am making."

"Then how are we to communicate with them?" I step next to her to watch her mix the ingredients.

Jasmine reaches for a bag in the cupboard. It's a leather-bound sack tied in a not. "Take this with you. Inside is a Soul Catcher. Neither of them will see you, as I have said, but you will be able to see them. Pull the object out of the bag and point. Their souls will be sucked inside. Then bring it back to me. It's the only way to bring them back."

"If this is the only way, then why have you not done it before?" Cole asks.

"I am not a druid." She looks at Rory. "I go in, I won't come back. If I had a portal stone from a mystic magician, I might be successful, but I cannot leave these crystal caverns unattended until Sarmira is once again capsulated."

"Capsulated?" Rory raises an eyebrow. "Are you saying she's been captured once before?"

"A few times, yes," Jasmine confesses. "The first time only held for only a few decades. The second time—"

"You mean more than once she's been captured and twice, she's escaped?" Cole is just as surprised as Rory and me.

"Three times actually. This last time—" She turns to face me. "Your mother risked her life."

"Yes, I know. She's somehow succeeded in trapping Sarmira in Earth's atmosphere. Do you have any ideas of how to defeat Sarmira?" I ask. "I mean for good?"

"There are a few thoughts roaming around in my head, yes. Long ago, we had finally trapped Sarmira. Tricked her, in fact." She beams in satisfaction, as though the memory brings her great joy. "That was one of the most fulfilling times of that era. But it was short lived. To this day no one knows how she escaped the mirror. It's important you find my sisters and their familiars."

"You mean through that mirror near the crystal?" I glance behind my shoulder to look at it briefly.

"No, not that one. As I said there are three. The one we think she escaped from is the Mirror of Fate in the Hall of Secrets."

"Which just so happens to be destroyed, now..." Rory spats.

Jasmine stops. "Destroyed?"

The concern on her face has us worried.

"Please tell me you are joking." Jasmine's heart speeds up. I can feel it.

"Sorry, I only assume," Rory explains. "One minute we were all having a conversation around the table and the next minute Sarmira appeared. Not physically of course but her voice, her laughter—" Rory veers to Cole. "She was using him as her vessel. The next thing I knew we're pulled from the portal and sent to this place, Elleirodal."

"Interesting. This goes deeper than I thought. All the more reason to free my sisters." She goes back to making her concoction.

"We haven't a clue what they look like," Cole says.

"Not to worry, I'm adding a pinch of photosynthesis to the mixture."

"That doesn't make any sense. Photosynthesis is a process by which plants transform energy in sunlight," Rory argues.

"Precisely. Light witches use energies from the elements in nature to gather power. Plants have memory, like water. It's all energy. This energy remembers what my sisters look like, therefore, when you reach the other side, you will be able to recognize them through photosynthesis." She takes down a jar labeled ground sunflower. "Four pinches of powder should do it." She adds lemon and moon water, before funneling the ingredients into four vials. "Are you ready?"

Jasmine hands each of us a glass vial. "This will taste awful. I suggest you swig it down fast but wait until you're ready to cross through the gate. You will have exactly sixty minutes to retrieve Cory and find my sisters."

Cole sets his watch. "That's' not nearly enough time."

Jasmine raises a brow. "You will with that." She points to my necklace. "Wynter's compass will lead you, or have you forgotten?"

I grin. "I suppose we did for a second."

Jasmine narrows her attention on Cole. "Clever watch. That looks familiar."

"My dad had them made for Cole and Cory," I say.

"Yes, Nyta and I worked hard to get them ready. There are several more where those came from." She rummages through a desk drawer. "Here we are." She hands two to Rory. "Clasp one of them around Redmae's leg. It will adjust when she shifts as well. This will protect you and her like it does the boys." She glances at me. "You do not need a watch as your necklace has the same protection. Like the tourmaline in the watches, the labradorite also protects you in Scarlet Hollow."

I touch my amulet and smile. "It protects in more ways than just one, I suppose."

Jasmine breathes deep. She pulls from her pocket two necklaces with black stones in the center. A small round purple stone sets above the black rock wrapped in silver wire. "This is black tourmaline and amethyst. These should bring you to my sisters. Please give these to them. It will help them *see*. I have done what I can. I wish all of you blessings and courage. Before you cross through this portal, I must warn you: do not veer off the trail." She places a token in Cole's hand. "Just on the other side of this gate is a path that will lead to another gate keeper. He prefers gold coins." She hands Cole in addition to the metal piece, a bag. "And a sack lunch. Give these to him as payment for you to cross through to the Crimson Moors. His name is Rhoan."

Cole stuffs both the coin and sack in the inside pocket of his jacket.

Jasmine adds, "The Crimson Moors is the physical world to that of Scarlet Hollow. The thin Veil that separates these realms is where you will find your brother. It's where the living is not dead, and the dead can still live."

"That's a riddle if I ever heard one," Rory says.

"I get it, Rory. She is saying that Cory, although he seems dead, he is in a coma-like state, and Jasmine's sisters, although they are alive, they live in spirit form in Scarlet Hollow." I look at Jasmine for confirmation.

"Something like that, yes. My sisters were not killed before being sucked into the Soul Catcher; they were alive. As with Cory, he is trapped by a vampire curse." She hands Rory a small vial. "Drink this before you go. It will help cure your ailment but remember you need a second dose that includes Waxlily. This medicine will not last, so remember to get it refilled."

Rory nods. "Thank you."

"Finally, as mentioned before, do not drink your illusion vials until you reach the portal to Scarlet Veil. The timer begins once you take the potion." She snaps her fingers, and a humming sound from the clear crystal echoes. The cavern lights up igniting prisms of light throughout.

We're in awe of its radiant beauty.

"Amazing," Cole says.

"Redmae," Rory calls.

Redmae gets up and grunts. *I was having such a good dream.*

"Let's go find Cory, my friend." I reach up and scratch her ear as the crystal opens a portal.

5
BRIDGE TOLL

W e enter a mountainous area. The moons are still full and bright, however, a rumble behind the dark red clouds alert us that another storm might be on the way. "This is such a bizarre looking place," I say. "It's as if we jumped continents. It looks so different here." Instead of green firs, the needles are vibrant orange, red, and golden. The ground is dark maroon, and the grass another shade of red.

"This looks all too familiar and it brings back memories I care not to revisit," Cole says.

"Where are we?" Rory asks.

"The foothills of the Crescent Mountains." Cole points. "There used to be a beautiful meadow with green hills and a raging river north of here, near Crescent Mountain with lush vegetation, butterflies, birds of all kinds, and unimaginable life. All that remains now is destruction and death."

"What happened?" Rory asks.

"The Underworld is what happened." Cole's face is cold. He marches past us down the path. "Crescent's Gate is behind that hill, and just beyond that, lies the ominous access we all seek—the House of Bloodbane."

"Crescent's Gate?" I ask.

"It's the gate to our world on Ladorielle," he explains.

Seeing Cole on our team is going to take time to process.

"This feels dreadfully eerie, Red. Do you sense danger?" I ask.

"Not at the moment, no."

"What about Cole?"

"He wants to reach his brother as much as you do."

"Do you know where we are going?" Rory asks.

"Down the path like Jasmine instructed us to," Cole answers.

Ash falls everywhere, reminding me of Dragonscale Island. "Why do I get the feeling you've been through this forest before?" I ask.

Rory nudges me.

"Don't worry, I'm not going to wander off." He pulls a branch out of the way so we can pass. "This is an identical planet to Ladorielle. You may have recalled a place named Songbird Meadow, Wynter."

"You mean there are two Songbird Meadows?" I ask.

He tilts his head. "Sort of? A gate used to separate Elleirodal side from Ladorielle side. As I recall, your father tried protecting the portal there with those birds. Very clever of him, indeed. I don't think Sarmira has figured out how to eliminate those vulture-like birds." Cole's body language radiates smugness. "Rest assured, there isn't any lulling songbirds on this side to put you to sleep like on Ladorielle."

"That's a relief." I reflect back when Cory and I, along with Aunt Fran and Dad, went through a gate that reached Songbird Meadow, and I check the small pocket on the outside on my jacket noticing I still have the ear plugs. "Where is this gate?"

"Gone. It was destroyed during the Great War. The only way

to Ladorielle now is either a druid or a Dragongryph. Although I have heard there is another gate access clear across the other side of the world where Wisteria Keep resides. I had always thought that place was a myth, but I have met people in passing, that have stated its existence and that it was their escape to freedom."

We walk down a moderate slope until we reach a clearing.

"Jasmine is taking us on the same journey. Hannah would have added a bit of trickery to her deal and at the sacrifice of Cory and me, but after talking with Jasmine, I'm beginning to think the choice my mother made might have been her only option at the time."

"How so?" I'm beginning to think Cole has many more secrets then I first assumed.

"It means I'm suddenly questioning everything. The House of Bloodbane is where they train the vampire assassins. Rhoan is one of them."

"An assassin?" Rory questions. "Cole Storm, you have some major explaining to do, buddy."

"Yeah, I know. Come on, we better make this quick else the nocturals will have us for dinner." He furrows his brows and points. "That valley below is where we must travel to reach the House of Bloodbane. There are two gates in the forest, one that leads to Vothule's kingdom, and the other is Scarlet Hollow's Veil."

"I thought you couldn't remember where your brother was or knew the way. Cole Storm, you better not be leading us into a trap." I pull at Cole's sleeve. "I may not have had the opportunity to know you very long, but I know that look. What are you up to?"

He nods in the direction of our destination. Smoke escapes from the soil, and the ground is dried and cracked. "We have to cross that, but first, we must find Rhoan. He has the key that will allow us to pass."

"What key?" Rory asks. "Jasmine said to give him the coin and the sack lunch you hide inside your coat pocket."

Cole grins as he continues to walk. "Indeed, that is true. Payment to open the bridge to the other side."

I glance across the vast deep valley. "I don't see any bridge."

"It's invisible." Cole picks up a rock.

I huff. "Of course, it is."

"Well, why not fly?" Rory asks.

"There's an invisible barrier from the ground to the sky." He looks up and we look with him. The same dark clouds continue to rumble with electricity, lighting them up every few seconds.

Ironically as crimson as this place looks, it isn't hot, but more of a tepid feel. Still, the thought of crossing these dead dreadful lands sends chills up my spine. "Uh huh. I can clearly see to the other side."

"Don't believe me? Fine." He tosses the rock, and it embeds into the invisible layer forking electricity like a spider-web. It crackles and sizzles upon impact and burns into gas-like fumes that dilute through the atmosphere. "How about now?"

Rory and I both swallow hard, stunned at what we saw. Red groans an unpleasant growl of frustration.

"Come on then. Rhoan's home is this way."

I don't like the sound of Cole's tone. "What aren't you telling us?"

"I hold no secrets, Wynter. Just know reaching the other side of that terrain will not be easy. I've been here before, both in the real world and Scarlet Hollow." He stares at me. "Both dangerous."

"This valley isn't like the crevasse earlier where there was a deep bottom to the ocean rocks below when we were attempting to cross and reach the lighthouse," Rory states.

"Not at all the same, no. It doesn't matter whether you jump, or port in there. House of Bloodbane is like a fortress.

No one goes in unannounced. And Rhoan has the key to let us cross. The coin is payment, and the lunch is so he doesn't eat us instead. Believe me that keeper of the invisible bridge has an appetite, but he cannot resist Moggle Pop Cakes."

"As in Moggle Pops the drinks?" I ask.

"Similar, yes, only it's a sweet cake. Like a donut, only different."

We continue to follow down the trail that leads to the gnome's house. Dead tree branches scatter the ground, and the soil is cracked like the valley. I hear the dirt crunch beneath my feet.

"And how far do we have to go?" Rory asks.

He stops, turning to face us. "It's not far. Stay on the path, and don't veer off under any circumstances."

The air is thick with ash. Bones lay half buried and tumble-weeds roll about, not aiming in any particular direction.

We reach the edge of another cliff, and there is nothing in front of us but a drop off to the depths of the valley below.

"Okay, Cole, so where is it?"

He smiles, pulling the gold piece from his pocket and placing it by his feet. A dinner bell appears out of thin air and he rings it.

"Are we someone's supper, Cole?" Rory sneers.

"Patience would do you some good, Rory. And yes, to answer your question...we would be dinner if not for the sack lunch." He smirks, holding up the bag.

She huffs, rolling her eyes.

Fog rolls in. "I don't like this," I say.

"Relax and watch." Cole chuckles. "So jumpy."

"You would be, too, if you had the whole universe after your soul."

"Point taken."

The fog clears, revealing a small log cabin structure. A

rocking chair sits on the front porch, rocking without anyone in it.

Rory's eyes grow wide. "Not creepy at all..."

I try to not be surprised. Cole's head is big enough as it is. He thinks he's so sly. I can tell he's waiting for my shocking response. "So, knock on the door," I say.

He rolls his eyes and curses, seeing I'm not playing into his childish cryptic games.

"Cole Storm, is that really you?" A man flickers into view, like a hologram.

I move my hand through his holographic image and his appearance swirls in and out like fog. "Who are you?"

"Wynter, stop being rude," Cole says.

A stern stare of venom draws attention to me. "Question is, who are *you*, my dear?"

I raise one brow, intrigued, not at all intimidated by his attempted fearful stare. "So, you're a hologram."

"Ha, hardly. I'm real as anyone. I'm just not in your precise location. Fortunate for you, otherwise I would have killed you by now."

Cole clears his throat. "We have come for bridge access."

Rhoan's attention narrows on Redmae. "Cole, I do say you've outdone yourself this time. You brought food with you, I see. A feast for a king."

"I'm not sure I like the sound of that." Redmae growls.

"They are not food, sir. I did bring an offering you might find satisfying, though." Cole holds up the sack.

"Hmm, I see. You assume I can be bribed by food? Tell me first before I accept your donation, who are these strangers you have brought with you? One can never be too careful when travelling to the House of Bloodbane."

"Ha! Strangers," Rory scoffs.

Cole turns to us and back to Rhoan. "These are my friends."

"So, you play with your food first, then eat them? That's a new one." His smile is wicked. "And where is your brother? You two are rarely apart."

"No, Rhoan, they are not food, I assure you. As for my brother, he is who we have come for. We have on good authority that he's in House of Bloodbane territory."

Rhoan seems surprised. "Ahh, I see. "Well, you know the drill. What is in the bag? It better be good, else you will not survive the next few minutes."

Cole drops the small bag Jasmine gave him, with a note tacked to the side by the doorstep.

Rhoan grunts. "Well open it, my boy. I want to see the contents!"

Cole opens the bag.

"Are those—"

"Yes, Moggle Cake."

"Very well, you may pass." The mischievousness in Rhoan's expression gives me a clue that he's hiding something and is up to no good. Rhoan veers toward us and eyes me closely. The gnome grins. His hands roll together as if he's about to receive something he's been waiting for.

"Rhoan, the key please." Cole puts out his hand. "Enough of the games. You have the agreed payment for safe passage."

"Fair...fair," he replies. "I see you made your choice; however, I do not guarantee anything safe in this world." He and the log cabin disappear and in its place the onramp to the invisible bridge.

"It looks like it's made of glass," I say.

6

UNCHARTED TERRITORY

"So, where's the key?" Rory asks. "I knew he was a double cros—"

Cole gives a hard glance at Rory. He holds it up. "Right here." He steps onto the ramp, and an invisible door appears that separates us from crossing. "We don't have much time before this bridge will disappear."

"I'm guessing this will unlock the door," I say.

"Among other things, yes. Crossing this area won't be without its challenges. Be on guard." He inserts the key and turns until it clicks. "Here goes nothing." Cole cautiously looks around. "Rory, I have an idea. Do you think we could do a jump across the bridge? It might save us time."

I'm suspicious of his motives. "Cole, what is it?" I look over the edge. "Crossing bridges are not on my list of favorite things to do."

Rory smiles. "Wynter, you're a dragon. You're not supposed to be afraid of heights."

Cole pushes through the gate, and we follow.

She glares at him then smiles. "You're a dragon now, too, Cole. Why don't both of you shift and fly us over instead?"

"I agree with Cole. Jumping across is a better idea."

Cole glares at Rory. "We're being watched. Wynter, can you feel it, too?"

"Of course I can. What concerns me more, is what's gotten you all shook up."

"Perhaps because this invisible bridge will fade before we get across, hence why I asked Rory if she could jump us across. Shifting into dragons is out of the question. You saw what happened last time when the dark dragons found us. I don't think we should risk it."

I grab Rory's arm. "You've got this my friend. We can all link hands and you can jump us across."

"I'm afraid," she says hesitantly.

I feel her tense.

"Don't be afraid. Like I said, you've got this. Jasmine gave you a cure. Trust that."

She shrugs off my grasp, as if something I said brought her back to reality. "A temporary cure. I—I don't know, and I don't trust so easily."

"You have magic from the moon phases. Trust that, then. You can do this," Cole reiterates.

"What if I shift us out of this dimension?"

A crack below the bridge startles us. "Make this quick, Rory." Cole grabs her hand. "We've wasted enough time arguing. Jumping is our only choice to make it across, now."

We link hands as Rory closes her eyes and concentrates. Like back in the Grengore Mines, we make a high-flying jump but it only gets us halfway.

I look down and gasp. Although the feeling underneath our feet feels like a solid surface, it has the appearance of us walking on air that catches my breath.

"Yeah, I forgot to warn you not to look down," Cole says.

I can clearly see bones scattered from decaying bodies

below us in the valley. "Most don't make it across the bridge, do they?"

"Except if you have the talent of speed," he says, looking at Rory. "Or in our case, a druid."

I look up to see a whirl of wind following us. "What's that?"

"Oh, no! Time is up. Run!" Cole flees ahead of us and we scatter after him.

"The bridge is disappearing," Redmae says. She grabs Rory by her cloak and summersaults her onto Red's back. *"Use your superspeed, Wynter, I'll be right behind you."*

WE REACH THE OTHER SIDE, AND THE BRIDGE vanishes seconds after Redmae's last paw lands on solid ground.

"That was close," Rory says. "I see now why you wanted me to jump us."

All of us breathe heavily and my gut churns at how close we came to permanently joining Scarlet Hollow. I look at Cole. "What now?"

Cole gives an irritated sneer. "We keep moving before the Shadow Walkers find us. Be on alert. We're close to The Veil."

"The Veil? I thought we were in the Crimson Moors?" I ask.

"We are sort of... this path will lead us to the gateway." He nods to the winding trail ahead. "Over there..." He points to where Rhoan's house used to be before it disappeared. "That is part of the Crimson Moors, and the valley, and the invisible bridge. House of Bloodbane is to the left, over there, and near the mountains, and is also the Crimson Moors. The Veil is part of both worlds, the Crimson Moors and Scarlet Hollow. The

Veil is all around us on either side of the invisible bridge where the living and the dead collide."

"That's sounds so creepy," Rory says. "Do you mean undead creatures can live in the Crimson Moors?"

"Oh no, Rory, you misunderstand me. Undead creatures are everywhere. The difference is you will see them once in The Veil where we presently stand. Meaning for the average mundane human who doesn't believe in magic, the veil is lifted from their eyes—" He looks at me.

"I'm not mundane, and certainly not human!"

Cole chuckles.

"But you thought you were, living in Blaine Washington."

I glare. "Get to the point, Cole."

"My point is the average nonbeliever of magic will suddenly see the truth once in The Veil, should they come across to this side."

"You're, saying everyone can now see ghosts, is that it?" Rory asks.

"Precisely."

Wolves howl across the lands echoing through the valley, warning us danger is near. Soft whispers penetrate my eardrums, and my body shivers sending goosebumps down my arms.

"I don't like the sound of that. Red, can you sense any danger?"

"What, besides the death and evil souls walking about?"

"Right...noted."

"If I have any warning, I'll let you know. I will say, I don't like the heaviness in the atmosphere."

Cole's shoulders pull back and he stiffens as if he knows what's hidden beyond the darkness. "We need to keep moving. If those Shadow Walkers catch up with us, we're in for a battle."

"I didn't realize Shadow Walkers were here, too. I figured Moyer created them," I say.

"She did. Her version, anyway. Moyer merely added to their population. Wynter, they're everywhere." Cole adds. "Where do you think Shadow Walkers came from?"

"Is House of Bloodbane their birthplace?" Rory readies a bow and arrow in her hand. "I mean, I knew they existed, but some of this doesn't make sense to me. I too, thought Madame Moyer created them."

"Sarmira created them. She used Moyer as her pawn on Earth." Cole pauses, circling around us and huffs, sounding frustrated. "Be ready to fight. When the physical part of you dies, such as an elf, Iknes Shaw...human, or whatever other species you were, you're reborn to the House of Bloodbane—referencing the Shadow Walkers. When I stabbed Cory, a part of him died, but the blade saved him somehow—and me, too. Normally we would be reborn into another Shadow Walker."

"Hang on." Rory stops him. "Are you saying when we were in the tunnels trying to release the Storms and other prisoners a couple weeks ago, at the Storm River Manor grounds, the Shadow Walkers we fought and killed that combusted into ash, have been reborn once again?"

"Something like that, yes. They may have a different meat suit, but their dark soul lives for an eternity. Scarlet Hollow was created for those same dark souls to be captured forever, without any possibility for escape."

"Light souls are there, too, though," Rory says. "Cory isn't a dark soul. Neither is Wynter's mother."

"This is true, Rory. In some cases innocent souls also become trapped in Scarlet Hollow."

I feel for the bag Jasmine gave me that houses the Soul Catcher she asked me to use when we find her sisters and a thought pops in my head, realizing that she must've been involved in the dimension creation, or knew who was. "How do you know about its creation, Cole?"

"My brother and I figured it out while in Scarlet Hollow."

Cole stops and smiles. "I found him—spirit him— while running from the soul suckers who hunt for innocent souls wandering outside The Veil of Scarlet Hollow. We both reached The Veil from different locations. That is how we found each other" —he gestures to the area we stand upon— "in our spirit forms, we met in this exact spot. Except, Cory fell ill. It was the strangest thing. We were both in spirit form, of course, but something was preventing him from stepping any farther."

"How does a spirit get ill, anyway?" Rory raises her eyebrows.

"He's not a spirit technically, Rory. He's basically in a coma," Cole corrects.

"Okay, but that still doesn't explain the phenomenon, Cole."

"I don't know, Rory. Maybe it's because he's got the blade in his chest of his physical body? He's in The Veil of Scarlet Hollow, on this side of the portal gate. Perhaps he's been poisoned?"

I gasp at Cole's words.

"He persuaded me to go on without him. It was more important that we reached you, Wynter. The goal was for both of us to be free. Like how Isalora was able to be by your side in the past. She was in The Veil. That was why you could see her. Why I was able to reach you. We were hoping you could see us as ghosts, and we could lead to where Cory's physical body was." He pauses. "You know, in the Hall of Secrets before it was destroyed...a second time."

"A second time?" I squint, trying to remember. "Oh, right, Cory mentioned many of the portals were broken after the

Great War." I cover my mouth in thought. "Wait, that's why we escaped with our lives. The portal naturally purged us out."

Cole nods. "In theory that's what I think, yes."

"Jasmine said once we enter Scarlet Hollow, we had an hour to find her sisters and get Cory out of there," Rory reminds us.

"I know exactly where my brother is. The harder part is finding the light witches." He nods at my neck. "But I think *that* is trying to tell us something."

I look down at my glowing necklace and open the clasp. "It's pointing straight ahead that way."

Cole groans. "Of course, what's an adventure without going through The Dark Forest of the Undead."

"Isn't it the way to the portal, though?" I ask.

"Not exactly," Cole answers.

Another howl cries out. This time multiple ones. Screams, evil laughter, ominous whispers, and growls.

"Not sure I like either of our options," Rory says.

"I'm with you there." Cole's right hand glows. A swirl of light funnels from his index finger as a cascade of light beams upon us and disappears. "A protective bubble will keep us hidden only for so long. One step out of this twenty-five-foot perimeter or if someone casts a spell of their own the bubble will disappear."

"I'm shocked, Cole. No camping tent?" I smirk.

"Cory can create physical things out of nothing, while I can create magical enchantments such as an invisibility shield." Cole pulls at my hand. "The demon Shadows, what you might refer to as Shadow Walkers—they know we're here. Believe it or not, The Dark Forest of the Undead despite the name, is the safer route."

7

THE DARK FOREST OF THE UNDEAD

Cole leads the way as we race as fast as we can to the safety of the trees ahead. Like before, the fir trees have needles in the colors of red orange and yellows—the colors of autumn. As we draw closer, tree trunks drip what looks like dark crimson sap. Maple-like leaves in the same shade twist and wave in the crisp breeze. The ground is another shade of red compared to that of the trees and leaves—almost amber in color. Dark ruby rocks with a brownish tint pop along the worn path. The grass has a rosy pigment with cherry-blush tips. The cracks in the ground become larger and deeper as we near the forest's threshold.

Cole takes the first step beyond the line separating us from the open field behind us. Owls hoot and the crows caw, annoyed that we've disturbed their home. Crickets sing and other odd sounds echo through the forest as we all slowly venture deeper.

"The air smells like sulfur and death," Rory says.

We come to a deep thick river of molten lava that spits and bubbles between us and the forest.

"We'll need to jump." Cole puts his hand out, to help me across.

"You're not my type." I leap over the fissure and then glance at Rory, rolling my eyes.

She snickers.

Rory hops over the same cleft. "Give it up, Cole."

"Offering a helping hand isn't a marriage proposal, ladies." He leaps across, joining us. "It must eat at you, Wynter, looking at me, knowing I'm not my brother."

His smug tone is irritating. "Conceited and arrogant. I see that never left your body." I smirk. "A trait that clearly isn't Cory.

Rory grins. "Shot down by your brother's girlfriend. She's chosen the right twin, wouldn't you say?"

He grunts. "Well, that's a first. I mean, I sort of have a way with...women."

"Gawd, Cole, you're exhausting. Erase the triangle fantasy you have going in that tiny brain of yours. Not going to happen." I march forward.

Rory follows, walking backwards, addressing Cole, saying, "Arrogant and conceited, like Wynter said."

"Anyone ever tell you that you have a mean streak, Rory?" he shoots back, glaring.

"Why yes, your brother Cory."

Redmae is the last to leap across and paws ahead, ignoring us teens hashing it out.

A clatter of different sounds echoes through the woods. Wailes, shrieks, and howls come from different directions. Tree branches shake vigorously, and the ground rumbles beneath our feet. The minimal light we have from the twin red moons darken, and shadows of different shapes and sizes move across the ground, imbued by the lunar light.

I turn to see the shadows racing behind us and pick up speed. "What is that?"

"Remember, they can't see us," Cole reiterates, "but they know we're here. As I mentioned before, do not cast a spell or shoot an arrow, else our invisible shield will disappear."

"Maybe it's time we drink the elixir Jasmine gave us," Rory says.

"Not yet. We need to get closer to Scarlet Hollow's gate." Cole races ahead of us. "This way."

The path winds down a slope until we are cut off by a burgundy river, drowning out the ominous sounds of the undead creatures that roam about in the darkness.

"They will be close behind soon." Cole points over at the opposite ledge, where the path continues up the side of a cliff. "That's the way to the portal gate. You can't see it from here, but once we get to the top, it's only a few hundred feet away."

"Won't your shield fade by Rory jumping us across?" I ask.

"Yes, but we have no choice. That's the way out of here. And another thing, we won't be able to see the gate without Jasmine's potion."

"They're getting closer," Rory calls. "What do you want me to do?"

"Go ahead, cast the jump spell," Cole answers.

A bubble forms around us. "Link hands now!"

The trees behind us shake and the ground once again tremors.

"Don't look back, whatever you do. If you look at their faces, you will turn to stone." Cole grabs my hand and wraps his other arm around Redmae. Rory grabs my other hand.

"You mean like Daniel would do to humans such as Chad's betrothed who is now a stone statue in front of Storm River Manor?"

"Yes, these would be those beings—Shadow Walkers."

"Hang on," Rory says, "We're about to jump."

We leap over the river that's about thirty feet wide, leaving behind our attacking enemies. I watch as Cole glances past my shoulders. "They're separated by the river. They can't touch the water."

Screams of annoyance echoes across the way.

"They're calling for reinforcements on this side of the bank. Rory, get us out of here."

"Link up again, guys," she says.

We jump a fair distance up the cliff making a good amount of space between us and the Shadow Walkers, landing deep into a thick clearing. Cole repeats our protective shield. The air is brisk, and the red colored grass crunch beneath our feet.

"I think we lost them for now," Cole says. "Stay close and quiet. Loud voices will alert more predators."

"Lovely," Rory says, taking out an arrow from her quiver set.

"And shooting will lower our shields, too." Cole narrows his eyes at her.

"Right, you already mentioned that." She returns the arrow.

Quietly we walk through the meadow. The grass is nearly as tall as us which makes for a great camouflage. "Cole, can you please tell us how Cory became ill? You never finished."

"My theory...he's been poisoned. Poisoned with the curse, that is. If you recall, back at the Hall of Secrets, all of you were questioning the curse, and magic being drained. I know those answers because I was in between both good and evil."

"The Veil," I confirm.

"Yes. You see, we fought our way to The Veil, a spiritual battle broke out. Cory was wounded as we crossed over."

"Are you referring to when Cory, Redmae, and I were at Storm River Manor trying to free the Storms while Wynter was learning to be a dragon shifter?" Rory asks.

"If you're referring to after I stabbed Cory with his own blade, yes. His soul was sent to The Veil, while his physical body still rested on the grounds of Storm River Manor."

"Are you suggesting someone moved him?" Rory looks at me confused. "When we ported out there, he was in Chad's arms. But when we arrived at the druid circle Cory wasn't there."

"I can confirm, Cory is still in The Veil. I'm still not sure how his physical body managed to arrive in The Veil on Scarlet Hollow's side, but Wynter, I assure you, he's alive. He's trapped from getting back to his body and cannot awaken until that blade is removed."

"That must be why I heard him in my dreams, when I too, succumbed to Sarmira's poisoned spell. Do you think it will work?"

"You mean pulling the dagger from Cory's physical body? It has to."

"I hope you're right, Cole. Knowing the magic is fading, I wonder if I'll be able to protect myself like before. And I can't shift—" I look at him. "Neither can you for that matter."

"Exactly. That's why Rory had to jump us across." He points at my jacket. "That medicine Nyta gave you, doesn't keep you from shifting, it only suppresses the symptoms. Your shifting also will not prevent you from ascending to the throne. You're the heir. However, shifting will summon the dark dragons and I think Nyta knew that."

"Are you telling me that's why my dad said not to shift? That by shifting the dark dragons would find me?"

"Your dad, Nyta—they did it to protect you. They knew what you were up against."

My anger grows from being lied to. "Why couldn't they just be upfront and honest with me?"

"I can't answer that, sorry. What I can say, the Blade of Hope that is impaled into Cory's chest is cloaking him from Sarmira. And as ironic as this sounds, he's safest where he is. If Sarmira catches wind of his whereabouts, he's toast." Cole pauses. "It wasn't until I was given the watch, burned to ash, and reborn as a dragon, did I understand that."

"Are you saying you're free from the Underworld now?" I ask.

"Yeah, I guess am. I'm cured. And we need to find my brother and free him from her grasp as well. I am cloaked from Sarmira because of this watch, but I also have dragon blood running through my veins, something that evil witch does not want the Storms to discover. I can feel its magic, but it is weak. The dragon magic that soars inside my body isn't strong enough to take on the magic that Sarmira has consumed for centuries."

"Wait, is it your theory that all Storms have dragon blood?" I ask.

"I didn't believe it until my old body died. As I was rising out of my ashes, the memories of who I truly am, then came back to me. Sometimes fragments of the history of our line come into focus, and I remember everything, but not all at once. Wynter, we're descendants of dragons. And you have it from both sides."

Rory wrinkles her forehead. "No wonder she's after your powers."

A thought hits me. "I have dragon blood, and witches blood both running through my veins, but as we all know shifting to dragons will summon her dark dragons."

"True," Cole agrees. "We must be careful. Try to keep your inner thoughts as secure as possible. She can hear us while we're in dragon form. At least until we go through training school."

"That must be why Dad kept this secret from me. I need training to keep the intrusive thoughts out." I think about how Cory's a master at getting into my head.

"It won't take long for Sarmira's minions to find us. We haven't much time. And keep the voices in your head down."

He looks to everyone. "She had my mind under her complete control. Trust me, you don't want her to find yours."

Howls echoes across the land once again. The feeling of death approaches, reminding me how I felt under Sarmira's dream stamp.

"Come on, they're gaining on us fast. We can't stop," Cole presses. "Rory, it might be best if you ride on Redmae's back. She's a faster runner."

Loud screeching sounds are close behind us.

Rory climbs on Redmae "Let's go!"

"Stay as close to me as possible to avoid losing our shield protection." Cole wastes no time getting started. We run for cover once again and zigzag through large undergrowth terrain and giant fir trees trying to keep up.

Cole stops. Looking up above the treetops Shadows skate across the red cumulous clouds. Frustrating howls and roaring thunder follow. "Everyone, remain quiet. My cloaking shield acts like a mirror. If they come upon us, they will see their own reflection."

The howling grows louder. Sneering and hissing noises hide within the trees.

"Cole where is this gate?" Rory asks softly.

"Beyond that path." He points. "Now would be a good time to run. They're attempting to close us in." He glances past my shoulders, his eyes wide with fear.

I turn around. Just like in my nightmare hundreds of wraiths appear between the trees, by the dozens.

"Get to the end of that path. Just beyond it you will see the portal." Cole shifts before I have a chance to stop him.

"No! You'll bring the dark dragons."

"Too late, they're already here," he says inside my head. *"Look up."*

He's right, there are three headed right for us. *"How will we know we've found the portal at the end of the trail?"*

"Trust me, you will know," Cole says. *"I'll hold them off."*

"Don't make it a habit to be in my head."

"It's not by choice I assure you, Wynter. I don't like it any more than you do." Cole ignites the ground around our perimeter, separating us from the demons allowing Rory, Redmae, and I to escape down the pathway.

"I should come help you."

"No, get yourselves to safety."

Rory sneers. "So much for his cloaking spell."

"I'd like to see you do a better job. This isn't the time for petty jabs, Rory." The demons behind us charge forward, not giving us much time to reach the portal gate. "Jump us out of here!"

Redmae grunts. She grabs my jacket and pulls me onto her back as well.

Rory quickly casts a spell, with her bow in hand, and leaps us forward a few hundred feet ahead of the Shadow Walkers.

The demons do the same and collectively make the same jump that Rory just made, catching up to us.

I'm beginning to understand why we didn't fly in our dragon forms to the Scale Café & Grill, that day I spent lunch with my dad. He mentioned he didn't want people knowing he's a shifter, nor does he like showing up in big cities as a human. Him being in public showed the dark dragons our location. Am I also a beacon to the dark side?

We continue to race through the woods. "They're still gaining on us," Rory says. "We need to do another jump."

"We can't outrun them," I say.

We come to a dead end, as though the Shadow Walkers knew we would be corralled in a mountainous cove.

A few demons catch up to us and Rory shoots, hitting one directly between the eyes.

Another appears behind her, and I throw a fireball, striking it down before it has a chance to bolt Rory back.

Redmae growls, pouncing onto a Shadow Walker as another leaps onto her back. It's about to sink its teeth in her when Rory nails it in the neck with an arrow.

"There are too many of them!" I shout. Rage builds and I feel my body change. I can't control it this time. A burning numbing feeling travels through my veins and scales appear changing my skin. This time there isn't pain. My shift completes and with it comes a roar so loud it grabs Cole's attention. Uncontrollable flames ignite through my mouth burning every Shadow Walker in sight. More multiply.

"Redmae, get Rory out of here."

"We're not going anywhere."

An arrow whizzes by my wing and I look up to see four dark dragons approach.

One by one, Cole and I fight them off. They circle in droves attempting to surround us. The wails of screams grow as Cole burns more creatures. We see one dark dragon aim for Redmae, gliding fast.

Rory draws back her bow and shoots.

Cole comes plowing forward roaring out blue flames, charring more Shadow Walkers on the ground. One by one, the demon vanishes only to appears seconds later.

"This is a losing battle, Wynter we need to get us out of here."

I flame a large circle of fire separating the demons from Rory and Red. *"You grab Redmae, I'll grab Rory,"* I say.

Cole swoops in and I follow his lead. *"As soon as we reach the portal, we need to down the potions Jasmine gave us and glide through the gate. If these elixirs are as good as Jasmine says, we will be invisible to the dark dragons."*

We sail up and over the high mountain range while the dark dragons' race after us. Cory and I hover over solid ground next to the side of a mountain crag. *"It's a dead end. We're going to be forced to fight them."*

"Not if I can help it. As soon as you can, drink your potion."

Cole lands first and shifts. He pulls from his jacket Jasmines potion.

Redmae tucks and rolls.

I drop Rory a few feet from the ground and shift as well.

"Drink your elixir now!" Cole grabs Redmae's bottle, pops off the cork, and helps her down the liquid.

Rory reaches for her container, and swigs.

I take out my potion and do the same. "Yep, just like Jasmine said, it tastes disgusting."

The wailing from the Shadow Walkers slowly fades as though they can no longer sense our presence. The dark dragons rage with breathing fire once they discover that we have disappeared. We've become invisible to the undead creatures of The Veil between Crimson Moors and Scarlet Hollow.

8

SANCTUARY OF SOULS

A hazy feeling comes over me and the color from my vision is replaced with a black and white. "Strange." I look over at my friends. "Can you see me?"

Rory nods. "Everything looks greyscale. There's no color palette."

"I think it's supposed to be that way," Cole says. He turns a full circle noticing for himself that our environment is different.

More Shadow Walkers approach but they do not see us and roam aimlessly about, confused. We stand back, observing their moves. A few of them walk through the mountain crag that we all ended up landing in front of and disappear.

A clear wall of liquid substance, ripples with each demon that passes through it. One dark dragon we managed to miss, flies right through the portal gate with ease.

"What in the world?" Rory says in awe. She reaches to touch the substance. "I've never seen something so strange. This defies the laws of physics."

"This is another world, Rory. We're not in Earth's realm," Cole says.

"No, we're in sister planets, realm, and I haven't seen anything like it," she counters.

"I have," he argues.

"Wait." I'm reminded by the electrifying display Cole demonstrated earlier. "What if it hurts us?"

"Harmless. It's like the invisible barrier from earlier, but this one is slightly different. This is Scarlet Hollow's front door," Cole says.

"Are they waiting for us on the other side?" I touch the substance. It feels like gel, but the gate itself ripples like water.

"Not sure," Cole answers. "We are temporarily protected by Jasmine's spell, though, so they cannot see us. I'm positive this is the correct way to Cory. What does your compass say, Wynter?"

I open my locket. "It says we're in the right place. The dial is pointing to that gel-like gate."

"If this is a portal, it's one massive entry." Rory looks up. There aren't any distinguished lines separating the portal door to the sky. "We should test it out first before going through." Rory picks up a rock and tosses it through the barrier. It plunges through the liquid wall, leaving a ripple in its wake. The fluid stays in place and emits a sound like rushing river water.

We don't see our reflections, but we do have a clear vision of the other side. The same trees we've seen throughout this hellacious adventure awaits beyond the liquid glass in front of us. It's as though the entire space we're looking at is water, starting from the ground and leading up to the sky. An endless amount of liquid acting as a wall. Yet it's clear as glass.

"Here goes nothing." Rory puts her palm through first and then pulls back. Her hand comes out dry, and arm still intact. "It may look like it's water, but it isn't, but whatever it is, it feels ice cold."

"We're wasting time." Cole slips directly through the watery liquid without warning.

Rory and I give each other a perplexing glance.

Seconds later, Cole grabs my hand, and before I have time to react, he pulls me through the liquid.

"Hey!"

"Oh, stop being such a baby," he teases. "I just saved your life."

"That's debatable." I shake off his grasp and look up. Black clouds rumble, and smoke and ash still rain down everywhere. "Not a place I expected at all. This is completely different than the side of The Veil that the Crimson Moors are on."

Rory and Redmae plunge through.

"Whoa," Rory says. "It's completely different on this side."

"Yeah, that's what I just said." As before, the land is filled with thick brush and an abundance of trees, except no sounds of birds or life. More like an eerie silence. A light fog covers the ground obscuring our view of the grass, if there is any. Whispers of random voices float through the stagnate air. Most of the time I hear voices of random souls in my mind, but this time my ears response to the creepy sounds. "Are we in The Veil, now, Cole?"

"We're still in The Veil, Wynter, we never left. This side is Scarlet Hollow, where the afterlife of magical beings go. Like I mentioned before, the Crimson Moors is the physical world of Scarlet Hollow. The Veil is the in-between dimension. A dimension where both the physical, and metaphysical meet. Like when we were on the Crimson Moors side watching the shadows and demons cross over, this side will have the same circumstances."

We watch as each demon penetrates through the gate and vanish into a puff of smoke once they touch the barrier, much like the demonstration Cole did with throwing the rock earlier before we crossed the invisible bridge. "That's really eerie."

"This is where the tourmaline comes in that Jasmine mentioned," Cole says. "It protects our physical bodies from the darkness. If we didn't have that protecting our mind, we could easily be possessed."

Cole's comments send goosebumps down my spine. I look at my hands. "And we're not ghosts—spirits—or whatever; we're still in our physical forms? Cole Storm, this is so bizarre."

He nods. "Stay close, though, there is no telling who we will run into." He looks down at his watch. "We have about fifty-five minutes to find Cory. We haven't much time, and remember, try not to have too many inner thoughts."

"I'm sure Sarmira hasn't thought we'd be brave enough to step into her world," Rory argues.

"Don't be so sure. You better believe Sarmira's minions who were chasing us earlier have already reported back to her. Count on it."

The demons continue marching around above our heads searching for us, their howls loud. Above the trees, I can see large shadows trace across the clouds, much like before except the Shadow Walkers have increased in numbers. Howls roar like thunderclouds and power through the sky in frustrated calls.

"We definitely made them mad, didn't we," Rory says.

"Definitely not happy, no. Come on, the Sanctuary of Lost Souls isn't far from here." Cole steps ahead of us, leading down a dark narrow path with the same trees on either side of us as before when we were running through the dark forest in the Crimson Moors. The grass is a shade less than the trees, with the path the only color that stands out in a different shade of greyscale. Even the bushes have a tint to them. It's like every shade of grey, black, and white imaginable on the rainbow spectrum of no colors.

"I imagine all these grey colors would be red shades if not for the illusion spell, am I right?" Rory asks.

"Correct. When I passed through here as a spirit when my body was possessed searching for Wynter while she was under her dream stamp, I saw a lot of red. It's The House of Bloodbane colors." He turns around. "Remember, much of Elleirodal is the parallel to Ladorielle, the difference is, this is the dark side of the realm."

We take a few more steps farther and come to a stop. A stone fence crosses our path with an iron gate. The door is in the shape of an oval and has an iron bar window where one has the option to use a knocker. He opens it and we walk through.

I'm stunned by a hidden garden beyond. Dead, dried up vines cling along the fence. A few trees look dormant or dead. Dried leaves scatter across the ground and the dirt paths are cracked from lack of moisture. "It's like Sara's Garden on the grounds of Storm River Manor. Except, there isn't any hints of life."

"Sort of, yes," Cole answers. "Before the war, this land belonged to a light witch coven. You may have heard of it. The House of Ashburn."

"Oh right, the House of Ashburn. We're supposed to find Jasmine's sisters." I feel for the necklaces that I carefully placed in the outside pocket of my jacket. The Soul Catcher is on the inside. "Do you honestly think we are going to find them?"

"I don't know. Let's get to my brother first then worry about them."

"No. Cole, we gave our word."

"You did. I didn't." He pushes forward past a large willow tree.

The hanging vines tickle my shoulders. I feel the tinge of magic from the leaves. *This tree is alive.*

A strong wind thrust Cole to the ground. "Who dares to trespass upon my sacred lands!"

Rory gives me a side eye. "I thought we were invisible?"

"Keep still," I say.

"Well, I do say I didn't think I would ever see visitors from the living realm..." the entity purrs like a cat.

"We mean you no harm," Cole says. "We've come for my brother, Cory." He nods. "Over there beyond the boulder and inside the cave lies his physical body."

"I see." The image of a black cat with leopard spots and white jawline reveals itself, and prowls around us in a circle. The rumble in his deep voice is eerie. "Hmm, I smell something familiar about you but cannot place it."

Although I can see him, he isn't quite translucent as a ghost. If I didn't know any better, I'd say his form is as solid as mine. "Are you trapped here like our friend we've come to claim?"

"Who said I am trapped?" His eyes dart to each of us.

Another growl comes from behind us. This cat has brought a friend. "Who have we found this time, Kaun?"

"Trespassers!"

"No, we're here to find our friend," Rory claims. She pulls out her bow. "I'm not afraid to use this."

"Oh no, an arrow..." Kaun shutters. "I'm so scared, whatever shall I do?" he purrs louder, unaffected by Rory's outburst.

She takes aim. "I mean it. Get out of our way."

"Or what?!" Kaun roars, and pounces toward her.

Rory shoots and the cat disappears into a puff of smoke.

Boisterous laughter comes from the other cat that has yet to reveal himself. "You think a little archery will defeat us?" The other cat appears. He's almost identical to Kaun. This one is all black. "You know, I'm not as spicy as my friend." He licks his front paw and purrs. "I take it you're Jasmines friends?"

Cole squints. "What?"

Rory relaxes.

Redmae is ignoring everyone and lying on the grass. "*I*

could have told you the cats were harmless but, I quite liked the entertainment."

"A lot of help you are."

Rory puts back her bow. "Yes, we have met Jasmine. She said you were trapped here. I don't see her sisters with you, though."

Kaun reappears. "They do not come out from hiding much. It's best they do not draw attention from the Shadow Walkers."

"Speaking of which...how is that you can see us, and the Shadow Walkers cannot? Jasmine said this spell would make us invisible to the spirit realm. I mean, I can see ghosts naturally, but my friends can't."

"That's easy," the second cat says. "We're familiars. It's hard to get past us." He comes closer. "I'm Sasha."

I nod. "Please to meet you."

A loud whistle pings our ears. Beyond the willows two figures stand still.

"Ah, that is our calling," Sasha says. He disappears along with Kaun.

"Great, now what?" Rory asks. "Aren't we supposed to bring them back with us?"

"Let's find my brother first." Cole isn't amused. He steps forward toward the big mossy boulder behind the large willow tree.

"How do we move it out of the way?" Rory asks.

"We don't need to." Cole walks the through the solid looking rock.

I look behind me to see Redmae still lying in the grass. *"Are you coming?"*

"Nope!"

"Why not?"

"Because I want to rest my weary bones."

"*Redmae, are you under a spell?*" I'm worried. This isn't like her.

"*Calm down, I'm fine. Someone needs to guard the entrance, right?*"

I sigh. "*Okay, good point. You had me nervous for a minute.*"

"*Go get Cory...*"

"Wynter, are you coming or what?" Rory calls.

9

MIRROR OF SOULS

Spiral steps greet me on the other side of the boulder. The hollow passageway is dark and creepy. "Hello? Where did you all go?" No answer. I take a step. "Come on guys, this isn't funny."

"Wynter, we're down here," Cole calls.

The stone steps wind around. It's like I am in a castle turret. Moss grows on the walls in-between each layered stone blocks. The musty smell invades my nostrils, making it hard to breathe. I nearly bump into Cole once I reach the bottom. "Sorry, it's so dark, I can't see well."

He snickers. "Turn on your night lights."

I nudge him. "I keep forgetting to use my eyes. I'm not used to being a walking flashlight. Where is Rory?"

"Over here." She gazes at something hanging on a wall.

"It looks like the same mirror we saw in Jasmine's crystal cove and in the Hall of Secrets. It even has the identical infinity filigree pewter loops on the frame."

Rory touches the mirror. "Well, I guess we found our way out of here."

Cole turns in the opposite direction. "That is the direction I came from when Cory and I tried to escape."

"Wait, what about the sisters?" I ask again. "We promised Jasmine."

"I told you; we'll get them out of here too but first let's find my brother. He's over here. I can feel him. Can't you, Wynter?"

"No, not yet."

Cole brushes aside some branches that our in our way.

"Another willow tree?" I ask. It blocks the entrance to a double door. Weird how they can grow in such dark areas.

"It's not a willow tree, although, similar. This one and the one out in the garden are some the few blue oak trees left that survived the war." He touches the long vine-like branch hanging before us. "I'm quite amazed it's down in this hollowed out area, too."

"That's because I planted it," a woman says behind us.

Startled, we turn together.

Two women, one with curly sable hair and the other a soft golden shade, come into view. Their facial features nearly identical. "I feel like I'm looking at Jasmine times two."

"We're triplets," the woman with brown hair says. "I'm Sage, and this is my sister Angelica."

I nudge Cole. "Jasmine didn't say they would look exactly like her. I'm so confused right now. How can they see us?"

"I'm not sure, myself," Cole answers.

"How do you know our sister Jasmine?" Angelica asks.

Cole steps forward, putting out his hand to greet them. "We mean you no harm, I assure you. The Raven sent us to your sister, and she led us to here. We're looking for my brother. He's just beyond those double doors."

"I don't understand. How did you get past the gatekeeper?" Angelica tilts her head looking a bit perplexed.

"Jasmine said the gatekeeper owed her a favor," Cole replies. "

The ladies look at each other, concerned. Their familiars come to their sides to comfort them.

The blonde woman named Angelica whispers, "That can only mean one thing—"

"Do you think he's been released?" Sage questions.

"Only one way to find out—"

I clear my throat interrupting. "Excuse me but who has been released? I don't mean to be nosey, but we have had our shared of released demons and we don't need another." I look at Rory.

She nods. "That's the understatement of the year."

"Whatever do you mean?" Sage asks. "Demons are after you, too?"

"Redmae, are you there?"

"I am. All clear out here."

"Thank you, but I need to know if you sense danger like these witches..."

"You mean Jasmine's sisters? They're quite innocent I assure you."

"Can you tell us why you're here? I mean neither of you look like any ghost." I hesitate to pull out the Soul Catcher, just yet. "Jasmine mentioned you have been trapped here."

"We have," Sage confirms. "Not sure how long, time isn't measured in The Veil. We were tricked. The night of a Super Blue Blood Moon in fact."

Rory, Cole, and I eye each other. There must be a connection between the current moon phase and their past moon phase.

"We were about to cage an evil sorcerous who had been wreaking havoc on our lands for what seemed like an eternity." Sage looks to her sister.

"I was captured first, sucked into the very thing that supposed to be used for the wicked witch herself." Angelica's facial features harden. "A Fae goblin grabbed my Soul Catcher and turned it on me." She reaches for her cat and scratches the top of his head. "Kaun was pulled in with me. I landed here in this garden thankfully. We don't venture farther than the entrance from the iron gate you passed through, from above."

"The demons cannot penetrate the garden as long as the blue tree out there—" Angelica points to the boulder blocking this part of the sanctuary- "and this tree between us, continue to consume magic. I planted both of them a while ago. These two trees were the only ones that grew out of the hundreds of seeds I had in my possession. The day I was confronted, I'd been picking blue oak nuts. Tiny seeds that can be used in many recipes or eaten on their own. That's how these trees rooted here."

"That is quite the odds to overcome. I can appreciate the tenacity it must've taken to keep it healthy." I look over at the mirror. Jasmine mentioned the Mirror of Souls would be hidden from The Veil. I wonder if the potion she gave us was for us to see the mirror? "May I ask, why haven't you passed through the Mirror of Souls to your freedom?"

"We have searched and searched," Angelica says.

I glance in the direction of where the mirror hangs in plain sight.

"We even sent out our familiars to look for the magical portal. We cannot find it," Sage adds.

All of us eye each other, knowing this must be why they have not escaped this horrid dimension.

"What do you see over there?" I point to the mirror on the wall.

Sage raises one brow as though I'm blinded by the obvious. "A... stone... wall?" She looks over at her sister and she shrugs.

Rory walks to the frame and touches the filigree silver craftsmanship once again. "You do not see this?"

"I'm telling you, all I—we- see is limestone walls." Sage's

tone changes to concern. "Are you telling me that you see a mirror and we do not?"

Cole nods. "We can help you leave."

I'm reminded of the necklaces Jasmine gave me and pull them from the small bag in the outer pocket of my jacket. "Here, maybe this will help." I hand the tourmaline silver wrapped inlay stone pieces to both women. "Your sister said I should give these to you to put on."

The light witches are stunned. "My necklace?" Anjelica looks down at the one around her neck. "It's identical to the one I am wearing. How did you replicate it?"

"My guess is the one that you're wearing is fake," I say.

"Fake? Impossible, we never take them off."

I pull out my necklace. "See this? I never take it off either." I come closer to show them. "When I was under a dream stamp, the same thing happened to me. I couldn't see the truth because the fake necklace was blocking the energy. If you can find a way to trust us, you will be set free, but only if you release the energy that is holding you here."

Sage is the first to put on the new necklace. The old one fades, allowing her to be consumed with light. The willow tree her sister planted responds to Sage and branches out. The leaves gleam from the faint glow of Sage's aura.

"Angelica, look." She points to the tree. "Can you see it?"

"No, I see nothing." She pierces a glare at me. "What kind of trickery are you trying to pull here?"

"It's not a trick, dear sister. Wynter is right." She notices the mirror and walks right up to it. "The Mirror of Souls has been here the whole time." She gazes at her reflection and it shimmers until it shifts into clear glass.

The crystal we saw in Jasmine's cave appears.

"I see Jasmine!" Sage's excitement grabs Angelica's attention.

"What?" she comes to Sage's side. "Honey, it's just a wall. There is nothing there."

Sage earnestly squeezes Angelica's hand. "Put the necklace on and you will see the truth."

Angelica wavers.

"Sage, what about this?" I pull from my other pocket the Soul Catcher.

She gasps. "That is what brought us here. Be very careful with that."

"I told you she wasn't to be trusted!" Angelica springs forward.

I brace myself without thinking and cross my forearms in front of my face, still holding the Soul Catcher, and Angelica is sucked into the device. "I—I –didn't—"

"It's alright. She's perfectly safe in there. Angelica is known for jumping to conclusions. I know the truth. I am not worried."

"But she's—I don't understand."

"My sister Jasmine is a clever woman, and I think she anticipated this was going to happen. She knew Angelica would be suspicious, so she gave you the Soul Catcher not only for protection, but should my sister not take the necklace, the Soul Catcher would be a second way to release her from this dreadful place."

"And how will she be released?" Rory asks.

"Wynter, bring the Soul Catcher to the mirror, and allow the energy to flow through your fingers." Sage helps with the power by also holding onto the handle. A swirl of light penetrates from the device to the mirror. Seconds later all of us see Angelica on the other side. The expression on her face says it all. She's stunned.

"Shall I do the same to you?"

"Not at all. I simply touch the mirror, and I'll glide right through."

I smile, "Here, then." I attempt to hand her the Soul Catcher.

"Keep it with you. My guides tell me you're going to need it."

"Guides?"

"The voices in your head, Wynter. That intuition. The thoughts that come to you, ideas, the sense that danger is near, or that you're about to make a wrong decision... all of those incidences are signs or guidance from the energies above. Learn to read the signs and understand the feelings that come to you. My feeling, my intuition tells me, you're going to need this." She pushes the Soul Catcher back into my hands. "I recommend you keep it safe and in a leather bag."

I hold up a bag that Sage just describes.

"Good deal." Sage smiles. "It was good to meet all of you. Now I must go home. I owe you, my life." She touches the glass reflection, and as she said, her body drifts into the mirror, where we can see she safely makes it through to the crystal cave.

Jasmine and Angelica stand on the other side greeting their sister, they wave back, and the portal mirror fades back to a looking glass once more.

SATISFIED THAT WE FULFILLED A PROMISE, I TURN TO Cole. "Let's go find Cory." My compass glows, directing us to the double doors behind the blue oak tree.

"How do we open them?" Rory asks.

"With this." Cole holds up a familiar key. It's the same one he used to open the door to the invisible bridge. He inserts it into the lock and opens it.

Before I step over the threshold, I notice something move.

Cole notices, too. "We're not alone obviously." He looks at

his watch." Ten minutes left on this spell. We better make this quick."

Beyond the entry is another garden-like room filled with hanging vines and ivy climbing along the stone walls. It reminds me of an old castle terrace. In the center of the room a dais where Cory's physical body lies. The Blade of Hope that Cole stabbed him with is still in his chest.

"I can't believe we finally found him." I know Cole already warned me about what he did, but seeing Cory's dead body puts the visual in perspective. I feel a familiar presence of something standing close to me and I turn to see it's Cory.

Rory sees him, too. She elbows me. "Look. It's Cory."

"Yes, I know."

"Do you think he sees us?"

"I don't think so. I'm guessing not while we're under this spell Jasmine gave us. I know he would have come directly up to me if he had."

"But Sage, Angelica, and their familiars saw us."

"They were witches," Cole says. He stands by his brother's body.

Tears well in my eyes. My instincts kick in and I climb upon the dais, grab the hilt impaled into Cory's chest and pull. "It won't budge."

"Here, let me take a stab at it." Rory chuckles. "No pun intended, my friend."

"None taken." I tuck my hands in my back pockets in anticipation.

"Nope, I've got nothin." Rory steps down.

"Here, let me try." Cole steps onto the dais. He places his hands around the hilt.

Cole hesitates before pulling the blade, glancing at each of us.

"What are you waiting for?" Rory asks, staring at him. "Pull out the blasted dagger."

"There's something I must warn you about before doing so," Cole confesses.

"Of course, there's a catch. I should have guessed." Rory folds her arms.

Cole licks his lips. "When I pull this dagger, it will trigger our location to the underworld. The only reason they haven't gotten to Cory yet is because of this blade. It's cloaking him."

I turn to look at Cory's spirit, then back to Cole. "And you waited until now to tell us this part...why? What do you propose we do? Cole Storm—"

"We port Cory out as soon as possible while the blade is still in his chest," Cole says.

"No, something tells me that isn't going to work. We've tried that already," Rory argues. "The day we fought the Shadow Walkers, after you stabbed Cory at Storm River Manor, we tried that, and Cory didn't land with us in Ashengale."

"Then we have no choice but to release his body here," Cole says. "Be ready for Sarmira to appear once I free my brother." He stares at us all.

I ball my fists in frustration.

"I'm not dead, ya know," Cory says, showing a lopsided grin. "It's about time you found me."

I nearly choke. "Wait, you can see me?" My heart aches and pounds for him to be real.

"See you? Why wouldn't I? Wynter, you're supposed to see ghosts. I mean I *am* a ghost, right?"

"Hopefully not for long, brother." Cole gets ready to pull the blade.

Cory appears confused. "I swear I just heard Cole."

"You did." I attempt to hug him, but my arms go right through his frame.

He laughs. "My sweet Wynter, pull the dagger from me first so we can do that."

"That is the objective, brother." Cole's tone of voice sounds frustrated.

Cory turns around. "Where is my brother hiding? I hear him, but I cannot see him."

"Rory and Redmae are with us too. Well, Red is out frolicking upstairs in the open field doing who knows what."

"I am not. I'm right here." She roams into the room.

"Hey, I can hear Redmae." Cory grins.

"Likewise, Cory." Redmae licks her paws. *"I will be happy to finally be rid of this place myself."*

I collect my emotions, trying hard not to be too excited. We are, after all, in Sarmira's world, and I don't put any surprises past her at this point. I turn around to still see Cory's body lying motionless on the dais. "You look so alive next to me."

"It's not as bad as I thought the afterlife would be, I suppose, but wow, do I have some stories to tell all of you."

Cole clears his throat.

Cory and I laugh. "Sorry, brother. I can't thank you enough for finding her for me."

Cole straightens. "What are siblings for." He gives a mocking wink. "Would you like me to pull the blade from your chest and bring you back to the land of the living, dear brother, or do you prefer to stay a ghost?"

He grins again. "Sorry." Cory steps aside.

"I know I should have said something earlier about Sarmira, but—"

"Just pull out the blasted thing. We can deal with the aftermath later," Cory says.

Cole looks at his watch. "Our ten minutes are up. Looks like the spell has worn off."

"What spell?" Cory looks over at his body.

"That, my friend, is a long story," Rory answers. "We need to focus on getting you out of here. It looks like our only option is to leave through the Mirror of Souls."

"Jasmine said we needed to do it before the spell wore off or we would be trapped in here. I think I know why, too. Like the sisters, we too, will not see the mirror now." I look at Rory. "You're going to have to port us out of here."

"I don't like the sound of that," Rory says. "My port abilities have been off, or did you forget about the medicine Jasmine made for me? Besides we tried that already, after the battle on the grounds of Storm River Manor the day we fought the Shadow Walkers right after you stabbed Cory."

"It isn't up for debate, Rory. I made this mess, now it's my turn to fix it. Bro, you have to know I had no idea."

"I don't think either of us had any idea that you had the Blade of Hope in your hands. Don't sweat it. I would have done the same thing if the roles were reversed."

"Be prepared for Sarmira to appear," I say.

"I'll make sure we are out of here before anything appears." Rory circles the dais as though she is measuring the circumference. "I only have one concern."

"Which is?" Cole asks still holding onto the hilt.

"This may not make for a pleasant landing. I'll try and take us to Storm Castle, but we must port out before Sarmira has a chance to attack. If she has an opportunity to disrupt our escape it can alter our route. Loop around the dais and hold hands. As soon as the dagger is free from Cory's chest, I'll begin my cast."

"Aren't you forgetting someone?" Redmae nudges at Rory's hand.

"Oh gawd, sis, I'm so sorry."

"Not forgiven." Redmae grunts, coming beside me.

"She says you owe her one." I scruff the back of Red's neck.

"You want on my bad side, too, Wyn?"

"Oh hush, we never would have left you behind. Did you have a good nap."

She grunts again. *"We're not done here; I will get even with both of you."* Her tone sounding mischievous.

Cole wraps his hands tightly around the Blade of Hope's hilt once again as I hold onto Cory's physical hand and lock my other arm around Redmae's neck. Rory sits upon Redmae's back waiting on Cole's cue.

"I'm pulling the blade on the count of three."

Rory prepares in her free hand and reveals the rune stone to Storm Castle. A blue glow with golden hues appears from the rock. She nods. "Do it now."

Cole pulls at the dagger and Cory's ghost begins to fade.

The wind kicks up and dust flies. "We're too late. She knows we're here," I say.

Rory engages the port. "Not if I can help it."

The blade is free, and Cory's grey cracked stone complexion begins to clear up. His skin softens and he slowly opens his bright blue eyes. He grins.

"You're back!" I kiss him to make sure.

He laughs. "I'm back."

I kiss him again. "I never thought I would miss you as much as I do now."

High pitch screams ensue along with stirring gusts. A funnel appears gliding at fast speed.

"Rory," Cole yells, through the stirring wind, "where's that port?"

"It fizzled." She attempts to cast again.

A ball of light shoots through the veil and Sarmira appears. Her evil laugh taunts us. "I knew you would eventually come for him, Wynter. I see you brought some friends. I think we can work something out. They will be quite useful. Especially the druid."

I throw a fire ball and fail to hit my mark.

Sarmira laughs. "You have no power here, Wynter. This is my world."

"Rory!" Cole calls. "Now would be a good time to port us out of here."

Rory's second attempt fails.

"My darlings, trying to get away from me so soon?" Sarmira lurches forward, blasting a powerful fireball of her own, but it implodes before reaching us into a falling snow.

"What? Impossible!" Sarmira shrieks in frustration. She casts again, and this time the powerful blasts reverts back to her, pushing her backward to the ground.

Behind her, Jasmine, Sage, and Angelica link hands around Sarmira trapping her in their shield. "This won't last long, Wynter, port out of here as soon as you can," Jasmine says as her sisters enchant a spell together.

"Hang on, this time I got it," Rory says, with a determined expression. A bubble illuminates around us.

Sarmira's cackle grows louder. The defeat of Sarmira is temporary. She flings upward, pulling out of the witch's spell. "You cannot defeat me!"

"Hurry up!" I scream.

Sarmira surges forward a second time and succeeds with tearing through the portal bubble, but Rory is faster, and we're lifted from The Veil of Scarlet Hallow just in time, except, Rory warned us that a portal disruption meant a destination disruption. We disappear into the ether.

IO
HOME SWEET HOME

R ory's portal gate isn't like the last one, when we stepped through— Scarlet Hollow. This one speeds us through a tunnel that winds and flows like a slide at a water park and the experience doesn't even register until after I land at our new destination.

Realizing I'm lying on the cold ground, I sit up. My fingers are numb from the icy snow, and I blow on the tips to warm up. I stand, turning a full circle but do not see any of my party. "Cory! Cole! Rory!" No answer.

My first observation is it's eerily quiet except for the whistling wind. Flakes of frozen snow part through the air. It's cold. I look up at the clear sky. Stars twinkle as though they have a secret message that they cannot relay to me. Part of the landscape is burned to ash, and I instinctively think Rory has jumped us to another area of Elleirodal, but the difference here, only one moon. Plus, the energy feels heavy. A heavy energy that swirls around me and feels all too familiar.

The crackle of burning wood and flesh make for an unsavory smell. A waft of smoke invades my nostrils, mouth, and throat that has me nearly gasping for breath.

Looking up at the bright red moon again, a whirl of fog pours from its glowing light with a feeling of dread that attempts to overpower my thoughts. Whispers of several voices call to me. They try to penetrate my soul and fail. My necklace glows. It's a glow I've grown to know and it's a sign of protection. I quickly realize where I am. It's a place I wish to forget and never return, but alas I fear that my intuition is not wrong. *"Redmae, can you hear my thoughts?"*

"Yes, I can hear you. Are you okay?"

"Yes, I'm fine. I'm alone, though. No signs of Rory, Cole, or Cory. Are they with you?"

"I'm alone as well." She pauses. *"I'm in some sort of building. I think it's a barn."*

"Really? Oh, come on."

"I know, right?" I hear her irritated grunt in my mind.

I can feel the pain in her telepathic voice. *"Redmae, you're hurt."*

"A little bruised, maybe. I'm a dire wolf. We tend to heal quickly. I think I've landed on hay, which may have softened the landing, and I have a massive headache. You?"

"I'm sore a little. Redmae, you won't believe where Rory sent us all to."

Redmae's tone changes dubiously. *"Where, home sweet home?"*

"How did you know?"

"I was joking, Wynter, but it might explain why I landed in a barn."

"Ha!"

"Good news, I do sense four heartbeats, including yours."

"That's a positive sign." I move through the smoldering woods hoping for any clue where our friends might be. *"Any sign of your best friend Casey?"*

"So far, no, but I haven't made it a purpose to look, yet. I'm

still trying to get the hay out of my fur." She pauses. *"Hang on, how did you know that Casey and I are best friends?"*

"Rory told me." I stamp at the ground trying to kick ice off my boots. Walking in the snow isn't easy. I definitely chose the wrong footwear.

"Figures. I think Casey is gone, Wynter. That night when it all went down, he had consumed as many souls that emptied from the full Blood Moon as possible."

"You mean the same Blood Moon I'm looking up at right now?" Another cold chill whips across my face and I close up my jacket. Clearly, I am not dressed for this weather.

"What do you mean same Blood Moon? That's concerning, Wynter."

"How so?" I come to a ledge and overlook a valley that appears in ruins.

"We may have gone through a time shift."

"You mean gone back in time?" In the far distance, Storm River Manor barely stands. It's been burned nearly to the ground. The only walls that remain are ones made of stone.

"Yes. The Earth's atmosphere shouldn't be going through a full moon phase right now. They just went through one before your long nap. Plus, I would feel something. Us dire wolves are connected to the moon. Something feels off."

"Redmae, you need to come see this."

"What is it?"

"Most of Storm River Manor has burned to the ground. And there is something else you should know. A dark cloud is swirling, around the moon like a ring."

"That's concerning. It means either my sister's porting abilities are off course significantly, or we've gone back in time."

"Redmae, do you think Aoes had something to do with this?"

"Most definitely. I don't think Rory has those capabilities. This is the work of a mage."

"We need to find your sister and the others." Rustling leaves followed by moans startle me. "Who's there!"

"Wynter, be careful. I'm coming to you now. Stay where you are please."

"Don't worry, Red, I have magical hands, remember?"

"Not on Earth you don't. You're not nearly as powerful here as you are in the realm of Ladorielle. The atmosphere is much too dense."

"Yes, I've noticed that." More moans follow. *"Redmae, I think someone might be hurt. I can feel pain that isn't my own."*

"One of us, or someone else?"

"I don't know."

"Wait for me."

More groaning sounds come from a few feet away. The bushes move. *"If this was some sort of predator, they would have struck me down by now, don't you think?"*

"It could be Sabretail Prowlers, or invisible hounds, or worse, Shadow Walkers. Please, stay where you are, I'll come to you."

"Redmae, I can't stand by and wait. This person is hurt."

"No, wait for me." Seconds later I hear her roar in what feels like a ripping sensation of pain in my mind. Far in the distance the cry of a wolf, echoes through the valley. I look down toward the barn and see no sign of movement which, signals to me, something is wrong.

"Redmae!"

The groans near me increase, as well. I hesitantly step closer to where the sounds are coming from. My heart pounds within my chest. *"Redmae."* Nothing but silence follows. She's no longer in my thoughts.

The bush moves again with more moans of pain. That isn't the sound of any animal. I pull back the branches of a large shrub. "Rory!"

"Redmae, I found your sister." Rory's head is planted face down in the surrounding grass. Thankfully the snow hasn't

touched this area much, otherwise she'd be frozen solid. I roll her over. Her cheeks are flushed and bruised, with a cut across her forehead, but other than that, she seems okay. Hovering my hands above Rory's face, I heal the gash. *"Redmae?"* She remains silent in my mind. Worry sets in that she too, has found an unpredictable situation. I tap at my best friend's cheeks. "Rory, wake up."

She moans a bit more before finally opening her eyes. It takes her a few seconds to focus before realizing I'm the one who has woken her. "What just happened?"

"I don't know. You tell me?" I kneel next to her.

She sits up and looks around. "Where are we?" She places her hand against the back of her head.

"Take a wild guess."

She shrugs.

"I'll give you a clue...it's not Storm Castle, but you did get Storm correct in your calculations."

"What? You're kidding?"

"Would I kid when it comes to that?"

Rory tries to get up.

"Careful." I help her to her feet. "Rory, you seriously need to check up on your porting compass."

"I know." She covers her nose. "And it smells like burning flesh everywhere."

"Yeah, much different than the last place we were." I glance back at the moon, and point. "Any idea why we're seeing that? Shouldn't that phase have passed a week ago?"

"And here I thought we were going back to Storm Castle," she says. "Surprise... Just kidding."

I give her the side-eye.

"Hey, I can kid too, right?"

"Not funny, Rory."

"I know. Sorry." She takes a quick turn. "Where's my sister? And the boys?"

"Good question. Redmae is possibly in the barn down there." I point to the ruins of what once looked like Storm River Manor. A few yards from there, the red barn remains untouched. "We had telepathic communication right before I found you, but I haven't heard from her since. Rory, I'm worried. Sabretail Prowlers roam the grounds of Storm River Manor and this compound, is in ruins."

Rory takes note of the smoldering coals beneath the frozen mounds of snow. "That's the scars of war, Wynter. We battled down below. Some of us retreated to these woods in hopes of weeding out our foes one by one." She takes a few steps forward and studies the ground as she rubs her arm. "I felt Sarmira strike at me right as we disappeared." She rolls up her sleeve showing me the burn.

"Talk about cutting it close." I lay my hand over the wound and heal it.

"Yeah, well, something tells me she won't be far behind."

"It's going to be difficult for her to find us, unless we lose the protective stones Jasmine gave us, remember? She said that it will cloak your whereabouts, Rory—like my necklace."

She checks her pocket for the stone. "It's still there."

I nod. "We need to find the boys and Redmae. Once we're under the protection of the Storm River cottage, it will be harder for her to find us."

Rory nods, at my necklace. "You're glowing again. What does it mean this time?"

I open it. "It's pointing to those dark woods."

"Guess we should follow it."

We come upon an open wrought iron gate. Old brown grass, and dead ivy vines creep in and out between the black rusted bars. "Well, this might be a good sign. Maybe we'll find them in here." I push the gate open more and it creaks. We quickly discover where all the dead bodies go to rest.

"Wynter, it's a cemetery."

A magical feeling comes over me once I pass over the threshold as though the presence of my mother is close. I don't see her like I used to, but I feel her love. "Rory, did you feel that?"

"Just a breeze. It's freaking cold!" She closes the cloak she wears tighter around her body. "But this doesn't look too inviting."

"Afraid of some ghosts, my friend?"

"Ha! Not in the least. Just wish I could see them like you can."

Heaps of snow spill over headstones lined in rows up and down the walkways. "Rory what is that?" The sole of a person's shoes lay between a pathway to our left.

"Please don't tell me it's a body."

"Well, I can say it isn't any ghost." We reach the figure and quickly discover it's Cory. I turn him over and check his chest. "He's still breathing."

"That begs the question, where is Cole?" Rory asks.

"Good question." I shake Cory. "Wake up."

Rory searches close in the area. "Wynter, I found footprints." She looks at me concerned. "And blood."

"We can't leave Cory here. What do we do?"

Rory pulls out her bow and arrow. "Stay here until he's conscious. I'll go look for Cole."

"Not alone, Rory. Have you lost your mind?"

"Heh, maybe a little. There is no telling where Cole is. What if he's hurt."

I look down at Cory. "Come on please wake up." *Maybe he's hurt.* I hover my hands over his body, hoping I can heal what I can.

Cory stirs.

I smile. "Thank goodness." I hug him.

"You know, every time you use your healing abilities, it drains your energy," he says.

"You're awake!" I kiss him. "Come on no time for jokes. Get up. Your brother is missing, and Rory went to find him... alone."

"What?" That got his attention. He stands as though nothing happened and looks around at his surroundings. "Which way did she go?"

I show him the footprints drenched in blood.

"Well, that isn't a very encouraging sign, is it?" He grabs my hand. "Come on, I think I know where he went."

"Wait you know where we are?"

"Yeah, I do, unfortunately. We're in the cemetery of Storm River Manor. My brother probably went to the kid fort we built a long time ago when we were little. We can't call out Rory's name either, else the Nocturnals will hear us."

"You mean the Shadow Walkers."

"And Sabretail Prowlers, or invisible hounds."

"You can see the hounds, as I recall."

"Yes."

"Wait what about my compass?" I hold it in my hand. "Lead us to Rory."

The compass glows showing us the way.

II
HIDEOUT

Just beyond a large evergreen tree I spot two of Rory's arrows sticking out from the trunk. Rory has followed the bloody tracks down a trail layered with brush, and dried pine needles so thick the snow never reached the ground. However, the blood still leaves us clues that we're going in the right direction. "Try not to sneak up on her. She'll not hesitate to shoot you, you know."

"Right." I pull out the stuck arrows. "Not like her to leave these behind, either."

Cory steals a grin before speeding away. It all happened so fast that my eyes take a minute to catch up. He has Rory in one arm and the quiver set in the other.

"Put me down, you big brute!" She half screams and half whispers at the same time, knowing full well the loud noises will bring on our enemies.

It forces me to giggle just a tad bit. "Rory, you're going to wake the dead."

Cory drops her near his feet. "You couldn't have waited just a few more minutes and allow me to come to before setting out on a dangerous nightly adventure without us?"

Cory's remark shuts whatever was about to come out of her mouth. She glares at him.

I hand her the abandoned arrows, then hold out my hand. "Let's go find Cole and Redmae together."

Rory stands. "I had a good lead until you spoiled it, Cory."

"Hardly. I know where Cole is."

She tilts her head, confused.

Cory shakes his head. "Follow me."

A few steps from where we bumped into Rory, the trail of blood stops.

Cory seems pleased. "Just as I suspected. He's in our kid hideout."

Rory wrinkles her forehead. "You feel alright, Cory? Perhaps you hit that petrified head a little too hard and cracked it. I see nothing but a tree trunk in front of us."

He rolls his eyes. "Whatever." Cory grabs my waist, and with his other hand grabs a rope that was slightly hidden from view and pulls. "Chao." We zip up onto a small platform attached to a branch. Small wooden planks nailed to the upper trunk, ladder up to a circular opening of an upper-level structure.

Rory is about to shout words, of frustration because we left her on the ground. Cory releases the pully and throws the rope back down. "Keep your shirt on Ror—"

I elbow him.

"Ow."

"Don't be so rude." I point at the circular platform above our heads. "I'm guessing Cole is up there?"

"Ladies first."

"Nope, you go first. Cole might attack me again," I tease.

"Ha!" Cory climbs the trunk and disappears through the opening.

Rory catches up to us and hooks the rope on a branch. "He's supposedly up there?"

"Yep." I step up.

The circular fort isn't anything too special. It reminds me of a bird's nest lookout from pirate ships.

The hideout is empty except for Cole who is sitting up against the wall clutching his side. Cory is kneeling next to him. Cole looks at me. "Guess being a vampire had its perks. I'm not regenerating like I used to."

"How did this happen?" I ask.

Cory rips open Cole's shirt. Three deep claw marks line the side of his chest.

"Sabretail Prowler?" his brother asks.

"How'd you guess?" he jokes.

"Not funny, Cole." I raise my hand and try and heal him.

"That isn't going to work this time, Wynter. He's going to need something stronger than that. These wounds are deep."

Rory leaps into the hideout. "What happened to you?" She kneels to check the lesions. "Those are definitely some nasty gashes you got there, my friend."

Cole grunts. "So, I'm your friend now, huh."

"Knock it off..." She reaches into her cloak and pulls out a pouch. "Nyta gave this to me a while back, when she knew we were going on our quest to find Redmae. I never needed to use any of it, but it might help you for now." She lathers some salve onto his wounds.

"I never made you out to be the healer type, Rory."

"I'm full of secrets. You just never stopped to learn about them."

Cory and I look at each other and raise our brows. *"Rory has a soft spot for your brother."*

He grins. *"Ya think?"*

"How did you get yourself tangled with a bunch of Sabretail Prowlers, anyway?" Rory asks.

"Landing around a nest full of Sabretail Prowers wasn't my idea. What happened to the smooth ride to a druid circle?"

Rory winces. "Yeah, I know. We need to figure that out, don't we?" She presses on the wound. "This might hurt a little."

Cole grunts in pain. "A little?"

"Sorry." She looks up at Cory and me. "Sorry for all of it. This is all my fault."

"Rory it's not." I squeeze her shoulder. "We will figure out what is going on, okay? Everything is off—"

"Wynter is right, the balance of the energies has been altered. We need to find the source of Samira's powers. It's the only way to get back the natural order of things." Cole places a hand on Rory, and she instantly pulls away.

"I'm fine. I'll be fine. We will all be fine." She stands. "Cole, we should really get you back to Ladorielle where Priestess Nyta can take a look at that."

He positions himself against the wall for a better pose than slouching. "Yeah, well, something tells me that isn't going to happen anytime soon." He winks. "The magic on Earth is heavier. Harder to use magic, and it takes much more concentration."

"You're probably right." I stand. "Anywhere else hurt, Cole?" I pull out the medicine Nyta gave me from my pocket. "I wonder if this might help you?"

Rory grumbles. "My sister is still out there somewhere."

"We'll find her, Rory," I say.

Cole pushes away my hand. "No, Wynter, she made just enough for you. Besides we don't know if that will work on me. I could turn into a dragon," he teases."

"Dragon?" Cory raises a brow.

I kiss Cory. "I still can't believe you're real."

"Clever girl. I'm not falling for it. Don't change the subject..."

I look down at Cory's chest. "Not even a scar remains of the blade. You're already healed."

"Vampires regenerate quickly." He nudges me, waiting for me to answer him.

"Right, I almost forgot. You're still a vampire."

"You're still not answering my question. What is this about a dragon?" He looks at his brother. "You said being a vampire *had* its perks, not *has* its perks.

My arm forms scales from the wrist to the elbow.

Cory is taken aback by my shift changes. "Wynter, your arm."

"Yeah, about that—" I collect my emotions, trying hard not to get too excited. Telling Cory that he's a dragon shifter might take a more strategic move. Last time we parted ways, I was going to Dragonscale Island to seek Dragonscale and his knowledge. Plus, Sarmira is still hunting us, so now may not be a good time for confessions. The scales slowly creep up to my shoulder, so I quickly take a couple swigs of elixir. "I still can't control my transition."

"Your transition? Are you telling me you're a dragon shifter?"

I give him a silly smile. "Surprise!"

Cory looks at his brother. "You knew about this?"

"Looks like we have some catching up to do." Cole tries to sit up further. I can tell he's in pain. He stiffens. "Don't worry. We can explain on the way."

"On the way to where?" Cory asks. "You're not in a position to go anywhere."

"To run after Rory." He nods toward the entrance. "She just took off."

I tuck the medicine back into the side pocket of my leather jacket. "Not again."

"If you think I'm staying here, you two don't know me as well as I thought." Cole struggles to get up.

Cory grunts and looks out the window. "Don't you think I know that?" He looks up at the full moon. "This isn't the night to be a hero, Cole." He veers to the left. "Rory is headed west. Son of a—" Cory leaps to the fort opening and shoots down.

"Cole, stay here, please." I hear him grumble and curse as I quickly follow Cory.

Crows caw alerting their friends, that the forest has visitors. "I don't like the sound of that, Cory."

"Neither do I."

"Can you spot Rory from here?" Although the keen eyes of a dragon can see as well as any vampire, we shifters don't have the ability to see warm bodies moving about. "Is this why Sarmira raised so many vampiric Shadow Walkers, because they can see extremely well at night?"

"I believe so." He nods ahead. "Rory is just beyond those trees. Step carefully... Wait." He instinctively holds out his arm to stop me. "Do you feel that?"

"I do. What is it?"

"Invisible hounds." Cory grabs my hand and pulls me onto his back.

"Just like old times, eh?" I clasp my hands around his chest and tuck my feet.

"The hounds cannot outrun me." He turns a full circle. "I see them. Through the tree over there. They have their eyes on us."

"Why are they not approaching?"

"I don't know."

Glowing blue eyes peek through the darkness. "Rory is out here alone, Cory."

"No, she's not. She's right in front of us."

My defenses go into overload.

Howls of wolves join the hounds, and the eyes in the forest multiply.

"Cory, I don't like this one bit."

"Remember what I taught you about the wolves—to stay perfectly still and not move a muscle?"

I'm reminded of the day back on Ladorielle when Dad, Aunt Fran, Cory, and I spent the night in the Iknes Shaw mountains. "Giant country. Yeah, I remember."

"Like mentioned before, the Earth's atmosphere is heavier so when you use your magic it will take more energy from you, and more concentration. This is about to get really ugly."

My stomach churns. "I was afraid you were going to say that."

Clouds cover the moon. The forest dims completely.

"Time to turn on some blue eyes of our own," Cory says. A roar comes from behind us and Cory darts out of the way. An arrow slams a wolf as it leaps in midair. A screeching sound of pain comes from the creature. It lands by Cory's feet. The wolf transitions to a man.

"That isn't any ordinary wolf," I say.

"One of Sarmira's werewolf Shadow Walkers. Where there is one, there are more."

Rory's legs dangle from a tree branch above our heads, saying, "They're everywhere."

The inner beast within my frame itches to be free. The frustration and patience of Rory's childish games grows thin.

She jumps down.

Cory releases me from his back. "Yeah, and it was your bright idea to come out here alone. Good job, Rory!" I pull the arrow from the dead man's back. "Here." I slam it against her chest.

"I have to find my sister."

"*We* have to find your sister. You know, Rory, sometimes I just don't get you."

"Easy, ladies, remember what I said about moving too quickly."

"Too late." The wolves and hounds move in and circle us.

"Now what, genius?" I look at Rory. "You know, for being a stealth-like druid, you sure have a way of easily getting caught."

Rory groans, annoyed at my comment. "Well, if you would just listen—"

A large dire wolf leaps to the center, frothing at the mouth, fangs extended. It slams Rory down to the ground, before she can get a shot off and then turns to the hungry predators circling us.

"That's one way to get our attention, I guess." I look at Cory and he shrugs.

Rory quickly gets up and takes aim.

"Wait, Rory, don't shoot!" I step in her way and watch the ferocious animal shield us between the enemies of the dark. "I think it's Redmae."

"No, that's not my sister."

"She's right, this one is a bit browner. Redmae has a white coat with a red stripe going down her back," Cory says.

The pack backs up with a few wolves still lingering. The creature protecting us growls more, then lunges, snapping at the leader of the group. They seem to challenge each other.

"Rory, back up slowly," Cory says. He hooks his arm with hers.

The two wolves engage.

"Run!" Cory pulls at Rory.

We make it back to the hideout where Cole is lying on the floor. "Back so soon?"

Cory grumbles.

"Did you find Redmae?"

"No, but we found Shadow Walkers, wolves, and invisible hounds."

Cole sits up, intrigued. "Fun times. I'm missing all the fun. Can't say I'm surprised."

"Now what do we do?" I look out the small window-like peep hole and see nothing but trees. The sounds of the wolves fighting carry out for a few more minutes before a painful sounding holler calls out. More howls follow. The clouds move away from the moon once again and on the snow covered ground the moonlight shows and injured man wearing no clothes, holding someone in their arms who is also naked, and another body bloodied on the ground. "Hey, come see this."

Cole stays put, but Cory comes to my side.

"Who is that?" I ask.

"I'm not sure."

The man looks up, making eye contact. "Please don't shoot. I'm not going to hurt you." He sets the body down and then races out of sight.

Rory looks out. "That's my sister!" She slings her bow to her back and slides back down from the tree house fort to aid Redmae.

I look at Cory confused. "Redmae isn't a wolf?"

He too, seems perplexed. We rush down the tree as well and meet up with Rory.

A naked woman with long red wavey hair lies still on the frozen ground. She's bruised a bit but otherwise looks okay.

"Redmae," Rory says. She moves some strands from Redmae's face. Rory takes off her cloak and wraps it over her sister.

"I heard her scream a little while ago just after we landed here. We had communication at first, and then she went silent in my mind. I thought the worst and didn't want to say anything," I say.

"She's alive and that's what matters." Cory picks her up. "Let's get her out from this open area, and back up in the fort."

12
PROWLERS AMONG US

"Can't you conjure a blanket or something, Cory?" I ask while watching Redmae sleep.

"I can try." He closes his eyes and concentrates. Unlike being on Ladorielle, it takes a bit more work for the object Cory musters, to appear. "Will this help?" He hands me a throw.

"It'll work for now." I lay it across Redmae.

She stirs a bit.

Rory sits next to her, humming softly and stroking her cheeks and head. "Wake up, sis."

Redmae smiles. Says something none of us can comprehend. Then she opens her eyes. At first, she has a blank stare, then pops up on her elbows. I think that surprised her the most. She looks at her hands, and balls them into fists and opens them again. "What—I mean, how did I—"

"Yeah, we're all just as surprised as you. Do you know what happened? How are you human, Redmae?" I kneel down next to her and Rory.

Her hair is tousled with leaves tangled between her red, curly strands. "I—I don't know. I don't have an answer for you. I remember stepping out of the barn as a wolf and now I'm this." She looks at her hands again. "I-I don't understand. Why now? Nyta has tried to figure out how to turn me back and now that we're back at Storm River Manor, I'm a human again? None of this makes any sense."

"Don't worry about it right now. What matters is you're safe." Rory tugs at the cloak, pulling it closer about Redmae's shoulders.

"I think I know why Redmae transformed," Cole says.

"Why? Please indulge us, Cole." Redmae isn't amused. She looks out the fort window at the moon as though it's trying to communicate with her. "Never mind, I think I know why, too."

Rory looks with her. "The last time you changed from your wolf form it was on a night like this. A full blood moon."

"That is what I'm getting at." Cole stands. Some of his strength returns and he goes to the window.

"Are you suggesting we have gone back in time, brother?" Cory looks at me, worried.

"That's the theory."

"This is close to the exact area where we all had a battle among the Shadow Walkers, right after I stabbed Cory with the dagger. I'm guessing we're minutes behind the final scene from when Rory ported everyone out of here. What other explanation is there?"

"Cole's right," Rory says. "It's nearly in the same position as when I ported everyone out to the safety of Dragonscale Island."

"Redmae and I were discussing that there was a possibility we may have traveled back in time, earlier before she shifted, when Rory first landed us here."

"The real question: how is that possible, though? I am no mage. I can't just cast a time spell and poof we are in a retro redo," Rory argues.

"No, but I'm willing to bet that Aoes had something to do with this," Cole says.

"That's what I said to Wynter." Redmae pulls the cloak tighter. "It's cold. Having fur does have its benefits."

"This is terrifying, what if we run into our past selves?" I look toward the open garden gates. "What if we're in a continuous time loop?"

"Interesting theory, Wynter. That would mean there could be an unlimited amount of 'us' walking around in different timelines. Logically speaking that idea makes my head spin," Cole says.

"Wynter is right, what would happen if we bumped into ourselves." Rory turns to each of us. "Cole would still have vampire blood running through his veins... my sister would be a–" She stops to rub the bridge of her nose. "Okay, sorry, sis, your situation totally has me befuddled. At any rate Cory would still be in Scarlet Hollow, and you—" She points at me. "Wynter, you would be dead."

"Rory, you sound a bit too excited about this." I thread my fingers through my hair thinking of the possibilities of how real this might be. "It puts a new meaning into the word doppelganger." My heart sinks at Rory's comments. "Who's to say that we're not dreaming?" My thoughts wander. "I mean, you're not a mage, so how has time been turned unless Aoes has had something to do with it?"

"No, true, I'm not a mage, but it isn't in the realm of impossibility for a druid to have such an ability, is it?" she counters. "It is said there is a rune that can do just that. A time travelers' rune, in fact."

"Rory speaks the truth," Redmae says. "I forgot about the druid that once had such an ability. It's rare, but not impossible. Question is, do you have that ability, my sweet sister?"

"I don't have the travelers' rune if that is what you're

asking. Perhaps that is something Aoes can answer when we go back to Ladorielle."

"If we can go back," Cole says.

I jab his arm. "Stop being so pessimistic. We will get back."

"Yeah? Look around..." He gestures to the area below and the dark forest around us. "How are we getting back." He points at Rory. "She's broken."

"I'm not broken!" Rory stabs a look at Cole. "I had no idea we'd land in a place without magic," she defends. "I'm not sure what happened. Apparently, I can port—randomly?"

"Apparently." Cole glares at Rory. "Why did you send us back here? Not to exclude the fact that Earth has little to no magic!"

"Not true, Cole. Earth has some magic. Your brother just conjured a blanket for Redmae!" Rory shouts back. "Like I have any control of that! I warned you even after Jasmine gave me this herbal medicine. And if you recall, Sarmira lunged through just as we escaped. It could have contributed."

Cory comes between them. "Okay, enough! The more important task is to get out of this forest, and I don't feel like fighting any more Sabretail Prowlers or Shadow Walkers."

I shiver at the thought of them coming back.

"Most Shadow Walkers don't come this far from the compound," Redmae interjects.

"Except the ones we saw just before you were dropped at our doorstep. The Sabretail Prowlers do linger in the forest. Keep your eyes out for the sneaky beasts. They love being up here in the hills," Cole says.

"Cory is right though, we can't stay up here forever." I look at Cole. "How's that healing coming along?"

"What? This scratch?" He lifts his shirt and winks at Rory. "The salve she lathered on is nearly gone."

I come in for a closer look. "Your wounds have faded. That's good news."

"Great." Rory pulls out her medicine and takes a quick swig. "We should get going."

"She's right, those wolves know we're here.," Redmae agrees.

"Come on. I know where we'll all be safe." Cory goes down the hideout ladder first.

Rory glares at me and grumbles. She holds her bow and arrow close, and leaps down.

Cole gestures. "After you."

Redmae follows.

The leaves whisper in the wind as they rustle along the dirt trail. Owls hoot above in the trees next to us.

Rory's eyes glint as she uses her abilities to see farther than we can for any approaching predators as we venture across the grounds.

The brightness of the moon guides us as we walk along the dark path. The heavy energy continues to weigh me down. Cole is right. Before, when I was back on Ladorielle I felt lighter and free, but this feels different than when I was still seventeen and not yet intuned with my spiritual abilities.

"It's because Earth is three dimensional and they haven't created the means to understand magic like we do," a familiar voice, answers.

I look at Cory and smile. *"I'm never going to get you out of my head, am I?"*

"Nope."

Rory, Cole, and Redmae follow along the tight trail behind us until we come back to where I first landed alone on these grounds a few hours ago.

Cole walks to the edge of the cliff and looks down on the barren lands of Storm River Manor grounds. "If I know Moyer, she knows we're here."

"Sarmira," I say.

"What?" Cole looks confused.

"Sarmira. You mean Sarmira. We all know Moyer is innocent. Just a vessel that Sarmira can use as she sees fit."

"Sarmira is possessing her soul," Rory adds. "Remember?"

"Right. Sarmira. It's going to take me time to get used to that. If Sarmira is the mastermind in all this chaos, then we better be prepared. We're no match for the Daughter of the Underworld."

Cory grabs his brother's sleeve. "The cottage is this way. We'll have to go the long way around."

"Cottage? What cottage?" Cole asks.

I smile and hook my hand with Cory's as the memories come back of when he first showed me the cabin.

The deeper into the forest we go, the stronger the smells of sulfur and burning flesh become. "It must've been one horrible battle," I say. I use my sleeve to cover my mouth from the smokey air and putrid odors.

"A lot of death, blood, and gore," Cory says. "The Storms put up a grand fight a few yards ahead." He points in that direction. "That's also the way down off this hillside."

Cole briefs us on his version of the skirmish. "What I still can't figure out is how... I–I mean the demon that once possessed me, how could it—what I mean is, I am confused as to how Moyer shattered into a million shards and yet there are clues that she's still alive. If she was truly a vampire, wouldn't she have turned solid—like petrified wood?" His voice softens. "Like my brother." He briefly glances at him.

"Or ash?" I grin, reminding Cole that he rose from ashes.

He points at me. "You might be onto something there." He ponders a minute. "No, that wouldn't be right. I don't think she was a vampire. Moyer came from a long line of dark witches."

"Are you saying witches can't be vampires?" Redmae asks.

"Not at all. But clearly, she isn't a vampire, or we're missing something."

"I'm not making a connection as to what you're getting at, brother."

"Neither am I," Rory says.

"Sarmira was killed by Bryce Storm with the Sword of Valor. There's a connection between both Moyer and Sarmira. There has to be. They both were destroyed the same way, yet they are both... *alive*."

Redmae tilts her head and squints. "I'm sorry, I don't follow."

"I am implying that the blade I was handling and the Sword of Valor must somehow be connected."

"I'm guessing you don't remember, Cole. It was explained back at the Hall of Secrets. Moyer was a clone. At least that's the theory," Rory says.

Cole chuckles. "A clone. How clever." The look on his face makes me wonder if he knows something and isn't sharing. He notices me staring. "We should keep moving."

We all follow Cory as he leads us farther into the dark forest when he steps on dry wood. The loud snap startles several birds high above in the trees.

I jump.

Rory smirks. "Scared of a few birds, Wynter?"

"Those aren't birds, Rory, those are bats," Cory corrects. "Shall we continue?" The trail before us is overgrown and hasn't seen much foot traffic in a while. "If my memory serves me right, this is also the back way to the catacombs."

"What?" I pull at Cory's sleeve. "I thought you were taking us down the hillside to the river."

"Relax, we are. It's not what you think." He cups my chin. "This is the only way down off the cliff. Other than going all the way around the property which is a few miles from the cottage."

"Tell me more about this cottage you speak of," Cole says.

"It's down this path," I say. "A place where we can regroup and rest."

"You'll see, brother." Cory grins wide.

Cole grunts.

Cory takes a few more steps and his eyes glow a deep blue.

"What is it, brother?" Cole's senses seem to catch a scent, too, because his eyes begin to glow blue. "Sabretail Prowlers."

"Do you think they're following us?" Redmae asks.

"Yes. Too much talking and not enough walking." Cory marches forward, irritated.

"We have nothing to protect ourselves with," I say.

"Your magic may not be as strong as it is on Ladorielle, but it will still do some damage, Wynter. You've turned eighteen and none of us have Valiancium cuffs around our wrists anymore. If we need to, we'll fight them," Cory says.

"I've gathered enough strength that I might be able to cast a protective bubble like before." Cole uses what little energy he has and musters up a shield. Parts of it glistens in the moonlight. "Just as before it won't hold long, so wherever this so-called cottage is, let's get there a little faster than this current snail pace we have going."

We follow the boys down an old trail. The full moon shades the ground making the night sky creepier than it normally would be. A breeze catches the air, and leaves kick up in the wind once more, and I zip up my jacket.

We come to the end of the pathway to a small ledge. Cole jumps off a large embankment and lands a few feet down and Cory does the same.

The rest of us stand above them, looking hesitant to follow.

"Come on, you guys. I'm sure you've jumped from steeper things than this." Cory puts out a hand to help.

Redmae urges us aside. "He's right. This jump is child's play." She leaps downward with zero effort.

I press my lips together. "You must be a wolf in another life or something."

"Ha! Or something..." she teases.

Rory jumps next. "Piece of cake."

"Now your turn, Wynter," Cory says.

I take a step forward about to jump as well, except my left foot trips my right, and I end up sliding down the cliff on my rear instead. "Awesome!" I snark.

They all laugh.

"That's one way to get down, I suppose," Cole says, "but I wouldn't have—"

"Oh, shut it, Cole!" I wipe the back of my butt and manage to make a bigger smudge. Now my hands are filthy. I grunt in frustration. "Come on, let's keep moving. I know where we are now."

"Are we that close?" Rory asks as we walk through the spooky woods.

"Yes, the cottage is just up the river here. Cory took me to this area once, after I escaped Storm River Manor."

"That was fun," Cory interjects sarcastically.

"Let's just hope no one is home," Rory says.

"Home?" Cole's eyes widen with suspicion.

Rory looks at me with concerned eyes.

"See right there." He points. "You looked at Wynter when you said 'home'. What is this 'home' that everyone is referring to?" He turns to his brother.

"Patience. You will soon see."

"Oh, you're enjoying this." Cole is not amused.

"Yes, brother, I am. I have waited for this moment for a long time."

I take a deep breath. "Cole, we can't trust you until we know for sure. This is the only way we know whether the demon inside you still exists."

"What's that supposed to mean?" Cole asks in irritation.

"She means if the evil side of you is truly gone then we'll know once we reach the cottage." Cory looks over at both Redmae and Rory. "Plus, I'm sure Red would like to get into something more comfortable."

"Ha! If it was my choice, it would be in wolf skin," she says.

"Which reminds me, I want to know your dragon secret, Wynter, you're not off the hook," Cory reminds me. "I admit, I was beginning to think you might have been a dragon shifter when we parted ways, and you were sent to Dragonscale Island."

"Wow, that long huh? And you didn't mention anything?"

"I didn't want to prematurely trigger something that might have backfired, and then you would never remember. You know, the side effects of the memory stamp."

"Right, yes, I remember."

As we continue down the overgrown path, the sound of rushing water greets my eardrums. I smile at the memories that come back when Cory first showed me the cabin.

We don't walk but a few feet down, when I hear a moan of pain. I put my hand up in warning and stop. "Shh. Does anyone else hear that?"

"I don't hear anything," Rory whispers.

"No, Wynter's right. I sense a faint heartbeat." Redmae holds her hands close to her ears and focuses.

A soft mutter calls out. "That's not the sound of an animal," Cole says.

"No, it isn't." Redmae follows her innate tracking ability. "It's coming from over here. They sound injured."

"Agreed. That's no Sabretail Prowler," Cory says.

Cole wanders ahead through some thick brush. He waves us over.

A man's frame lies face down, like when I found Rory. "Help me flip him over."

13
UNEXPECTED ENCOUNTER

Steam emits from his scorched clothes. "Dad?" Instinctively my hands glow and I hover them across his burned body, hoping I can heal him. His face is dirty with soot and ash like he'd come down a chimney. If it wasn't for the tone of his moans of pain, I may have not realized it was him. The strength in my body isn't enough to heal him completely.

Cory creates a rag out of thin air. "Here this might help wipe away some of the sweat and dirt from his face."

"Dad, can you hear me?" I brush debris from his forehead. A deep gash above his left eyebrow begins to bleed. I dab at it with the cloth. "Dad, wake up."

Rory's mood shifts. "Do you think any of the others from the Hall of Secrets survived, too?" She observes our location. "We really need to get to shelter. I sense we're being watched."

"Of course we are," Cory confirms.

"Question is why are we not being attacked?" Rory asks.

"Good question." Redmae kneels and touches the ground around his legs. "Doesn't anyone find it odd that he landed here instead of where we were, on Elleirodal." She sniffs the air. "I smell fresh blood." She turns around. "There is someone else injured as well. Worse off than your dad, Wynter." Redmae steps away, tracking the second victim. "Whoever it is, they're alive, but I can't seem to clear my senses enough to find the location."

Cole glances at all of us. "I hope that cottage of yours is as good as you say it is. We're going to need it now more than ever."

Redmae travels farther away, almost out of sight.

"We should travel in twos, sis. Wait for me and I'll search with you." Rory looks back at us.

Cory nods. "We've got Jeff. Go find the other one you say is still alive."

Rory isn't but a few yards from us when she and Redmae disappear. "Rory?"

"We're okay," she confirms. "We may need your help, though."

"Go," Cory says. "Don't worry, we have your dad. They need help."

I reach Red and Rory. They're in a small ditch about four feet deep. "Is everything alright—Blair?"

Rory stands after checking her pulse. "She's alive."

"But she's badly hurt," Redmae adds. "Can you heal her?"

"I can try. I used a lot of my energy to heal my dad, though." Blood seeps beneath Blair's body. "You know she can't die though, right? I watched Casey bleed her dry once, while she was chained in the torture chamber below Storm River Manor. She's a vampire."

"Right. Except by fire, Wynter." Rory kneels next to Blair.

Like Dad, Blairs clothes are adhered to her skin. Steam emits from her clothes. Her face is covered in burns and soot streaks across her forehead. Her cotton jacket is seared to parts of her arms. "She's barely recognizable." Redmae attempts to peel away some of the burned fabric.

Blair screams.

That attention brings one of the twins our way immediately. "That scream sounded like my mother," Cole says, looking concerned.

"Yes, it is and she's badly burned." I kneel beside Blair and hover my glowing hands over her body. "This is giving a repeat vibe of Cole, when we—" I stop and look up at him.

Rory looks at me then at Cole. "Yes, I know."

"What are the odds of finding Blair and my dad so close together?" I ask.

Rory looks at Redmae and gasps. "Mom...what about Mom? Do you think—"

"Rory, don't go there. Not now," Redmae says.

A not so comforting thought comes to the surface. "I'm betting the Hall of Secrets has been destroyed." Remembering the electrical force sends me shivering.

"Wynter, please, we don't need the grim concepts right now," Redmae says.

"How are things over there?" Cory shouts.

"Fine," I say. I look at Cole. "Are you going to go tell him or shall we show him the horror of his mother's condition here and now?"

"I'll go break it to my brother on my own."

We watch him make his way back to Cory.

"At least the cottage will have a fireplace to warm all of us, and herbs to help them heal. Plus, it will give all of us peace of mind to know for sure if the demon in Cole is really gone." I look back, observing Cole talking with his brother.

"Can you walk, sir?" I overhear Cory ask, in a rushed but easing tone.

Dad gasps painfully. "I think so." He favors one leg as he hops toward us.

"We should try and do the same with Blair. Being out here where many predators hang out doesn't rest easy on my chest." I pick her up under her shoulders. "Grab her ankles, Rory."

Redmae centers in the middle. "She's heavier than she looks."

It takes a bit of maneuvering, but we manage to get Blair out of the small ditch. "How are we going to do this? The cottage is still quite far from here," I say.

"Very carefully," Redmae says.

We all regroup. The silence among us is deafening.

"We need to find this so-called cottage you all claim exists, and, soon." Cole looks up at the angry sky. "We don't have time on our side." He points. "See those swirl-like streaks across the Blood Moon?"

"Yeah, I saw them earlier," I say.

"Looks like swirls of smoke to me," Rory says.

"Those are not clouds, my friends. Those are dark entities entering this world. When I was under Sarmira's control I remember hearing about her plans. She was going to use this phase of the moon to move through the worlds. I wouldn't doubt if she' already succeeded."

"Which is probably why she was able to finally travel to Elleirodal," Rory says.

"But my mother cast a spell to trap her here. That can't be right," I say.

Cole looks at me with a heavy heart. "Unless Sarmira managed to finally capture Isalora's soul."

"Impossible." Tears well in my eyes.

"Is it?" Cole eyes turn a glowing blue. "Sarmira is free."

"No, she's not free yet," Cory says. "She was projecting. Her body is still anchored here." He turns a full circle. "Somewhere on these grounds. I feel it, don't you?" A glow emits around his waist.

"Perhaps you're onto something, Cory." I point.

He pulls from his sheath the Blade of Hope. It glistens in the moonlight. A message reveals itself along the blade in another language.

"Can you read it," I ask.

"No."

My necklace responds with a glow of its own. "What do you suppose this means?"

"I believe our thoughts are linking with the magic of these items," Cory answers. "I have a strong feeling we'll find out soon enough."

"You're probably right, brother. I'm tired of being Sarmira's puppet. It's time we figure out this Storm saga, once and for all. Question is where we do start."

I smile and nod at Cory. "The loft in the cottage may have some of our answers."

He nods back.

My dad's eyelids are heavy with exhaustion. "Where am I?"

"You're safe, Dad." I kiss his cheek.

"Cole, I'll carry our mother if you can help Wynter with her dad," Cory says. "Redmae, shall we switch places?"

Redmae hands Blair into his arms and then she helps Cole lift up Dad's other shoulder. "I may be in human form, but I still have the strength of a dire wolf."

"Wynter, you lead the way. Cole can assist Redmae," Cory says.

SNOW PATCHES SPRAWL ACROSS THE GROUND AND the smell of death still fills the air. To the left of us are the hills that lead to the Storm River Manor and to the right, a foggy haze fills the woods.

Rushing water tells me we're near the cabin. A small ledge separates us from the river below. "We can rest here for a few minutes to catch our breath." I bend over to stretch my back while looking over at the valley.

"No," Cole says. "We need to keep moving. The quicker we get to that cabin the better. There are predators everywhere."

"Wynter is right, Cole. We should rest here for a few seconds and catch our breath," Cory says.

Cole grunts in disapproval.

I walk along the ledge. This one is not as high as the last one. Although it's dark, there is enough light to see smoke escaping from the chimney of my mother's cottage. A part of me wonders if she's in there. It feels like yesterday, even though it's only been a few weeks since I've been inside. I glance back at Cory who is looking toward the valley too.

"What?" He creases his nose looking at me like I'm crazy.

"Nothing."

"Where are the others?"

"Resting against the logs behind me."

He pushes through the tree branches to see what I see. "It feels like we never left."

"I know."

He grabs my waist and pulls me in while we both overlook the view. "I thought I would never find you."

"But you did find me. I never had any doubts." He kisses the back of my head.

Cole walks up and stands next to us. It takes a couple seconds before he sees the structure below us. "Hold up."

I smile, knowing what is coming next.

Looking rather perplexed, he says, "Where did that come from?"

"Where did what come from?" I smile inwardly trying not to acknowledge what he sees.

"Oh no, don't play with me, Wynter. I know we're on the grounds of Storm River Manor... And I know that house down there didn't just build itself in a matter of days. My brother and I used to fish from the bridge over there." He points.

Rory comes walking up. "Are we almost there?"

I turn and smile. "See for yourself."

She smiles back. "I cannot wait to be inside beside a warm fire."

"This is the cottage you spoke about earlier... is this it?" Cole turns to his brother, for clarification.

"Come on, let's go get the others." Cory walks back to Redmae and our injured family members.

Rory tucks her arrow back into her quiver set and slings her bow onto her back. "Here, let me help." She grabs my dad's other arm. "Let's go. We're almost there, sir. Just a few more steps."

Long grass lines the shallow walls of the cliff that separates the woods from the shoreline. Everyone sets foot after me onto the rocky riverbed shore.

Dad continues to slip in and out of consciousness. "Water." Dad sits down on a large rock along the river shore and splashes water against his face. "How much farther?"

"Not far, Dad. We're almost there."

Dad looks in my direction and sees the rocks that line across a small area of the river.

My dad is a fairly large man, and I don't doubt it's hard on Redmae and Cole's backs as well. Cory shows a little fatigue, too.

"Just a little farther." I take the first step across the river, followed by Cory carrying Blair.

Dad nods. "Okay, I think I can make it across. I might be slow, though."

"It's fine, Jeff. Redmae and I will be with you." Cory helps Dad up.

One slow step at a time which feels like forever, but we all make it across in one piece. The sound of wolves in the distance warns us they are watching us closely.

"What if they see us go into the cottage, Cory?" I'm concerned that they will know our secret hideout.

"To them we would simply disappear. Not To worry, Wynter. Just like an illusion Cole would cast upon us, the cottage does the same thing."

We reach the front door and immediately notice the music playing inside.

We give each other perplexing glances.

"A light is on. Someone must be inside," Cole says.

Rory raises a brow. "Guess we're about to find out who."

"Well, we know it can't be my mother."

Cory squeezes my hand to assure me I'm not alone in the grieving of our lost family members. He opens the front door. "Let's see who is living in your mother's cottage."

I nod at Cole. "After you."

Cole crosses the threshold. "This place is amazing. Just like you said, a little cottage in the woods."

Like all the other times I've stepped into the small house, nothing appears to be out of the ordinary. I feel the warmth of an inviting fire. The smell of herbs permeates the room, just as it did the last time I visited. *Mom.* My first reaction is to search every inch of this house for her, but I know it's not possible. She isn't here. I haven't heard from her since before I fell ill from the pill Miles gave me when he pretended to take the place of Dragonscale. He too, has mysteriously disappeared. I know from the expression on Cole's face he hasn't a clue how comforting it is to me, knowing that he's no longer tied to Sarmira.

"We're safe in the cabin for the time being," Cory says. "No evil may enter here. It's protected." He helps my dad to the winged back chair that sets near the fireplace.

"A test," Cole says.

"More or less. That's why Wynter and I gave that look earlier. We knew by coming here, we would know once and for all whether the demon that possessed you was truly gone or not." He looks over at Redmae, as she gently helps Cole lay unconscious Blair on the couch.

"You haven't disintegrated to dust, so all is well," Rory teases.

"Hah! Funny, funny girl. Glad I could reassure all of you."

I fluff a few pillows for Dad's head and a few more for Blair's.

Rory walks to the kitchen. "A kettle of warm water is on the stove."

"Who is living here?" I ask. Tears glaze over my eyes. "It can't be my mother. I'd feel her presence."

We hear sounds of someone coming up the basement steps.

Cole's eyes begin to glow bright, his muscles flex, and he extends his teeth as though he's going to change into his monster self. Redmae's throat rumbles in human mode, and Rory pulls her bow and arrow, getting them ready.

"Stand down, everyone." I put my arm out to hold them back. "Whomever it is, they cannot penetrate through these walls if they mean any harm." I look at Cole. "You of all people should know that."

"She's right," Cory says.

Cole relaxes.

Rory lowers her bow, giving me a wavering expression.

The knob of the basement door turns, and the resident of the house crosses the threshold.

14

ASHES AND DUST

I raise my brow, seeing a familiar face. "Derek?" He appears different. I can clearly see he looks the same but isn't. I mean yes, I briefly saw him when we were still in the Hall of Secrets, but there was too much going on, to notice... His complexion is smooth like any average vampire, and his looks are stunning, but he still appears old. His hair still white, but there is something about him that is...off. I can't quite place it.

"You're all alive? Tell me I'm not looking at illusions." He's holding onto an old, tattered book, and looks stunned to see us standing here.

Cole is dumbfounded, too. "I thought..."

Derek tilts his head. "That I was dead?"

"I admit, not one of my best moments," Cole confesses. "I was possessed by a demon."

Derek stares at him sternly. "You don't say." He sets the hardcover down onto an end table and crosses his arms over his chest, studying us.

"I must agree with my brother, I can't believe I'm standing here staring at you, I watched you die."

He chuckles, looking at Cory. "I imagine the last you saw

me alive was just beyond the river, stabbed by this young man…" He veers his eyes to Cole. "I confess, I was about to give up hope that any of you survived the catastrophic electrical surge of the Hall of Secrets. Everything happened so fast."

"Wait, what surge?" Cory looks back at us.

"Oh, they didn't tell you?" He furrows his brow, confused. "Odd indeed." Derek moves his right hand pinching his chin with his fingers in thought.

"We haven't had a chance to catch a breath ourselves," Rory defends. "We found Jeff and Blair, alive—barely. Brought them here." She gestures to Dad in the chair and Blair on the couch.

He rushes to them. "How did you—"

"Find them?" Rory answers. "Not sure. We think that we traveled back in time, though."

"You're not alone in that theory, I assure you of that." Derek feels both Jeff and Blair's foreheads. "No fevers. That's good. How long have they been out?"

"Jeff has been mostly conscious since we found him. I'm guessing he's exhausted from walking the far distance it took us to get here. We assisted of course. Blair, she hasn't woken up yet. Cory carried her most of the way," Cole says.

"Derek, how did you escape?" Rory asks. "We didn't have time to digest that you were still alive when you entered the Hall of Secrets, before we were purged from the portal." Rory looks back at Cory, who seems confused. "Sorry, we'll try and fill you in as we go along, my friend."

"Purged is such a strong word, Rory," I say.

"Do you have a better explanation, Wynter?"

I shake my head.

"To answer your question, Rory, I'm not sure." Derek goes to a door in the hallway and grabs a couple blankets. "This should help them stay warm until they awaken. We haven't seen anyone for days."

"We? You mean, you're not alone?"

He ignores my question, saying, "Come sit by the fire and catch me up to speed." He grabs his book off the end table, taps the cover, and sits in a chair opposite of the couch. "I was down below doing some research. Where did you find them, exactly?"

"Near the Storm cemetery," Cole says. His eyes glisten.

This is the first time I've seen Cole have any empathy. The impression I had all this time was his hardened thoughts and manners, never having any consideration for others, but seeing his mother like this has changed my perspective. Perhaps his recent transformation has changed him more than I thought.

Cole kneels next to Blair. "I've made a mess of things, haven't I, Mom." He brushes strands away from her face. "Uncle, I–I–" Cole gulps. "I watched helplessly from the spirit side..." He looks over at his brother.

Dad mumbles incoherently. Blair remains unconscious.

"Cole, it was a helpless situation," Derek answers.

"I nearly used up all my strength to heal them," I say.

"You did good, Wynter," Derek says. "I'm still wondering how you're all alive." He looks at both his great nephews. "That blast back at the hub should have killed everyone. We've been worried. And Cory, your alive as well."

"We?" Rory asks.

I bump Rory's arm. "I just asked that question, and you didn't answer me, Derek, so I'll ask again. We're over here trying to figure out how we're alive" —I point toward Cory, Cole, Rory, and Redmae— "how we survived the collapse of the portal hub and you're alluding that you're not alone? Who else is with you?"

Derek smiles. "All of us have so many questions. Geneviève and Drena. They're downstairs." He gestures to the door leading to the lower level.

"Wait, my mother's here, too?" Rory asks. She looks at Redmae. "Our mother?"

He nods. "She is. Geneviève has been so distraught since she ported everyone out. She was the only one that appeared at the druid circle below the house. Drena and I appeared up in that loft." He points to the upper-level balcony.

"Hang on a second. I thought Rory ported us out of the Hall of Secrets. Are you saying Geneviève did too?"

Rory is stunned. She looks at her sister. "Our mother must've ported everyone out." She runs to the basement door. "I need to go to her. Are you coming, Red?"

Redmae hesitates. "I—I'm not sure?" She looks at Derek for approval. She adjusts the cloak tighter about her body.

"Go on, we'll be fine. She may also find something more comfortable for you to change into."

"Wait, I need to process this. I get that I'm behind with all the twists in my life including the drama that just unfolded, but are you saying there is a druid portal below us?" I ask.

"Yes," Derek answers, "One that can take us directly to the Hall of Secrets. Except, it is no longer working. In fact, the druid circle has been inactive for years according to Geneviève."

Rory holds up her hand. "Sorry, I'll be right back."

"Why are you hesitating, Redmae?" I ask.

"Because the last time my mother saw me as a Shadow Vine Elf it wasn't but a few hours later that I transformed back to a wolf without any warning. She's been through enough heartbreak. I'm worried that seeing me will send more confusion."

"Or relief, my friend. Go with Rory. Your mother will be thrilled to see you're alive. I gather the three of you have a lot of catching up to do. Don't waste the moments of the present, trust me."

Redmae bows. "Thank you, Wynter. You have a way of shedding light on something others can't see."

Cory points to the book in Derek's lap. "What kind of research were you doing?"

"Finding a way back to Ladorielle."

"Any luck?" I ask.

"Alas, no." Derek's frustration shows. "The druid circle seems to still be out of commission. We thought perhaps it had been fixed because Geneviève found herself landing there, but it hasn't activated. There is much more about this small cottage that will surprise you." He opens the book and flips through the pages. "I found an interesting entry of notes written on the edges." He hands me the literature to read. "Have you seen this language before?"

I shake my head. "I don't recognize it."

Cole comes to investigate. "I don't recognize it, either. Maybe Rory might? It looks like it might be in Elvin."

"I'll ask her when she comes back." Derek closes the book and sets it aside. "So, tell me what happened? How did you come upon the cottage? We thought the worst, I'm afraid."

"Well," I begin. I swallow hard, not sure how to start. "It seems that Cole is no longer a vampire. We can't explain why. All we know is that he's not what he once appeared to be." I look at Cory and can clearly see he's intrigued.

"What...not a vampire?" Cory asks. "I hadn't noticed." His sarcastic tone tells me Cole needs to explain himself. "You said you would clear up a few things. Here's your chance, big brother."

"I noticed the same thing, Cory," Derek agrees. "How can you no longer be a vampire? This doesn't make any sense, Cole."

"We don't understand it, either," I say. "It all started when we landed on Elleirodal after the blast from the portal hub. Cole's body was burned badly—"

"Which explains why I can no longer sense your presence up close," Cory says. "Your scent has changed. I thought it was me, that somehow being petrified for weeks caused a temporary symptom."

"I'm the common denominator, Cory. Believe me, it's not you."

Cory stares intently at Cole. "What are you saying, brother? Every vampire knows fire of any kind will kill our kind. I don't see a single scar on your face, hands, or neck. When were you burned? How are you still alive right now?"

"All of us have been trying to find a way to tell you—" Cole's attention is diverted. Several footsteps hurry up the basement stairwell and the door swings open.

"Is it true?" Geneviève finds my dad peacefully sleeping against the lounge chair and races to him.

The worry on her face leads me to believe that her and my dad may indeed be more than just friends. I should be angry, but I'm not. My dad needs to move on.

Drena, Rory, and Redmae who are dressed in more appropriate clothing, soon follow, having their own conversation. They halt in midsentence when they see how distraught Geneviève appears.

The room grows quiet.

"Trust me, it is not what you're thinking," Geneviève says, interrupting the awkward silence. "Jeoffrey is my dragon. No other can break that bond. Wynter, you of all people know that."

"She's right. Namari is my warder. I'd feel the same way if he was hurt." I'm embarrassed that I thought the two of them were romantically involved.

Geneviève sits next to Dad, checking his forehead again. "Rory said you found him and Blair a few yards from the house, correct?"

"Yes," I say. "Well, closer to the cemetery."

"I cast my portal spell right before you four disappeared and a split second later we vanished from imminent devastation. I saw the portal dissolve at the last moment before I landed in the druid circle. At first, I thought I was the only one who survived, until I went upstairs to find Derek and Drena. Although deep down I knew Jeff was alive; otherwise I would have felt his passing."

"What about the others? Uncle Chad, Zak, Thom, Dom, Arryn, and Akira are they—" My heart sinks to think what might have happened to the rest of them. I gasp. "Nyta—"

Derek looks up at me. "We don't know. We're worried the blast killed everyone. Seeing the four of you lifts our spirits a little."

"We hoped all of you were fine, but we didn't know for sure." Drena smiles, taking Derek's hand, and sits. Her long chestnut hair flows to her waist, and her eyes are the brightest amber complimenting her high cheekbones, small rose-colored lips, and heart-shaped face.

Cory puts a hand on my shoulder. "Don't worry. We will find them. All of them."

"Have you seen their spirits pass, Wynter?" Redmae asks.

"No."

"Then there is still hope that they're alive."

A tea kettle on the stove in the kitchen whistles, disrupting the tension.

"If you will excuse me, I was attempting to make some tea before you arrived," Drena says, and gets up. "Sounds like we have some catching up to do." She walks to the kitchen to get down some cups. "I do admit, it brings me comfort in seeing all of you. Perhaps we can put our heads together and come up with a concrete solution to the unfortunate predicament we're all facing."

"I'll help you," Geneviève says. "Would any of you care for some tea?"

"That would be lovely," Rory says. "Thanks, Mom."

Geneviève pulls a jar of tea bags from the cupboard while

Drena carries a tray of cups along with the hot kettle to the coffee table. She divvies out a teacup for each of us.

"Anyone have any idea how Sarmira was able to penetrate through to Cole's soul in the first place?" I ask.

"That's the big question, isn't it?" Drena smiles and looks over at Derek. "Surely Sarmira hasn't that much power to destroy a portal hub like the Hall of Secrets?"

Rory's eyes flit back and forth, studying everyone's reaction.

"You'd be surprised," I say. "I've experienced her power firsthand. It's not going to be easy beating her at her own game."

Geneviève places the tea container next to Drena. "We have an array of delicious tea. Chamomile, mint, apple cinnamon, blackberry—"

"Black tea is fine," Rory says.

I take a seat opposite of Derek, and Rory sits next to me.

Cole and Cory stand against the fireplace with their arms folded across their chests. A faint memory of the two of them flicker in my thoughts, when they stood against the wall outside on the basketball court of Storm River Manor. I shake off the recollection.

"I still can't believe you're alive," Cole says, looking at Derek.

"Same," Cory repeats. "I thought for sure my brother killed you.

Derek's stern stare is evident that he himself is surprised. "He nearly succeeded." He changes positions in his seat. Drena hands Derek his tea and then pours Rory her cup. "I wish we had an answer for you. It was a strange moment for all of us."

"A horrid moment," Cole says. He presses his finger to the bridge of his nose as if the memory was traumatic. "I remember the shooting pain that drilled into me."

Our eyes focus on Cole as he explains his experience.

"Most of the memories are foggy." He looks up at us. "It went dark...I mean like I closed my eyes one minute and the next instant I was rising in the sky like a dragon."

Cory unfolds his arms, stunned by Cole's confession. "A dragon? You mean to tell me you're a dragon shifter, too? I admit, the clues were obvious."

Cole grins. "Try and keep up, brother." He looks over at me, for confirmation. "Sometimes I think I imagined it all. It was indeed an awakening moment."

"Like a Phoenix rising from the ashes," I say.

Derek's eyes perk up. "Hang on a second. Is this what you were trying to say earlier?"

Cory wrinkles his forehead. "I'm hearing this for the first time, too, Derek."

I nod. "After the portal hub blast, we were sent somewhere else. We think it might have been a place near the Crimson Moors on Elleirodal. Redmae, Rory, and I found Cole. Nearly his entire body burned. Much like Blair." I glance over at her still sleeping. "Minutes later he dissolved to ashes. Shortly afterward Sarmira appeared. She tried to destroy us. A dragon rose behind her."

"We thought we were all toasted marshmallows," Rory says.

Derek looks at Cole. "Are you saying you were that dragon?"

"Yes," he answers. "I soared in the sky as a dragon." He huffs as if the words coming out of his mouth is unbelievable on their own. He looks over at his brother. "Yes, apparently I'm a dragon shifter, which begs the question... are you one too, brother?"

"Wait a minute..." Cory tries to wrap his head around the news. He looks over at me. "This is what you were trying to tell me earlier, but it wasn't the right timing. Am I correct?"

I nod.

He turns to Cole. "We're identical twins."

Rory Smirks. "Obviously."

"Then we must assume that I'm a dragon shifter, too," Cory adds.

"That would be the consensus, I imagine." Derek stands. "But that would be impossible." He paces back and forth a few seconds, mumbling under his breath as if trying to figure out a mathematical equation. "When Maura—yes, I know Sarmira, but before any of us knew Maura was possessed, she would spend hours in her laboratory. One by one our Storm bloodline began to erase all evidence of our dragon DNA…" He looks up as if he had an epiphany. "She turned most of us into vampires." He shakes his index finger at Cole. "This changes the game plan indeed."

"Wait, you didn't know?" I ask, stunned. "But clearly you must've known when Chad came back rising from the ashes after my dad burned him?"

"Okay, stop." Derek puts a hand up. "What are you talking about, Wynter? Chad is a vampire like me. His shifter DNA was stripped along with the rest of us."

"Was…" I turn to see Rory is just as surprised as me. "He was a vampire. He's a dragon shifter. Just like Dad." I look over at him. "At least that's the theory. And I'm willing to bet Blair is, too." I look over at Derek again. "And me."

"You?" He's clearly stunned. "Hmm…" He grabs a pipe from the mantle."

"Uncle, how do you not know this?" Cole asks. He stops to ponder a minute. "If you didn't know, and my birth mother Blair didn't know, that means—" He looks at me and Rory.

"That must mean Sarmira doesn't know, either," I say.

"Oh no, I most certainly knew," Derek says. "Well, suspected at least. Those who knew simply kept it to themselves." Derek prepares the pipe to smoke. "Memory stamp.

Everyone has been under a memory stamp. That has to be the explanation. It's the one big factor playing into this."

"Like a dream stamp?" I ask.

"Indeed. My how the tables turn when revelations appear." He pauses to smoke his pipe. He blows a couple O-rings. "This could work to our advantage, ya know."

"What are you implying, Derek?" Drena asks.

He stands. "Okay, hear me out." He briefly glances at my dad and then paces around the couch until he finds the words. "My guess there's a memory stamp that's been placed upon me, as I mentioned—" He looks at Cole, Cory, then me. "Like you. Your mother placed one, as did your Aunt Fran, to protect you." The gleam in his eyes tell me he's excited about his thought process. "What if before we were placed on this Earthly plane, years ago, Sara somehow managed to position a memory stamp of her own on all of us?"

"You're talking about when we all escaped the Kingdom of Storm Castle when Sarmira tried to kidnap Isalora as a baby and poisoned Francesca, aren't you?" Geneviève asks.

"I remember this, too," I say.

Derek raises a brow, confused. "How? You were not even born yet."

"My mother showed me in a dream once. Ian, at the time, stayed back. Allowing all of you to escape."

"Yes, I remember," Derek confirms. "I was only a boy then. Shortly after, the Storm family discovered Ian had been handed down as the next Dragonscale."

"Where is all this revelation going? Please enlighten us," Cole says.

"I think all of the Storms are dragon shifters," Derek says.

"If that were true, then why are you not a dragon?" Cole asks. "Better yet—" he looks over at Blair. "Why isn't she a shifter, herself?" He laughs, still not accepting that Derek's theory could be rendered as facts. "I could name quite a few people who are Storms and not shifters. Daniel, Uncle Arik, Great Uncle Gavin, and Bram. Better yet, Great Grandfather Ailbert." Cole points to me. "Her mother Isalora. She died trying to save her. I don't buy it. I need proof."

"But Chad and Jeff are dragon shifters. You yourself claim to be one, and Wynter, too," Derek points out.

"I think Derek is on to something, Cole. Both you and Chad were charred to a crisp before rising as a dragon," Redmae says.

"Something isn't adding up," I say. "Dad and I never burned to ash. We transformed naturally. Aunt Fran had fire capabilities, and she is a Deagon. A dragon shifter as well. You're a vampire."

Derek nods. "I think we've established that. Isn't it obvious from my appearance? What are you getting at, Wynter?"

"If vampires turn to dragon shifters, eliminating their vampiric side, is it safe to say that all the Storms in this room are either active shifters or dormant?"

Blair moans, distracting us from the conversation. "Water," she whispers.

"Finally, one of them is waking up." Geneviève gets up to grab a glass of water. "Maybe she can shed some light as to what happened." She tips the glass to Blair's lips. "Here, love, drink this."

15
DRAGON SISTER

Blair chokes on the water spitting it out, screaming in agony, as it flows through her like a river. On the surface of her skin, orange and red embers travel across her body singeing her like fire to paper, while bubbles form underneath appearing on her lips first, and increase down her body, bursting randomly, leaving behind holes where steam rises off her frame.

"Mom!" the twin's scream. They're powerless to stop it. "You're killing her!" Cole knocks the glass from Geneviève's hand. Water splashes all over the floor and onto Drena who stands behind Geneviève.

"What have we done?" Drena watches in horror.

I turn away, not able to watch any longer until Blair's screams cease.

The utter quiet is deafening.

Cory looks frustrated. "Please, what just happened?"

I turn back around to see Blair dissolved to dust and ash, leaving a figure formed hole in the cushion where she once rested. A brush of air swooshes in from the fireplace, exploding small embers from the logs, startling us.

"She's gone," Rory says.

"No, she's still very much alive." A faint aura of white and gold swirls in the air. An aura only I can see. Blair's ashes lift from the scorched cushions and spin with a glow of light.

"What do you mean? Are you blind? I saw Blair disintegrate before my very eyes." Derek obviously cannot see what I see.

Geneviève smiles. "Wynter can see ghosts, my friend."

"This is more than a ghost sighting. We're watching the rise of a dragon, I'm sure of it," Redmae states.

Blair's spirit stops, and stares at me intently. *"I see the truth, Wynter. They're telling me to go outside."*

"Who is telling you?" I turn in circles watching as Blair's spirit swirls around the room in a dance of freedom before she whisks by me, into the fireplace and up the chimney leaving sparks of fire spitting out the hearth as she goes. *"Follow me."*

"This is exactly what happened to you, Cole," Redmae says. "Minus the fireplace of course."

"Blair is keeping in theme with her dramatic persona, apparently." I open the front door. "Well, what is everyone waiting for? Let's go after her."

The night sky is still lit up by the bright Blood Moon as all of us pile outside. Blair's spirit whirls in the sky reflecting off the moonlight. To my revulsion, evil apparitions still pour through the Blood Moon's portal behind her. "Can you see them while in human form, Redmae?" I whisper.

"Yes, I can. So many specters. We need to find the source of it," she answers.

A breeze circles us, forming a funnel of fog that kicks up leaves, and it temporarily distracts our view. When it clears, Blair's spirit transforms into an ash covered dragon. She stretches her body and roars like Cole did when he changed. I'm in awe at her magnificent wingspan. She shakes off the dust, and in the moonlight, a silvery white shade glistens off her scales, giving a golden shimmer.

Geneviève, Drena, Derek, and Cory step back, stunned.

"I can't believe my eyes," Cory says.

Redmae bumps his arm. "Told ya!"

"How is this possible?" Drena asks.

"How is anything possible anymore?" Cole answers.

Derek puffs his pipe. "How magnificent."

"That... Uncle..." Cole begins, "I believe is your theory."

"Cole my boy, I do believe you're right." Derek takes another puff.

Cory looks at me, surprised by what he's witnessed. "I concur, Uncle, I believe you might be onto something."

Derek looks over at Drena and sees her concerned expression. He hugs her tightly to him. "Don't worry, dear, I think this is strictly a Storm bloodline trait." He grins. "A complete game changer, though."

"But Derek you're a Storm, too," she argues. "The common denominator—all of those who have transitioned have been Storms." We need to seek out Sara's journals up in the loft."

Blair roars again. Her wings wave and heave in swift strides. The swooshing sound is loud but strong. I smile knowing this revelation that my family have stumbled upon is—in Derek's words—a game changer.

A swirl of wind surges in, sweeping Blair's dragon form away, and as quickly as she formed into a dragon, she shifts back to her human self. She lies on the ground looking stunned as she struggles to get up. Her confusion turns into fear seeing all of us stare at her.

Drena comes to her aid. "It's alright, dear. We'll explain inside." She helps her daughter to her feet. "Put this around you before you catch a chill." Drena takes the shawl she is wearing and places it around Blair's shoulders. Derek and Geneviève follow them.

I look back up at the evening sky, still mesmerized by the pouring of malevolent souls coming through the Blood Moon portal that isn't visible to the average human. "We need to stop them."

Cory, Cole, Rory, and Redmae look up with me.

"Agreed." Redmae says. "I don't know how, but we will stop them."

Cory touches my shoulder.

I jump and gasp.

"Hey, it's just me," he says. "Stop what?"

"Wynter is referring to the immortal entities piling through the moon," Rory says. "Can you not see them?"

"No. Actually, I can't. It looks like an ordinary moon."

Confused by Cory's admission, I look at his brother. "You either?"

Cole shrugs. "I'm not sure why Cory can't see them."

I look at Rory and Redmae. "Yet you two can?"

Rory grins slightly. "We're wolves. We're guided by the phases of the moon. Like Redmae said, we will stop them." She looks at Cole. "And I'm guessing because Cole is a shifter—"

"Dragons can see through the façade of what people interpret as real, verses metaphysical," Dad says, coming from behind. "Preferably without trying to get themselves killed of course."

"Dad, hey, you're up and about all on your own." I come by his side and lean in for a hug. "How are you feeling? Are you in pain? Can I help?"

"My ribs are tender. Nothing too bad."

I look for the area that gives him discomfort and hover my hands over the painful spot. "Better?"

"Better than I was, thank you. Like many supernatural beings, we can regenerate with time, but not as quickly on

Earth." He nods, turns to study his surroundings, and makes eye contact with everyone. "Looks like I missed the party. I'm curious, how did we stumble upon your mother's cottage?"

"Not sure how it happened, really. We were just discussing a link to the Storms and the Blood Moon. Someway, somehow, all of us have gravitated to here. But Dad, you missed it... Blair is a shifter, like us."

He tilts his head, nodding slightly. "I knew this day would come; I just didn't expect it this quickly."

Stunned, I say, "Wait you knew?"

"Many know except the ones still under the memory stamp." He looks at Cory. "Let's hope your memory doesn't lay dormant."

"I understand," Cory says.

"I don't. Enlighten me, please." Something in the pit of my stomach grows. I have a funny feeling something not so funny is about to emerge.

"Wynter, remember when we were going through Songbird Meadow, and we had to wait for your Aunt Fran to wake on her own from the comatose state she was in?" Cory asks.

"How could I forget."

"This is similar. And what your dad is trying to say is, I didn't suddenly learn on my own. Circumstances, such as tonight, may have prematurely triggered a dormant state. I may never shift." He looks over at my dad. "Isn't that right, Jeff?"

Dad's subtle nod confirms it. "Not impossible. Cory could still shift but purposely sending him into a fiery inferno would not be a good option right now."

"Everything will work out, brother. We should tell the others inside about the Blood Moon."

"Cole's right, they need to know this," Dad agrees.

"So, you can see them, too, Dad?"

"Yes. We're in for a bigger battle than what I have foreseen."

The sky crackles and once again, dark dragons appear.

"They've found us. Just like when you transformed, Cole," Redmae says.

"Quick! We need it get into the cabin, now, before they see us," Dad says. "At least inside the cabin we can figure out a plan of attack."

Before I turn to go in, two dark dragons let out a loud screech and then dissolve into nothing. The riders fall to the ground. "Guys, did you see that?"

"Now that, I saw," Cory says. "Those were the dark riders of the House of Zhir."

"Remember, dragons cannot withstand Earth's atmosphere," Cole says. "It's why Blair and I both transitioned out of our dragon forms. The atmosphere is to dense for magic to freely soar. "The riders are still alive, and they will be lurking, so unless you want to seek them out and fight, we better get inside the cottage like your father said."

WE STEP BACK INSIDE, AND THE OTHERS ARE huddled in the living room tending to Blair's needs. She's obviously disoriented.

Drena stands as we come in. "What do you two make of all this?"

"Well," Cole says, as he motions everyone to sit. "I'm betting we have a much bigger problem than this dragon drama or the aging curse. There are wraiths, apparitions, and demons of all kinds pouring into Earth's realm."

"It's true," Rory says. "The question is, why all of a sudden now and not a week ago? Do all these events have something to do with the Blood Moon?"

"Perhaps now is a good time as any to explain?" Derek looks at Drena.

"Explain what?" I ask. "You mean, you know about the evil beings flooding through the portal of the Blood Moon?"

"Yes, and like you, I can see them, too," Drena says. "Derek cannot."

"And what do you make of that? Forget the transitioning of Cole and Blair for a moment. What are we going to do about this string of evil plaguing us right now?" I ask.

"That was why we were all downstairs when you arrived," Geneviève answers. "We were trying to find any clue to stop it from happening."

"Did you find anything?" Rory asks.

"Well, we know that I transformed to a human as soon as the moonlight touched my skin," Redmae says. "That should be significant enough evidence to prove something strange is happening."

Geneviève points to her daughter. "We need to write down these details. Can someone find me a pen and paper."

Derek rummages through an old antique desk against a wall near the hallway that leads to the back bedrooms. "I saw something in one of these drawers." He holds up a pad and paper. "Ha! Found it."

Geneviève writes down a couple theory points. "Okay, what else?"

Derek huffs. "I can only conclude that it's a Storm bloodline connection. Drena isn't a Storm. She hasn't got the necromancer gene."

"Yet, I am a Storm and haven't the aging skin as the rest of you. Is that your theory?" I ask.

"I don't think the Blood Moon is the only reason for this aging phenomenon most of you are experiencing." I look at Blair. "It appears her aging curse has lifted."

"It's the only common denominator, and I see your point, Wynter, but something still isn't adding up," Derek says. "After seeing what has happened today to Blair and Cole, I'm beginning to think it has something to do with the Storm gene."

I look at my hands. "Again, I haven't aged. We're missing something."

"Agreed," Drena says. "The source by which the magic is being drained is still a mystery. Plus, we need to find the source of why magic is fading. This cottage cannot hold for too much longer before the magic protecting it will fade."

"Which means if we don't find a solution fast, we'll all be fighting off thousands of demonic entities," Redmae says.

"Wait a minute, I think you're onto something." Blair adjusts her blanket and looks at Geneviève. "What does your list say so far?"

Geneviève Reads:

Blood Moon
Transition—Redmae, Cole, Blair
Aging curse
Dragon bloodline?

"I agree with Wynter. We're missing something," Blair says.

"Perhaps it's time I shed some light on what I've been forced to keep to myself for years. I think it's time I explain," Dad confesses.

16

A STORM CONNECTION

"Are you saying part of the connection is indeed the Storm bloodline, Dad?"

"It is an interesting theory," Blair says. "I mean, after all, I'm apparently a dragon shifter myself." She looks over at Derek. "Dad, if I'm a shifter, you must be as well."

Derek nervously answers, "I'm not confident enough to test that theory just yet."

"I wouldn't expect you to either, cousin," Dad interjects.

Cory seems frustrated and asks my dad, "Tell us, please, what happened the day Uncle Chad *died*?"

"The rumors are true," Dad admits. "However, I didn't know at the time Chad would rise from the ashes. After we realized the possibility that this is what broke the vampire curse, we didn't want to tell anyone until we knew for sure. Chad pretended to play the blood sucking creature although I don't think we fooled you, did we, Blair?"

She shakes her head. "No. I had my suspicions, but I kept them to myself. Knowing Moyer, if she found out it could've added more tools in her toolchest."

"But we all know it's really Sarmira behind this façade, so, what now? Where is the real Maura Moyer?" Cole asks.

"That's the golden question, isn't it?" Dad answers.

Uncle Derek—" Cole stops. "Wait, this is all too confusing. I was raised to think you were my uncle. That you, Chad, and Jeff were brothers."

"Cousins, actually," Derek corrects. "Chad and Jeff are brothers, and Maura Moyer's biological sons." He looks over at Blair. "She really did a number on our family, didn't she?" Derek looks sad. He reaches for Drena to sit with him.

Cole places his hands against his temples. "You're Blair's biological parents and you're our grandfather." He looks at Cory. "This family tree is so large I don't think I'll ever figure out how everyone is connected—"

"Moyer took your mother from me right after she was born," Drena interrupts. Her eyes glisten, looking at Blair.

Derek places a hand on Drena's, and she quiets. "Yes, Blair is our daughter, and Cory, Cole, and Casey are our grandsons."

I gasp. "Casey. I'd nearly forgotten about him."

Redmae's eyes glisten. "Casey is the only one who took care of me when Moyer—"

"I'm sorry. We'll find him, too, Red," I say.

Derek sighs. "It would be nice to repair what was lost."

I glance at the flames flickering back at me. "Lost," I whisper.

"What was that, Wynter?" Derek asks.

I continue staring into the fire as though it is hypnotizing my every thought. My mind travels through ideas as I think of the riddle that has been placed in front of us. "Sarmira comes from the Underworld, right?"

Both Derek and Drena nod.

"What can you tell me—us—about her? Is she a witch, dragon, vampire? What is her genetic make-up." I turn to the twins. "Do you know that answer?"

"She's a witch. A dark witch that has a gifted power in necromancy," Cory says.

"And Maura Moyer? What about her?" I ask.

"Hmm, what are you thinking, Wynter?" Derek appears confused.

"Maura Moyer's husband Arik was of dragon blood, too, right? I mean, he's a Storm, correct?"

"Yes, of course," Derek answers. He still looks confused.

"Was she a dragon, too?"

"No, she comes from a long line of witches, as well," Drena says. "She was my mother's student as a teen."

"Okay, now we're getting somewhere," Dad says. "I never knew this about my mother. She didn't reveal much of her past to any of us kids."

"Her mother was a light witch and her father a dark witch," Drena goes on. "Her parents were cast out from their covens because they had fallen in love. It was quite the scandal. Moyer's father created his own coven called the House of Shadow Raven. But that is an entirely different story. What we're trying to figure out is the connection between the Storms, the dragon bloodline, and the curse."

"My grandfather, a dragon shifter, married a witch. There is a connection to all of this, I just can't figure out what," I say.

"In theory, yes," Drena affirms, "it's a good probability that whatever happened to Moyer affected the entire Storm family line."

"But what if it wasn't just Moyer," Cole says. "I'm not related to her by blood."

"Hang on a minute. I just remembered something. About a week before my eighteenth birthday, Cory showed me this cottage and we were walking along the river, and I suggested we should burn the manor down and destroy Moyer with fire."

"What are you getting at, Wynter?" Redmae asks.

"What if every Storm that was or is a vampire, burn to

ashes, would then rise and turn into dragons?" I point to Cole. "He was a vampire." I point to Blair. "She was a vampire." I look at Dad. "You just admitted that you torched your own brother because he didn't want to be a vampire. And then a few days later he appears alive."

"I think I know where you're going with this," Cory says.

I breathe in deep, knowing we're on the same page.

"What I mean is, I think I know how we can get our family back, and defeat Moyer—I mean Sarmira—once and for all."

"The suspense is killing us. Wynter, spit it out already," Rory spats.

"Beat Sarmira at her own game and set all her vampiric Shadow Walkers on fire."

"Oh, I do like this theory indeed," Blair says mischievously.

"However, the source by which the magic is being drained is still a mystery," Drena adds. "Seeing the twins, it's a good probability that whatever happened to Moyer affected the entire Storm family line."

"I'm beginning to think she never had any intention of allowing you to live, Derek," I conclude.

"Why is that?" Rory asks, curious. "I don't understand. You would think Moyer would want all the allies she could get."

"Ah, but see, Derek wasn't her ally, and she knew it."

"Interesting theory, Wynter," Derek says. "And correct. I despise her."

"I think you're onto something," Drena states. "You see, the first twenty-four hours, even though vampiric blood is running through someone's veins, they look, act, and smell mortal. If Moyer did something to Derek's blood, say gave him an antidote to counter act the vampiric bite, then he wouldn't change at all."

I look over at Red, suddenly connecting the dots. *That might be how we can cure you.*

"How do you know about this?" Rory asks.

Drena smiles, a little devilish grin. "I'm not just a vampire, darling. I still have my light witch powers. However, I don't think she gave him any antidote. He was nearly dead when I found him."

"I know I'm changing the subject slightly, but its relevant. Do all vampires have youthful bodies?" Rory asks.

"Yes, but it's not just a vampire trait, it is also a Nytemire trait —a cross between a Storm vampire and a necromancer — rather, I used to be a vampire." Blair looks down, viewing her new body. "I was born a vampire through my mother." She glances at Drena. "It doesn't explain why suddenly I'm a dragon shifter and no longer a vampire." She looks at her son. "Or Cole, for that matter."

"To answer your initial question, Rory," Drena says. "Whether they drink blood of their victims or take their essence, either way it keeps us young looking. It doesn't matter what age a human or any other species is, because the moment they are turned, their youthfulness comes back. But to answer Blair's question: as far as the dragons on the Storm side, Derek has the bloodline in his veins through his parents, Clairice and Bram. She was a light witch, and Bram a dragon shifter on his mother's side."

"Queen Sara, right?" I ask.

"Yes."

"And who turned you, cousin?" Dad asks.

"You noticed?" Derek chuckles.

"Hard not to. You forget we shifters can smell vampires from miles away."

I take in a surprised breath. "That's how Aunt Fran knew the Shadow Walkers chasing us the day I was kidnapped!"

"Yes. I knew, too, but your aunt's talent is much better than mine." He glances back to Derek. "So, who turned you?"

"I did," Drena says.

"Well now, I didn't expect that." Dad gives a stern grin.

She places her hand on Derek's. "He lost a lot of blood and clearly wasn't a vampire."

"I'm not sure Moyer knew Chad's attempt to turn me was staged," Derek adds. "And well, we all know Chad is a shifter like you mentioned, Wynter. He couldn't turn me even if he wanted to." He looks over at Cole and Cory.

"Ah, I get it now," Rory says. "You boys didn't know he wasn't a vampire?"

"I knew he wasn't," Cory says, "but Cole assumed he was, which has me wondering—who staged this? You, or Uncle Chad?"

"I see where you're going with this, Cory. Please let me explain. It's not what you think." Derek takes another puff of his pipe. "When Cole stabbed me, Moyer thought I'd turn stiff like all other vampires that are staked, but she soon discovered I was still human."

"And now both her and Sarmira know Chad isn't a vampire." I cross my arms. "How did they not know, anyway? Thought vampires have a sixth sense about this sort of thing?"

"Ah, that's easy," Dad says. "I kept slipping him potions Nyta would brew. We were able to keep his little secret for a while, at least."

"Ha! So, you staged this coup!" Blair calls out. "I knew something was awry, but I couldn't put my finger on what it was." She grins devilishly. "Next time let me in on the scheme, will ya?"

Dad chuckles.

"Wait, I watched Chad change Derek myself," Cole argues. "His body physically changed."

"I guess I'll take that as a compliment. I should credit my drama instructor for such a profound performance then," Derek says. "Like Jeff mentioned, Nyta made up a brew that left Moyer/Sarmira convinced her plan was falling into place."

"Wow, you had me fooled. And so, you found him bleeding, Drena?" Cole asks.

"Yes. Derek saved me from Moyer's chopping chamber, all those years ago, so it was my turn to save him." Drena smiles and squeezes his hand.

"I woke with a hole in my chest, and I was very weak," Derek adds. "For whatever reason, the stab wound didn't kill me. After collecting my thoughts, I glanced around among the melting snow and spots of debris to see the woods burning from the battle. Some trees singed, and piles of charred cinder all around me with raining ash that caked the compound, and yet it was freezing cold from the blanket of snow. As a vampire I would have felt nothing. Flakes fell in large chunks. In the distance, I saw the mansion had burned to the ground."

"I know why you didn't die," I say. "It's because you have dragon blood running through your veins."

"That is yet to be determined, Wynter. I'm not going to jump into a fire willingly though, trust me." Derek winks.

"We have all seen the current blackened stone structure of Storm River Manor above the hill when we arrived," Rory says. "How did you find shelter?"

"I laid there on the bench under the gazebo for who knows how long—I might have fallen asleep for all I know. Perhaps that's why I woke hearing a whisper. A voice called to me, and I opened my eyes to her." He looks at Drena and smiles.

Realizing the connection, I say, "You turned Derek at the moment before he woke up?"

She nodded. "I don't regret it. I'm mean, I always said I would never turn a human being into a vampire; it was a promise I made long ago. The choice was taken from me, and I wasn't ever going to do that to someone else, but out of selfishness, and my deep love for Derek, I turned him. I couldn't go on living without him." She pauses. "So, yes, it was me."

"Sounds more like true love, if you ask me," Rory says.

"This coming from someone who despises vampires," I scoff.

"Yeah, well, people can change, Wynter."

"Once my brain caught up and I realized I was staring at the love of my life, I sat up, and we held each other for a long while and cried. At first, I thought I was dreaming, but soon realized I was in the exact spot I'd wobbled to before blacking out." He gazes at her. "You saved me."

She smiles. "And you saved me."

"Once I gathered my strength, we began to walk around. Rummaging through the ruins of Storm River Manor to see who or what survived."

"Did you find anything?" Rory asks.

"This book." He points to the hardcover resting on the coffee table that he'd brought up from the basement. "Among a handful of other ones." He looks up at the loft. "Lucky for us, we found a lot of literature up there."

"Okay, this is a wonderful romantic story, but I want to know how you came upon the portal to the Hall of Secrets," Rory says.

"And the cottage?" I ask.

"After rummaging through the ashes, we realized we should probably find shelter. The wind was picking up, and fresh snow began to pelt the ground, so we made our way back to Sara's Garden. I knew about the cottage, but I couldn't remember the secret passageway."

"Wait, a secret passageway?" I ask.

Derek smiles. "Sara intended it that way."

I raise a brow.

"Anyway, at this precise moment I had a familiar feeling come over me. A hunch if you will. Like something was telling me to go beyond the trees into the woods. I don't know, maybe I was still having some hallucinating aftereffects, but whatever

—whomever—it was, it led us to this cottage." Derek puffs once more on his pipe.

Mother comes to mind.

17
A VAMPIRE WITCH

Rory glances to Drena. "The stories we were told said you were dead. How are you still alive?"

"I imagine there is a lot in the history books that are incorrect. The winning side writes the narrative. Truth is, I was buried six feet deep for centuries. It was purposefully done. And your grandmother Moyer played a role in the planning. I do regret I haven't been around."

"What do you mean? Moyer knew? I'm so confused right now." My mind whirls.

"Moyer sacrificed her soul to save you, Wynter, before you were even conceived."

I wasn't ready for this twist. Flashes of memory flit through my head, as though much of Moyer was misunderstood.

She looks at me. "If your theory is correct and every Storm that is a vampire turns to a shifter, then Derek can be cured from this vampiric curse." She looks at Cory. "And you as well."

"Great, who's going to be the first volunteer to test the theory," Rory says with enthusiasm.

"Not funny, Rory. What about Casey? Have you seen him?" Redmae asks.

Derek shakes his head. "We haven't seen him or anyone else."

"Everyone is just gone?" Cole asks. "All the servants, too?"

"Gone, they're all gone. Either perished in the fire or turned to a Shadow Walkers," Drena says.

"We managed to save a few that were imprisoned in the basement, during the battle here before the manor was destroyed," Rory says.

"If there are any children left, they're not on this compound. We have scoured every inch of this property. I don't think any of you quite understand that according to our calculations, all of this happened in the past, like a week in the past, but—"

"But what?" Rory says. "You're about to say we've gone back in time, aren't you?"

"Yes, how did you know?"

Rory glances at her sister.

"We all felt like it was déjà vu," Redmae says.

"I can't explain it, but this present moment we're in now, is the exact moment I discovered Derek out there in the snow right after the deadly battle," Drena says.

"Then our initial theory is correct and we have jumped back in time." Cole looks concerned. "The Super Blue Blood Moon is still happening."

"That explains the demonic beings pushing through the moon's portal, currently," I say.

"Yes, an army of them it seems," Drena confirms. "And this does not bode well at all." Drena stands and paces the floor. "I think, when Sarmira tried to destroy the portal hub, something must've set us back in time a smidge. It's the only thing that make sense. Because it doesn't explain why we're all here at the same time. We were not part of Rory's group when she ported out of the Hall of Secrets." She looks over at Jeff.

"That's a good point, but the one to ask this question isn't here.," Dad answers. "Aoes wasn't present when the explosion at the hub happened."

"I have heard that when certain energy forces come together it can cause a dimensional shift," Geneviève adds. "There are billions of paths before us. Each choice we make shifts us into another reality. This one happened to bounce us back here."

"We've been given a second chance to do this right. They need to know how to fight back," Dad says.

Derek laughs. "I hope you two know what you're doing."

Geneviève nods. "It's time." She looks at Drena. "What we're about to tell you might clear up a few things. Things that all of you have been questioning for quite some time."

My heart beats quickly. "I think most of us want to know why, Moyer—Sarmira—has targeted the entire Storm family line."

"And we'll get to that, but the biggest threat we face at this present moment is this aging curse. It's affecting our magical abilities. And if we don't find the source of it, this cottage will be vulnerable very soon." Geneviève looks over at Drena to add her thoughts.

"I fear that Geneviève is correct. To defeat Sarmira, you need the Sword of Valor. To locate the Sword of Valor, you need to find the three daggers. If you remember, Queen Sara mentioned this in the Hall of Secrets."

We nod. "Go on," I say.

"Queen Sara said that Cory's dagger would lead to the others," Redmae says.

Derek looks at Geneviève with concern. There is a long pause before he speaks. "Years ago, when Queen Sara instructed myself and the others to seek Ashengale and assess the area after the battle of the crown, I requested to return to Storm River Manor, instead."

"Why?" I ask.

"Because Drena was still here on the compound somewhere."

I look in her direction.

"I left her when…" He again takes a long pause.

"When what?"

"When I stabbed her in the heart with the Blade of Truth."

"Hang on a second…what? You killed her?" I looked at Drena again. "I mean clearly, you're not dead. Clarify, please."

Derek tilts his head, lips curving. "Technically, she was never…dead. I mean, yes, she should be, but well, you know as well as I, a stake to the heart doesn't kill a vampire so, why would a blade?"

Drena smiles. "It's a long story. Just know, I was forced to give up Blair." She looks at Cole, Cory, and her daughter. "I tried to protect you, but I see I failed. Sarmira still rages on." Drena's eyes glisten. "She figured a way to produce a naturally born vampire. Blair was the result of that."

The room grows quiet.

"That's when I made the hard decision to have Derek stake me and hide my body. We knew by protecting the blade we could slow the prophecy and if they couldn't find me, Sarmira and her minions wouldn't be able to break from the Underworld."

"The rumors say that you were pregnant with Blair when Moyer captured you. That's how she got the idea to produce the Shadow Walkers. So, you were captured a second time?" Cole asks.

She takes in a deep breath. "Yes."

"Hang on a second, am I missing something?" I ask.

"My dear, Wynter, don't you get it?" Drena presses.

"Obviously not, so spill it."

"The three shall be one." She stares at me intently. "The Sword of Valor, of course."

I take in a breath. "How do you know about that?"

"Because my mother was one of the witches that cast the spell."

"What?"

Drena walks to a bench standing along the wall near the front door and she paces to collect her thoughts. "Many of you may know that the witches in our world of Ladorielle and Elleirodal are immortal, like that of dragon shifters." She looks at Cory, Cole, and me. "As well as druids and wolves."

She glances over to Rory and Redmae. "Vampires are an extended version of that immortality. People think that once you turn to a vampire you cannot grow, or have children, but that is incorrect. For a magical creature they are already immortal in their own right, and receiving a lethal bit from the fangs of a vampire merely transfers that being to use a different innate power. Our true born nature will remain dormant. Earthy humans are a different story, for their magic isn't as strong, but I digress. What I mean to say is I was present when the Sword of Valor was split a thousand years ago."

Shocked by Drena's confession, I say, "That would mean you're older than my grandmother Maura Moyer."

"We're nearly the same age, actually. To put it in your perspective to understand, I would have been about five when my mother prepared the ritual spell. Again, I must reiterate, the years on the sister planets is much different than the years here on Earth."

"Perhaps that's the reason for the aging curse," Rory says. "Earth is just too dense."

"You're partially correct. Earth's atmosphere is extremely heavy for us magical creatures. And we must learn to adapt to live in these conditions," Drena agrees. "But Earth isn't entirely to blame. I think the aging curse that is currently happening on Ladorielle and Elleirodal has something to do with the Blood Moon that both those planets and Earth are experiencing at the same time millions of light years apart—" She stops and looks at Cory. "And the power of The Sword of Valor that was split into three blades, have something to do with it."

Cole straightens. "You mean the Blade of Hope is somehow connected to both worlds?"

Drena nods. "Along with the Blood Moon Eclipse, yes. A rare event that hasn't happened in a thousand Earth years." She lifts the lid on the bench. "There are so many theories written in books, through the years and rumors of the prophecy, in reference to, 'the three to be one,' that I will shed some truth for all of you to swallow."

Inside the bench a white linen cloth covers items beneath it. Drena gently pulls back the cloth. "Before splitting the Sword of Valor, we realized that utilizing the magical talent from three witches from three different bloodlines would enforce the foundation of magic of the spell that we were about to perform. It was the only way to ensure the bond would hold against the powerful magic Sarmira would try to consume. This way if she tried, it would counteract her own magic, bonding the Sword of Valor stronger."

"You mean like a counter spell. If she should cast a spell, it would bounce back onto her instead?" Redmae asks.

Blair gasps. She looks at the twins. "That's why the Blade of Hope did what it did? Cole, essentially possessed by one of Sarmira's demons, used it against the owner of the Blade of Hope, encapsulating them both. As though in some twisted way, protecting them?"

"In a matter of speaking, yes," Drena says. "Only the descendants of those bloodlines would be able to bring the sword back as one. So, we enforced the odds of that happening by adding vampire, dragon, and wolf blood to seal in the spell and with the help of the Dryads made sure the Sword of Valor would never surface again until it was time."

"I don't understand. This doesn't make any sense," Rory says.

"Sounds all so very complicated," Blair says. "Why are these blades so special?"

Drena lifts her chin. "Together these blades will forge the Sword of Valor."

"The three to be one," I whisper. "It makes perfect sense, Rory."

Cory pulls from his waist the Blade of Hope. "We believed this was part of what caused the catastrophe upon the magic world."

Drena lifts out an item bound in more cloth. "My mother, along with her coven sisters, and with the help of the Dryads, made sure the sword would never be found. After the splitting and reforging each of them would receive a third of the sword." She comes forward and places the object on the center of the coffee table that sets in the middle of the cottage living room. "You see, Sarmira was very powerful in her time—still is in her apparition form. Her daughter pushed back."

"Hang on a second...Sarmira has a daughter?" Rory asks, shocked.

"I'm sure you have heard of the story, Rory. Most of us have," Dad says. "Sarmira's daughter was Petra. Bryce Storm's wife."

"She's the mage that came through the portal of the Crimson Moors in the Hall of Secrets before the portal hub catastrophe," Redmae reiterates.

"I remember Eleena, my grandmother told me. She didn't elaborate too much, though," I add.

"Hang on a minute," Rory interrupts. "I just realized something. You're related to Sarmira?"

"Yeah, I guess I am."

"And you didn't think it was important to say anything?"

Drena hangs back before revealing what's under the cloth and pours herself another cup of tea.

"When have we had time? Rory, I just woke from the dead about thirty-six hours ago. Besides, it didn't really sink in until now."

"She's right, cut her some slack," Cole defends me.

"You said necromancer witch, Drena. Are you saying Petra was one of the three witches?"

18

THE BLADE OF TRUTH

Drena sits back in one of the chairs around the coffee table holding her cup before answering. "Yes, including my mother Sage, and a dark witch. A witch none of you know personally but may have heard of her. Some call her The Raven."

My eyes meet Cole's.

"The Raven? Do you think Drena is speaking about the same witch we met before being led to the crystal caves?"

"Are you inviting me into your thoughts now?" he asks, sarcastically.

I roll my eyes.

"Are you saying you have met The Raven?" Cory asks.

I look at his brother and he nods. *"We have,"* Cole says."

"Well, that is interesting, because I met her too, except I was in Scarlet Hollow. When I still had the dagger in my physical body."

"I'm suddenly not too confident with trusting this Raven witch," I say. The letter she had instructed me to give Cole still hides inside my pocket. I knew there was a reason not to give the note to him.

Geneviève grunts bringing me back from my thoughts. "She is a rather neutral character. One who doesn't play by the rules when it comes to magic." She comes to sit on the floor next to Drena. "A character who doesn't fit the mold of the average witch, I would say. Wouldn't you agree, Drena?"

"A vigilante?" Cole asks, still standing next to the fireplace.

"Something like that, yes," Drena admits. "Geneviève is right. The Raven always has her own agenda. Anyone taking a deal from her may as well have sold their soul."

I swallow hard. My stomach turns to knots.

"At the time, the Underworld was gaining power, and the Dryads knew the only way to keep the peace was to break the sword's curse. We need the magic of an oracle. What our forces didn't anticipate was it started a prophecy." Drena looks directly at me. "Yours."

"Me?"

"You, my dear, are one of those bloodlines, as is Cory and Cole. If the Underworld got a hold of all three of you, the prophecy would be fulfilled. The oracle required a certain ingredient. She convinced us it was the only way to stop Sarmira."

I remember when Aoes gave me a gem, placing it in my hand, saying, *'This will help you on your journey.'* "It all begins to make sense. Aoes knew, didn't he?"

"About the stone, yes. He wouldn't know where the daggers were, though," Drena says. "That was up to the covens to find a way to hide them."

"Nobody suspected the Blade of Hope was part of the Sword of Valor. I mean, how else would Moyer be free with Cory unknowingly releasing her," Cole says.

I look at Cole, making a grave connection. "No, not possible..." I can see he, too, is making the connection.

"My grandmother Maura was clever, but I think Sarmira thought she got the upper hand. It's only a guess, but what if

Maura knew all along that the Blade of Hope was part of the Sword of Valor?" I look at Cole.

"What are you getting at, Wynter?" Dad asks.

I shake my head. "It makes perfect sense."

"What does?" Cole presses.

I take in a deep breath, looking up at them. "I'm surprised we didn't see this; it's so blatantly obvious." I shake my head in annoyance. "Maura Moyer knew about the magical elements of the dagger, that much I'm sure of." I stare at Cole. "She banked on Cory stabbing her with it. Because if she was right, she would be free from Sarmira. Of course, Sarmira didn't know that. Somehow Maura was able to hide her thoughts from Sarmira. I think, knowing that Cory was wielding the Blade of Hope, Maura would sacrifice her body if it meant that it would freeze Sarmira along with herself. However, it backfired."

"Okay, Wynter, we sort of established this already back at the Hall of Secrets," Rory says.

"Much of it, yes, but we were missing something. I think this is it."

Rory nods. "Okay, I think I follow you."

I look at Cole. "Neither you or your brother knew what that dagger really was, but Maura knew, and she somehow tried to tell us. I think Maura was afraid that Sarmira would gain that dagger's power along with yours. Maura Moyer stopped that from happening."

Drena nods. "I believe the Elementals foresaw Sarmira's cheating scheme, too. At least that's my theory. None of us knew where the other person's magical item was to be. Call it an insurance policy, if you will."

Derek nods. "Everything is connected. I had overheard Sarmira's plans, mentioning I was her bait. She had Cole stab me on purpose to provoke Cory, so she could get her claws into him. Sarmira thought I was still weak. If you're theory is correct, Wynter, it must mean real Maura Moyer, the light witch part of here is alive and well."

"Then we must find a way to free here as well," Cole says.

"We're Storms with the blood of Petra's powers. If Sarmira turned us, we would lose our magical abilities and become useless to her. But the difference between myself and the rest of the Storm bloodline is I have an added magical bonus," Derek says. "I'm beginning to understand where Sarmira's mind is going." He presses his fingers against his forehead and closes his eyes.

"What are you getting at, Uncle?" Cory asks.

"His mother Clarice was part Dryad and light witch and had the gift element of Terra," Rory says. "Clarice was my grandmother's best friend."

Derek clears his throat. "My mother Clarice's bloodline traces back to Earth elemental descendants, or if we are speaking of our world on Ladorielle—Terra—we take a little longer than most to regenerate. But there's something else you should know. Drena and I don't know for sure because of Sarmira's 'little experiments,' we don't know if Blair is one hundred percent my biological daughter. Her shifting to dragons gives us hope though."

"Mom, did you know about this?" Cory asks.

"I did, but I didn't care if he was my biological dad or not. He raised me. He took on the dad role and that is what mattered to me."

"Something doesn't add up," Cole says. "The demon part of me would have known about this scheme."

"What are you getting at?" I ask.

"I don't think Sarmira knew about this secret."

"And you're thinking only Moyer did? How? Isn't she under the spell of Sarmira?"

Drena smiles. "It appears the Maura Moyer I knew was a

little more powerful than she led on. That could go in our favor." She takes a sip of her tea.

"You mean Moyer knew, but Sarmira didn't? Is that your brilliant theory?" Cory asks.

Cole gives his brother the side-eye. "I did mention that. Were you not listening as usual?"

Cory grunts, annoyed.

"Moyer comes from a long line of witches. Her father was a dark witch and her mother light. It's the only thing that makes sense. Moyer's body may have been controlled by Sarmira, but Maura made it perfectly clear Sarmira would never get inside her mind and take away her family. As sick and morbid as that sounds, I quite agree that we're onto something here." Drena takes another sip of her tea.

"When I was..." I look over at Rory and Redmae, "asleep."

"We thought you were dead," Rory says.

"Hear me out." I hold up my hand. "I remember seeing a door in my sleep saying 'private,' and I wonder if Maura keeps a similar door?"

Drena's eyes grow wide. "But of course. I don't know why I didn't put this together before. It's starting to make sense. Now I know why Moyer had all the Storms under her thumb."

"Why?" Rory asks.

I face my friend and answer for Drena. "To protect us."

Rory drops her hands to her side. "What are you saying?"

Drena sets her cup down. "This whole chase isn't about saving just Wynter—"

I shake my head; I don't like where this is going.

Drena looks at me, then to Cory and Cole. "I see now, none of you know." She stares at Derek. He looks as amazed as we do. "If you fulfill the prophecy, you will become next in line, but not for Ladorielle, but for the Underworld. This is why Sarmira needs all three of you. You're the Child of Darkness, Wynter."

———————⟨✦⟩———————

I FEEL LIKE I'VE BEEN HIT IN THE GUT. DEEP BREATHS are not cutting it.

"Wynter, we won't let that happen," Rory says.

"I imagine having this watch on, severely disrupts Sarmira's plans," Cole adds. "I can visualize her seething with fury."

"I'm not sure we've disrupted her plans at all. I think we're playing right into them," Drena says.

"How so?" Rory asks.

"I don't know, it's just a feeling."

Looking at Drena, I ask, "Please tell us more about these daggers."

"They protect the one holding the blade." She reaches over and begins removing the cloth from the hiding object.

"It's a long brown box!" Cole jokes.

Drena smiles. "Not just an ordinary box, Cole. Why don't you open it?"

He huffs. "Me? It isn't a snake that is going to jump out and bite me, is it?"

"Just open the dang box, Cole," Rory presses.

He opens it and pulls from the compartment an identical blade to Cory's except it has a brown stone embedded in the hilt.

"This is the Blade of Truth, one of the three daggers," Drena confesses.

"It's so beautiful it hardly looks like it should be used for war," I say.

"As I said before, The Sword of Valor was melted into three different daggers. There was a labradorite stone attached to the Sword of Valor." She smiles. "You hold that stone within your locket. Why do you think that necklace protects you so well?"

I grab my necklace. "Dad?"

"She speaks the truth. I didn't know it came from the Sword of Valor, but I did know it was a very important stone imbued with magic. Eleena gave it to your mother on our wedding day. She had it made into a necklace. Eleena insisted your mother should wear it always, and to never take it off."

"That sounds strangely familiar, Dad."

He smiles. "Your mother wanted you to have it. It makes sense now, looking back."

Cole holds up the dagger. The hilt glows slightly.

"How do you feel?" Drena asks.

"I-I'm not sure." Cole sways with the blade and dances softly, as he waves his arms about pretending to be in battle.

"This blade will give magical gifts to those wielding it. For example, holding these daggers will allow the person insight. Such as seeing the undead." She eyes both the twins, and then me as though expecting something to happen. "Using the dagger on an undead creature will disintegrate them. And the blade also gives the handler sight to see people possessed by a wraith. But there is a downside to this blade."

"Which is?" Rory asks.

"Should a person die while holding the dagger, its power transfers to the victor."

A chill runs up my spine. and I look at the twins, making a grave connection. "No, not possible..."

"What?" Rory asks. I sense her heart race.

"Now I understand." I look at the twins. "Neither of you knew what that dagger really was, and in Sarmira's twisted mindset, I think she thought she would gain that dagger's power along with yours." I shake my head. "We came really close to losing all magic that day."

Cory looks at Drena. "There is something I haven't told any of you prior to the encounter with my brother."

"Go on..." Drena says.

"I was visited by the Elementals before the battle at Storm

River Manor. They asked to see the sword, and did some sort of magic ritual, then they vanished."

Drena looks pleased. "It seems my assumptions were right that the Elementals foresaw Sarmira's cheating scheme after all. Terra, wind, water, and fire. It's all beginning to make sense. Like I said, before, my mother and her sisters vowed to keep the sword safe. That blade has a tiger's eye embedded into the hilt. It's a grounding stone that will help keep you grounded, Cole. It will protect you from evil spirits." Drena looks at Cory and me. "The Blade of Hope in combination with Wynter's necklace it will make all three of you stronger when facing Sarmira."

"And what exactly are these blades used for besides killing Sarmira during the Super Blue Blood Moon?" Blair asks, looking toward the window. "Which we're experiencing as we speak."

"The dagger will choose its owner, Blair. Cory's blade has Lapis Lazuli on its hilt," Drena says. "It will give the holder wisdom, power, and truth. This truth connects to Cole's blade. Cory will have a stronger connection to his conjuring abilities while Cole will have added courage and strength allowing him to enhance his illusion-based skills. Together the twins will share their capabilities along with your necklace. Wynter, the three of you will be nearly unstoppable. It also will give the holder of that blade some sort of longing to carry it in their hands."

We all watch Cole continue to be mesmerized by the blade as he carries it in a simulation of battle moves. The dagger glows brighter.

Drena grins. "I do believe the blade and owner have been found."

I see an aura of white glow about him. He closes his eyes as though to soak in its power.

"How do you feel?" Drena asks.

"Like I suddenly know who I am. I have clarity." Cole swipes the air once more.

"That's similar to what I felt when I found my dagger," Cory says.

Drena smiles and folds the cloth that the dagger was wrapped in, places it in the box, and puts it back in the bench. She grabs a sheath and hands it to Cole. "Guess that's yours now, too."

My necklace glows brighter along with the blade as does Cory's dagger. "What's happening now?"

"You hold the link to the three daggers, Wynter, the same magic that is in your locket," Drena says. "Why do you think that necklace protects you so well? Like your father said, the labradorite comes from the hilt of the Sword of Valor." She stands.

"The Blade of Hope and the Blade of Truth have been found. Only one blade left to discover. The Blade of Peace." She looks at me. "Yours. It will have labradorite on the hilt. That blade will protect the minds of your entire group from negative energies and keep Sarmira from getting inside your heads."

"Well, it does appear the pieces of the puzzle are coming together quite nicely," Dad says.

Cole continues to pace with his dagger in hand, as though he's not listening to a word we're saying. I catch Cory's eye and nod toward Cole.

"Brother, is something wrong?"

Cole stops. "Hmm?" The right side of his mouth curves into a grin. He looks at us and back to the dagger. "I think I know where the Blade of Peace is and this dagger is going to lead us there."

19

THE TRAVEL STONE

I straighten, my posture eager to hear what he has to say. "Where?"

"I can't be positive, but I think in the catacombs here on the grounds," Cole answers. "I think the blade is trying to communicate with me. It's weird. It's like suddenly I have insight, where otherwise I wouldn't."

"Like my necklace." I touch my chain. It still glows, and the closer I move to the dagger the brighter it gets. Cory moves closer to Cole as well and his blade glows brighter, too.

"See, your necklace and the daggers are connected," Drena says. "I'm willing to bet with the help of your necklace and both your blades, we will be able to locate the Blade of Peace." Drena walks to the basement door and opens it. "Come with me. Isalora has a working alchemy station downstairs. There's something else I want to show all of you...specifically Rory. Something that might pique all of our interest, and it may get all of us home."

We're startled by the whistling of the wind outside. I jump slightly, and Rory, too. "The howling reminds me of the past experiences when Sarmira was near."

"She's closer than we think," Drena says in an ominous tone. "We are going to have to act fast. I sense we don't have a lot of time." Drena looks at Blair. "You're a Shadow Walker, tell us...is she near?"

"Former Shadow Walker," she corrects. "And yes, she's near...I think. Something in me has changed, though, after I shifted. It's as though a part of me died forever. I can't seem to connect to any of them like before."

"That's what happened to me, too, when I was temporarily cured from the potion, my sister gave me the moment the Blood Moon rose," Redmae says. "I still can't hear them—the wolves that is. I mean, I can't communicate like before, but I can still sense when they are near. And they are watching us closely. At least in this vicinity. I don't think they can see this cottage, but they do sense our presence."

"Same thing happened to me when the old me died in a combustion pile of ash, back on Elleirodal," Cole says. "And I too, like Redmae said, I could feel the Shadow Walkers close. And like what Mom mentioned, I can't communicate telepathically anymore, but I can still sense them."

"That is useful information, you two," Drena says. "Come, we have much work to do."

When we reach the bottom step to the second living room, a lit fireplace fills the cozy space. It hasn't changed much since the last time I stepped into this area.

Looking out the windows I can see the snow flurries kick up and the trees sway fiercely. My gut is telling me something isn't right. "Red, you feel that?"

"Like some sort of dread is upon us? Yeah, I do."

"I think we all feel it," Geneviève says.

My necklace continues to glow, grabbing everyone's attention.

I see fear in Drena's eyes. "Your compass is detecting

danger. My protection spell won't hold long, we are on borrowed time." She looks at Derek and Dad.

"Protection spell? But I thought this cottage was already protected from my mother's magic?"

"Isalora isn't here to keep it up. When Derek told me about the story how this place was protected, I knew I needed to get the shields up, immediately, because it was clearly visible in the woods."

"Do you think Sarmira knows it's here, then?" I ask.

"Yeah, she knows," Cory says. He looks at his brother.

Cole nods. "This dagger acts as a messenger in a way. Whispers of the past. As though souls of the fallen are trapped within it, and they are speaking to us."

"I feel it, too," Blair says.

Drena goes to a small corner of the room that is an extension of my mother's workstation. A sit-up island bar takes the place of a worktable, and hidden inside the cabinets isn't liquor, but herbs like dried rosemary, thyme, oregano, mint, and lavender. More herbs hang above a window looking out onto the river. Her wash station isn't for dishes but potted plants, soil, and plant food. Instead of beverage glasses hanging on hooks and sitting on the shelves, it's mason jars, alchemy bottles and ramekins. The small area looks like an indoor greenhouse rather than a working laboratory.

Cole raises a brow. "Really?"

"Welcome to my office," Drena says. "Wynter's mother had it set up already."

"How clever," he remarks. "What are you planning to do now?"

"A spell," Drena says. She points to a window with hanging herbs. "Wynter, grab a few sprigs of lavender and crush the flowers with this mortar and pestle." She scoots it toward me.

Drena roams from one end of the family room area to the

other, rifling through random drawers. "Where is it?" she mutters.

I do as she instructs, while watching her rummage through some drawers.

"What are you looking for, my love," Derek asks.

"A travel stone." She turns around and looks in a desk drawer. "I had one left. I was saving it for a special occasion. Travel stones are unique. Rarer than some of the largest diamonds ever recorded. There are so few of them that it's become a legend that they even exist at all."

I glance at Rory, and she shrugs.

Drena moves to the closet down the hall, and we hear more drawers open. "I know it's here somewhere because I'm the one who hid it. Now, if I could just remember where it is."

"Can you tell us about this travel stone? What does it do?" Cole asks.

"Well," she says, briefly glancing at us and then back to her task at hand. "It isn't any ordinary stone." Drena stops. "Ah, I remember now." She moves a painting from a wall, and behind it is a built-in safe.

"The oldest trick in the book," Redmae says. "I guess if it works, then it works, right?"

Drena cups her hands putting her index fingers together and closes her eyes. "I don't have much magical energy left. This world is so draining that magic loses strength each time I use it. Travelling to Ladorielle, albeit short, still gave me a good recharge." A breeze whisps through her hair, even though all the windows are shut. The lock on the safe unlatches and the door swings open. Drena grabs a box inside. "The trepidation is coming upon us quickly." She sets the box on the counter near me, where I continue to grind the dried lavender.

Drena stops to stare at my necklace, as though she can detect what each color shade of blue means. "Sarmira is near." She looks at Rory. "If we're going to make this work, we need to get it right the first time." She lifts the lid revealing several pebbles.

"Rocks?" Cole asks.

"Not any ordinary rocks, my dear. In here are several semi-precious stones, crystals, and gems." She rakes through them searching. "Hidden in plain sight. Nobody would think to sift through this rubble to find a stone so rare. Ah... I found it." Pulling out a round navy-blue-grey stone with a black stripe down the center for all of us to see, she says, "Here we are."

"I remember when we decided to hide in that box," Geneviève says." She meekly smiles at Drena, and nods. "It's time, my friend. We have waited long enough."

Drena holds it up. "Only a druid porter can acquire a travel stone such as this." She looks at Geneviève and she nods. Drena pulls out a leatherbound sack tucked inside the box. "This should help you, Rory. "You cannot expect for everyone to survive bouncing around from one world to the next, when infected with Gate Rot."

Rory gasps. "How did you know?"

"I'm a witch, we know things. Question is, who gave you the potion elixir you're taking to curb the symptoms?"

Rory looks over at Cole, Redmae, and me before answering, "We met up with a light witch who helped us rescue Cory."

"Impossible, all light witches are gone. I mean I'm a light witch, but I never completed my training, so I never received the elemental stone each light witch acquires to fulfill the rite of passage, but I have enough knowledge to get by."

Drena's confession sends a realization of how close magic has been disrupted. "Hang on a minute. Are you saying there are no more light witches at all? You have magic still..."

Drena huffs in irritation. "Sarmira took care of every light witch that ever existed. I may be a descendant, but I do not have the elemental magic like my mother. Your grandmother, Maura Moyer is...was... a light witch."

"That's why Sarmira is so powerful," Blair says. "I bet my last breath on it."

"Now, that makes complete sense," Dad says. "I bet that has something to do with the magic dying, and this aging curse."

Drena covers her mouth and thinks. "Hmm. The last time I saw someone making a spell like that—" She looks at Geneviève.

"But we saw her through the mirror years ago," she responds. "It can't be her, can it?"

"Who was this witch that made the potion, may I ask?" Drena looks concerned.

"She called herself Jasmine."

Drena's eyes widen. "Impossible." She cups her hands and tears form.

Rory is worried. "Who is she to you?"

"Jasmine is my aunt. My mother Sage's sister. They all disappeared when I was sixteen." She looks at me. "In Ladorielle years, of course. At the time I was living on the sister planet Elleirodal. My mother disappeared the same time as my sister Eve. Our house burned to the ground. I could hear the screams of pain." Tears fall down Drena's cheek. "I ran for my life that night, and into the arms of my sire."

"That was the night you were turned?" Cory asks.

Drena nods. "I remember being shot by an arrow in the chest. The next thing I remember is waking up different."

"I'm sorry we didn't put the clues together sooner, Drena. I can confirm—your mother is alive. We will take you to her, if we can manage to go back home," Rory says.

She nods. "That would be lovely. Perhaps there is hope for the light witches after all." She turns back to the box of stones. "That was such a long time ago."

Drena closes the lid and drops the stone into the leather bag, tying it with a shoestring and hands Rory the bag. "I hid this under uncertain times before I made myself disappear for centuries. Something tells me, now is the right time to give this to a druid." She smiles. "You."

Rory pulls out the item inside, taking it between her forefinger and thumb, inspecting it. "Wait, this looks like a—" Rory stops her mom.

Drena grins. "It is."

"So, what else is it besides a travel stone?" I ask.

"That's the informal name," Drena answers. "This stone doesn't work like the other porting runes but it's so rare people don't even bring it up in conversation, unless of course, you're a storyteller and wish to gather the children around you and speak of folklore. So, an exceedingly rare stone, some people never see them in their lifetime. It's also an insight stone."

"A Hawk's Eye is the other name for it," Geneviève answers.

"I don't understand." Rory looks at her mom and then back to Drena. She tries to hand it to Geneviève. "Mom, you should be the one to have this."

She pushes it away. "It's true I could have taken it, but I want you to have it."

"Each travel stone has an added bonus and serves a different purpose, depending on the person's talents that's in possession of it. They give the extra boost of healing, cure poison, provide peaceful clarity, or swift speed," Drena adds.

"So, not only will you have the ability to port anywhere, Rory, but you can also gain target precision when using your bow and arrow. Like the sight of a hawk."

Cole smiles. "Very cool."

"But Mom, you really should have this, not me. Plus, you're more experienced."

"Drena tried to give this to me centuries ago, but I said it was something that should be kept for a special event."

"Events like today," Cole says, quietly.

Rory shakes her head in protest attempting to hand it back to her mother with her palm upright. "I can't take this from you. It's too rare." The stone begins to glow blue, and in seconds sinks through her palm absorbing into her skin. Rory gasps in pain.

"Too late now," Geneviève says. "The stone has chosen."

A faint impression of the rock, like a scar, blends in with the color of Rory's skin behind her neck. One would miss it entirely if they weren't looking for it. "Does it hurt?"

"Not now, no. Only when it first absorbed through my skin. I'm okay." Rory's face reflects concern.

"What is it?" Cory asks.

"It also puts a target on my back now, doesn't it? If anyone were to suspect I have this tattoo behind my neck, all they would have to do is kill me for it. One reason why the stone hides behind my neck. Harder to be detected."

"I have the perfect item for that." Drena reaches into another drawer and pulls out a choker necklace. A simple black ribbon with a center stone. "It will also protect you. Obsidian."

Rory pulls out a round stone in her pocket. "Jasmine gave me this to me."

"Excellent. Two obsidian stones. Even better." Drena turns to look at the crushed lavender. "Now let's finished this spell. You can't wander into the catacombs without the proper ammo. You have a compass that will show you a pathway to anywhere you would like to go, Wynter. This spell will help all of you."

I hold the family heirloom in my hand, reminded of how it has changed from a simple locket to a compass. "If only it would lead us to where Sarmira has Dragonscale."

"I'm sure it will. Ask the compass to show you. You have

the tools to seek whatever you wish to find, all you need to do is learn how to use them." She glances at the twins "And you have the Blade of Truth and Blade of Hope now. Those daggers will guide you to the third. Cole mentioned he already can feel the energy."

I close my eyes, take a deep breath, and concentrate. "Show me where Dragonscale is."

My necklace glows, and I open the locket. The dial points. I look to the others with curiosity.

Rory's eyes are wide, and she's just as surprised.

Drena nods.

We all look toward the open curtain bay window that overlooks the rushing river.

"That's the way to the closed-up catacombs," Cole says. His dagger also glows behind the sheath strapped to his hip as well as Cory's.

"Adventure awaits in the catacombs," Drena says. "We must prepare and put an end to this magical curse before the Blood Moon descends. Something is causing this chaos, and those daggers are the key to it all."

20
SECRETS REVEALED

"I agree," Derek says. "We need to think of something quick." He looks out at the moon. "What time is it?"

Cory looks at his watch. "Twelve thirty, why?"

"Because if our theory is correct, this curse will be permanent after the moon descends. We need to break it before the Blood Moon ends."

"No pressure, Uncle."

Derek heads to the stairwell. "Blair, Jeff, Geneviève, all of you come with me, please." He points toward the stairs. "In the loft library. Isalora has some great literature up there. Maybe we can find something worth using."

"What are we looking for?" Blair asks.

"Anything you can find about the Super Blue Blood Moon," he says. "There is a connection between Blood Moon and this curse. We just have to find it."

"Are you referring to the phases of the dire moon realms?" Blair asks.

"Yes, how do you know about that?"

"I'm a historian as well as a math teacher, Derek. Remember?"

"Fair." He nods. "Please indulge us."

"You won't find anything about the Super Blue Blood Moon up in that loft," Blair says.

"Why not?"

"Because I took and hid them." She grins a devilish smile.

The room grows eerily quiet.

Derek raises one brow, Drena tilts her head, confused, and Dad grins back as though he isn't surprised by her comment.

"You took them?" Derek says sounding irritated. "Blair those books are—"

"Yes." Blair interrupts. "They're safe, I assure you."

"So, where are they?" he demands.

Her grin widens. "A place no one would think to look." She looks at Cole. "In the catacombs."

"Clever," I say. "It's looking more and more like the catacombs need investigated."

"What, you have them locked in cages?" Derek asks, surprised. "I mean that's all that's there. Cell blocks, cages, and a few laboratory specimens."

"Are we talking about the dire wolves or the spell books?" she jokes. "Like I said they're safe–all of them." She stretches her neck and straightens her back. "I feel so different than before." She looks over at us again. "I feel like I need to sneeze."

Cole and I chuckle.

"Hang on, no changing the subject. Did I hear what I think I heard?" Rory asks. "Are you saying you found survivors?"

"No, of course not. I mean, yes, there are survivors, but I didn't find them. We hid them." She grins more, loving the fact that she's given all of us a plot twist.

"Blair, this may be amusing to you but none of us are laughing. Spill it," Drena says.

She rolls her eyes. "Gawd, you're all so exhausting. I was waiting until we got there."

Drena gives Blair a stern look.

"Okay, fine. Before the battle began at the manor a few weeks ago—ha, right the time jump thing—I mean a few hours ago, Chad and I managed to safely hide the children. They are not converted Shadow Walkers like some of you might think."

"I admit I didn't see this coming," Cory says. "How did you manage to pull this off?"

She smiles. "I have my ways. A woman doesn't give out all her secrets, son." She looks at Drena, Derek, and the rest of us. "At any rate, they are safe, they are fed, and they are, I imagine even scared."

"Who are they with?" Dad asks. "By themselves?"

She grins again and chuckles. "They're with Aoes, of course."

"Aoes!" we all say at once.

"I knew he was behind this," Rory says.

"And when did you have time to do this?" Geneviève asks.

"When we all landed after the battle, I had orders to see Master Aoes. He wanted to be briefed."

"About?" Dad asks.

"Sarmira, of course."

"Why would he need to be briefed about Sarmira?" Dad presses.

"Hey, I'm just the messenger."

"Don't play coy with us, Blair. What are you not saying?"

"I—I've been secretly passing through dimensions to update him on Storm River Manor. Nothing nefarious, Jeff, I assure you. If I had ill intensions, would I be able to stand under this roof right now?" She looks up at the ceiling.

Dad grunts knowing she has a fair point. "Then why the secrecy?"

"Aoes didn't know who to trust. Too many people acting on both sides." She looks over at Cole.

"Don't look at me. I'm on the right side of the line this time."

"He knew I could fly under Sarmira's nose undetected." She twirls her necklace. It's a princess cut ruby, encased with copper filagree weaving around pinhole sized black stones.

Obsidian. That must be how she protects herself.

"What are Aoes's intensions?" Derek asks.

"He didn't tell me. My job was to keep him updated." She looks down at the floor." Her voice is low as she adds, "It was his idea to turn back time."

"See, I knew it! I called it! I called it!" Rory puts her fist in the air.

"Oh, stop being so juvenile, Rory," Cole says.

She elbows him.

"Ow."

Drena takes a deep breath. "Well, this enlightens things a bit. I do have to agree with Jeff and Derek. It would have been nice to know this earlier. Any reason why you kept this to yourself?" She points at her. "And no aloof comment. The truth as you see it."

"Aoes didn't want an overhearing ear to know about the children. He was afraid Sarmira would find them."

"You think that's why the manor was burned down?" Geneviève asks.

"No," Blair answers. "Chad gave the signal once he knew all the children were safe. Aoes's brother lit the manor on fire."

"His brother?" Dad asks, shocked. "Sam is alive?"

"Who's Sam?" Cole asks.

Oh no! I keep forgetting to hand him the letter.

"What letter?" Cole asks.

"Once a very powerful magician," Blair answers. "He was exiled years ago for a crime he didn't commit. His powers were stripped, without any memory or means to even come back home again."

"Dang it, I keep forgetting you can read my thoughts now, too." I grunt.

"Wynter, is there something you'd like to share?" Drena asks, staring at me curiously.

"Um—I—no, ma'am."

Drena squints. "Hmm."

"I sort of peeked at a letter that I was to give to Cole before finding you. I'm sorry for being so nosey."

"What did the letter say?" Cory probs.

Cole too, looks concerned.

"This changes things..." Derek says, "by a lot."

"How so?" I ask. I briefly glance at Cory.

"Because if the brothers are together once again, something major has happened to make Aoes break his contract."

"What contract?" Cole and Cory say at the same time.

"The contract that sealed his brother's fate. Aoes was the reason he was banned in the first place," Blair adds.

Gasps and stunned reactions flit around the room.

Brushing away the initial shock, Derek pulls off his glasses and eyes Blair. "You're telling me that the children have been left in the catacombs with Sam?"

The fire crackles, startling many of us.

"Like I said, they're safe. But we won't be if we don't find the source of this curse. We've stumbled onto something I don't think we were supposed to discover. We're getting closer to figuring out how our magical world has gotten off balance. We know Sarmira is involved. The question is, how do we correct it?" Blair asks.

Redmae groans and plops herself in a chair in front of the hearth. "When Cory killed Moyer, something changed in all of us."

"Agreed," Rory says.

"We found Cory, but Dragonscale and Eleena are still missing," I say.

"Along with your mother and Aunt Fran," Cory points out.

"And Chad. If we have gone back in time like you said, then where is Chad?"

"We'll find them," Geneviève says. "Don't worry."

"Not if I don't finish this spell that we're all going to need when entering the catacombs." Drena adds a few more ingredients to the bowl. "Last ingredient: Waxlily." She looks up. "Please tell me one of you has some?"

Cory grins. "As a matter of fact, I do." He wrinkles his forehead and pulls out a bag of the herbs. "When we were at the Lake of No Return, I may have...sort of...stashed away some on a rainy day. I figured it may come in handy." Cory hands the Waxlily to Drena.

"Perfect!" Drena says. She puts on gloves and opens the bag, pulling out one leaf.

"Well...when we... were at the Lake of No Return, I may have...sort of...stashed away some on a rainy day, too," Rory says. She pulls out another small bag of herbs from the hidden kangaroo-like pocket of her palm."

Drena grins. "Aren't you two full of surprises."

I shake my head. "That hide-a-way pocket still has me baffled. How does that not bother you?"

"It's a druid thing." Rory hands her Waxlily to Drena, too.

"How were you able to pull that plant without gloves?" Cory asks.

"After I touched the Waxlily, my body became tolerant, I guess. I noticed when I accidently touched it a second time, there wasn't a reaction, so, I took the opportunity to pull a few while you and Cory were talking."

"How long before that potion is ready?" Dad asks.

"I need to boil these ingredients like tea leaves." She gathers vials and fires up the kettle.

"Now, while she's working on the elixirs, tell us about the letter you were given," Cory says.

Most of my family is distracted with tasks. Blair and Geneviève are helping Drena make the several potions we will need entering the catacombs while Rory and Redmae work on the few arrows Rory retrieved when we engaged in our previous encounters. Derek and Dad strategize together, while leaning over a table that has a map of the catacombs.

"Cory."

"What? Don't change the subject."

"I'm not." I nudge him in Cole's direction.

Cole lifts his chin, eyes the stairs and nods. He pulls away from leaning against the wall and walks to the steps. *"Shall we take this conversation elsewhere?"*

Quietly the three of us make it upstairs without anyone noticing. "The loft might not be the best place to speak freely," I whisper. Suddenly I feel like I am about to be judged for reading a private note.

"So, we'll keep our voices down," Cory says.

"Let me see it," Cole demands.

Carefully I reach inside my jacket and pull out the previously sealed envelope. "I—I am sorry, Cole. It's just that—"

He holds up his hand. "It doesn't matter. You're never going to trust me anyway." He squints. The irritation in his tone crawls under my skin.

We huddle together as Cole opens the letter. It reads:

> *Cole,*
>
> *I know you probably have many questions. If you want the answers, seek out the Keeper of the Light-house, they will tell you how to find me. It is of grave importance not to share this message.*
>
> *Sam*

The letter ignites in flames, causing Cole to drop the note as it crumbles to ashes. In a panic he smashes at the flames.

"That's what happened to me when I got nearly the same letter," Cory says.

"You mean you got the exact letter too?" Cole eyes the ashes on the floor.

"With the exception of the last sentence, yes." Cory looks with his brother as the embers slowly burn the paper. Remnants of a few words still exist. Scorches mark the paper revealing bits of different letters and words. "Hey, take a look at this." He picks up what's left of the charred note. "The words are mismatched."

Se rets foun in the cata ombs

"Secrets found in the catacombs," Cole says. "Do you think the letters were a decoy?"

"Quite possible." Cory glances back to his brother. "Thoughts?"

"I find it a little suspicious that both of us received the same letter. Wynter, who did you say gave you this note, again?"

"The Raven." I look at Cole. "You remember, the raven shifter that showed us the way to Jasmine?"

"Yes, I do remember. Question is why did she give the note to you, and not me directly?"

"Good point. I don't know."

"Something tells me The Raven is more than just a shifter." Cole folds the now-delicate pieces of papers and tucks it into the back pocket of his jeans. "I'm willing to bet Sam didn't write either one of our notes."

"What are you going to do with those? They're basically a pile of ash," I say.

He shrugs. "Hopefully some of it will preserve until we can clarify who wrote this."

"Do you think the lighthouse was a trap?" I ask.

"Looking back, that was the direction we intended to go until The Raven appeared. I agree, Wynter, something isn't adding up," Cole answers.

"There you three are," Dad calls from the below the loft. "What are you up to?"

"Research," Cory says. He eyes us and shrugs. *"Well, I'm not lying."*

Cole and I both smirk quietly.

"Drena finished the elixirs."

"Be right down, Dad."

21

DRUID CIRCLE

"Now that we're all here we can prepare our next strategy phase," Dena says. She makes her way down a hallway in the basement. "Down this way is something I would like all of you to see." She opens a door at the end of the corridor.

In the center of the room stands a pedestal just like in the Hall of Secrets, except there isn't a book present like there should be.

"A druid circle?" Rory walks to the platform first.

Rectangle stones appear, sliding upwards from out of the floor, and surround us after Rory steps onto the raised platform.

Drena comes next to her. "This was the exact spot where Geneviève arrived after porting out of the Hall of Secrets. We have tried to activate it again, since, but nothing happens."

Blair looks at Geneviève, saying, "I don't understand. This portal gate has been closed for years."

"Geneviève activated it somehow." She touches one pillar with her hand. "I feel the magic flowing through it."

"I spent years in this tiny cottage when Moyer ruled the

manor, and I never once found this here," Cory says. "I've been in this room before and all it's ever been is an empty room.

"Stepping on this circular stone pattern, activates the pillars to open from the floor," Drena answers. "We can't explain how Geneviève landed here after the Hall of Secrets incident."

"Which is precisely why you've brought all of us here, because something is working within these large stone pillars, but you cannot figure it out?" Rory touches the pedestal where the missing portal book should be laying on top. "What makes you think any of us would know?"

Drena points to the pedestal. "The ancient druid circle can then be activated. Find the missing book and we can go home."

"But it can be anywhere," Cory argues.

"This cottage isn't nearly that old, is it?" I look back at Dad.

"It's as old as the cabin at Mount Rainier. And like this one, it's hidden from the outside world. The portal at our cabin is also in the basement."

I raise my brows. "Clever."

He nods toward the druid circle. "And like this one, it's also dormant and not working."

"So, you knew about both portals and never said anything. Why?" Rory asks.

"It wasn't important at the time. The less anyone knew, the better I could keep my family hidden." Dad looks at me.

"Geneviève, perhaps you should tell the story why. You were a witness to what happened," Drena says.

Geneviève folds her hands. She hesitates, to answer as though the memories bring back great pain. "It's a portal like all others, scattered across the universe. Except this one hasn't worked since the day we all escaped here long ago. What isn't known in the history books is I had a friend die. It was then that the druids shut down this portal circle."

"Which is how you acquired the stone, isn't it?" Rory says.

"Yes. I mean sort of... A druid will collect portal stones during their lifetime, and once they die, all the stones they've collected are released."

"I'm guessing," Rory clarifies, "all I need to do is trigger the stone, and we will get to the destination we need to."

"Sort of," Drena counters, looking at Rory. "The reason the Hawk's Eye travel stone is so rare is because it can take a druid and her surrounding party to anywhere in the galaxy." She goes to the pedestal. "However, there is no book. Someone has taken it. Without it, no one can use this portal gate."

"No wonder you thought to give it to my mother." Surprise fills Rory's face as she looks over at her mom.

"I didn't need it, Rory, trust me." She turns around and lifts the hair from her neck.

Rory and I stare at the tattoo.

"It's a crescent moon," Rory says. "I don't understand. That doesn't look like a rune tattoo."

"That's because it isn't. It's a birthmark. And although I still do not know why, when I activate it, I can simply think where I would like to go, and we go there." She turns back around, letting down her hair. "So, you see, I do not need the Hawk's Eye Stone."

"Wow, that's incredible," Cole says.

"If the portal isn't working due to the lack of magic and missing book, then how do we get it to work now?" Rory asks.

"Your guess is as good as mine," Drena answers. "Which is why I am suggesting we find the book. Gen and I were down here trying to figure out this conundrum when you arrived."

Geneviève agrees. "Yes, why did it suddenly work when we jumped to safety from Sarmira's powerful blast in the Hall of Secrets, to an entirely different universe, but now, not work?"

"Let's not forget how she was able to penetrate through the Hall of Secrets in the first place," Dad reminds us.

"She must have Dragonscale," I say. "How else would she be able to do that, Dad?"

"It's a question we all would like to know," Rory says.

I look again at the pedestal and then to my locket as it begins to glow softly. "Are you all seeing this?" I open the clasp, and the needle is pointing directly at the podium.

"Hmm, I wonder…" Drena says. "Place your hands on the pedestal. Let's see what happens. Maybe it will show us a clue."

"What if it takes us to some unknown universe?" Cole says.

"I'm guessing the Super Blue Blood Moon draws from the magic," Drena says. "Trust the process. But stay within the circle."

"At least we will be together, this time," Geneviève says.

"How do we know the compass is guiding us in the right direction?" I ask, uncertain, because of all the other porting mishaps. "Do you think it will lead to Dragonscale?"

"Only one way to find out," Rory says, and she puts her hand over the podium. "That magic is dying and we're running out of time."

The wind whistles through the cracks of the windows, and something hits the side of the house with a crash.

"Sarmira is near," Cory says, looking towards the wall the sound came from.

I shiver, and seconds later a feeling of dread and evil magic begins to penetrate through the cottage barrier.

"You feel it, too, don't you?" I ask.

Drena's look of worry has me concerned that we need to leave. She nods.

"We better get going before it's too late," Cole says.

"Okay, Rory, whenever you're ready." She looks at Derek and he nods.

"Tell me again, how does the travel stone, work?" Rory asks.

"Place your palm flat on the surface of the pedestal. Think

of the location you wish to go and the portal should work without the book present. Your druid power will help boost Geneviève's.

"Catacombs it is," Rory says.

All of us glance at each other, stunned as the portal starts to spin.

"Oh no. This isn't the idea I had when I told Rory to put her hand over the podium." Drena looks worried. "Everyone, off the platform now!"

Blair attempts to step off first. "I can't."

The force of the spinning increases, forcing each of us against a pillar. "I can't move."

"Hang on, everyone. We're about to engage in another adventure. Try and grab hands." Rory links hands with me and Redmae, while my other hand links with Cory, along with Cole, Geneviève Dad, Blair, Drena, and Derek forming a complete circle.

The spinning increases, and a loud swooshing sound— like an engine humming as we all spin like a top.

"This is not what I expected!" Drena calls.

The stone pillars around the pedestal light up and the room fills with a bright light, and in seconds we're sent on our way.

Everything happens so fast that my brain doesn't register until we land on the ground somewhere outside the cottage. I look up to see the same Blood Moon, cluing me in that we're still on the grounds of Storm River manor.

The good news is we're all together.

"Looks like the portal circle is still broken," Dad says. He looks at Geneviève, confused. "This has never happened before. I don't understand."

"I think I do, and I don't think Rory has a problem with porting at all," Geneviève says.

"Why do you say that?" Blair asks.

"I specifically triggered my mother's gate to the Shadowvine Forest knowing we'd be safe in her kingdom, and we ended up out here in the middle of nowhere. I don't think it's about Rory having Gate Rot. There's no reason for my porting abilities to not function properly."

"Redmae, what do you make of this?" I ask.

"I'm at a loss. I too don't understand. I think we're all confused."

"I agree with Geneviève," Drena says. "I think it's the magic of the Sword of Valor pulling the daggers to each other. Cole and Cory have a stronger pull of magic than any of us. And together with Wynter, their force is stronger. I'm betting if we find the third dagger, we might be closer to putting an end to this curse. Which means that another dagger is near us, and the Blades of Truth and Hope are answering," Drena says. "Wynter, open your compass."

I do as she instructs and note the compass is pointing north.

Cole leans over my shoulder. "That's the way to the catacombs." He turns around. "I know where we are. We're on the other side of the forest of Storm River Manor."

"How many times do we need to take the signs of the universe before we start believing it? Obviously, we're being guided toward the catacombs," Rory says. "We're stronger together then split up."

"She's right. We're better equipped to fight as a team." Drena nods. "Let the compass lead the way, Wynter. With all of our magic combined we should be able to survive any attack. Stay alert. The nocturnal creatures are out."

"You mean the Sabretail Prowlers?" I ask.

"Not just them, but Shadow Walkers. Sarmira's summoned demons, wraiths, and the hellhounds."

"Awesome," Rory says, as she takes out her bow and arrow.

"I can cloak us." Cole moves his hands like before and

shields the group. "Stay close and the spell should protect us. It won't mask our smell, but it will hide our whereabouts."

My compass glows bright as we follow through the thick woods to where the abandon catacombs remain. I look up to see black swirls in front of the vibrant orange-red moon and point. "They're still coming in masses."

Drena stops and shows concern.

"What is it," I ask.

"The moon hasn't formed into a full eclipse yet. This is good news."

"What are you saying?" Cory looks with her, a little apprehensive.

"I remember seeing all this before, too," Blair says. "We're still in our Super Blue Blood Moon phase on Earth, which means, we need to find a way to close the demon portal before the Blood Moon descends and wreaks havoc on the world forever." She steps ahead of us. "We should keep moving."

"I agree, I think the Earth is still going through the motions. Ladorielle hasn't quite started theirs yet," Geneviève answers.

"Which means we still have a chance to stop Sarmira," Dad says. His eye widens with hope.

Cole and Rory's faces show worry.

He chuckles. "There are ten of us. Odds may not be in our favor."

"Dad has jokes."

"Do you think we still have time to save everyone?" Rory asks, changing the subject.

"Yes, but it must happen tonight!" Drena says. "We've been given a second chance, thanks to Aoes."

"What if the aging curse has something to do with this— the Super Blue Blood Moon?" I ask.

"I'm not sure whether I like or dislike where this is going, Wynter. Care to elaborate on your thoughts?" Blair asks.

"Dom and Arryn mentioned something about the Tora'-Nari Plague; any chance it was around a Super Blue Blood Moon? If so, it might be the link we need to figure this out."

"Go on, we're listening," Dad says.

"What if that plague had something to do with a Super Blue Blood Moon phase as well? Clearly this isn't the first time there was such a cycle, right?"

"Who would know more about this?" Rory asks.

"You want my honest opinion?" Cory asks.

We all nod.

"The Hall of History," Blair finishes.

"Of course," Rory says, sarcastically.

"Cory's right. I don't see any other way. We need to find the history book of the Tora'Nari Plague," Blair says.

"Who would have been around back then to write the book?" I ask.

"Aoes," Drena answers.

"Well, first we need to find our way back to him," Rory adds. "He's obviously not here on the Earth's plane."

"We need to keep moving, like Blair said," Dad says. "If it's true that Aoes has managed to mess with our timeline, then we are on borrowed time. The evening sky isn't going to last much longer. And if the Earth is still experiencing the Blood Moon phase, then we need to figure this all out before the moon goes down." Dad walks to the edge of the overgrown trail and points through the winter wooded trees. "That's where we're need to go to get to the catacombs. The trail is going to get a bit steep. Be alert and try not to fall."

22

CATACOMB ENTRANCE

I follow behind Drena, and whisper, "Can you tell us more about the three blades?"

"What more would you like to know?"

"How did the elders know that melting down the Sword of Valor would work?"

"They didn't at first." Drena leaps over a dip in the ground. "Watch your step." She continues, "It took a lot of planning and meditation. We asked The Elementals for guidance." She turns back at me and smiles. "It has worked so far."

"Until now." I jump over the same dent.

"Well, I would say now is the right timing." Again, she looks up at the moon. "It's been many centuries in Earth years since the last eclipse this world has had in conjunction with our world of Ladorielle."

We take a few more steps and stop on the pathway. It drops dramatically into a steep ravine.

"Okay, now what?" I ask. "We can't exactly transform into dragons here. We would draw attention to ourselves. Jumping isn't an option, either."

"Don't look at me," Rory says. "Last time I cast a spell it sent us onto Storm River grounds...*again*...remember?"

I smirk, realizing she's right.

Cole laughs, pats Rory's shoulder and says, "Down this way, my friend."

A growl rumbles in Rory's throat. "I'm not your friend. Kindly refrain from such condescending tones, Cole."

"Sure, okay." He bows respectfully and disappears through the soft foliage before us. Only the sound of his footsteps keeps us abreast of his location.

"That was kind of rude, don't you think?" Drena says.

"Agreed." Blair brushes past Rory and glares.

"At least try and make an effort to get along, Rory. We're all on the same team." Dad follows up with Blair, as does Redmae and Derek. I follow behind them, as Rory walks alongside me and Cory.

"Whatever you two have going on, may I suggest you wait until after this is all over?" Cory says.

"What's gotten into you? You have been brash with Cole this entire time. Am I missing something?" I ask.

"It's nothing. I don't want to talk about it."

"Okay, fair, I understand. At least try to put your differences behind you for now. We have enough to worry about."

She answers with a deep breath and pushes ahead of us.

"It feels like we're on a steep hillside," I say.

"We are. Don't worry I won't let you fall."

"Ha!"

Cory pulls back more branches and steps downward. "Careful, it's about a four-foot drop."

Derek is hesitant to take another step. "We're not prepared for a fight through the catacombs with the Shadow Walkers, should they appear. I don't care how many of us there are," Derek says.

"The cave is dormant," Cole says. "And I can re-cast the

invisibility spell if needed. Trust me, Uncle." He clears his throat... "Grandfather?"

Derek grumbles. "Uncle feels more familiar to you. Go with that, Cole."

"Why were the catacombs boarded up, anyway?" I ask.

"I don't know the details; what I can tell you is Maura Moyer never goes back there," Cole answers.

"That we're aware of, anyway—" Derek interrupts.

Cole pats Derek's shoulder. "We will be fine."

Derek takes a deep breath, ignoring Cole's optimism. "It was where Sarmira killed her husband Arik." Derek pauses, realizing his statement needs correction. "Rather Maura's husband. Looking back on it now, she must've been heartbroken...The real Maura Moyer, that is, who was trapped within her body."

"I think I remember Rosie mentioning something about that," I say.

"She witnessed the entire scuffle," Dad says. "I don't want to talk about my father's demise, let's keep moving."

Dad pushes forward with Geneviève by his side, comforting him.

"In the spring and summer these woods would be filled with green foliage," Drena says, changing the subject. "This is where Derek buried me."

We come to the bottom of the ravine and leap over a small creek and finally reach a stone fence with twisted wrought iron sticking out from the structure, making it evident whatever is inside doesn't want outsiders.

"Is this a really good idea?" Blair asks. "I sense dread."

Cole turns around. "I sense it, too, but our daggers and that compass Wynter's wearing tells us this is the way."

"Catacombs it is then," Blair says. "It's been a long time since I have stepped in there."

Cole smiles mischievously. He reaches for the latch

attached to the oval iron gate. Wood planks are set in between the bars, making it impossible to see what is beyond the door. A knocker is attached to the center of the entrance. Cole opens it without any effort and walks through.

"It's not locked?" I ask, stunned.

"It hasn't needed to be. Like mentioned previously, this place has been abandoned."

"It's another hidden garden," I say.

"Only there isn't any hints of life anywhere," Rory says.

Vines grow along the back fence. A few trees look dormant or dead. Dried leaves scatter across the frozen ground. Patches of snow heap in clumps here and there. Thankfully there is little to no wind now. The chilly evening has already seeped to my bones.

"It's not a garden," Cole corrects. "It's a cemetery." He points to the tombstones in the distance. The leaves mixed with snow, crunch beneath his feet as he walks ahead of us. "Where vampires rest, ghosts hide, and zombies come up from the ground—"

"Cole." Dad's stern look tells him now is not the time to freak everyone out. He reaches for some branches in our path and pulls them aside and out of our way so we can pass. "I almost forgot this place existed."

"This is the back way through to the catacombs," Cory says.

"Yes, I know it well," Dad replies.

As we draw closer to our destination an eerie feeling comes over me. Goosebumps travel up my arms. A sudden coldness enters our presence. "Do you feel that?" I turn my head and suck in a startled breath. A shadow hides near a maple tree. "What's that?" I point.

"I don't see anything," Rory says.

Blair and the others look over my way. "Probably a ghost,

Wynter," Rory answers. "You know that thing you can do with your eyes."

"Haha, right. I'm a paladin warrior. I see ghosts, It's my thing... I get it, but it doesn't mean I'm used to it."

"Besides," Cole adds, "we're hiding behind my invisible protective bubble, remember? Nothing should be able to see us."

Ignoring the apparition, one by one we follow Dad, Cole, Cory, and Derek as they lead toward the catacomb entrance.

Cole stops and stares ahead. A shed-like structure blends into the side of an inclined hill with many boards nailed against a framed-up hole. A sign above says, 'Keep out.'

"What's wrong?" I ask.

"Nothing. Annoying is all. Angry and maybe a little anxious. I'm not sure what we will find down there, honestly."

"Do you have knowledge of something we don't know about?" I ask.

"No, nothing like that. I feel a sense of dread, like my mom said."

"I feel it, too, brother," Cory says.

"And me," Derek agrees. "This reminds me of when Sarmira came for us at Storm Castle." He looks at Dad and he nods slightly.

"I think we all feel it," Redmae says.

Dad pulls at the first plank boarding up the doorway. Derek, Cory, and Cole join him.

"Isn't this where vampires rule?" Rory jokes referencing Cole's comment earlier.

Cole huffs. "Sort of, but I've heard stories from my mother that the House of Bloodbane is worse." He briefly glances at her.

"This is true," Blair confirms. "It's where I went through training as a girl." She looks at Drena with regretful eyes.

"Training?" I ask.

"Blair's been hiding a secret," Rory says.

Blair grunts, ignoring Rory's comment.

I raise my brow, and smile. "Oh, do tell."

"Not much to say." She steps in to help pull off the planks. "It's not something I'm proud of. I've seen things, is all…" She pauses, turning to look at me. "I've done things I wish I could forget. Let that resonate for a minute, Wynter."

"We've all done things we regretted, Blair. Things we're not proud of. I get it if you want to keep that part of your life to yourself, but believe me, I understand." I attempt to help them.

Rory looks over at me. "You act as though we haven't had our share of regretful actions."

"Rory, I'm not making light of what Blair is saying, but you seem to be holding out. What gives, Rory?"

Blair glares at us both. "Okay, enough. That's not what I mean, Rory, and you know it. Care to enlighten your friend or do you want me to do your dirty work now?

I look over at Redmae. She stays still.

More secrets.

Redmae shrugs. Although she can't read my thoughts in her humanoid form, I feel like she can still read my body language.

Blair glares at Redmae this time. She rubs her hands together to brush off the dirt from helping remove the planks against the entrance.

"She was raised and trained to hunt me down and kill me," Drena replies. "Now if we could all focus, perhaps we might sever this curse before the moon descends?" She points at it, referencing that our time draws short.

My mind reels at Drena's confession. "Oh, come on, you can't leave us hanging without telling us why."

"They're not ready," Blair mumbles to Drena.

Is she a trained assassin? It can't be. I've read in Sara's journals and remember reading about the twelve houses within the realm of Ladorielle. I'm filing away this new information and keep it to myself for now. My great-great-grandmother also warned that a trained assassin belongs to a guild of many others. No one knows the true identity of one.

A loud crack pulls me from thoughts as the last plank is yanked from the entrance frame.

A growl echoes within the hollow entrance.

"Did that come from inside?" I ask.

"I smell my former pack," Redmae says. "They know we're here."

23

THE CROW MAN

"I thought you said you can't communicate with them anymore," Rory asks.

"I can't understand their communications within the pack, but I can still understand their tone as wolves, though, dear sister. They are not pleased I am human. That much I know."

"Be on guard," Cole says. "My shields are still cloaking us, but if anyone steps outside the circle of protection, it will be broken."

One wolf howls, then another, followed by the entire pack and they sync together in a calling chant.

"That's a battle cry," Redmae says. "Something tells me they don't care that you have a shield up, Cole."

A flock of black birds scatter about and swirl into a funnel-like cloud. The cone shaped mass of birds grow bigger and bigger, increasing in speed as more birds add to the stack that collectively take shape of a human-like figure. The wind howls. Or is it wolves? I can't tell.

"This looks way too familiar," Drena says. "I've seen this before. My gut is telling me we need to huddle close and stay as still as possible. No one say a word." She looks at Geneviève.

She nods. "I'm afraid you may be right, my friend. If this is *who* I think it is, we're sitting ducks."

"What are you all talking about?" I ask. "This looks incredible. I've never seen anything like it." I'm distracted by the breathtaking formation of birds.

Drena's face hardens. Her eyes stone cold. The vampiric beast she's hidden beneath her skin is set free. Her body changes as black veins appear along her cheeks, neck, and hands. She's changing to the same type of beast Cory transitioned to the day Cole tried to sink his teeth into me. In an icy tone, she says, "That's because you've never met The Crow Man."

Birds continue to add to the form of this strange apparition. A top hat grows on his head, boots develop on his feet, a long cape-like coat covers his back. He holds a long wooden staff in one hand that has a pulsing, green, glowing stone that caps the top, while in the other hand twirling a set of skeleton keys. A raven sets upon his shoulder of that same hand. It's chained to the staff. His facial features are the last to take shape. Dark eyes and hair with a square jawline and thin lips add a sinister feel to his handlebar mustache and pointed beard.

"Oh, my dear, you cannot hide from me, you are after all, marked. Did you think you could escape me?"

He walks closer and turns to stare at us as though he sees right through Cole's shield. "Come now, Geneviève, do come out and play. I quite like the chase. I admit you are somewhat of a challenge to locate, but alas that has come to an end."

Drena cups her hand over Gen's shoulder. "He's baiting you. Don't fall for it."

"I have no memory of this creature. He's terrifying," she whispers.

"No memory, you say?" the Crow Man replies. "Ah I see now. It all is beginning to make sense."

"He can hear us?" I ask.

"Of course I can hear you, Wynter." He chuckles at my shock. "I can see you, too!" He steps closer and grins.

I turn away, and his face pops right in front of me. "Boo!" He laughs louder.

I jump, but not enough to make me scream. He's going to have to do better than that. I turn back around to see he has vanished.

"The Crow Man can hear the slightest sounds," Drena says. "It's why rarely anyone can escape his presence."

"Your mother escaped me once, but it would be her last time." He revels. "Your sister on the other hand—"

Now it was Geneviève's turn to hold Drena back.

"What do you want!" I shout. "You're just a bunch of collective birds made into a coward, out to frighten people, intimidating them into thinking you have some sort of power over them.

"Crows," he replies close to my ear.

"What?" I squint. I turn a full circle and he's nowhere to be found. Fire within my veins burns to be free.

"Wynter, don't egg him on," Dad says. "He thinks he's untouchable."

"I am... untouchable, Jeff." His sinister laugh crawls beneath my skin. "I led your mother Maura, right to Sarmira, and I see that plan worked out perfectly as predicted."

This time it took Cory, Cole, and Derek to hold Dad back from stepping from the invisible barrier that is shielding us.

"Dad, don't."

"Crows," the Crow Man repeats. "And you, my dear, are one feisty little bit—"

"Watch it there, Thane, you'd be wise not to antagonize my granddaughter like that. Do not underestimate a Storm!"

"I know that voice!" He sneers.

A flash of light zaps through him and the crows disperse scattering about the treetops with a few of them dropping dead at our feet. Laughter echoes through the air. "You will pay for that. I will take the souls of your loved ones for each dead crow."

Petra Storm stands in the exact spot where he was a moment before, only this time she's much older than our last meeting. "Good luck with that. As long as I am here guarding, you can't touch any of them."

"We shall see about that." The crows reform in front of her, slowly reappearing one by one until the Crow Man once again is put back together. "Well, if it isn't my favorite person."

Petra stands between us. "Aww, so I am your favorite, now. I'm flattered."

"You broke my heart, you know." He stamps his staff on the ground. The raven on his shoulder aims for our group and fires blue flames from its mouth.

Petra deflects the move with her cloak. "I didn't think you had one to break."

He grunts. "You ruin all the fun."

Petra looks past his shoulders and eyes the crows gathering behind him. "I had a feeling you would show up here sooner or later looking for her."

"And who would that be?" A second funnel of birds form behind him and begin to take the shape of a dragon.

"Don't play coy with me. What do you want, Thane? We had a deal, remember?" She steadies herself as she watches closely the formation of birds.

"Cole, I thought you said your shield would cloak us?" I whisper.

"It's been a while since I used that ability. Cut me some slack, will you?"

"Yes, a deal." The stranger disparages Petra's reminder.

She stiffens. "Then what are you doing here?"

"Ah, a Fae never tells their secrets. You of all people should know that."

She looks at me as though that remark wasn't for my ears. *Fae?*

"What is he talking about?" Blair asks, nudging Geneviève's arm.

"Nothing, just stay quiet," she answers.

"Hmmm... I see," the Crow Man says. "She's been released." He chuckles again as though the pieces he's been searching for are finally coming together. "You know, Petra, it will never work. You can't protect them all."

"Who has been released?" I ask.

"Shh..." Drena nudges.

"Oh, the plot thickens." He hums a chuckle. "They don't know your side of this little scheme, do they?" He walks around our protective shield but doesn't get close. "I wonder why?" The raven squawks and flaps its wings.

"You don't have any power here, Thane. Geneviève has no magic therefore she is of no use to you. You and I know it." She steps in front of him. "What are you really after?"

"Ah right, you would like that, wouldn't you? I don't give up my cards that easily." He disburses into a thousand birds, and they flock to the treetops.

Petra comes forward. "We don't have a lot of time. I'll explain more inside. The catacombs will protect you from him, but not his spirit. The birds won't enter enclosed spaces."

"How did you figure that out?" Geneviève says. "Speaking from experience?"

"Something like that. Now move!" We hesitate to follow as Petra steps inside.

"I THINK I CAN SPEAK FOR EVERYONE HERE WHEN I say you're the last person I thought anyone of us would see in such a short time, Petra," Derek says, being the last one across the threshold.

"I'm still collecting the portal books, Derek. My last finished quest brought me here. I knew immediately once I landed that the Crow Man was involved."

"Tell us more, please? Who is he?" I ask.

Petra breathes in a heavy breath. "At one point, he was my betrothed. It didn't take me long to figure out he wasn't 'The One.'"

"You found something that changed your mind, didn't you?" Blair asks.

"Something like that, yes. Long ago, I snuck into my grandfather's study. I was looking for a book that was said to be hidden there. At first, I didn't believe the rumors, until I found the book."

"The book?" I ask.

"Yes. The same book that is missing now. The Book of Secrets. Which one of you started this cycle all over again?"

"Wait, wait, wait..." Drena begins. "Are you telling me the reason we're in this entire mess is because someone stole the book in the Hall of Secrets all over again?"

"Why else am I here?" she looks directly at me. "You have opened the gate, Wynter."

"Me? But how?"

"No, don't blame her. Sarmira had taken possession of me." Cole step between us. Sarmira broke the portal by using me. And it killed me."

"Really?" Petra looks at him suspiciously. "Are you a ghost then?"

A few of us chuckle.

"No, more like a dragon. I was a vampire before I transformed. We're all trying to figure out the connection."

She stares at him, deep in thought. "I see." She rubs her hands together and then places them under her chin as though to mull over his words. "This might be why the Crow Man has appeared. He's made a deal with Sarmira. Question is, what has he sacrificed?"

"This time shift and different dimension stuff really has me questioning a lot of things. My mind hurts thinking about it," Rory says.

"Imagine being me," Petra jokes. "The last you saw me, I was younger, yet according to my ordinance, I look older to you, yes?"

"Not by much."

"We don't age rapidly like the humans on Earth. I assure you this is how I look now. When you met me in the portal hub, I had a younger illusion, but I've remained like this for centuries."

"Centuries? Never mind I don't want to ask right now," I say. "I'm still trying to wrap my head around being from another world, a dragon, related to witches, and using magic, let alone time travel."

She smiles.

"So, what are you doing here?" Blair asks, "you never finished explaining."

"Apparently the Book of Secrets portal tome is close to our presence. One that I must find in order to seal Samira for good and begin re-repairing the portal hub in the Hall of Secrets."

A cold brush of air crosses over my skin and stench assaults my nostrils as we venture into the dark cave-like underground structure.

"That smell. It's horrible," Rory exclaims.

"You will get used to it," Cole answers as he too steps inside.

Debris falls from the walls like sand. "It doesn't feel very safe to me," she counters.

Cole chuckles. "Of course it isn't. We're entering a tomb. No telling what will jump out at you."

I jab his back in retaliation.

"Ow." His smile fades. "Fine."

The catacomb's entrance descends into a dark stairwell.

"I can't see my hand. A little more light might be nice," Rory asks. "I don't have the innate ability to see in the dark, like most of you."

The light from our eyes carries a few feet, but all we see is darkness beyond. The sense of dread is all around. "This is so eerie," I say. Chills creep over my skin.

Cory looks down at our feet. "Watch your step, everyone. The stair risers are shallow and will make it difficult to plant our feet down steadily."

Derek comes from the rear of our group. "It's been a long time since I've been here. If I recall, there are sconces attached to the walls. "Someone have a light?"

"Hang on, as a matter of fact, I do." Cory pulls from his pocket a lighter. "I forgot I had this."

"Is that the lighter Rosie gave me?" I ask. "I have been looking for it everywhere. I thought I'd lost it."

Cory winks. "It is. You left it on the mantel at the cottage. I had intended to give it to you. I'd forgotten it was in my pocket until now."

"May I?" Derek asks, and Cory waits for my approval before handing the lighter to him.

He lights a torch tucked inside the frame of a wall by the entrance.

"Wait a minute, Petra. Where is Bryce?" Derek asks, randomly.

She pauses a minute. "I don't know. He and I were separated when I retrieved the last portal book."

Geneviève gasps. "It was you who activated the druid circle at the cottage!"

"If it's the one that leads to Shadow Vine Forest, then yes, I found the portal book to the realm."

Geneviève looks at Drena. "Guess that explains why it's suddenly working. That part might be resolved, but I still wasn't able to take us to the forest."

"This changes things," Drena says.

"What do you mean?" I ask.

"It means we can go home," Rory says.

"Not yet," Blair says. "We need to break the magical curse."

A howl comes from outside.

"Sabretail Prowlers," Dad says. "Sounds like the Crow Man brought friends. Be ready for a skirmish."

"Hiding in here might deter the Crow Man, but not the Prowlers or the wolves from approaching," Petra adds. "And it might give us a better advantage to fight them off should it come to that."

I shouldn't be afraid—and deep down I'm not—but the sense that Sarmira will show up once again reigns in my mind.

Cory and Cole's eyes light up like they're both ready to compel. "Stay close," one of them says.

Rory, Red, and I follow close behind, along with Drena, Blair, and Geneviève. Dad and Derek fall back, lingering near the steps to make sure all is clear.

We reach the bottom step to the crypt; I half expect to smell death. But on the contrary, I detect a musty odor instead —like entering the average basement. The heaviness filters through the air, and I can see my breath cloud when I breathe. It's cold, and not that I mind it—I mean I can, after all throw ice bombs—but this is different. It's like a vindictive spirit— many of them—and they're surrounding us. Cold air brushes across my skin and I jump.

Derek reaches more old patina sconces that hang on a hook to the right and left of us and lights them. "Here we go."

"Not exactly an inviting room. What is this the 'Catacombs of many Doors?'" Rory says.

It's a circular room like the Hall of Secrets. Skulls line the walls from floor to ceiling. "This is horrid."

"This is the way Shadow Walkers cleaned up after a meal," Derek says. "Moyer would bring me back here, take a sip of essence, and then have me hang out with the monsters as they fed on live flesh."

"Gross." Petra steps between us and passes through to center of the circular opening. "Unfortunately, there's more beyond those doors." She points to another boarded-up entrance.

"I'm guessing you have been here before, Petra?" Cole asks.

"Briefly. I had a little squabble with a crow, once."

Cole nods toward the double door entryway ahead. "Beyond there is another circular room with several doors leading to different passageways. It's like a maze. Luckily, I have a map of the tunnels." He smiles again and points to his temple. "Shall we proceed?"

I roll my eyes. "Wonderful."

Cole opens the doors.

The circular room is like he said, but not as many doors as the Hall of Secrets. "Which one do we try first?" I ask.

"This one." Cole reaches for the knob and pushes. "It won't budge."

Outside of the entrance the Sabretail Prowlers' howl.

"They're getting closer. I thought you said we'd be safer in here," Rory says. "Your shield didn't protect us from the Crow Man. Why should it protect us now?" She takes out her bow and arrow.

Cole recasts another shield protection. "Rory, do you ever have anything nice to say?"

Growls from the entrance to the outside grow louder, distracting her rebuttal.

"It's unfortunate that I can't understand their communication, but I can still sense their rhythmic tones. They're waiting on more *friends* before entering, that much I'm sure," Redmae says.

A shadow moves, bumping something in the far distance opposite of us and it shatters onto the stone floor, startling everyone.

The figure in the dark laughs. "You think a shield will protect you?" It moves forward, reveals itself, lashes out, and pushes us backward.

24

THE OTHER BROTHER

Dazed by such force, I struggle to stand. Déjà vu kicks in as I reflect on a not-so-distant altercation. The veins beneath my skin warm, and the scales I've managed to hide thus far, appear. *Not yet. Too soon.*

Cory transforms into the beast he tries so hard to avoid being, while Cole remains in his human form, but his eyes have changed to a liquid gold. *That's new.*

"Not so fast, brothers!" A roar so fierce it pushes them backward again.

"Wait!" Redmae stands between them, and the beast. "Casey," Redmae whispers. "Is that you?"

"Oh, that's rich coming from you." He moves closer. "As if you're amazed that I'm still alive? You abandoned me, Redmae!"

"I am amazed. We all are. I—I didn't aband—"

"Silence!"

She flinches. "Casey, please let us explain."

Rory raises her arrow. "You're the traitor, Casey, not us."

"Careful with that, it could hurt someone." Casey tilts his head and smiles revealing yellowed teeth, not at all afraid of her threatening arrows. A patch that covers one eye is slightly shifted, revealing a nasty looking scar. His clothes are torn exposing oozing pus wounds about his chest and arms.

"You're not helping." Redmae nudges Rory. Redmae braves the beast in front of her. "You should have someone take a look at those wounds, Casey."

"Don't act so concerned, Red, you're no longer part of the team. You left! You're not the beast I know you can be."

She backs up slightly. "I don't want to be a beast, Casey. I don't think you do either."

He laughs again. "You have no idea what I want."

"Redmae is right. Casey, this isn't like you," Cole says.

Casey growls. "You have no idea what I have been through, brother!" He puts out his hand and with some unknown force, shoves him back against a wall a third time.

"That was the wrong move, buddy." Cory moves forward to pounce and he, too, is blasted backward once more.

"Anyone else want a go at me?" He puts his palm up, motioning with his fingers for more of us to try.

Rory shoots an arrow, and misses. It pings to the floor.

She's shoved back in retaliation. "You're losing your touch, Rory," he says, amused.

Dad pulls his sword. "Those are some big fighting words, Casey. Care to tell us why you are still here?"

"I'm the Keeper of the Crypt. The Stable Boy of the Barn, and the Guardian of the Manor. How you don't know this, Jeff, is beyond me. You tasked me with this burden long ago, or have you conveniently forgotten?"

"Dad, what is he talking about?"

Dad shakes his head. He ignores my question. "It's over, Casey. Sarmira is gone. The manor has burned to the ground. You're free."

"Free?" he laughs louder. "Free, you say?" Look around..."

He gestures to his body. "Look at me...does this look free to you?"

"Casey, it's a curse," Redmae steps in. "Sarmira has been planning this for a long time. What you're experiencing is a curse, darling."

Darling? I glance over at Cory to see if he's hearing my thoughts.

He shrugs and focuses back on Casey.

"Listen to Jeff. He's right, you're free from Moyer's clutches. We can be together again soon. I promise," Redmae adds.

All of us step back, but not Red, she isn't afraid of him.

"Empty promises!" He steps out of the darkness more, revealing deeper features. His balding head with a few reddish blond threads hang to the side of his right ear. His complexion is covered in pimply green and yellow pus. His entire body is riddled with infected lesions. "You never came back for me!"

"Casey, I would never leave you." Tears well in her eyes. "Honestly I thought you were dead."

"Dead?" he gives a dissatisfied grunt. "I'm not easily killable. You know me better than that."

"I do, which is why I am concerned by your behavior."

Cory relaxes. His body slowly turning back to his gorgeous self. "Brother, we're all here for you."

"Brother? I'm your brother now?" He sneers, irritated at Cory's response. "I have never been a brother, according to you. I'm the outcast, remember?"

"Let's get this hashed out, shall we?" Cole rolls up his sleeves. He races forward. I can see the invisible shield that separates him from Casey. Though, Casey can't see it himself because he attempts to slam Cole with his fist and fails.

Casey falls back as though his blow toward Cole bounced back to him. He clutches his injured hand. "Ah, you come prepared this time, I see. Get out!!"

"No. Wait. Stop. Both of you, please," Redmae pleads. She reaches to help Casey up. "We can help you, I promise."

"Again, empty promises, Red. You promised to come back for me when I tried to save you from being captured."

"But I'm here now. See? It's me. I'm here now, my dearest love... I'm here now...Please let me help you." She opens her hand, welcoming him.

Casey posture softens.

"We will find a way to lift your curse, too."

Confusion coats Casey's face. "Too?"

Rory stands down and tucks her bow and arrow away. "We're all cursed. The Storms, my sister and I, even the Deagons."

"It has something to do with the Super Blue Blood Moon, Casey. Would you know anything that might help us?" Drena asks.

Redmae smiles. "This is the last light witch, Casey."

"One of—" Drena stops and bows instead. "I might be of assistance with those wounds, Casey."

He grabs onto Redmae's hand to stand. "That would be kind of you." He nods in return to Drena. "How can I repay you?"

"By granting us permission through these tunnels," she answers.

He nods looking at all of us and stops at Petra. "Here's a face I haven't seen before."

She nods back. "Petra Storm of House of Storm."

Confusion crosses Casey's face.

"It's a long story, my friend," Redmae says. "Tell us, please. What happened after Sarmira was released from Maura Moyer?"

"I don't recall much," he answers. "The last I remember I was near the barn. Sarmira jumped from Moyer to me." He quivers briefly. "I could feel every soul that entered me. Every painful thought. I felt a searing touch within me until I realized I was being burned from the inside out. The demonic souls could not acquire my body any longer and they boiled to the surface of my skin and escaped into the ether." He looks down at his arms. "These open pus wounds remain as a reminder of what happened to me."

"Interesting," Drena says coming forward. "May I?"

Casey shrugs. "Be my guest. There are no herbs I have tested that will help with the pain, nor heal them. I have tried."

"Ah but see, you are not a light witch. I may be of some assistance." She reads his palm, front to back. "May I see your back?"

Reluctantly Casey turns around and pulls up the back of his shirt. Two large scars remain near his shoulder blades.

Rory gasps. "Is that—"

"Wings. I was born with wings. Moyer, who you all know by now was possessed by Sarmira, had them removed."

"You're a dragon shifter," I say. "Obviously I should know that. Blair is your mom."

"Yes, but I have never shifted."

Blair clears her throat. "Shortly after his birth, while I was distracted, Casey was taken from me. For years I was told he died, but on the contrary Moyer experimented on him as a boy. It sickens me to this day. I found out years later Casey was my son. I was bound to secrecy." She looks at the twins. "She said she would have both of you killed if I uttered a word."

Drena grins as though the mystery has been solved. "Casey, it would seem that you're immune to Sarmira's possession. And although the healing is slow, you should make a full recovery."

"Can you elaborate please?" Blair asks.

"He has dragon blood running through his veins."

"That makes no sense at all," I say. "I'm a dragon shifter. I've been running from Sarmira's possession for years."

Cole steps up. "I was possessed, if you recall, Drena."

"All of that is quite true." She stands, and digs into the bag she brought with her, and pulls out a jar. "Layer this upon your wounds. It's a salve. It should help with the pain." She hands it to Casey.

"Okay, but that still doesn't answer our question," Cory presses.

She firmly directs her eyes to Cory. "Vampires."

Cory tilts his head and squints, confused.

She huffs. "I can't believe I didn't think of it before."

"But of course." Jeff touches the bridge of his nose with his index finger and paces in thought, muttering under his breath.

"Care to share with the rest of the class, cousin?" Derek asks.

He holds up the same index finger. "Hold on a minute. Gathering my thoughts." He stops. "That's it!" He turns to Cory. "You, Drena, Derek—" He looks over at Petra. "Even you..."

"Dad?"

He puts up both hands. "Drena, you're a genius. Forgive me for the interruptions. I'm on the same page as you, I think. Carry on."

She bows. "I'd quite like to know your thoughts first, if you don't mind?"

"Very well." He looks at Cole. "It's like Drena said. Vampires." He turns to everyone else. "And witches, druids, wolves—anyone who does not have dragon blood running through their veins can be possessed."

"Well, this wasn't on my bingo card today," Blair says.

Cole attempting to sink his teeth into me a few weeks ago comes to mind. "That is why you tried to turn me."

"Hey, in my defense, that was the demon possessing me. Not me personally. Besides, I'm a dragon shifter." His eyes light up. "Wait—"

"That is a huge clue, it seems, to solving this curse," Geneviève says.

"Partial puzzle solved that is," Drena says.

"Dragons cannot be possessed. Which explains why Fran and I were never her vessels," Dad says.

"Precisely. Her only avenue was to create her blood suckers. If they latched onto a dragon shifter it would entrap them for an eternity." Drena turns to Cole. "Except you tried to turn Wynter."

"Clearly that was mentioned, yes. It's not a secret that I tried. I wish it could be a buried memory and forgotten already."

"Cole, I think what Drena is saying is I'm a shifter and had you tried to turn me, you would be trapped as a vampire forever without any chance of shifting."

"Now there is a twisted theory indeed," Dad says.

"Or so she thought, as we have possibly discovered fire will break the curse," Cole adds. "Blair died by fire but was brought back just like what I experienced." He points to Dad. "Your brother Chad had the same experience. He was bitten, not born."

"True. At any rate, I'm seeing a pattern here," Dad confesses.

Cole faces his brother Cory. "Care to test the theory?" He grabs the torch.

"Ha, no!" Cory hops out of the way. "Nice try, not it."

Cole laughs. "Okay, fine, but I think we're onto something."

"I agree. And if your theory is correct, Drena, that means Sarmira cannot possess me. She's been taking advantage of our fear this entire time." I look at Cory. "I seem to remember we talked about this theory down by the river the day you showed me the cottage on these grounds.

"I remember," Cory replies. "Question is, where do we go from here?"

"I think I might know," Casey says, "but you're not going to like what you see."

My locket glows once more along with Cole and Cory's daggers. I open it. The needle points to steel double doors down a dark corridor, instead of one of the other doors that line around this circular room.

"Why does our next clue always refer to dark hallways, Wynter?" Rory says.

Dad grunts. "Someone want to come help me open this door."

"That's odd," Cole says. He stands next to my dad.

"What?" Rory asks. "Don't tell me you know what is behind there."

"Sort of, yes," he answers. "It's full of storage items."

"Storage items protected by an armor of Valiancium steel," Dad adds. He reaches for the knob. "It's locked, of course."

"Well, that compass is clearly indicating we need to investigate," Blair says.

"If I had to guess, the Blade of Peace is in there," Drena says.

"Agreed." Redmae puts her ear to the door.

"What are you doing?" Rory asks.

"Listening... shh."

The compass brightens and the tiny sword that is secured behind the silver rose on my locket, glows. It was the secret key that opened the leather-bound coffer that had secretly been place behind the stone fireplace in my room at Storm River Manor. It draws Dad's attention.

"Of course, why didn't I think of that before? Go ahead, try it. Worth a shot," Dad says.

I pull the small sword-like looking key and I insert it into the lock. "It's not doing anything."

"That's because it's the wrong key," Petra says. "What about the one dangling from your chain?"

I touch it and realize that was the item that was glowing, and not my locket. The labradorite stone that sets in the center of the handle brightens. "My Aunt Fran gave me this back at my room on Dragonscale Island. She said it will open many doors. I thought she was referring to metaphorical terms. Do you think this is a master key that opens actual doors?"

"Only one way to find out," Drena says.

Pulling the chain from my neck I take the skeleton key and insert it into the lock on the door and turn.

Dad reaches for the handle, opens the door, and walks in first.

25

THE TOMB OF STORMS

I was half expecting something to jump out at us once we opened the door, but what stands in front of us are glass coffins that line the room and along the walls. "Casey, is this what you meant when you said we wouldn't like what we'd find?"

"Yes."

"There must be a dozen or more of them in here," Blair says.

"What is this...the vampire tombs of Storm River Manor?" Petra asks.

"Something tells me this room was made to look like a storage area for a reason," Dad says. "These must be the Storms and its court that never reached our magical born world." He looks in awe. "I don't think many of us knew this existed.

"How do you know they're of the Storm Court, Dad?"

He points to one glass coffin. "I recognize some of their faces."

Cory turns a full circle and moves further into the room. "Maybe we can find some more sconces like earlier."

"Over here," Rory says. She points to the opposite wall.

Dad goes over and lights them. The dank, dark room lights up showing the horror.

"And here I thought the skulls lining the walls in concrete was creepy." Rory gasps and points. "Is that—"

"The queen." Petra puts her palm against the lid. "I feel like I just spoke to her hours ago."

"Theoretically, you did," Rory answers. "We all were there." She turns to my dad. "Jeff, how can this be Queen Sara? I'm confused."

"If you recall, she mentioned she has an illusion spell cast upon her and the kingdom, making one think they are all physically alive, when in fact—" I glance around at all the coffins. I breathe deep. "When in fact they are not."

"Did Sarmira move an entire kingdom in here?" Redmae asks, confused. "I thought they were all supposed to be on Ladorielle at Storm Castle."

"Yes, they're supposed to be," Petra says. She traces one coffin with her fingers. "But why?" She trails over a few more coffins. "I am shocked to see all of them here, too."

"Someone should guard the entrance," Dad says.

"I will." Blair positions herself outside the doors. A blue glow filters through the darkness, from her eyes while she stands watch.

I hadn't ever laid eyes on my great-grandmother's physical body before, and I'm taken aback by her beauty. "She's stunning." Long blonde hair flows over her arms and her flawless porcelain complexion. "No wonder great-grandfather was so smitten with her." I look out over the other caskets once more, that line the walls. "Is he in this room, too?"

"I would imagine so." Redmae walks to the other end of the room looking through all the glass coffins.

"Ailbert Storm is here on the other side of the queen," Dad says.

"And Isobel," Derek interrupts, looking at the coffin next to Ailbert. He turns around. "And Sir Gavin, My Lord," Derek says.

"Please Derek, formalities are not needed here." Dad comes to investigate. He does a brief scan of the room. "There's so many." He focuses on another coffin. "My father Arik, too." Dad's face changes to a shade of red. "All of our missing family members have been here on Earth the entire time?"

"All of them look like they're just sleeping," Rory says.

"Wynter." Cory is standing over another casket. "It's your Aunt Fran."

"What? Impossible. Her body is supposed to be with Nyta."

"Then she's a clone," Cory says.

"I doubt that. Clones don't sleep," Drena says. She investigates Aunt Fran's casket. "She was just put here, look." Drena shows us by wiping her finger on the lid. "No dust."

I weave in and out of the aisle of coffins and shed a tear. "So many family members." I wipe my cheek.

"Wynter, it would make sense why you have not seen her, though, wouldn't it?" Rory asks.

"Rory is right, it's been a while since we have heard from your mother or aunt," Dad says.

"Speaking of my mother?" I ask. "Do you think she's here, too?"

"I'm still looking for her." Redmae is clear at the far end of the room now. "I've come across so many familiar faces." She looks down and stops.

"What is it?" Drena asks.

"There is a light coming from the other side of that threshold." She points to another silver steel door. This one isn't doubled.

Curious, Cole moves to investigate first and places an ear to listen. "I don't hear anything from the other side."

"Should we open it to find out?" Rory asks.

"What if it's Shadow Walkers?" I ask.

"What if it is?" Rory teases. "With my arrows, your fire and ice blasts." She grins. "Cory and Cole's daggers—" She turns to Drena. "And we have a light witch on our side—we can handle anything." Rory looks at her sister. "We've got this."

Redmae nods.

"I have a gut feeling that is the direction your compass is leading us, anyway," Cory says. He unclasps his dagger, and grabs the hilt, pulling out the glowing blade. "See? We're on the right path." He nods at Cole for verification. His blade mimics the same glowing light.

"Wynter, you just asked where your mother is. Don't you find it coincidental that suddenly there is a light under the door beckoning us to open it?"

"I don't believe in coincidences," Petra says.

"Neither do we," Cory adds.

"Who is going first?" Rory asks.

"Well, you're the stealthy trained assassin," Cole teases. "Be our guest, please." He bows, taunting her.

"Come again?" I ask.

"Whoops, was that too soon?" His sarcastic tone doesn't set well with many of us.

"What aren't you two telling me?" I look over at Redmae.

"Nope, not it."

"Rory?" My stern glance has her hesitating to answer.

Dad, Derek, and Drena, stay quiet. Even Blair standing guard, is silent, and she's the first person to usually open her mouth. I look at Petra last.

"Don't look at me, I know nothing of this."

Rory sighs. "Before I was assigned to you back in Blaine, Washington, I was enrolled in a school that train—" She stops, not wanting to answer.

"Quit with the drama, Rory, spit it out," I say.

She stiffens, puts her shoulder back, and looks at everyone else. "Please let's not all talk at once," she says in a sarcastic tone, still hoping someone else will speak up instead of her. "Everyone here, including yourself Wynter—although you don't remember—we all belong to The Guild of Shadows."

Petra raises her hand. "Except me, of course. I'm a traveling mage. The Guild of Shadows was incorporated after the mess I created."

"And me," Casey says. "I've never stepped foot off these grounds my entire life."

"We will bring you back with us to Ladorielle," Cory says.

"But first we deal with Sarmira," I say. "Petra, can you explain what you mean please."

"The short answer...The broken gateways, remember those? I need to find all the book portals."

I look at the others. "Right, that I understand, but Rory, what is this secret I'm not supposed to know about?"

"Not a secret per se, just something none of us wanted to reveal until you had less on your plate." Rory rolls her eyes. "I mean saving the world and all."

"Ha! Now you have jokes, and at a time like this. You know what? Forget I even asked!"

"No, wait. Wynter, you're right." Drena turns to my dad. "Jeff, she should probably know enough to get us through these catacombs. It might trigger her memories, because so far everything we've tried hasn't worked."

Dad grunts. "Remember when I mentioned an academy for dragons?"

I nod.

"It's the Academy at House of Bloodbane. It's a place where Shadow Walkers train to be assassins, where warriors train to be... well warriors, where dragons learn their magical skills and where witches learn their craft. The healers like Nyta, and the wizards like Aoes go to the City of Dark Shadows, near Wisteria Keep."

"And the mages such as myself—"

Dad puts a finger to his lips. Not yet. "She's not ready."

Petra's eyes grow. "Not ready?" She chuckles under her breath. "We're in the middle of—"

Dad holds up his hand. "Not. Yet."

"You know, Jeff, eventually you're going to have to tell her." She storms off, looking through the lines of glass coffins.

"Assassin. There, I said it. I'm a trained assassin," Rory bursts.

"Is this true?" I ask Dad.

"Yes." He glares at Rory.

"When were you going to tell me?"

"When the time was right."

"No time like the present, I guess," Rory says under her breath.

I raise my brow and turn to Cory. "This is the secret you were trying to tell me back at the ranch before we went to the Grengore Mines."

Cory bows his head. "Yes. Remember I told you that I'd done some terrible things I wasn't proud of—"

"Well, I don't think I saw this coming. And you thought Rory would eventually tell me the truth."

"But I had no intension of telling you...until now." She squints at Cole.

"I'm no assassin but I know enough to know that you can't reveal your true identity to another soul without risking your own life. Which means either one of two things: you have to kill me, or I'm also an—" My heart sinks. How did I not know this? Dragonscale showed me my past. He gave me all my memories. He did say that he would show me everything. Is this why? "Have I killed people?"

None of them answer me, except Dad. "No, you're not an assassin. Like mentioned before, you are a paladin knight like me. The House of Zhir have assassins, and the House of Storms have death knights."

"So, I'm a death knight, then?" I squint. "What's a death night exactly?"

"A unique dragon shifter paladin," Casey mumbles. "I read about them in the books I stole from the library in the manor when no one was watching."

"Ah, that's where those books went," Blair peeps from the guarded doorframe.

"But now isn't the time for explaining this," Dad scolds. "I tried to mention this to you earlier when we talked about the dragon academy. Once you finish high school you will ascend to this school for further training. Right now, our focus is to a more imminent threat—Sarmira."

"I know it's a lot to take in, Wynter, but we really need to sever this curse plaguing our magic," Cole says.

"Fair enough," I say. "But none of you are off the hook."

Redmae feels around the frame some more. "Wynter, I know you have been through a lot, and if I was in your shoes, I would be livid—of which I am sure you already are but considering all the things we as a family have gone through, this is just one more hurdle. Together we can face Sarmira and beat her at her own game." She continues investigating the door to an adjacent room, feathering over the surface inch by inch. "I sense whatever is behind this door is the key to unlocking the curse, though."

Cole raises a brow. "What are you up to?"

"Nothing nefarious, Cole, I assure you. I will say, though, something isn't adding up. It's almost like we're being lured here on purpose. This is too easy. The prowlers outside are quiet." She looks over at Petra. "The Crow Man didn't put up much of a fight, only intimidation, of which didn't work. He simply vanished into a thousand birds." She takes a deep breath. "I smell a trap."

Dad wrinkles his forehead. "A trap, huh?" He pulls his sword. "Ready when you are, Red. I have a feeling we have more unfinished business."

"Hold on. I agree with Redmae. If she smells a rat, it's a rat," Cole says, "but let's go at this with caution."

"What do you suggest we do?" Rory asks.

Cole's concerned look has me worried. "We can't open this door until we know what we're dealing with, Jeff."

"Cole is right. As powerful as we all are together if there is something more than what we can handle, we can kiss saving the *world* goodbye," Cory looks at me and smiles. The dagger in his hand glows in response.

Rory points to Cole's hip. "The blades don't lie." Then she points to me. "Your necklace is glowing, too. I have no doubt that whatever is behind this door is what we've set out to defeat. We need to have a plan."

"And although I trust what those blades are steering us to, I also have a gut feeling that beyond these doors is a trap," Petra says. "I have to agree with the rest of you."

"So, what do we do then?" I ask.

Cole grabs his blade, pulling it from its sheath and holds it upward. Letters in another language light up along the sharp edges revealing a message.

> *Behind the door is what you seek,*
> *be swift, be cautious, else it will render everyone*
> > *weak.*
> *The blades, the compass and arrows are one,*
> *but be aware of what already has been done.*

"Gawd, I hate riddles," Rory says.

"That's cause you're not a genius like me." Cole laughs.

"Okay, smarty-pants, what does it mean?"

"Well, your arrows, Wynter's compass, mine and Cory's blades are powerful. Which means—"

"Which means we're dealing with some sort of undead creature," Cory interrupts. "Oh, I'll tell you later. Just open the door already and let's get this mess over and done with!"

26

A GLASS COFFIN

A musty smell assaults my nostrils as soon as we cross the threshold. A coldness sifts through the air like the area hasn't been touched for centuries.

I take a couple steps forward. "This room feels drearier than the others." I gasp as soon as I see her. "Dad!"

Dad looks upon a clear casket with white trim. "I can't believe it's really her."

"This must have been the glow we saw under the crack of the door," Petra says.

My mother's casket glows blue, matching the same color as Cole and Cory's dagger. "Do you think the third blade is in there?"

"Only one way to find out," Cory says.

I attempt to lift the lid. "It won't budge."

Cory traces around the lid with his fingers. "Perhaps there is a lock keeping it closed." He stops. "Hah! I think I found it." He looks closer. "Try the key your Aunt Fran gave you, again."

I insert the key and turn the lock. "It still won't budge."

"The coffin is too strong we cannot get the top off. Casey will you help us lift the lid?" Redmae asks.

"You have the strength of a giant," Cole says. "Like Red said, we could use your help."

He nods. "I will try." He attempts to push open the lid. "Nope, it won't budge."

Cole, Derek, and Dad aid in helping Casey. The lid still doesn't move an inch.

"None of us have the strength to pry it loose," Dad says, stunned.

"We'll be here all night at this rate," Cory says.

"Agreed, this is going to take forever," Cole says.

"It's made of glass. Why not break it?" I ask.

"Great idea." Cory uses his talents to create a hammer. He swings expecting the glass to shatter, except the opposite happens and the hammer retracts with such force Cory flinches back in agony. "Well, that backfired." He looks at his hand and rubs it. "That glass is unbreakable."

"Let me see your hand." I hover my palms over Cory's, hoping I can mend any damage. "Let's not try that again, okay?"

"Agreed." Cory winces as he stretches out his fingers.

"Magic," Drena says. "It's what is keeping you from opening it. Let me think. There must be something I can do."

"What about a reverse holding spell?" Petra suggests.

"Genius idea." She closes her eyes. "I don't have the recipe. Let me think a second... Going off memory here: I need thread, a candle, and a simple incantation."

"Sort of like a binding spell?" Petra asks.

"Yes, but in reverse."

Petra whispers in Drena's ear.

"That might work." She moves closer to the casket. "Someone find me a candle."

"Will that work?" Derek asks, pointing to a sconce on the wall.

"It will." She smiles. "Who has some string?"

Rory cuts a hanging thread from her cloak. "How about this?"

"Perfect." Drena melts the wax onto the lid of the coffin so the candle will stand and then ties the string around the stick. She nods at Petra and begins the incantation. She repeats the verse three times.

"Why is nothing happening?" I ask.

"Patience, Wynter, the string needs to burn first," Drena says.

We all watch with intense trepidation as the flame inches closer to the string Rory gave to Drena. It sizzles and pops. A few sparks fly. A faint hiss finishes the threads at each burning end.

"Now try," Drena says.

We all push again, and the lid moves slightly.

"It's working!" Rory says.

"Yeah, but it's still hard to move. What if we can find something to pry it open..." Cory holds up his dagger. "Like this... I mean, it's Valiancium steel, right?"

"It's worth a shot," Derek says.

Cory wraps one palm on the hilt and places his other hand atop his firsthand and pushes the hilt against the lid.

He inches the opening more.

"Here, let me try." Dad takes the hilt using both his hands and presses it forward more, jarring the lid enough to allow us the leverage we need to finally pry the lid completely off. It falls onto the stone floor.

"I've never known glass to be so strong. How has in not shattered?" Not even a crack.

"It's made of a certain mineral found in the Crescent Mountains. Clear like glass, hard like a diamond, and heavy as steel," Geneviève says.

"Grab the dagger, Wynter, and let's get out of here," Cory says.

Looking inside leaves us breathless. Like my great-grandmother, my mother's skin is flawless. A dim blue light glows under her garments. Brushing away the layers of lace and satin, I find the lustrous blade tucked away inside a deep pocket of her dress. I pull it out and look upon the dagger, mesmerized by its beauty. A surge of energy flows through my veins. A power that consumes me like no other. This power is different. Not like when I turned into a dragon, or when suddenly I knew all and could see all, no, this power is much different. I can feel both love and evil from it. A power if not careful will consume me. It takes a minute for me to decipher. Wait, this isn't just magic I hold in my hands, it's the lost souls of the fallen. The hilt is made of labradorite with a green stone embedded in the center and a letter S engraved at the top of the blade. "The stone is beautiful."

"It's tsavorite." Drena answers. "A healing stone that is said to bring health and enhance your consciousness. Possessing this dagger should bring you more clarity, Wynter."

"Wynter, I can feel your fear," Cory says. "What is it?"

"This power. The blade is so strong. I hear voices, Cory. So many voices."

"Yeah, I know. You will get used to it. Try and focus on our objective. It will help a little."

"If I may suggest," Cole interrupts, "I visualize putting the voices in a room, and shutting the door, locking them in."

"You hear voices, too?" I ask.

"Yes. All the time."

I try what Cole suggests. In an instant after visualizing the door shut, silence follows. "What a rush." I shake my head to focus. The dagger still glows bright blue. I look at Cole and Cory. Theirs glow, too.

A howl—not Redmae's—interrupts us. Redmae growls in her human form.

"Guys, we have company!" Blair calls from the other room.

Dad, Derek, Cole, and Cory circle shoulder to shoulder with their backs facing each other, and ease in and out between more family coffins.

"Be on guard," Dad says.

Rory nocks her bow and arrows in preparation for a fight.

We rush toward the first entrance where Blair guards the door to the family coffins.

Redmae takes a stance behind the second door opposite from the one we entered from. "They're behind that door over there." Cole points to the left.

"Someone definitely doesn't want us near these coffins," Petra says.

We hear another creepy howl, followed by strange whispers that consume the catacomb.

"I think we're about to find out who else is in here with us. And I don't mean our family of coffins. There isn't just one entity in this catacomb with us—there are several. I can feel them," Redmae says.

The glowing from all our blue eyes bounce off the stone walls around us, lighting the way as we follow around the room. A sudden movement to the left, startles us and we all turn towards the noise.

"Yes, someone else is in here, I can feel it, too," Drena says.

The first Sabretail Prowler patters through the entrance, followed by the next. A third stays behind, guarding the entry. They sniff the corners of the walls, lift their snout, and growl.

"Stay still," Dad whispers.

"They know we're here, don't they?" Blair asks.

"Yes. Don't move a muscle."

One of the cats moves slowly circling the outer edges of the room, appearing annoyed that it can't see us. It roars. My heart pounds and I swear it can hear it beating.

It wanders over to us and stops right at the edge of Cole's

protective bubble. Almost as though the barrier he cast moments earlier prevents it from moving into our space.

Rory grabs my hand and squeezes it. I squeeze back to let her know I understand her.

"I bet we wouldn't die if I shifted into a dragon and torched those fu—"

"Wynter!"

"What? Am I wrong?"

The prowlers pounce, breaking the protective barrier.

"So much for keeping quiet," Dad says. He pulls out his sword hidden inside his long coat and swings.

"Our magic isn't as strong on Earth as it is on Ladorielle," Blair shouts.

"Do your best. You have newfound dragon powers," Derek replies.

"Right, like I know what those are yet," Blair says. She swings forward with a high kick to the side of one of the beasts.

"Any idea on how to get rid of them?" Rory asks.

"I can try and blast them with ice," I say.

"It's worth a shot, I suppose," Cole replies. He jabs his weapon toward another prowler and misses.

"There's ten of us and three of them," Blair says. "This should be a cake walk."

"Eleven," Petra reminds us. "I have a few magical skills of my own." She winks. She flicks her wrist and sends them both flying backward against the opposite wall.

Casey shifts. He roars and pounces a third prowler.

"Make that twelve but who is counting." Petra pulls her wand out and flicks it slowing the creatures moves.

I smile. "Nice." I flick my wrist outward as the blood in my vein freezes instead of boils, and right as I'm about to throw my weapon of choice, Cole disappears from our view.

"Where did he go?" Rory asks.

Seconds later a yelp is heard from the entrance and the Sabretail Prowler guarding the entrance goes down.

"Nothing like cutting to the chase," I say.

I blast one of the distracted beasts with ice, freezing him instantly while Rory takes an arrow and impales the other prowler. Dad shatters the beast I froze with his sword.

"Well, aren't you just full of surprises," Petra says, looking at me.

"I concur," Blair says.

"And you, Cole, when were you going to tell us about your rogue-like moves," Derek asks.

"Oh, cut me some slack, will you?" He pockets his switchblade.

We walk back to the other end of the catacomb where the caskets of our family lie. I revel, feeling a little triumphant that we defeated the Sabretail Prowlers.

"I don't think we'll ever be ready for something like this, but we're prepared for whatever comes our way, even if it kills us," Cole says. "I'm not going back to the dark side—ever."

We exit the doorway and back into the room my mother rests. Dad, Derek, and the brothers comb every square inch of the other room where we feel the presence of more shadows could possibly be hiding.

Redmae grumbles. "There is still something lurking. Can you feel it, Wynter?"

"Yes. I suspect this is a distraction."

"Agreed, " Cole says.

"Who's there?" Dad calls. "Show yourself. We know you're in here." He laughs. "Unless you're the one who is scared."

"Can you give a sense of how many, Redmae?"

"Besides us? No. What I can say we're the only ones with a heartbeat."

"So, you think it might be spirits?"

"Most likely, yes.

"There's movement ahead of us." Casey points.

Something crashes to the floor, and glass shatters.

THE WIND KICKS UP AND DUST FLIES, WARNING US Sarmira approaches.

Cole takes advantage of the approaching threat and immediately cast his invisible bubble.

A ball of green light shoots through the walls and she appears with a taunting evil laugh along with two Shadow Walkers. Both dressed in assassin gear, wearing masks so we can't see their faces.

"One thing is certain, they reek of vampire venom or wet dog, I can't be sure. Either way this confirms that she's alive and roaming the grounds of Storm River Manor still," Blair says.

"Trying to get away so soon?" Sarmira's voice echoes through the hollow tombed walls before she appears.

"She can't see us," Cory assures through my mind.

We huddle together waiting to see her next move. She focuses her gaze, and her smile turns stone cold. "No!"

She looks inside the coffin of my mother and seems to be searching for something. Rage fills her eyes, and she screams. She has the form of a wraith, yet she looks solid. *Has she shed Maura's body?*

"Madame?" one of her minions asks.

"Where did it go!" she screams in frustration. "Impossible! The coffin was spell proof!"

Cole's plan is working. We're successfully cloaked.

She pushes and opens a stone coffin between us and my mother's coffin and looks inside. More rage consumes her and she screams in fury. She slams the stone coffin into the wall inches from where the rest of us are hiding. Skulls crumble to the ground, shattering from Sarmira's force of strength. How can we defeat this evil witch? She's stronger than ten men.

"Find them!" She shrieks in more anger and blasts the covers of several glass lids shattering them and the glass-like pieces come hailing down upon the crypt. "We cannot complete the ritual without those daggers!" A gust of wind blows through the catacombs forming dark clouds and just as quickly as she arrives, she disappears, leaving behind fire and ash. The Shadow Walkers remain, scouting the area before they too, disappear.

"Well, that was fun," Rory says, smirking, after the dust clears.

Still holding the dagger in his hand, Cory asks, "Is everyone okay?"

"I think so," I say. "Rory?"

"I'm fine. She packs one powerful punch, doesn't she? Wait, where is Redmae?" Rory's eyes show complete fear.

I hear a sneeze, followed by an answer, "I'm in here."

The destruction Sarmira left reveals another room. "Why do you get to discover all the cool places, Red?" I tease.

The new-discovered area isn't as large as the other one. Disrupted dust particles float across the blue beams of light from our eyes as we move through the widened hole.

Redmae gets to her feet. "That was some serious magic."

"Ya think?" I smile. "I mean Sarmira did just blast the tops off of many coffins."

I look inside one of the solid stone caskets that nearly killed us all by the force from Sarmira's tantrum.

"Wynter, do you recognize these two?" Rory asks. Standing next to two other coffins.

I come over to observe. "No, but she looks a lot like Drena," I say. "And this other person looks like her aunt ."

"Me?" Drena asks.

I nod. "She looks like you."

Intrigued curiosity gets to her and she looks inside. She gasps "My mother? I thought you said you saw her in Scarlet Hollow."

"We did. And we saw her reunited with Jasmine. Her and Angelica both," Rory confirms.

"Then they are still spirits. My Aunt Jasmine is a master at alchemy. She must have created an immortality spell of some kind." Drena stops. "Hmm..." She glances at me and then paces about for a few seconds.

"What is it? I can see the wheels in your mind, Drena," I say.

"I think she had some sort of insight that you would find the bodies that were laid to rest." Drena turns looking at both her mother and aunt. "Here they are—" Drena steps into the other room. She gasps. "There are so many of them."

I'd almost forgotten about the other room. Beyond the encased skull stone walls has all of us gasping in awe.

27

HIDDEN ROOM OF LOST SOULS

"I don't have a good feeling about any of this," Rory says.

"It's shelves. Dozens of them." Except it isn't books set upon on the ledges, but jars. Some empty, however most of them are full of some sort of substance I don't recognize.

"This isn't disturbing at all," Rory says in a sarcastic tone. She picks up one jar and looks closely at it. "It's filled with a clear liquid."

"Not all of them." Cole holds a jar with blue fluid. "There are more over here, some yellow, and others lime green."

The jars with the clear solution have blue smoke swirling inside, while others have white or green. "What is this place? I mean I understand we're in the catacombs, but this feels so… not right." I turn to Cory for validation.

"Yes, I feel it too. Something feels wrong," Cory agrees.

"Because it is wrong," Drena says. "These jars on the shelves are filled with souls. That's why this place was hidden, so she could carry out her plans in secret."

"'She' meaning Sarmira?" Blair asks.

"Yes. She must've been planning this power takeover for

centuries." Drena weaves in and out of the multiple shelving units, studying each jar.

Casey drifts over to Drena and follows her. He seems just as intrigued. "This must be why Sarmira tasked me to stay down in the crypt. She never mentioned anything like this."

"That was the point. This was her little secret. She didn't want anybody to know." Drena picks up a jar. "Anyone know of someone by the name of Margaret?"

"My brother's fiancé," Dad says. "The moment our mother found out they were engaged she had Daniel turn the poor woman to stone."

"And here we thought it was because of an affair between Daniel and a maid," Cory says, looking at his brother.

"Don't look at me. I always thought it was just a rumor."

"That is beside the point," Dad says, and he takes the jar from Drena. He studies the swirl of white smoke dancing inside the glass container.

"It can't be," Cory says. He goes to one of the shelves that holds the jars of smoke and picks up one. He looks at his brother horrified. "Cole, take a look at this one."

I look closer to see the smoke inside reflects from the light of our glowing eyes. "It sparkles?"

"The ones with reflective sparkle, means there is magic still left in the soul," Drena adds. "Which means there is still life left in the body."

Cole reads the label; his expression has a look of panic.

"What is it?" Blair grabs the jar from him. "You're not going to believe this." She turns the jar around for us to read: Maura Moyer.

"Wait, are you saying my grandmother's soul is in this jar?" Stunned I pick up another jar and read the label. "This one says Daniel Storm."

"Clearly Daniel Storm is walking around at Storm River Manor, though," Cole says. "None of this makes any sense."

"He's possessed," Blair says. She grabs a jar. "This one says Arik Storm."

"And he's dead," Dad says. "Or at least that's what was witnessed."

"Wait a minute…" I squint, pointing to them. "I wonder if you boys were once in jars like these?"

Cory raises a brow. "Clearly, we're right in front of you. What are you getting at?"

Cole grabs another jar and stares at his brother, with concern. He quickly glances at me then back to his twin.

"What is it?" Cory asks, reaching for the container. He reads it, and he too shows a bit of concern.

Cole again glances at me and quickly looks away once more.

My stomach sinks. I reach for the container. "Let me see it."

Cole pulls away. "I'm not sure that's a good idea."

I lunge forward, but Cory holds me back.

"Show me the damn name!" I struggle out of Cory's arms and grab the jar from Cole's hands and read it: Isalora Storm. "She's trapped my mother's soul?" I look over at the twins and take a moment to read another label on the shelf behind them. "Bram, Ailbert, Gavin…" I look up at my friends. "These are my great uncles on the Deagon side."

Rory moves to me and looks at what I see, saying, "There's more in the back." She reads the labels. "Clarice, Laurawyn…"

"I find all of this appalling. We must figure out how to free them," I say.

"Carefully though. We need to think this through," Drena says. "And I have an idea of how, too."

"How?" Derek asks. "Does this mean they can be brought back to life?"

Drena chuckles to herself. "I am no necromancer, and light witches don't deal with raising the dead, but if we could find the Book of Immortality and the items to perform the ritual, it could be possible."

"Is the spellbook the only way to revive them?" Cory asks.

"Sort of, yes. I could go off of memory, but it wouldn't be safe. One wrong measurement and I could permanently keep them in a state of death. Good news is usually where there is a Soul Jar, there is a body, and something tells me those caskets out there filled with our family members are key to the mystery of why our magic is fading."

"Hang on a second..." I look at Dad as I remember his explicit restriction about raising the dead when Aunt Fran was stabbed by his sword. "You said there is no way someone could raise—"

Dad has a concerned look on his face. "That would require a necromancer and Wynter isn't prepared."

Shock implodes within me. "What?"

"We don't need a necromancer, Jeff. This only requires a witch. If they were dead, yes, but these are souls in a jar. They are still very much alive, as long as we can find their bodies, and a Soul Catcher, we can bring back everyone. If we can manage to awaken them, maybe we can finally have answers to what we're all seeking." Drena turns, putting out her right arm and points. "I think we have stumbled upon Sarmira's soulless army. If we can connect body and soul, it will be like a resurrection. The only difference, the bodies have been preserved."

"I may be of assistance," Petra volunteers. "You would need a Soul Catcher"—she glances at me as if she knows my secret— "Plus we will need to find the spell book, as you mentioned Drena. Do you need any extra ingredients?"

"I won't know until I see the recipe."

"I don't understand this light and dark witch stuff," I say.

"It's something I haven't gotten around to explain to you, but your grandmother Eleena was half dark witch." Dad looks over at Derek and he nods. "Before I was born, when my mother Maura was still innocent from Sarmira's wickedness, the Deagon cousins Ian, Arik, and Derek, set out on a quest to find the evil witch—Sonjah. They met with two women…"

"Let me guess, Lira and Eleena," I say.

"Yes," Derek answers. "My cousins, Ian before he became the next Dragonscale, and Arik before he married Maura Moyer, we allied with the coven House of Shadow Raven witches. A guild made up of both light and dark witches. The dark witches were morally grey, so to speak. They did not see eye-to-eye with the House of Zhir." He grunts. "You, Wynter, come from that bloodline. Necromancy must be learned…" He looks at Drena quickly before continuing, "However, what I think Drena is trying to say is if there is a body still intact and is matched to the correct Soul Jar, the body will come back to life."

"Brilliant," Cole says in a sarcastic way. "Shall we get started?"

Cory's eyes focus on another shelf. "Wait, there's more jars." He makes his way over to the shelf and tips them forward. "Francesca Storm and Ian Storm."

"Something isn't adding up though. How are some of these souls in these jars walking in the physical world, while others have passed on?" Cory asks.

"Unless they never did pass on and they were trapped, like Cory was," Rory says. "I mean Drena said as long as the body is preserved or alive, the soul can reunite with it."

Drena nods. "Correct."

"I see something way in the back." Stretching my arm as far as it can go, I touch the jar with my fingertips, inching closer until it cups my palm. I pull it out and read the label. "Impossible!" My eyes fill with tears. "No!" I back away.

Cory takes the container from my fingertips before I risk dropping it from my shaky hands. He's rendered speechless and looks at both his brothers. He tips the jar and shows them. They avoid eye contact with both Rory and Redmae.

Dad notices our concern and comes over to investigate. The label reads: Geneviève.

Is GENEVIÈVE POSSESSED LIKE COLE WAS, OR LIKE Maura? She has been quiet throughout our entire time in the catacombs.

Cole looks at Rory, Blair, and Cory, then quickly gives the jar to Drena, and she reads it. It's a stare I know all too well. I've seen that look with Cory. "I found a jar that might interest you, Rory."

"Really, me? I can assure you I am alive and well."

Geneviève comes to investigate. The concern in her eyes has most of us troubled. "What is it?" She tries to read the label.

Drena huffs a bit. I can tell by her body language that she is trying hard to play the role of an ignorant witch. "It's nothing. Just another family member's lost soul."

Is this impostor a Trek, like the last time they tried to impersonate Geneviève? If it's a Trek, then it begs the question, where's the real Geneviève?

Dad stares Derek down. It's like an unspoken language between them. Blair sees it too. I think Dad is going to stealth his way into trapping Geneviève.

"Cory, can you read my thoughts?"

He nods.

"And Cole?"

Cole also nods.

"What do we do?" It's going to have to be a game of charades with the others who cannot get inside my head.

Cory motions for me to move behind her. He points to my

hands. I get it. He wants me to use my magic. Cole gestures the same thing. *Good, we're on the same page.*

"This room suddenly got very quiet," Geneviève says. "What's going on?" She turns to face me. "Wynter, what are you doing?"

My hands flex. "Nothing. My wrist feels stiff suddenly," I lie. *"This better be quick, before she catches on."*

Geneviève takes a step back. Her eyes dart to each of us.

"Cory, she knows something is up. I don't want to provoke her."

Geneviève raises one brow. "How did you figure it out? I was flawless. I know I was." Geneviève pulls her hand outward to open a portal.

Right before she disappears into the nothingness, I zap her back with a cold spell. Ice catches her wrist, pulling her back to our present. "Nice try. You won't escape this time, Lira."

She laughs. "Lira? Is that who you think I am?"

"Who else would you be?" I enforce the ice more with it slowly creeping up her arm.

She grunts in discomfort. "Think again, dear Wynter. Oh, I am indeed Geneviève, just not the one you think I am."

Confusion skims all our faces.

"You expect us to believe that?" I ask. The ice reaches up her neck and down to her feet, rendering her immobile. "Déjà vu indeed. I feel we've been around this battle before."

"You don't get it, do you?" Fake Geneviève snarls. "I'm a clone. I had you all fooled. At lease now we know it works."

"What works?" Dad asks. His eyes glow blue.

"If she's a clone that means she has no soul," Cole says.

"How do you know that?" Rory asks.

Fake Geneviève squirms. She isn't pleased that Cole knows this information.

"I've spent enough time with Madame Moyer to know

who's a clone and who isn't. This is how she builds her army of Shadow Walkers. Question is, I should have sensed it."

"Hmm…" Petra comes forward and squints. "Clones can't lie, either." She pulls at the impostor's hair. "A wig, just as I suspected." Black hair slicks back atop the woman's head. Petra grabs a cloth and wipes the faux Geneviève's cheek. "Cloaking makeup." She looks at the rag. "I've seen this before. "She's not a clone. She's Fae." Petra's tone changes. "Where is it?"

"What are you talking about?" the stranger impersonating Geneviève looks confused.

Petra comes nose to nose with her. "I know you have it. I won't ask you again."

"Have you seen this fraud before?" Dad asks.

"Yes, only she wasn't in this form before. She was in the form of me. She's a Fae, an illusion bender. She manipulates illusions with makeup." Petra wipes away the rest of the woman's face, revealing her true features.

Her eyes change to black, and her skin glows with green undertones. She has high cheekbones and sunk-in jawline. Her thin lips and pointed ears make this Fae look more like a goblin —the goblins Cory, Rory and I experienced at the Gren Gore Mines. "You're half goblin. I knew there was something about you I couldn't put my finger on."

"That explains why we couldn't sense her, "Cory says.

"If she is impersonating my mother then it means the real Geneviève must be here somewhere." Rory steps back and lowers her bow. "Where is she?"

The fake Geneviève smiles. "You're a fool if you think I'll tell you that."

I raise the ice to her lips and her ears. I turn around to the others. "What do we do with her?"

"Keep her here while we look, I guess," Cole says.

My stomach churns. "I think I'm going to be sick." I look

over at the icicle mound. "I'm done playing nice. This ends, now." I cover the clone's entire head.

"Wynter, trust me, we will figure this all out," Cory says. "This minion might be able to help us."

"Right, because we've made so much progress until now." I strengthen the ice with another layer. "Rory?"

"My pleasure." With one blow of her arrow, the ice statue obliterates in frozen ice crystals.

"Now there's a dark side of Wynter I haven't seen. I think I like it," Cole says.

"Don't egg her on, brother." Cory is disappointed I allowed my anger to get in the way of logic. "We could have use her for information, you know."

"She was a Fae, and we all know Fae cannot be trusted." I scowl at him. "

"I think I'm beginning to like you, as well, Wynter." Blair grins.

"Not the best move," Petra says. "She took the portal book that I'm looking for. I do believe that is why I am here. How am I going to find it now?"

"I—I'm sorry. My anger got the better of me."

"We will help you find it," Drena says.

"Realistically, that Fae didn't know anything. She was placed here to study us. What I would like to know, is when the transformation happened," Blair says.

"Same," Dad says. "The cottage would have protected us, from such evil."

Drena picks up one of the frozen goblin pieces and places it into an empty jar. "I wonder if this will give us some clues?" She throws in a few more pieces. "This is a laboratory of sorts. Perhaps I can study this. I have an idea. I might be able to create a spell from this. Or better yet locate the nest from where this creature came from."

"What are you saying, Love?" Derek says.

"I might be able to find a spell in here that will help us fight against Sarmira." She takes the specimen to the lab table and sifts through the jars."

"Hmm, that is a good point. Maybe a locator spell to find our mother." Redmae wanders over to a bench and sits. It activates a switch of sorts, and a bookshelf randomly moves into a pocket wall revealing a hidden passageway beyond.

"Perhaps that's our answer?" Rory says.

"This place will never cease to amaze me," Cole says. "The catacombs that I have grown to know as a maze, has a maze within its secret passageways." He ventures toward the secret room. "Any of you coming with me, or am I doing this alone? We aren't going to find Geneviève standing in one place."

"Count me in," Dad says. He and Casey follow after him.

"I'm coming with you, too. Don't have to ask me twice," I say. Redmae, Rory and I follow Cory and the rest of our party through the dark passageway to the next mysterious room across the threshold.

28

HALL OF SECRETS MAURA'S WAY

The wood surface floor creaks beneath our feet as each of us walk into the secret chamber.

"That's strange," Derek says. "The stone flooring ends at the door frame. Perhaps something is below us."

"I haven't been through here before." Petra stomps on a couple planks. "You might be right."

Still carrying the lighter from earlier, Dad lights another sconce mounted to the wall, and it brightens the area more than just by all of our blue eyes. "There is another lamp over there." I point across the room where a bookcase filled with an array of old books lines the entire wall space from floor to ceiling.

On the opposite wall, more jars filled with liquid set upon other shelves. In the center between the two shelving units is a large prepping table that could seat about twelve people. On top of it, some dusty old empty mason jars are filled with dried herbs, wrapped bundles of lavender line the edges of the table, and a mortar and pestle set in the center. Braids of garlic, onions, and sage hang on hooks from the rafters above us while wooden barrels filled with who knows what, sets against another wall with burlap bags leaning up against some of them. A second table butts up against a wall a few steps ahead with another mortar and pestle as a center piece along with a dozen more jars with additional herbs. This second table is next to an ancient cast iron stove with a cast iron kettle on one burner while a cauldron-like pot on the other. Charred wood is still present in the fire box.

"What is this place?" Rory asks. She looks around, stunned by what we've discovered.

"I don't know," Cole answers. He walks to the shelf of dusty books and pulls one, flips through it and coughs. "It looks like this area hasn't been touched in years." He puts the book back as he waves at the dust that's invaded his lungs.

Stained glass covers the ceiling and top edging of the walls. Flecks of moonlight seeps through despite it being nighttime. "Where do you suppose that would be if we were above ground? It's like we're inside a below ground turret."

"Under the gazebo of Sara's Garden, I would imagine." Cory points. "It looks like the same glass that is structured around the skirting of the gazebo in her garden."

Previous burned candles scale the high windowsills encasing the decorative glass.

French doors are decorated in more stained glass and open up to a larger room that reminds me of an underground garden cellarium.

Ivy intertwines around many pillars and herbs of all kinds growing in pots lining the walls. An altar at the opposite end of the room expands the entire length of the back wall with communion pews several rows deep position between us and the platform. "This seems like an odd spot to place a church." I sit in one, studying the position. "Clearly, they're not placed this way for a sermon. It makes no sense."

"I don't think it's a church," Cole says. "More like an altar of worship."

"That's a little ominous," Rory states. "Why so many benches, then? Clearly there is enough seating for a congregation in here." Rory sits next to me. She shifts a moment and squints. "Quite odd, isn't it?"

"Makes you wonder if that's how Madame Maura knew Stella's whereabouts when she wandered too far from the grounds. I remember the story Stella told of her punishment." I point to a clear view of a window that faces the manor.

"Maybe they're just simple benches." Cory smiles, and he too sits down.

Not satisfied by Cory's answer Rory looks behind one. "Hah! Bibles."

"What?" Both Cory and I look, too.

He pulls out the book. "This isn't a Bible." He flips through the pages. "This is a spellbook."

Cory hands a copy to Cole.

"Spellbooks?" Cole flips the pages, too.

"You're kidding." Dad puts out his hand. "May I?" He takes the book and reads the inside heading. "The Spells of Lost Souls." He looks up. "I bet this is the exact book you might be looking for, Drena."

"Let me see... I've looked at a lot of books these days. Each book usually has a page ripped out. The exact page that I need to awaken our family."

"And this one says, 'Spells and Curses,'" Cory replies, pointing to a recipe.

Rory's eyes light up. "Do you think there is a cure in there for my sister?"

"You know what this means, don't you?" I ask. "We may have very well found a way to lift the curse. It looks like Maura Moyer purposely hid these books."

"It wasn't Maura," Blair confesses. "It was me. I hid these books."

"What?" Drena is shocked. "How did you pull off such a feat without being detected?"

"Remember back at the cottage I said I had hidden the book of Immortality in the Catacombs? It was here in this room. I found this place by accident one day. It obviously had been hidden for years. I knew we would find the place eventually, but I didn't want to show you until I knew for sure who to trust. I'm glad we discovered the faux Geneviève when we did. I think she was sent here for the location of other books."

"Such as the Book of Immortality," Drena says.

"Yes." Blair walks to the front row, pulls one side of the legs that opens up to a hidden pocket of the seating bench and pulls out a book. "I believe Drena, this is what you're looking for." She hands The Book of Immortality to Drena."

"I love a good twist." Petra grins.

"The game isn't over yet, dear. We still have a lot of work to do." Drena quickly reads through the book. "This is the book I indeed need. The Spellbook of Immortality will lift the curse Isalora placed on herself and the rest of our family." Drena quickly leafs through the pages.

"Wait what do you mean placed on herself and our family? Are you saying she's responsible for the curse?" Cory asks.

Drena looks up. "She cast it herself, darling."

"But why?"

"That is the big question, isn't it?" Drena's face shows despair. "Oh no. Blair, I'm afraid this book has the recipe page ripped out as well."

Realizing it was probably time to retrieve my kept secret, I reach into the inside pocket of my jacket tucked deep down, and I pull from it the spellbook my mother gave me that she kept hidden under the floorboards of the cottage. "Do you think the spell you're looking for is in here?"

Drena's eyes grow wide. "Who is the clever witch now?" She smiles.

I think to correct her and quickly realize she's right. My grandmother Eleena and my grandmother Maura were both witches. Was this the plan all along? I mean this prophecy everyone keeps saying. The bloodline of a witch, a dragon, and a wolf—wait, no, no, no, please don't tell me I'm a wolf too.

"Wynter, I hear you and no you're not a wolf."

"That's a relief. I can't handle any more surprises. Wait who is speaking to me?"

Silence returns. I look at Redmae. "Did you hear that?"

Redmae looks puzzled. "Hear what?"

I look at the twins. Both of them shrug, looking at me, confused. "You okay, Wynter?" Cory asks.

"Fine, I think. Someone spoke to me in my thoughts. I have no idea who it was."

Rory comes to my side and hugs my arm, whispering, "I'm sure you will figure it out. You always do."

Drena reads further in the book I gave her, flipping through it until she lands on the page she's looking for. She points. "Look here. This is it." She looks up at me. "Your mother was a genius. It's the list of all our ingredients needed. Waxlily is one of them."

"But of course." Cory winks. "Don't worry, I didn't give you all of my stash earlier." He grins. "I've learned to listen to my inner voice and not question it. I've been burned too many times, by not listening." He hands the bag to Drena. "Will this be enough?"

Drena's eyes perk. "An Endless Bag! You have the Waxlily in there?" She takes the small leather pouch, looks inside, and gasps.

"Yes, it's an Endless Bag." He winks. "A faux Endless Bag that is."

"A what?" I look over at Rory.

"Cory's created a knock-off," Drena explains. "I'd say

enough for an army. I don't want to know how you managed to get this much."

He looks over at me. "It wasn't easy."

"I imagine not." Drena tucks the Waxlily bag into her pocket.

"And what is an Endless Bag?" I look at him oddly. "It looks like a giant purse, Cory."

He laughs. "A purse? My dear lovely Wynter, this isn't just any ordinary purse.

Drena takes the book she's holding and places it inside the bag. "The real ones are rare, especially since the great war. Shadow Elves from the Elvin city on Elleirodal make them. It's basically a weightless bag that can hold endless items without feeling weighed down. Except this bag doesn't have the exact capabilities. It will wear down after a few weeks and then disappear."

"Which means," Cory adds, "we need to be quick with what we accomplish here, or these items will also disappear along with the bag." He looks behind the pew and pulls two more books and plops them into the sack.

"I admit, that is quite the magical item, indeed," Rory says.

"Will we be able to bring them all back?" my dad asks.

She nods. "This does look hopeful. I will need some help finding each coffin that matches their Soul Jar. This will take some time. Wynter, I'll need your help with this."

"Me?"

"You have the bloodlines of both witches and although you haven't had the proper training, your ancestor magic will still help."

"Who is first?" I ask.

"Your mother." She holds up Spells and Curses. "But this book—this one will lift the curse we're currently dealing with."

"Wait a minute. Where is Casey?" Redmae asks.

"I'm over here," he says. "Behind the several aisles of bookshelves." He hides well, sitting at a desk, reading. "I think I found something that might be of interest to all of us."

There are piles of notebooks on the surface of the desk. "What have you got there?" Redmae asks.

"Journals upon journals, dating back two hundred years or more."

Stunned, Dad investigates. "What?" He picks up one. "Casey is right. There are all kinds of notes, maps, and drawings in here."

"Who wrote them?" Cole asks.

"They're in my mother's handwriting," Dad says.

We all pick up a different notebook and skim through the pages.

"Here's one about the twelve portal stones," Casey says.

"Can I see that?" Rory asks. She flips through the pages. "This will come in handy for Petra I bet."

Petra gasps, grabbing the book. "I think this is what I have been looking for."

"Does this mean your quest to find all the twelve books is done?" I ask.

"Not nearly, no, but it's like a map. Can I keep this one?"

"No disagreement here," Dad says. "Anyone else?"

"Go for it," Rory says.

"Thanks." Petra tucks it inside her cloak.

"Hey, I think I found something, else," Redmae says, reading. "It says here something about a room full of hidden hearts."

"What?" I ask.

"Can I see that?" Dad asks. He reads the pages, and his faces goes sheet white.

"What is it, Jeff?" Redmae asks.

"She's written in here the locations of all the hearts she's taken and placed in coffers."

"Does it say where?" Cole presses.

"Near a secret passageway I don't recognize."

"Well, this is a nice distraction to the task at hand. Shall we see how this curse can be lifted first? We don't have but maybe a few more hours before the Blood Moon has completely descended. Dawn is approaching," Cole says.

"He's right. First things first, we need to find the source of the curse," Dad agrees.

"There is too much literature to go over it all now, and we need to be very careful. The night will end soon. We have to stop the demonic forces flooding through the Blood Moon gate. That takes priority," Drena says.

"Wynter, come."

I veer in the direction of the altar. A sheet covers up the wall above the shrine.

"Wynter, what is it?" Cory threads his hand with mine.

"What is behind there?" I feel compelled to tug off the drape.

"Probably her deity." Drena pulls off the cloth and gasps. "The Mirror of Souls. The portal gate to Scarlet Hollow. Geneviève and I came across this mirror when we were girls. We've been looking for this for years."

"It looks just like the mirror we saw in Jasmine's cave," Rory says.

"It looks identical to the mirror in the Hall of Secrets, too," I say.

"You don't think our mother Geneviève is in there, do you?"

"I hope not. This is the other side from my aunt's world.

This is the mirror that also enters Scarlet Hollow, and the other mirror in the Hall of Secrets, that has been dormant for years, because this one has been lost."

"It's a three-way mirror?" I ask.

"Four," Drena answers.

"Wait," Cory begins, "are you saying that the souls lost in Scarlet Hollow can potentially be freed?"

Drena smiles. "Key word, 'potential.' Several elements must come into play to allow that to happen."

"Which is?" I ask.

"A Soul Catcher that holds a soul, whether in physical or spiritual form, when they get sucked through the catcher they are held there until they're released into The Mirror of Souls. It is the vehicle that holds the souls. Only a trained witch in alchemy that has the recipe for the ingredients can perform the ritual to release or free a soul in the device. The mirror used to be a common way to speak with the spirits until Sarmira found a way to use it for her own gain. The House of Ashburn are responsible for closing the passageway. This was how they were able to trap Sarmira last time she came to wreak havoc on our lands."

"That must be why Angelica and Sage were surprised to see us. They mention something about, 'she escaped.' This must be what they meant? What do you think, Rory?"

"I think you're right, Wynter."

"That would make sense," Drena says. "Angelica, Jasmine, and my mother were responsible, along with The Raven, in binding her powers and sending her to Scarlet Hollow for a time." She lightly touches the edge of the filigree infinity loops surrounding the frame. The Spellbook of Immortality is needed to release the souls that we found in those jars, and bring them back to consciousness, by matching the preserved bodies in those caskets. I don't think you quite understand—The Mirror of Souls is the gateway to Scarlet Hollow, and we just found the missing mirror to connect all of them once again."

"I'm guessing this means we can finally send Sarmira back to the hell she belongs in," Rory says.

"Precisely," Drena says.

Petra walks to the mirror. "If you were to look at your reflection you would see other souls instead."

Dad investigates, as do Cole, Cory, and Casey.

"I can make out some of their faces. And I see Sage as we speak. Can none of you see her?" I ask. I see spirits walk aimlessly across the window of death.

"I can," Drena confirms. "It's the witch's blood that runs through your veins, Wynter. That is why you can see the undead." She glances back to each of us. "It is either a blessing or a curse, indeed."

"The mirror shifts from scene to scene. Why is that?" Sage has disappeared and now the headshots of several souls push forward as though they're all looking into a camera lens up close. I step back. "That's a bit freaky."

Our reflections fade and Jasmine appears. "I knew you could do it." She smiles. "You found the other half of the mirror. Did you find them?"

"Find who, my lady?" I ask.

"My sister's bodies," Jasmine clarifies. "Are they there in the catacombs?"

"Yes, but how did you know—"

"Aoes said they would be there. At least it has always been our theory." She stops. "Is that—"

"Yes! Drena is with us."

Tears form in Jasmines eyes. "Give her a message for me, will you?"

"Auntie, I am right here. Can you not see me?"

"I cannot see you clearly, only an outline, but I can hear you. You must lift the curse to free us. We are still spirits and while not trapped in Scarlett Hollow, we cannot leave the mirror."

"I don't understand," I say. "We saw them help us escape Scarlet Hollow." I stare at Drena. "We saw Jasmine in the cave."

"Yes, because you were still in The Veil," Drena answers.

"Do you still have the Soul Catcher I gave you, Wynter?" Jasmine asks.

I verify the Soul Catcher is still on the inside pocket of my jacket. "Yes."

"Good, now you should have all the tools you need to release them. Soon, the balance of power will be restored." Jasmines image fades.

Drena snaps her fingers, and the mirror returns to normal with us seeing our reflections. She giggles softly. "I still have the magical touch. That's encouraging."

"Does this mean the mirror in the Hall of Secrets is now active?" Dad asks.

"I believe so, Jeff." Drena covers the mirror back up. "Until we figure out how to free the souls in the jars in the other room, we should avoid this undead portal and keep it hidden."

"It also means we can venture into Scarlet Hollow in our physical forms, too," Petra answers. She moves down the long altar to one end of the edge of the mirror and stops. "Hey, I think I just found something." She tries to pick it up, but it doesn't budge. An aura around Petra begins to form.

"Um, you're glowing," I say.

She points to a closed book that is butted up against the wall under the frame of the mirror. "Perhaps this has something to do with it. I can't lift it up."

Cory comes to investigate and touches the outer gold edging of the book cover and gets zapped. "Ouch!"

"Something is wrong. I should have been able to vanish just now. At least that's what has happened in the past." Petra walks back toward the other end of the small room and looks through the shelves of books and grabs a copy. "It's not healthy for either side to voyeur for too long." She pages through the book. "It seems Maura had many detailed notes."

"What are you getting at, Petra?" Drena asks.

"That book lying on the mantle that zapped Cory a moment ago is the portal book to complete my quest, yet it's not allowing me to time travel to my next quest. Something is wrong."

"May I see, please, Petra?" Drena puts out her hand and reads. She moves to the bookshelves, next to the altar. "I think we should take these books in the next room in Maura's work area. It's the best place for me to set up a workspace."

29
FINDING GENEVIÈVE

We follow across the threshold, and what sets in front of us still leaves me in awe. The glass coffins. A blue glow from our blades illuminates the room. "Do you think they are all really alive?"

"Only one way to find out," Drena says. "These are light witch spell books. They are the ancient books that have been missing for centuries. I must find a way to free our people—family. Isalora's soul is among the jars. Which means—"

"There is hope you can bring my mother back from the dead."

"My theory is she was never truly dead, so, yes there is hope. We must match the Soul Jar with the bodies. There's one catch, though."

"Which is?" I ask.

"We need the Soul Catcher," Rory says. "Don't we?"

"We can use the one I have in my pocket, can't we?" I pull out the pouch containing the Soul Catcher.

"Is that the one Jasmine gave you?" Drena asks.

"Yes. She said we would need it."

"And she was right."

"I have another one." Petra reveals her Soul Catcher. "I'm guessing it belongs to either one of your sisters or you. "I had found it once while questing a different portal book."

"You have a Soul Catcher this whole time and didn't tell us?" Rory seems annoyed.

"To be fair, my friend, so did you. I couldn't tell any of you for fear of risking it all. The more I tell you on this timeline the higher chance it will change your future."

"Keep it. We will need it. This is fantastic. We can awaken our family in half the time now."

"I'd bet money Sarmira has another one stashed somewhere," Cole says. "How else would she be able to do all this."

"You know, I bet you're right." Drena looks back at the shelf full of souls. "And by the looks of those jars, I'm guessing Scarlet Hollow Gates have been breached. Francesca was one of the guardians." She looks at me. "And your mother. Which leads me to believe they're in Scarlet Hollow as lost souls instead of guardians.

"Drena, do you think you can safely bring back Isalora?" Dad asks.

She nods. "I think I can, yes."

"Let's get this spell started. Grab some jars and bring them back to Maura's workspace.

"Our mother is still missing." Redmae picks up her jar. "She's here among the coffins; I can feel it."

"The best way to find her is to do a locator spell. I need something personal of hers," Drena says."

"What about this?" Rory pulls from her quiver set a hanging charm. It's a bow and arrow made of copper. "They're earrings that she made as a girl. She said that her father gave them to her, and that I should have them." Rory looks at her sister and shrugs. "Redmae has the other one."

"It's true." She lifts her tunic and shows her navel. "I pierced my bellybutton with it."

Drena smiles looking at the earring in Rory's hand. "Yours should work just fine."

We set our jars down on the center table.

"Jeff, will you go back to the room where we found the books and Soul Jars and search for a candle, please?"

He and Derek take off down the hall.

While they are away, Drena begins to mix the ingredients in the mortar and pestle. "Once we have the candle, we can take the crushed herbs and sprinkle them on this saucer." She adds a bay leaf.

Dad comes rushing back. "Will this do?" He hands her a white candle.

"Perfect." She lights the wick, drips wax on the saucer, and places the candle on the melted wax. Then ties twine onto the candle. "The earring please."

Rory hands her the jewelry piece.

"Wynter, open your compass and watch closely for the direction it tells us to go. With the help from your compass and this earring we might be able to find Geneviève."

Just as Drena predicted, my compass leads us in another direction.

"It's a wall, Drena. My compass led us to a wainscoting wall."

Drena feels the wood panels. "This can't be right." She pushes on it, but it doesn't budge.

"So now what?" Rory asks. "Obviously it's a dead end." She leans against a picture hanging on a hook, and it teeters sideways. It prompts the wood panel to spontaneously pop open. "Why am I not surprised. What's a creepy haunting catacomb without secret doors."

"Who's going first?" Casey asks.

Rory huffs. "Not it."

Blair rolls her eyes. "Can't be any scarier than what we've already been through." She pushes the door open farther.

The darkness in the room lightens as we cross the threshold. A small cot with a pillow and wool blanket butts against the same wall at the entrance. "This is like a studio apartment setup. It's almost as if it was a hideaway." A swirl of blue light gleams before my eyes. "Did you see that?"

"See what?" Redmae asks. She looks over at Rory and shakes her head.

A closed green wooden door mysteriously opens behind the head of the bed.

"Now... that, I saw..." Rory says.

"Where does that lead?" I ask.

Rory shrugs and looks at everyone else. "Cole?"

"Not a clue."

"There is no draft in this room, so the chances of it opening on its own should be impossible," Drena says. She investigates by pushing the door open farther. "It's just a closet." She widens the door more, to reveal old clothing. "See?"

"Wait a minute, let me see that." Petra grabs one of the hanging items and inspects it zealously. "It can't be..." She looks at another hanging garment, and then another. "I don't believe it."

"What is it, Petra?" Derek asks.

She turns around, showing us. "These are magical garments made by Shadow Elves." Her eyes widen. "You know what this means?"

Confusion rests on all our faces.

"No, what?" Dad asks, curious.

"Whomever left these garments was a traveler like me."

"You mean a travelling mage?" Drena asks.

Blair comes to examine some of the clothes herself. "I've heard the stories about travelling mages."

"Yes, I'm one of them. One of the few left, that is." Petra hangs up the item she's holding and reaches for a hat. "Oh my!" Pulling it off the shelf, she puts it on. "This once belonged to someone very special to me." A tear falls from her cheek. She looks inside and reads the label.

The hat doesn't look like anything special. It's black and looks a lot like a beret.

Petra tucks it into her pocket. "I will return this to my friend." She sniffles and changes focus. "We should search for clues. Look through those books and see if there is any other information we can use—" The floor opens, and without warning Petra let's out a quick scream and falls through a trap door.

Rory gasps.

"Where did she go?" I come over and observe.

"She just disappeared," Rory says.

I step aside allowing Drena to investigate. She looks down at the solid wood floor and taps with her foot. "There has to be a trigger to the trap door somehow." She turns around. "Did anyone move something to prompt the opening?" She feels the inside walls of the closet. The floor opens up and Drena shrieks spontaneously as she too falls through the chute.

Dad walks to the closet and inspects the frame. "This is getting ridiculous."

Derek comes to Dad's side. "It seems we have a trap door."

"Dad, careful." While everyone is focused on the closet, a flash of blue light skates across my vision a second time.

"It's a distraction," Cory says.

"You saw it too?"

"Yes." He watches it move.

The blue light glides around the room until it lands on the spine of a book. It pulls from the shelf and crashes to the floor, startling the rest of our group.

"What was that?" Rory calls. She makes her way to the noise.

"I think I found it," Dad says ignoring the commotion behind him. There's a loud click. The closet floor opens for a

third time followed by a loud thud. Dad tries to keep from falling, attempting to grab Derek's hands, but fails. He loses his
grip and down he goes.

"Okay that's three of us gone in less than two minutes," I
say. "Let's stop and think. There is a light no one sees, a closet
door that impulsively opens, and now this book falls from a
bookcase no one is standing near. Something or someone is
trying to communicate with us." I pick up the book and blow
off the dust.

It reads:

The House of Storm

Cole comes to my side. "That looks like a grimoire."

I open the cover. The pages have gold edging and near the
bottom the name Laurawyn Storm.

"I know that name," Blair says.

"Of course you do, She's my great-great-grandmother.
Queen Sara's mother. I'm confused. Laurawyn is a Deagon,
not a Storm.

"Is there a date?" Blair asks.

The pages in the book begin to flip on their own before I
can answer. "What's going on?"

"I think we're about to find out," Redmae says.

The page lands on a brief paragraph rather than a spell. I
read aloud:

*When the year was young, and I was a
youth, I used to run along the river chasing
magic. The Fae frolicked in the meadows and the
fairies' granted wishes. Mermaids played by the*

sea and dragons protected our lands. There was no sadness or evil plaguing the lands, only love and joy. The House of Zhir and the House of Storm were one, until the day our world split in two...

For the first time our realm began to experience lust and greed. A type of magic we hadn't ever seen. It would change our lives and future generations, forever... until the Child of Darkness returns.

"Okay, so that is disturbing," Rory says. "Didn't Petra mention something about you being the Child of Darkness?"

"Not going to happen. Sarmira is not getting possession of my body." I slam the book closed. The blue light bolts out of the closed book and zips and zings about the room. "Are you guys honestly going to tell me none of you can see that?"

"I see it now," Redmae says. She turns a full circle following the ball of light as it zips around.

"Me, too," Rory adds.

The blue light bolts to the closet and the floor opens up. This time, it stays open revealing a slide beneath the hatch.

"Down the hatch I go!" Blair braves the unknown first.

"Your dad did say we're stronger together." Rory goes next, then Redmae.

"I am not letting Redmae out of my sight again, if I can help it." Casey shoots down the slide-like mechanism.

"Don't be too long, brother." Cole falls backward with a smile as though he's excited where the mystery trap door will take us.

"If you're afraid perhaps I can cast an illusion on you," Derek says.

"No need," Cory says. "We'll be right behind you."

Derek disappears into the ether of darkness.

"Guess it's just us again." Cory smiles and kisses my forehead. "We're going to get them all back, I feel it." He takes my hand. "I'll be right behind you."

"I've heard that before but somehow this time I don't trust it. Sarmira is out there. We go down together."

He wraps his arms around me and we slide in sync to the dark abyss beyond.

30

SECRET LAIR

We land butt first on a stone floor. Someone grabs my mouth to silence me before I have a chance to let out a discomfort groan. It's Redmae. She puts a finger to her lips and releases me.

Four wraiths wail and fly about a cold spacious room that is about the same size as a ballroom.

"What are they doing?" I whisper.

Blair shakes her head, and Rory shrugs.

"No idea. None of us can see anything but them," Redmae says. "Apparently neither can you."

"Stay close, I've cast another invisibility protection shield. We're safe if you don't move," Cole says.

We watch the intensity unfold as these two wraiths become agitated at something none of us can see. One wraith lashes out, carrying with them a scythe and swipes at its target. While the other wraith reaches out its fingers to touch whatever it is. "What do you think they are fighting, Redmae?"

"I don't know. I can't sense a heartbeat. So, whatever it is, isn't physically alive."

"It's the death touch," Dad says. "Remember to protect yourself with those daggers. They will protect you."

"Death touch?" I ask.

"One swipe, of that weapon—just like your dagger or Rory's arrows— it will also turn your opponent to ash. Do not allow their armament to touch you."

"Well, that's comforting," Rory says sarcastically.

We're distracted by the rising swirl of smoke. Not the blue one that led us here. This haze is different. Familiar. It funnels in and out between the wraiths with each of them attempting a stab at the entity and failing miserably. The sound of crows caw in the distance and soon a swarm of them swoop through the room. Collectively they form into someone we have seen before. Someone Petra already warned us about.

I bump her arm. "I thought you said the Crow Man doesn't like to enter the catacombs."

"He doesn't. I'm just as intrigued as you. The magic is weaker with less energy from the Blood Moon. It doesn't make any sense. He's more vulnerable inside this crypt."

I point to the window off to the side. "Unless he's getting it from there."

"A skylight." Her tone sounds irritated.

"Let's hold off and see how this plays out." Petra motions us to move back. "We'll be safer in this dark corner."

The Crow Man uses his staff and zaps wraith one, then two. It took all but a few seconds to destroy them. "Oh Maura, dear Maura, where are you hiding?"

"What did he just say?" I whisper.

Rory nudges me to stay quiet.

"Come out, come out, wherever you are. I know you do love to play that silly game." He circles the room. His staff clanks against the stone floor and the chained raven on his opposite shoulder and squawks in response. "You know you cannot hide from me. Maura, I have come for my payment."

One of the crows pulls away from his collective bird frame that forms his body shape and transforms into an old woman.

Petra gasps softly and covers her mouth, hoping they didn't hear her.

"What is it?" I look closer. "Wait, she looks like the woman we saw in the forest." I nudge Cole.

"Yes, I see."

My stomach churns.

"Raven, you said they would come." The bird on his shoulder squawks again. He focusses his attention on his feathered friend. "Yes, my sweet, patience."

"If I know one thing about that witch, she's never late," the Raven answers.

The Crow Man reaches into an outside breast pocket and pulls his watch. "She has thirty seconds before the deal is off."

"She'll be here—"

"What deal?" Maura Moyer appears behind them. "Careful, Thane. I know your weaknesses." She shimmies, moving her hips and swaying as though she is the one with the clever wit. "I do say, I didn't think you could pull it off."

"Pull what off?" Thane asks.

She smiles, looking at the old woman.

The old woman bows. "Your Majesty, he is asking for payment."

"You owe me, Maura." He sneers not at all pleased with her trickery. "Or should I say Sarmira!"

The vision of Madame Moyer fades and is replaced by Sarmira. "Oh come now, Thane, you're not still angry that I killed you? What has it been, over a thousand years or more? You know it's not healthy to hold such a long grudge."

"A thousand years of torture, you mean. We had a deal!"

Sarmira rumbles in wicked amusement. "Have you found the book yet?"

"You mean the one your daughter Petra stole from Vothule's study?"

She laughs. "How would you know?"

"I was there. I saw her do it, but instead of Vothule catching her, he caught me in the office instead. Petra stole the book and she has hidden it. Hidden it well, I might add."

"What book are they talking about?" I ask.

"The Book of Secrets," Petra answers. "It's been lost for a thousand years. I'm the reason the Hall of Secrets was destroyed and the reason for most of the portals being broken. That's why I'm here, to find one of those lost portal books."

"Which one?"

"I don't know. I never know, until I find it. Then—"

"Then you're sent to the next path to find another portal book."

"That's right."

"Find the book, and I'll connect your soul with your ashes, Thane. Nothing has changed," Sarmira continues.

He thrusts her against the wall. His power is much stronger than I anticipated. "You started this mess. I. Will. End. You." His finger turns into a blade pressing against her neck. "Give me what I have earned. You owe me."

Sarmira struggles. She can't move.

"I want what he has," I joke. Although both are clearly the enemy, I do enjoy watching her squirm. Question is, if she's a ghost-like entity, how can he have such strong power to do that to her.

"Alright!" She caves. "But you need a Soul Catcher first."

"Do you play me for a fool?"

"Your soul must connect to the Soul Catcher, and I need your ashes, to connect with your Soul Jar. But I need a Soul Catcher to do it.

"What have you done with my ashes?" he screams.

"They're back at the House of Zhir."

He releases her with a growl. "So go get them."

"I can't. I'm trapped on this earthly plane because of Isalora. Bring her back to life first."

I gasp. The noise catches them off guard.

"Did you set a trap?" He laughs. The Crow Man dissipates into thousands of crows. They sail through the room and fly in all different directions until each one is gone.

The old woman turns to face the corner where we're hiding.

"Not so fast, Raven." Sarmira freezes her with only the movement of her eyes. She circles her. "Where are they?" She releases her lips to speak.

"I am not sure what you're talking about, Your Majesty."

"I see, so you wish to suffer the same fate as your sister. Very well."

"*What is she talking about?*" A question I don't dare ask aloud.

Both Cole and Cory shrug.

Sarmira zaps the old woman, and she turns to fallen ash before our eyes. She scoops up the remains into a glass jar and seals it. A steel door opens opposite of us, and she enters. Voices and whimpers call from within. "Silence or you all will receive the same fate! Your precious Raven is dead!" She throws the jar but instead of hearing shattering glass, something, or someone snags it with a firm catching sound.

Sarmira exits and slams the steel door shut. She chants a spell and uses a wand to enforce the magic. She disappears in a puff of smoke.

"Do you think the staff and children are behind that door?" I ask.

"Most definitely," Blair says. "We need to find a way to get them out. How did she find them? We were so careful."

"I'm guessing someone, is playing both sides," Dad says.

"Perhaps it was The Raven. Sarmira just turned their secret weapon to ash."

The magic swirl of light is back. It dances in front of us like last time. "Dad, do you see that? I tried to show you last time, but you were too engrossed with the closet that led us to here."

"Yeah, I see it."

"I think we all do," Petra says.

"Do we follow it again?" I ask.

"No." Rory's eyes scowl.

"It led us to those captives behind that steel door. Something tells me it is here to help us." The light zips by my nose and sails down yet another dark corridor. "Shall we follow it?"

Blair looks at Drena. "Maybe we should."

Drena casts a protection spell. "Guess we can see where it goes."

Dad looks at me. "What does your compass say?"

I open it and look in the direction it's pointing. "Through there, the same path that the swirl of light went."

We come to a door at the end of the hall.

This time it isn't a blue glow under the cracks, it's green.

"Last time a saw a light like that, your mother was turned to dark magic, Jeff," Drena says. The concern in her eye is frightening. "Which has me thinking that behind this door is an invisible entity. And they want you to come after them."

"But what if it isn't. What if it's leading us to Geneviève?"

"Hmmm, good point, Wynter," Derek says. "Cory, do you think you can peek at what we're dealing with? You know, do that thing you're not supposed to do here on Earth?"

Cole smiles. "Oh, I know where this is going, and I like it!"

Cory appears uncertain. "To summon a Dragon Eye? Uncle—"

"Oh stop, brother, you know you want to."

"A Dragon Eye?" I ask. "Like an actual dragon's eye?"

"It's a medallion," Cole clarifies. "The name of the device

used to spy on something undetected. It's forbidden to use because it's taking from dark magic."

"Huh? I'm not sure I like the sound of that."

"Relax, it will be fine." Cole nods for his brother to move forward.

This time Cory grins. "Watch this." Like all the other times before when Cory would conjure something, he does it again and opens his palm to reveal a cabochon glass Dragon Eye. "This one is blue and black. Blue represents our eyes and the gift of seeing in the dark. The black represents darkness and the ability to be invisible to anyone."

"Like a crystal ball?" I ask.

"Similar, yes. The nice thing about these Dragon Eyes is they disappear once we see what we need."

The Dragon Eye grows into a spherical glass ball. It indeed looks like a dragon's eye.

"Just like old times," Cole grins, looking at his brother.

Cory gives the ball to Cole and he releases it. The Dragon Eye flows through the door and disappears.

"How do we see what the Dragon Eye sees?" I ask.

"Like this," Cole says. He holds out his hand and a clear crystal ball appears. All of us watch as the eye travels through the dark room on the other side.

"Well, that isn't good at all," Cole says, worried. He looks over at Rory and Redmae.

"You know this is a trap, right?" Rory says.

"Most definitely. Are you in?" Cole answers.

"Of course, I am."

Dad twists his neck until it pops. "Guess it's time to clean this place up. Ready?"

"Wait, I have an idea," Derek adds. "I can cast an illusion spell upon you but be warned it will wear off in an hour." Derek snaps his fingers and turns into Maura Moyer. "I can create illusions, remember, or did you forget?"

"Clever," Rory says.

I smile. "He's right. How could I forget. Derek did the same thing to Cory and me when we came through the library after being chased from the field the day by a pack of wolves the first time he showed me the cottage. We were trapped after hours, and Cory took his cell phone from his pocket and asked for a helping hand." I look over at Cory.

He nods. "Derek has this. And we will find the source of the negative energy pouring through this world."

Derek snaps his fingers again and instantly we're all wraith illusions. "Can't beat them, then why not look like them?"

Dad smiles. "Like Rory said, clever." Dad is the first one through the door, following the light.

31
UNDEAD BATTLE

We exit the doorway into another room. Dad, Derek, and the brothers comb every square inch.

"See anything, Wynter?" Cory asks.

"Not yet."

The swirling blue smoke flashes before our eyes and zips through the dark.

"Correction, I see the spinning flash of smoke."

"Follow me... In here," the swirl of smoke says.

Redmae grumbles. "There is a presence in here. Can you feel it, Wynter?"

"In addition to this spirit-like smoke thing fogging around us? Yes. I suspect this is another distraction."

"Agreed," Cole says.

"Can you give a sense of how many, Redmae?" Dad asks.

"Besides us? No. What I can say we're the only ones with a heartbeat. If they truly have our mother, she isn't in this room."

"So, you think it might be more spirits?" Blair asks.

"Most likely, yes," Redmae answers.

"There's movement ahead of us." Casey points.

A cold brush of air crosses over my arms. "Did anyone else feel that?"

"Yeah, I felt it," Rory confirms. "We're definitely not alone."

We inch our way farther into the dark crypt. The sounds of falling dirt and rock scatter across the ground ahead, like before when we first entered the catacombs.

"Isn't there someplace where we can light another torch or something?" Rory asks. "Your glowing blue eyes don't give much to the depth in this area."

Dad hunts for a wall lantern. "Over here." He lights them.

The dark crypt illuminates, immediately making it easier to see.

"Amazing what a little light can do, huh?" Rory smirks.

"Yeah, sure, but what isn't amazing is that." I point to a wall lined side-by-side of human skeletons encased in grout.

"Are you kidding me?" Rory stammers. "That's just... wrong."

"It was done years ago, way before you two were born," Dad answers.

"It's disgusting just the same," Rory scoffs. "And barbaric."

Now that the crypt is partially lit, I can see the ground is made of cobblestone.

"Here's another sconce," Cole says. Dad tosses him the lighter.

A sound in the distance interrupts us and we all jump.

"Wynter, can you sense anything, now?" Rory asks.

"Like seeing ghost? No. Redmae is right though, we're not alone. There is a presence here other than that swirl of blue smoke we've been following."

Redmae points with her chin. "They're down that corridor."

Several hisses echo off the confined hall. Rory stares at me.

"I don't like the sounds of that. What do you think is down there? Iknes Shaw?"

"No," I say. "Red already said we're the only heartbeats she can sense. That wouldn't make sense."

"Then her senses are off because that was a hiss of an Iknes Shaw," Cole says. "An exact sound Nora would make before engaging in a meal."

I shiver at the memories. "Apparitions in the form of Iknes Shaw, I presume."

"Great. Hungry lizard Shadow Walkers." Rory swallows hard. "Your sense of smell should have detected something, sis."

"I know. I don't like it any more than you do that I've missed something as important as that."

Rory does a full turn, scouting the darkened crypt. "Do you think it has something to do with the curse? Your loss of intuition, I mean."

"No clue, but we're going to figure it out." Redmae's throat rumbles as though she's still in wolf form. "Can't you see them, Wynter?"

"You mean ghosts? Yeah, sure if they would come out for me, *to* see them. So far, I see nothing." I keep my hand lit with fire. At least then, if I need to, I can throw a fireball.

We inch our way deeper and deeper through the underground crypt and come upon another door. Iron bars separate us.

"These are the cells where prisoners go," Dad answers. "I mean... meals. Moyer kept the food for the Shadow Walkers, and her magical meals separate. Redmae, can you sense anything now?"

"Six beings," she whispers. "They're multiplying and they're watching us."

"Six?" Dad questions.

My gut cringes. "Redmae, there are more than six, isn't there?"

"Yes, there is now, anyway. I'm sure of it. I think they're porting here."

"A druid from the dark side?"

"No, a Shadow Walker that took the talents and gifts of a druid," Cory clarifies.

"I remember hearing how Shadow Walkers take the essence of their victims for their talents," I say.

"It's true," Dad confirms. "None of us know what we are dealing with. I have a feeling whatever is beyond this gate isn't going to go down without a fight." Dad unlatches the lock and opens it.

We pass a dozen or more empty cell blocks, but what is past them leaves me in awe despite the cold eerie experience. "It's a grand room that is bigger than all the other rooms put together. It's like the size of a warehouse," I say. "I can't believe all of this is underground at Storm River Manor."

"I'm beginning to think these are beings of a different kind," Rory says. She looks at me.

"Dragons can't stay in their natural form here, Rory, remember?" Cole says. "Earth is too dense." His face changes, and he furrows his brow. "Wraiths." He pulls out his dagger and so does Cory.

"What? Where?" Rory turns. "I don't see anything."

"Redmae, what do you see this time?" Cole asks.

She grumbles. "There are four beings. That much I sense. But there are two more beings farther back. Plus the six with heartbeats."

"Lovely. What are they?" Rory asks. "A mix of some humans, spirit, vampires, and werewolves? If Wynter can't see them as ghosts, they must be mortal, right?"

"I wish I knew the answer to that, Rory," I say. "I haven't seen anything yet."

We hear Rory gasp as several glowing blue eyes appear in front of us from a far corner of the room. "This confirms we're not alone."

"Shadow Walkers, as suspected," Cole mumbles.

They come into full view.

"Who are you?" one of the vampires comes forward. "This is a restricted area."

We still have our illusions shading our real identity.

The vampire eases close. "Your eyes look familiar." He sniffs. "You smell of a vampire, and yet you are not? How is that? Unless—"

"He's onto us," Cole says. *"That illusion was short lived."*

"And you brought friends. I sense you are not who you say you are." He tests his theory. "Send in the hounds."

"So much for the illusions." Cory pulls his dagger and Cole follows.

Our façades fade.

"Well, isn't this a shocker. You should know by now Derek's illusions never worked with me, Cory."

"Can't fault us for trying."

Cory flips his blade outward, hissing. "Are you not satisfied with your last loss in the underground tunnels a few days ago? You had to come back begging for more, Oskar?"

Oskar laughs. "And I see he failed, as usual. You're still alive."

"Who is he talking about?" I ask.

"A little scuffle between vampires, Wynter. They retreated like cowards."

Cole stands beside his brother. "Ah, I get it, you missed us." He extends his blade as well, ready for battle. "I see you brought some friends of your own. You should know Storms' don't back down without leaving destruction behind."

"Just coming to finish what you couldn't, Cole. Except this time, it looks like a two for one deal." His grin widens.

Casey steps in front of them. "Three." He transforms, shocking everyone, and changes into a ghastly beast. Scarred wings riddled with charcoaled holes sprout from his back and yet he stands on four legs. A tail grows outward with spikes on the end, and he whips it forward, growling. It's almost as if Moyer had genetically modified Casey as a half wolf, half dragon, and a touch of Sabretail Prowler blood.

"Well, this is unexpected," I whisper to Cory.

"Family secrets revealed, I guess. Surprise." He half grins as though he too is shocked.

"Looks like you upset our brother," Cole says. "It's rare to see him come out." He smiles. "This is going to be so much fun."

Oskar gives a scornful grin, and sneers. "Is Casey your pet now?"

Offended, Casey enrages and makes the first move, pouncing on Oskar.

"Wrong choice of words, dude," Cole says and he, too, engages.

More Shadow Walkers join in, and soon six become twelve.

Rory begins shooting arrows as fast as she can while Cole, Cory, and Dad engage in hand-to-hand combat.

Drena cast a spell to slow the many creatures behind the battle that are ready to mob all of us, while Blair tosses small healing spells to help our bodies regenerate energy.

Redmae throws up a blast of magic herself. I half expected her to add some damage but on the contrary, I feel a boost of energy sore through my body. She smiles. "A little healing magic of my own. I can only heal others, while in battle."

"Aren't you full of surprises." I grin and throw a fireball to Oskar's back as he tries to sink his teeth into Dad's neck, which in turn, has him gunning for me. I keep firing at him one by one, but it doesn't stop him. He sails through the air, knocking me to the ground. I do my best to push him off, but he's stronger. *How is this possible?*

Right as Oskar is about to finish me off, Cory stabs him in the back with the Blade of Hope, and he dissolves into a pile of ash.

"Nice," Cole says.

Cory pulls me up, and we tag team the next opponent, but nothing we throw at them seems to stick. "Cory, I think the only thing that will work are these daggers."

"Don't forget my arrows." Rory makes a direct hit at one of the entities. It too dissolves to ash.

"You might be right, Wynter." Cole curves a devilish grin. "Hang on a second, I have a plan. Jeff, can you distract them?"

"What do you think I'm doing? Dancing for the fun of it?" He stops a blade just in time before it reaches his neck.

Drena recasts her holding spell. Every remaining enemy is stopped in their tracks. "We have approximately two minutes before this spell effect wears off. What's the plan?"

"Wynter, you distract them with your fire power while Rory shoots. We'll circle around them, and I'll can come up from behind with my dagger." Cole looks at his brothers.

Cory nods. "Let's do it."

"Once attention is drawn to me, you all circle them."

"I'll cast a slowing spell while you're at it," Drena says.

"Where do you want me?" Derek asks.

"Can you help Drena by adding more slowing power?"

"Absolutely." Derek grins. "I haven't used that spell in a long time."

"Blair, can you spot heal us?" Cole asks.

"On it."

"Pick them off, one by one," Petra says. "I like it. And for an added bonus—" Petra clasps her hands together making a loud thud...

I feel added strength enter my body. "What was that?"

She grins. "A little boost. When you get hit, not only will none of you acquire damage, but what damage you would have acquired, will return to your opponent."

"Oh, I could get used to that." Cory grins.

"Guys, a little help, please?" Rory struggles with two wraiths, coming at her fast.

"They're breaking free from my spell," Drena says. "Recasting now."

Cole leaps into the air, striking the first, and Cory impales the second. Both Shadow Walkers dissolving to dust as all the others before them. Cole put out his hand to help Rory up.

Two more wraiths appear in their place and target us. Dad swipes them both from behind which directs two more wraiths onto him. An Iknes Shaw comes out from the shadows, hissing. It's so fast that I miss a striking blow. It strikes at Dad, and he moves just in time. Rory stabs it in the back with an arrow. It doesn't stop the Iknes Shaw from approaching. Casey comes from behind, mauling the snake, but not before it bites Casey in return. He yelps and yanks the snake in two.

The two more wraiths obliterate by blows from the Blades of Hope and Trust. The boys grin.

The strategy is working.

Slowly, one by one the band of twelve become a band of none.

"Well, that was fun," I say, trying to catch a breath. I bend my head between my knees.

Casey falls to the floor.

Redmae rushes to his side. "Iknes Shaw venom."

Blair's hands hover over his wounds. "I need more energy, it's not working. I'm drained from the battle."

I join her, but the wounds remain open. "Nothing is working."

"Someone help me get him to the other room where the coffins are," Drena says. "It will be easier to heal him. I can make a salve that can temporarily halt the poison from reaching his heart.”

“His heart?” Redmae says, concerned.

“Red, it’s Iknes Shaw poison…” Blair helps Drena along with Derek.

A cackling laugh followed by a howl comes from another room.

“It isn’t over,” Dad warns. “More are coming for us.”

The blade in my hand glows blue as well as my necklace. Cole and Cory’s daggers follow suit. I push the fear down, thinking we’re about to face Sarmira once more. “Let’s get this over with.”

“Get him out of here, Jeff, we can handle this until you return,” Cole says.

He and Drena along with Blair, and Derek, move Casey out of the way of danger and back to the other room where Drena can help tend to his wounds.

Cory leads the pursuit down the hall toward the cackling evil laugh and charges through another door. “It’s time to send these soul suckers back to where they came from.”

32

THE LAST STAND

As we cross the threshold the door behind us slams shut.

"Well, that's comforting," Rory says, and pulls her arrow.

Voices in different tones laugh while others whisper.

"I knew you'd come for her. You're all so predictable, it's pathetic." Maura appears in the middle of the dark room. She slowly glides toward us. "I've been waiting for you."

Redmae snarls and pounces forward, as though she's back in her animal form. Maura's magic stops her, holding Redmae in place.

"Ah, poor pup—human. Looks like you've got yourself tangled up with the wrong crowd, my friend. The blood moon curse working just as Sarmira said it would. You're less of a threat this way. I must say I am impressed with her work indeed. She and I have been going back and forth about how to destroy each of you."

Redmae's throat rumbles more. "You don't fool any of us, Sarmira."

"Give it up. You can't hide behind my grandmother's face any longer." Fire ignites in my fingers.

"Fool you?" She laughs. "I'm not here to fool any of you. Don't you know luring my prey is a talent?" She steps closer to us. "Whatever shall we do with you." She glides to the side as though checking out her opponents.

"It's over, Sarmira." The fire within me grows, traveling through my veins. I can feel the scales begin to surface. Flames shoot from the tips of my fingers in the other hand.

"How precious is it you think you can defeat me, Wynter." She chuckles. "Seriously, what do you take me for? I made you who you are."

"Lies!" I throw a fireball and miss.

Rory attempts to pierce Maura, but she turns just in time preventing herself from being impaled. "Oh Rory, that was a deadly mistake." Maura releases Redmae, and fires with a magical fireball force of her own, slamming Rory against the wall, knocking her unconscious. "Anyone else care to make such bold moves? I admit I didn't see that one coming." She laughs louder, taunting us. "Come now, there are six of you—" She looks over at Rory. "Well, five, but who's counting. There is just little ol' me. Surely, you can do better than that?"

"You're going to regret that, Sarmira!" I shout, clenching my teeth. A fireball forms in my palm again.

"My dear, can you not see, or are you blind? Do I look like Sarmira to you? Ah, ah ah." She waves her index finger. "I wouldn't do that if I were you."

"So, what now? Can you read her mind, Cory?"

He nods. *"Sort of."*

Cole seems to catch on to whatever his brother has planned.

Petra seems to catch on, too.

"She's a hologram," Cory says. *"Can you see through her, like I can?"*

I stare into my grandmother's stolen face. She doesn't get uncomfortable like most people would. *"She's solid looking to me, but there is something off, about her. How can she wield powers if she' projecting?"*

"Because she's not alone. Someone is doing it for her."

"Distraction. That's what we need to do," I whisper to Redmae. "She's projecting."

"If that's true then her body is vulnerable," Redmae says, softly.

"What are you two whispering about?" Fake Maura swings forward and we dart out of her way.

Cole distracts her. "Too slow, Joe. I mean Maura." He laughs at his own joke.

Maura isn't pleased.

Cole attempts to stab her, knowing full well she's not real.

She flinches like a loose wire connection on a television and disappears.

"The closer they are to their body the more powerful they are. Which tells me she must be somewhere in here with us," Redmae adds.

"I get it now," I say. "That's why I had such a hard time finding my way back to my body—my energies were focusing on projection."

"Good observation, Wynter." Redmae spins in a full circle searching for Maura to pop up. "Something tells me Maura hasn't caught on that we know about this."

"Let's keep it that way." Redmae eyes her sister who is still unconscious. "We need to drain Maura's energy. That way when we do find her true body, she will be weaker."

"Where do you think she went?" Cole asks.

"Back to Scarlet Hollow would be nice," Petra mumbles. She goes to Rory and checks on her. "She's out cold, but alive."

Two wraiths appear on either side of Petra.

I fling a magic fireball at them. "Watch out!" The wraiths fade before I can land a hit. Petra flings her cloak about herself and Rory to protect them from my fire.

"Wynter, something tells me it's not a good idea to miss," Cory says.

"Ya think?" I draw my hand back, rethinking my brash reflexes.

The wraiths reappear behind Cory.

Cole leaps forward and slashes them both with the Blade of Truth. They dissolve to ash.

Four more apparitions take their place.

"Not this again." Redmae stands in front of us as though she's going to charge them.

"You do realize you're not a wolf, right?" I form another fireball behind my back.

"Of course, I do." She forms a bubble around us. "Don't move."

"When were you going to let us in on your secret, Red?" Cole asks.

"Not something a wolf pack shares too candidly. Honestly, I didn't know if it was going to work. It's an invisible shield that is supposed to lower the aggression of my opponent. I usually only cast it if I'm trying to get away. My mother taught us long ago to use it if we ever came across danger that was too much for us to handle."

"Which means..." Cole looks at the wraiths waiting for us to make the first move. "You think we're about to bite off more than we can chew."

"Precisely. We need to find out where Maura's physical body is. Otherwise, we will just be spinning our wheels while she wears us down."

"Agreed," Cory says. "You two go find her, we can play tag team with the undead creatures. We need to stop her, she's the source of this, curse. I feel it," he says.

I'll stay with them," Petra says. "These wraiths are not easy to fight but be quick about it."

I smile. "You read my mind."

"I think we all know the assignment." She winks.

The wraiths multiply once more, to eight entities.

"This is going to be fun." She pulls from her cape a wand hidden from an inside pocket. "Pure onyx. The gold you see laced throughout is exactly that." She whispers in a language I don't understand, and it lights up in response.

Stunned I say, "What is—"

"I'll tell you later." She points it toward the wraiths, and they are encircled in a white powder.

"Salt?"

"Not just any salt. Ethereal crystal salt that comes from the crescent mountains on Elleirodal."

"I didn't know such a thing existed."

"Wynter, let's go!" Redmae hides behind stacked wine barrels, gesturing me to come to her.

Behind me Rory moans. "I'm coming with you." She rubs her head and tries to stand.

"You're awake!"

"Hurry up! This salt won't last long," Petra calls out.

"Awake and ready." She grabs her gear. "Let's find this witch."

"Do I sense a little hostility?" I tease.

She grunts, pushing past me. "Are you coming, or not?" She sprints over to where her sister hides.

Redmae and I look at each other and grin.

Maura appears again right as I move behind the wine barrel. "Where did your friends go?"

The three of us hide in the shadows against the wall behind her.

"Looks like you've been abandoned. Guess they know when you're all outnumbered."

Maura blasts a powerful spell toward the boys.

"Nice try, witch!" Petra slows down her magic, giving ample time for them to dart out of the way.

"Quick, let's get out of here. They can handle this. We need to find where Maura is meditating," I say.

"Where do we look first?" Rory asks.

"This way," Redmae says.

We come up on a door that reflects green light between it and the floor.

I nudge Rory. "You see that?"

"Yes."

"We need to be careful not to alert her," Redmae says. "She's tricky." She points to the right. "You and Rory go that way, I will go this way."

A loud crash comes from the other room where the rest of our team are fighting. Redmae takes that opportunity to push the door open further, avoiding a creaking sound. *Clever wolf.*

We quickly hide behind a shelf storing more empty glass jars. Peeking through the gaps, Rory and I observe Maura cross-legged on the floor at the opposite corner. Her palms are up with her fingers and thumbs clutched together. "She's meditating, projecting, just as I suspected."

"Which is a perfect opportunity to blast her with my arrow right now." Rory takes aim.

A blaring crash from the other room warns us that we might be on borrowed time. Moans, grunts, and shrieks of pain follow.

Rory fires a shot.

Maura tilts her head to the side with an unnatural jerk.

Rory misses. Maura lets out a laugh. She looks straight at us with her eyes glazed over like a blind woman. "I knew you would find me." She stares at us as if to compel.

"Don't look at her eyes." Redmae tucks and rolls pushing us from Maura's attempted trance.

Maura screeches like a banshee and comes at us with full force, knocking Redmae off her feet.

Something isn't adding up.

I blast her with ice, barely touching her fingertips.

Maura flicks her wrist in pain. "Nice sting. I see you're improving."

The crackling of ice tells me I still connected with her. "Not so fast, Sarmira!"

She enrages more. "I'm not Sarmira!" Maura blasts her famous sonic blast knocking all of us back. I hit my head hard and blood runs down the side of my face.

I manage to get one last freeze off aiming for her chest before everything goes black like before in the war room.

33

A DARK TURN

"Wynter, wake up! We got her!" Rory pats my cheek. "Please wake up."

The pain in my skull pulsates. I touch my head. "Ouch."

Cory, Cole, and Petra come running.

"Ah, Cory, is that you? I see you escaped your cage."

Cory growls and his veins bulge from anger but seeing me on the ground distracts him. "Hey, you, okay?"

"I'm fine... I think." I take his hand as he pulls me to my feet. I glance at Maura to see I succeeded in encasing her entire body in ice, except her head.

"Sarmira! At last we meet again," Petra says. "I did warn you that you would soon face the error of your ways."

"How many times must I say, I. Am. Not. Sarmira!"

Somehow, I am thinking that Petra has more business than just finding the portal book, but unfinished business with Sarmira.

"And we're supposed to believe you?" Cole crosses his arms over his chest.

"Where is it?" Petra seethes. "You have had plenty of time. I told you the consequences would be massive if you did not adhere to your end of the deal."

What deal? I nudge Redmae. "What is she talking about?"

She shakes her head.

"Shall I tell the others of your plans?" Petra pulls from her cloak the wand we saw her use earlier. She chants as she points her wand at Maura's head. The gold letters on the wand light up.

Maura laughs and breaks free, shards of ice scatter.

Petra again uses her own cloak to shield us, while the boys dart out of the way from being impaled.

Maura casts a shield of her own separating us from her. "I'm not so easily fooled this time."

Redmae and I step forward.

Rory touches the invisible barrier. A sizzle sound reacts to her fingers, and she flinches. "Ouch."

"Pathetic little heathens. You will not escape my curse." She laughs more, enjoying the mockery. Her eyes move to me. "Did you find Dragonscale? I know where he is, of course."

I grumble at her taunting. "You escaped me last time, but you're not getting a second chance."

"Oh really? I mean it seems you would have to break my shield to do that."

"Where is he?" I demand.

"And my mother!" Rory takes aim.

"Rory, go get the others," Redmae mutters.

Maura isn't pleased. I can tell by her expression she liked it being just us. "He's safe and sound," she says. The tone in her voice tells me there is some slight fear, knowing Petra's leading this battle.

"Right. I want proof." I form a fireball.

"Enough of the games, Maura," Cole calls out. "Where are Dragonscale and the others?"

"Finally, someone calling me by my given name!" She

smiles. "I'll bring you to your precious Dragonscale and lift your curse at the same time, but it will cost you a trade."

"What trade?"

Maura pulls from her waist a crystal globe and puts it near our divided line to show us. The world looks distant. A lot of red clouds, and the mountains are of the same color. The globe takes us to the inside where in a large deep dark cave, he lies on a stone floor chained to a wall. It looks like a dungeon.

"Crimson Moors," I say.

Maura snatches the globe away. "Yes. Deep in Bloodbane territory."

"She's lying. I sense it's a ruse," Redmae whispers.

"I'll take you to him," Maura says, interrupting.

"What's that supposed to mean?"

She shrugs. "Nothing. My life for Dragonscale."

"Huh?" we all say at once.

I squint. "We're not easily fooled by your trickery anymore, Sarmira/Moyer/whomever you are."

She snickers. "All of you are fools."

Dad and Derek come running in, followed by Blair, Drena, and Casey.

"I take it Drena slowed the poisonous bite?" I ask.

"For now, only temporary though." Drena casts a quick shield separating Maura from us.

"Ah, good, the whole family is here," Maura revels. "A reunion of sorts. How lovely."

"She says Dragonscale is locked away in a cave near the Crimson Moors." I look at the wicked witch. "Where exactly is he? I want exact coordinates."

She groans, irritated by my calm manner.

"I brought you here on purpose Don't you see? I knew you would come. Bringing upon the curse was the only way I would get all of you to seriously listen."

"And we're supposed to believe you, why?" I ask.

"You need to kill me, but it must be with the Blades of Hope, Trust, and Peace or it will not work."

"What won't work?" Dad asks dubiously. He laughs she the stupidity.

"The curse won't break. And magic will remain weakened, until it disappears forever. You all must know by killing me, the curse will be lifted, right?"

"Somehow I believe there is an ulterior move coming," Dad replies.

"I told you. You must kill me. Sarmira cast the spell, used me as her subject, like she does with anyone that comes upon her path, and—" She looks directly at me. "Like your mother, death broke the spell, trapping Sarmira on Earth's dense plane."

"Let's say for a split second you're not Sarmira possessing Maura's body. What exactly are you getting at? We all know Sarmira has taken over Maura's soul." Dad's tone shows he's annoyed.

"The dragon blood does run through your veins, does it not?" She pauses as though to carefully choose her words. "Your ancestry follows many lines, one to the Deagons, one to the Storms, and one to the Ashburns. You, my dear, are a very rare breed indeed."

"What does this have to do with the other? Why volunteer your life as sacrifice? How do we know this isn't another one of your tricks? Like Jeff said," Cory says. "We don't trust you, Maura."

"I imagine not, but you really have no other choice. You want the curse broken, and I want death."

"That sounds a little morbid if you ask me," I say.

Redmae elbows me. "She is lying. She's not telling the entire truth."

"I can't penetrate her mind," Cole says. *"I think she's a clone."*

"Put the Soul Catcher to her face." Cory says. *"I'm going off a hunch here. Clones are soulless, which means a Soul Catcher cannot catch their soul—"*

"Therefore, they would be immune to its power," I add.

"Exactly."

I look at Petra as I move my hand to the inside pocket of my jacket. She nods. *Good, we're on the same page.*

"Believe what you want. I cannot do it myself. It must be by the daggers, and Sarmira tripled down by making it all three," Maura continues.

I get that she 'thinks' she needs to somehow sacrifice her soul, but why. "This is a trap."

Blair glares. "You're not fooling anyone. I've lived around you long enough to know you're not the real Maura—I mean Sarmira."

Maura smiles. "A trap for us all."

She rushes forward and I whip out the Soul Catcher, forcing it in her face, and when there is no reaction, Cole stabs her with a switchblade instead, in the back. "This time there will be no shattered glass shards."

Maura stumbles forward and falls to her knees slowly melting into green liquid, oozing into the cracks between the grouted stone blocks.

A swirl of dust kicks up in its place. "I knew she couldn't pull it off. I warned Sarmira it wouldn't work." Lira appears in Maura's place. "If I want something done, I guess I need to do it myself! You won't win this, Wynter, I assure you of that."

Casey doesn't waste any time, and still in his half wolf/monster/whatever he is form, pounces, slashing at Lira's left shoulder.

She shrieks. Pulling Casey off, she takes a stab at him, injuring his jaw and Casey falls to the floor in pain. "I told you, you will not win this battle. I'm too strong for any of you. Even your pathetic beast."

"We're not using our weapons on you, either, Lira."

"Oh, come on, Cole, I'd be an easy kill, and you know it."

"Yeah, and that's just it. This is too easy." Cory pulls back and tucks his blade back in the sheath.

She appears annoyed by his actions.

"How do we know that you're not Sarmira in disguise?" Rory says, Steadying her bow and arrow. "Or a clone."

That's a good point. I hadn't thought about that.

Cole puts his palm to his ear. "What's that? I didn't hear a response. Cat got your tongue?"

"Revenge is such a sweet thing." Cory stands next to him. "We're not going to do it your way, Lira. We're doing it ours. I knew this whole charade was a bogus from the start."

I can read between the lines. It's a distraction. Quietly I prepare my ball of ice, this time I will not miss. I take Lira by surprise and blast her, encasing her body up to the neck in ice, like I did Maura. "I feel a bit of déjà vu coming on." I place my index finger to my lips. "Now where have I seen this before? Oh right, just before you nearly killed me—in the War Room."

"That was unintentional," she says.

"Was it now?" I look over at Dad. He says nothing.

Lira is now frozen solid from head to toe. This time I reinforced it with double the ice. "Something that may help in our quest for answers." I inch up to Lira's face, nose to nose. "You see, one thing about dires is they can sense when someone is lying." Redmae growls, still in her human form. "Here that? I'm sure you have heard about the silver dire wolves. And I'm about done with the games. Do you still have your conjuring skills, Cory? It appears Lira isn't going to talk."

He nods. "What do you have in mind?"

"Perhaps something to make ice cubes with?" I sense Lira flinch.

He smiles. "You got it." He proceeds to magically provide a sledgehammer of my liking. "Is this what you had in mind?"

I curve an evil grin, clicking my tongue. "You know me well, my love. I need a therapeutic release about now." I can sense Lira cringing at the sound of the hammer grinding across the floor, with each step Cory takes, bringing me my weapon of choice.

"Wait. You don't want to kill me, you need me. I told you where Dragonscale is."

I come close to her ear. "I don't know what kind of ruse you're trying to pull, and I don't buy it. But then you decided to play with our heads by cloning Maura. I see the games you're trying to pull and I'm not playing them." I pace the floor. "If I didn't know any better, I would say you want to die so you can thwart plans the light witches are working on in the spiritual world." I look her straight in the eyes. "Am I close?"

"How do you know about that?" Lira's brows sweats.

I'm close. "Oh, you see, I figured that out when I went to Scarlet Hollow. I saw things, heard things..." I pull out the dagger. "Funny thing about this blade—once you hold it in your fingers and absorb the power it holds, the voices within the blade of the souls it killed, sing like songbirds, and tell stories of their own."

Lira's eye dart from me to the boys. I don't think she was expecting that answer.

"Wait, Wynter, she'll talk. Trust me." Petra's wand brightens. "Thaw her body."

"But—"

"Trust me, she isn't going anywhere." Petra points the wand to Lira's throat.

"If I recall correctly, my mother banished you to the planet Xanterra." She inches the wand close to Lira's throat. "I remember you now."

"And you're alive," Lira counters. "I see my advice worked." She looks at Derek.

Petra grunts. "Oh, you mean have me fake my death? Yes

well, you see how that turned out, don't you? Your trickery won't work with me anymore, Lira. You've stabbed too many people in the backs, including family."

Lira gasps for breath.

"Oh, this is going to be so fun," Petra adds. "I haven't gotten to play the villain in so long. I mean, when someone messes with family there is only a certain level one can take. This is my family, and you have taken quite more than your share."

Lira grabs her throat. "Ca—" she struggles. "Breathe—"

"You see, dark witch, I found my calling, my purpose, and when I figured out how to use this wand you so conveniently gave me, I learned to wield it. What you intended for my demise, turned out to be for my good. I didn't die that day—" She steps closer. "As you are well aware, seeing as I am not... dead. This wand chose me, therefore you couldn't use it for the purpose you had intended to. It wasn't your wand to give."

Petra tilts her neck, popping the stress points. "Haven't you heard the saying fool me once shame on you..." She steps closer, lowering her tone to barely a whisper. "But fool me twice, shame on me."

I swear I saw Lira shiver. I look at Drena and smile.

Lira falls to the floor unconscious.

The shield barrier fades.

"You killed her," Cole says.

"No, she's in a deep sleep." She winks at Cole. "I kill in silence, when no one is looking." She kneels to check Lira's breath. Whispers something in her ear, and says, "You are going to a place far, far away, where you can't hurt anyone again." Pulling a mirror from her pocket, she places it above Lira's face and chants more words in another language, and Lira's body disappears into the device.

I smile knowing Petra read my mind, even though she isn't telepathic like me.

"She isn't going to be bothering anyone anymore," Petra says. She stands. "Now, if we can get Sarmira into this we'll be in business."

"She really did a number on us all," Cole says.

"'She' meaning Lira or Sarmira? They're both evil," Rory says.

In this moment the blue swirl of smoke like light appears once more. We all stare at each other. "I'm beginning to think whatever this haze that keeps appearing randomly is on our side."

"Agreed," Dad says.

The light guides us through the catacombs until it stops to show us another empty room. "Nothing out of the ordinary in here," Dad says.

The blue swirl slams into a wall in front of us and fades away. "That was strange."

The force of the energy it gave off pushes dust and debris down to the ground, leaving small pin size holes.

"What do we have here?" Dad swipes at the grout with his fingers. "Something is behind here."

Dad uses his glowing eyes to his advantage to investigate. He takes a pocketknife and scrapes the grout more. It crumbles easily. So easily in fact that he's able to pull the stone out of the wall. When he does, a stone door pops ajar. "What is this?"

All of us are stunned. I hold Dad back by the pinch of his sleeve. "What if it's a trap?"

He scoffs. "As opposed to the others we've encountered? Are you telling me you're not the least bit curious?" He pushes the hidden door open more. "It's safe, I'm sure."

We all gasp. Inside is money, jewels, and... "Coffers."

Dad reaches for the first one, turns to me and the others.

"Is that—" My eyes glisten. "The swirl of blue light led us to them."

"It's Queen Sara and King Ailbert's hearts," Dad says. He

turns around and assesses the room a little more. "Look. There is another coffin behind you, a few feet away."

We gather around one more glass coffin.

"And to think her real body has been here the whole time," Rory says. "Perhaps our theory of her being a clone was true after all?"

Cory comes over to peek. "I must admit, it makes sense why she didn't seem to be affected by the chaos when we were fighting upon these grounds a week ago..."

"You mean hours ago, according to Drena. The time shift, remember?" Rory reminds us.

"Right, yeah, that..." Cory agrees.

Maura Moyer lies motionless. Her resting face looks much younger than what I am used to seeing. Not a gray hair in sight. Her complexion appears soft. I touch her skin expecting to feel flesh. "It's stone cold, like porcelain."

Drena comes from behind my shoulder. "She's in a cocoon-like state. They all are." Drena turns to the next coffin and touches the body inside. "This one has the same markers. They're *still* alive."

"How can, you be sure?" Derek asks.

"They would have decomposed. This is dark magic at its finest I am afraid. If I'm not mistaken, Sarmira figured out how to preserve the body, separate the soul, and steal their magic for her own."

The swirl of smoke hovers over Maura's body. "Guys, I think this is Maura Moyer's spirit."

"I think you're right, Wynter. This blue swirl is probably on our side. Question is, why can you not see her?" Dad asks.

"Maybe we will have some answers soon, Dad." I tilt my head against his shoulder. Something inside me knows this is my grandmother soul, and she led us straight to her body.

"Rory, Redmae, come look at this." Blair kneels next to another glass coffin around the corner.

The person sleeping inside has us all dropping our jaws.

Rory comes over. "Mom." She places her hand on the lid. "Redmae, it's our mom."

"She looks so peaceful," Blair says.

Drena races out of the room.

"Where are you going?" Blair asks.

"Back to the lab. It's time we raise our own army."

34
PERFECT TIMING

Drena set down on the herbal table the book I gave her and glances at the recipe. Maura's Soul Jar sets in the center. "I need a little more light, please."

Cole comes to her side, and she takes advantage of his glowing blue eyes. The glowing green jar filled with Maura's name on it brightens, and the swirling blue smoke that has guided us throughout the catacomb tunnels hovers above us as though waiting in anticipation.

"I'll look for more sconces," Derek says.

"I'll look with you," Dad says. "My eyes might help in your search."

Cory comes to Drena's other side to light the room a bit more as she reads the ingredient list. "Any luck in communication with our ghostly friend watching us?"

"No, not a whisper," I say. "Do you think it knows what is happening?"

"I don't know." Drena collects the ingredients and adds them to the mortar and pestle. "I had first imagined the souls in these jars had no clue what has happened to them, except now I'm rethinking that observation by the reaction we're getting from our ethereal friend here." She looks up at the hazy smoke-like figure.

"You think it's Maura's spirit too, don't you," I say.

"It's quickly becoming rather likely." She adds lavender oil to her mixture.

"Perhaps they think their dreaming, or perhaps when they all wake, they won't know how much time has passed," Blair adds.

"Only time will tell. We can ask Maura when she wakes." She crushes the leaves along with a few other herbs and then adds boiling water she already had ready. "Have you girls done your homework?"

"Yes, we have," Rory and I say at the same time.

Rory clears her throat. "We have read all the literature. We're ready."

"Very well." Drena scoops a teaspoon of her concoction into a tincture bottle with a dropper lid. "It's almost ready."

"Do you think it will break the curse?" I ask.

"Only way we will know that is to wait for Maura to wake. Will you girls go to Maura's coffin and open the lid please. This recipe won't take long."

"You work fast," Blair says.

Drena smiles. "Most of the remedy is in the Waxlily. I must warn you though, Maura and the others will have added abilities after this." She looks straight at Dad. "Her rising will bring Sarmira right to us, as well. Be prepared."

That sends a chill down my spine.

"Do you think she will wake quickly?" Cole asks.

"I don't know." Drena tightens the tincture lids and follows us to the lower level of the catacombs where we also found Geneviève.

"For them, it will come with side effects at first," Drena warns. "However, they will be stronger than most of us because they have been sleeping for decades, if not centuries."

It takes Rory, Redmae, and I together to lift the heavy lid where Maura sleeps.

Drena inspects her patient's eyes, mouth, and ears. "I had a feeling after I saw all the coffins earlier before Cole opened the door to that other room, we may need this." She pulls out a water bottle. "I never go anywhere without it." She pours a small amount of fresh water into a cup and two drops from her tincture concoction. "Blair, the jar please."

She places it on a wine barrel the boys rolled in from the other room so that Drena could have adequate space to work her 'magic.'

The smokey haze has followed us to Maura's coffin.

"Petra, have the Soul Catcher ready, please."

"It's within my grasp." Petra hides it behind her cloak.

Drena glances at all of us. "Here is the tricky part. It's all about timing. We only have one chance to get it right. Remember do not look at the Soul Catcher when Petra pulls it from her cloak. I want all of you to see how this delicate procedure is done. This way you can learn how to do it, and we can wake all of them in half the amount of time. We haven't much darkness left to perform this spell. We must awaken them all before the moon goes down otherwise they will remain sleeping until the next Super Blue Blood Moon."

Rory and I nod.

"Petra will hold the Soul Catcher above Maura's head right as I drop the antidote into her mouth. I repeat, do not look in the mirror."

"Are you sure this will work?" Blair asks.

"Yes," Petra answers. "I have seen it done many times."

Many times?

Drena smiles. "Hold steady. Everyone ready?"

She looks at Petra sternly. "Whatever you do, do not let go of it. This Soul Catcher has a strong pull—"

"I know, Drena," she counters.

Drena glances at each of us once more. "And please, for the love of Ladorielle, do not look into the reflection."

"Yes, we know!" Dad raises his voice.

"I recommend everyone else closing your eyes or looking away, less of a chance that you will get sucked in yourself."

Her comments make me nervous.

"Blair, loosens the lid of the Soul Jar, leaving it intact, and hands it to Rory slowly." Drena sucks up the tincture liquid in the dropper. "All together at once. Ready?"

We nod in unison.

I hold up the casket lid to keep it from falling with Cole and Cory's help.

Petra carefully places the Soul Catcher over the opening of Maura's mouth. "Ready for the droplet."

Rory lifts the lid off the Soul Jar.

A bright light gleams from the Soul Catcher along with a screeching sound.

"What is that?" I ask.

"It's the sound of a tormented soul that has been in that jar entirely too long," Drena says. She squeezes one drop of tincture liquid into Maura's mouth.

"I'd hate to experience this with the others that have been in there for an eternity," Derek says.

"It's something we will need to prepare for, indeed," Drena agrees.

The screeching subsides quickly as the soul passes through the Soul Catcher and is pulled into Maura. The rise and fall of her chest confirms success.

The swirl of blue smoke stays. *Nothing is happening.*

"I don't think it worked, Drena." I watch as steam emits through the garments of Maura's body. "Something is wrong. Look."

Drena gasps. "This is a clone! How did I not catch this before performing the spell?"

"Do you think Geneviève is as well?" Rory asks.

"No, she would have done the same as this body just did, dissolve. Be on guard. We have just opened a beacon to our location."

WICKED LAUGHTER ECHOES THROUGH THE corridors.

"She's back!" Dad sneers.

"She's toying with us," Cole says.

"We still need to awaken the others." Drena's hands shake nervously as she tucks the water bottle and jar of elixir back in her pockets. "I must return to the other sleeping bodies and perform the rituals before the Blood Moon rests, else we will have to wait another thousand years."

"Leaving you alone doesn't sound like a good idea," Rory argues. "Besides, what about our mother? She is still asleep."

"What choice do we have?" Drena gathers the rest of her necessary ingredients. "Your mother will be safe for now. I must return to the other sleeping bodies."

"I'm not leaving her," Rory says.

"She has a point," Cory says. "If Geneviève wakes with no one around she will be vulnerable. Cole, you go with her. I'll stay with Wynter. We can communicate with our minds if we need help. Derek is good with illusions, and you have a cloaking ability that can hide all of them, should you need it."

Derek nods. "We will need a Soul Catcher."

"Take mine," I say.

"I'll go with my mother. She will need help with the awakening," Blair says. "How are you holding up, Casey? Redmae and the others will need you at full strength."

"The medicine is doing its job. I'll be fine," Casey says. "We have no choice but to split up. Resurrecting Wynter's mother is important. We need her."

A rush of air passes by, and I sense a cold chill. Swishes sounding like rustling leaves scrape against the floor, only I know that's not possible.

Derek immediately cloaks him and his group. "I feel another trap coming."

"Go, we've got this," Dad says.

Two wraiths charge forward, screeching.

"Get ready for another round, guys!" Dad pulls his sword. He swipes at them both in one swift move and they disappear. "That was too easy. Show yourself, you miserable witch." Dad turns a full circle, and we're all thrust off our feet from Sarmira's powerful magic blast.

She allows herself to be seen once more. Her body has changed to a wraith with two distinctions; blood red fingernails peek out from under her sleeves, and she is in physical form. Yellowish brown jagged teeth, hollow black eyes, and a bone skull face, sends a haunting chill down my spine. She isn't any beauty queen like when she revealed her true self in my dream stamp nightmare. "It appears Cory and Cole have found the Blade of Hope and the Blade of Truth."

Dad grunts, realizing Cole is still here.

"*You were supposed to leave with Drena,*" Cory says.

"*Derek is with her. He can cast illusions to hide should he need to.*" Cole pulls his dagger. "*Besides I'm not missing out on this.*"

Cory side-eyes his brother.

Sarmira turns her gaze onto me. "Just one final step before I will consume all of your souls. You must claim the Blade of Peace, Wynter."

"*I don't think she knows I have my dagger, guys.*"

"*Good. I always love the element of surprise.*" Cole moves opposite of Cory and me. "*Keep your dagger hidden for now.*"

"You won't take my soul. Or theirs." Fire grows again in my hand. "Where's your body, Sarmira? Did you get tired of your old look?"

Sarmira tilts her head. She coos. "I'm looking at it."

"If you think you're going to acquire my soul that easily, try again." Hastily I throw my fireball and miss. Quickly, I draw ice in my other hand.

"Oh, I see." Her calm and cool nature purrs spiteful venom. "So, because you can finally use magic in both hands, suddenly you're a pro. Impressive. Let's see how you play with the adults in the room." She throws the first punch, spinning electric bolts throughout the crypt, forcing us to take cover.

I jump out of the way, diving to the floor while Rory takes a shot at her and misses.

"Awe, how sweet. You're like a toddler trying to fight back. You can't defeat me, Wynter. You're just like your mother. She, too, tried to kill me—unsuccessfully, I might add." She glides vigorously around making it difficult for us to latch onto her. "Isalora pleaded for her life right before I ripped her heart from her body." Sarmira lunges forward, missing me.

The unexpected charge thrusts me on my rear.

Her wicked laugh calls out once more. "Here you go, as promised, Thane." She disappears.

"I knew it was a trap," Cory says.

"Where did she go?" Cole asks.

"She'll be back. A little scuffle isn't going to keep her away that easy," Petra says. "Something tells me she's projecting from someplace else, just like Maura's clone did."

"That's a great theory," Casey says.

Winds pick up in the confined room with a swirl of a thousand black birds or more behind us.

"Crows," Petra says. "Here we go again."

The Crow Man appears as a collection of birds. His form not as solid as outside and the birds sway and move about his frame, keeping in sync with his movement as he walks about in a feather-like profile. "Well, this is going to be easier than I thought," he says. He physically charges forward toward Petra. "Finally, I can bring you home!"

Petra uses her wand to zap the Crow Man, freezing him in place. All of the crows that make up his silhouette also freeze in place. Icicles form off his nose, ears, and chin. Frost lines trace the feathers coating each bird within his structure. "I have a few tricks up my sleeve as well, Thane. And my reflexes are much quicker than yours." She smiles. "You didn't see that coming, now did you? Skills are like fine wine. Looks like mine have aged gracefully." Anger fills her eyes, but her composure remains calm.

Ice thickens around him and his precious birds.

She can freeze creatures like me? That's interesting.

Petra clears her throat. "You're a little too cold for my liking. Thank you." She pulls from her pocket a Soul Catcher and shines it at the Crow Man. "It's time you go back to where you came from."

His eyes glaze over knowing what comes next, and just as quickly as he appeared, he disappears into the void along with the thousands of crows he brought with him.

"Well, aren't you full of surprises?" Cory says. "I was expecting a little more action."

"My, are we spoiled, Cole?" Petra tucks her wand away. "I knew it was only a matter of time before he showed up again."

We see Drena, Derek, and Blair follow back in the room.

"We're fine," Cole says before either of them asks. "Petra is a sneaky traveling mage. I'll give her that. Better skills than she leads on."

"I couldn't let you all have the fun." She places the Soul Catcher back in her pocket. "He shouldn't be bothering us for a long time. This device will send him back to Scarlet Hollow."

"I managed to bring back two more people from a deep

sleep while you were battling more enemies. It shouldn't be long before they wake up," Drena says.

A gasping sound comes from the hidden room where we found Geneviève and the clone, Maura.

Redmae gets to the chamber first.

Geneviève sits up, her older daughter helping her stand.

"Mom?" Rory says. The hope in her voice is reassuring and she runs over to her. "We were so worried about you. How do you feel?"

"Fine... I think?" She rubs her head. "I have a little headache."

"Do you remember anything?" Cole asks.

"I don't know. The last place I remember is porting out of the cabin." She stops and looks around. "How did I end up in the catacombs?"

"Great question," Dad answers. "We don't know.

"It's a long story, Mom," Rory says. "What matters is you're alive." She hugs her again.

"Okay, my turn," Geneviève says. "I found Aoes and the others."

35

FAMILY RETRIBUTION

It doesn't take but a few minutes to brief Geneviève.

"We're so glad you're back," Dad says. "I think this plan will work out perfectly."

Casey and Redmae stay with Geneviève, while she gathers her strength and the rest of us go back to the other room where our family rests, where Drena reveals the two family members she resurrected.

As soon as I cross into Maura's apartment-like quarters, my eyes well up in tears. "Aunt Fran? Please tell me I'm not dreaming, because if I am I do not want to wake up."

She pulls her red wavy hair away from her face. "It's me. I'm back in my body."

"But how— I mean, your heart was in a coffer—"

Aunt Fran looks at my dad. "Jeff had the coffer in his possession, apparently."

"Dad?"

"I didn't know who to trust, and with the destruction of Ashengale, Nyta slipped me the container. We already had a strong feeling this crypt existed because of the briefing Drena gave when she and Derek came to the Hall of Secrets. We had no idea the catastrophe that would follow. We had planned to come back here anyway. And thanks to Petra, we've managed to put a wrinkle in the timeline."

I hug Aunt Fran. "There is so much I want to know."

"Me, too." She laughs. "But we have a lot of work to do, still. How long have I been out?"

"A few weeks, but what you might find a little odd is all the other members of our family are lying in coffins like you were."

She raises a brow. "Intriguing."

"Something even more intriguing is in the other room," Drena adds.

"Oh?" Geneviève wrinkles her forehead.

"Yes," Drena goes on. "Something I predict you haven't seen in years."

She makes her way to the other room, and we follow.

Geneviève goes to it and gazes at her reflection in the Mirror of Souls. "Does it work?" She glances quickly at Drena.

"Yes, and we have already spoken with the keeper of the Crystal Cave," she answers. "Can you tell us anything about it? I know you and Maura had an encounter with it as teens."

"We did, indeed." Geneviève stays quiet for a few minutes before answering. "I thought I had those memories buried years ago." A tear falls from her cheek. "My father—" she drifts off and doesn't finish her thoughts.

"Your father?" Cory asks. "You have never mentioned him before."

"A memory I had long forgotten." She turns to face us. "You must cover this mirror. Souls from the other side can possess you."

Her words are concerning. "What do you know about it? Drena mentioned briefly you and Maura, before she was possessed by Sarmira, came across this mirror."

"Yes, we were young girls then. Your grandmother Maura tried to hide me from her mother Sonjah." She takes in a deep breath as the memories come back. She looks at me with saddened eyes. "Sarmira had taken Sonjah's soul when Maura was a little girl. Sonjah had marked me for life. Maura tried to hide me. We found this mirror in a strange cabin that, at the time we had no clue who it belonged to, and this mirror was hanging in the hallway—or one like it. Thermyah." She turns back around looking at the mirror. "Also known as The Raven, or Eye of the Raven."

Cole, Rory, and I acknowledge that we had encountered her on Elleirodal and that Sarmira turned her to ash not long ago, here in the catacombs. *"Are you thinking what I'm thinking?"*

"That the Raven died too easy? Yes," Cole answers. *"I also find it too convenient."*

"I thought that story was folklore," Rory says.

"Oh no, my dear, it's a true story, and I barely lived to tell it." She drifts off in a blank stare. "The Eye of the Raven sacrificed herself to save us both."

"Are you saying she's in there?" Blair says the quiet part out loud. "Because we watched Sarmira turn her to ash."

"Yes, she and the Crow Man." Geneviève's eyes grow wide. "Messing with this mirror is like opening Pandora's box. This 'thing' needs to remain hidden."

"Hang on, did you say the Crow Man?" Cory asks. He turns to Petra. "We just watched Petra send him back there. How can The Crow Man be in two places at once?"

I've never seen Geneviève so scared before. "Oh no."

"We met him already," Rory says. "Here on the grounds and in the crypt."

Cory's concerned stare has us all on edge. "The Crow Man was cast into the mirror tonight, so what do you mean by he's in there? Do you mean he somehow escaped previously?"

"He must've," Drena says. "And I'm betting his soul is in one of these jars." She files through the shelves, looking.

"He can't possibly be a clone like Maura, was, can he?" Cole asks.

Geneviève covers her mouth as though the words coming from her lips are burning her.

"Mother, what is it?" Rory comes to her side.

"My memories have returned." She chokes down the horrific thoughts. Her emotions are in complete turmoil. "She will come after me now. She knows where I am." She looks at Rory. "Your grandmother Laveena is in severe trouble. Sarmira will know how to reach her and the kingdom. She'll know her weakness."

"How do we stop her?" Cole asks.

"You don't. Whatever happened recently—" she looks at the other coffins where the rest of the family still sleeps and a tear falls down her cheek. "My memories are back. I had Thermyah wipe them. It was the only way to save my father's kingdom, and my mother's because I was marked."

"How did she mark you?" I ask.

"By luring my family pack to Sonjah's property where she could cast her curse." Her words seem to trail off. "Redmae." Tears fall more. "Oh, my sweet Mae. This is all my fault. I tried to shield my family."

"How is this your fault, Mom? You couldn't have known."

"I don't think you quite understand, Rory. You see, Thermyah told me the only way to save my family from the curse that Sonjah bestowed upon us was to eliminate my memories."

"As I recall, it was only to save you from the mark, not the curse," a voice says behind us.

A man looking much like Ian steps out of a coffin. It isn't my grandfather however, but they could pass as twins.

"Arik, is that really you?" Geneviève asks.

He looks down and pats the front of his body to test her theory. "In the flesh, it looks like, yes. But tell me, how is this possible? The last I remember I was sucked into that wretched Soul Catcher." He looks at the Soul Catcher lying on the chemistry table.

Geneviève gives him a warm hug.

"They're all starting to wake up," Blair says.

Drena looks at Geneviève. "We will need help to comfort them as they wake."

"What do we do in the meantime?" Cory asks.

"We need to get everyone back to Ladorielle," Dad says.

"And we need to place the hearts of Queen Sara, King Ailbert, and Isalora. If we can bring them back..." He turns to look at me. "I know your mother's heart has to be on these grounds somewhere. Rosie told me, once, that she had hidden it down in her working chamber." He looks toward the other room. "Her heart has to be in this place somewhere."

"Isalora's heart is the last piece to the puzzle," Drena says. "Ask your compass, Wynter."

THE AMOUNT OF WORK WE HAVE DONE IN JUST A FEW hours amazes me. Of course, most of the resurrections we've finished are still in a sleeping state, so we wait in anticipation. Geneviève has been busy porting family members as they wake, and escorting them back to the cottage, with each of them gaining strength and magical abilities which has also strengthened the cottage shield barrier. That's fantastic news since Drena can now focus more on tending to the remaining sleeping family members here in the catacombs.

"I don't know if you've noticed, but I feel like I have more energy," Blair says.

"Come to think of it, me too, and your complexion looks more refreshed." Drena turns to my dad. "And yours."

"I bet it will be daylight soon," Cole says. "Something tells me when we killed Maura's clone, the curse lifted."

"Yes, I agree. Something has changed." Drena looks at her watch. "It's about six in the morning. The sun will be up soon. Queen Sara and King Ailbert resurrections have been completed." She moves to the coffin where Isalora lies. "Without her heart I cannot connect her soul."

"We will find it," I say.

"I sure hope you're right. Your compass has not yet shown us the way," Blair says.

"Perhaps it needs a bit of cleansing. I mean, it has had its share of dark energy tonight. May I see it?" Drena grins. "Or a wash. I found moon water Maura must've stashed away. Here, dip it in this."

"What about putting it out on a windowsill?"

"You do not want this full moon's energy." Drena hands me a glass jar of clear liquid.

"How do you know it's moon water?" I ask.

Drena taps the lid. "She labeled it."

I hand her the necklace and Drena sinks the stone in the liquid.

I look down at my mother and gaze upon her sleeping face as she lies still between dimensions. "She hasn't even decayed. Her skin looks soft to the touch. I'm so glad we're breaking the curse."

Dad comes to my side. "We will find her heart, I promise."

I smile inward, knowing how much I dislike that word. An unexplainable pull has me drawn to her beauty and I feel the urge to part her hair and touch her soft porcelain looking skin. I trace my mother's face with my finger and lean in to kiss her. A tear falls from my cheek hitting hers, and when I go to wipe her face, I touch something hard underneath the pillow supporting her neck. "Dad!"

"What is it?" He comes to investigate. Moving her head to the side he pulls out something solid. "It's a box?"

My eyes widen.

He tries to lift the lid. "It won't open. It's locked."

My necklace glows inside the jar filled with moon water. I smile. "Something tells me that isn't going to be an issue."

"Guess the compass works after all." Drena pulls the necklace out of the container. "You might want to put this back on."

Dad hands her the coffer.

She inspects it. "Quite heavy, isn't it?" Setting it down, she adds, "Magic is keeping it closed. Try the key, Wynter. It's worked before, so why not this time. I think that's a sign, don't you?"

I insert it until I hear a click. The lid springs open and inside leaves us all breathless.

36

HEART AND SOUL

"Do you think this will work?" Blair asks.

"We have to at least try." Drena places the box on the working bench in the next room that have shelves filled with remaining jars of souls not yet matched to their sleeping bodies. "Isalora is a different type of situation. I can't easily match her soul until I have the recipe to reunite her heart with her body."

"Could it possibly be around where we saw the other books in the pews?" Cory asks.

"Possibly," she answers. She flips through the spell book I had given her earlier. "Wait, I found something." She looks up and smiles. "See, right here." She points to an inscription. *Be aware of what already has been done.*

"What does that mean?" Rory asks.

"It's speaking about the Blood Moon Curse, isn't it?" Blair's face goes white. "Drena, we don't have those ingredients to make a spell for protection from that."

"I thought you said that killing Maura's clone was the end of the curse?" Cole says.

"Perhaps not but keep reading..." Dad encourages.

"It says find the source and the spell will be broken," I say.

Drena's eyes light up. "Exactly."

"And you think Maura was only half of the source of all this chaos?" I ask.

"Does it mean the curse still stands?" Rory asks.

"No, I don't think so. Something has happened. I feel different," Blair says. "Drena's right. It says in detail how a curse like this is started and how to break it. This recipe is for added protection. Without it you must have a paladin of the undead—"

"That would be you, Wynter," Cory says.

I gulp.

"A conjurer of magic. I'm guessing that's you, Cory."

"Keep reading," Drena says.

"A stealth knight in sheep clothing." Blair looks up from reading and squints. "A what?"

"I'm a rogue, by definition standards," Cole says. "I would have thought you would've figured that by now with all my trickery."

"Hah!" Blair continues.

I huff. "Right. So, basically you can't be trusted."

"Now, come on, family always comes first. No one messes with family and I'm always loyal there." He grins.

"What about you, Casey?"

"I'm just a stable boy," he jokes. "No powers, or if I do have them, I've no clue what they are."

"That's really sad, Casey, that you think that," I say. "We will help you find your true gift, but from what I've seen so far you're a bad ass."

"Is there more?" Rory asks.

Blair smiles. "Yes, one more line. A wave jumper that blindly defeats their enemy."

"Haha, I get the reference. Seaspike." Rory grins back. "Not exactly clear on the wave jumper part though."

"It's a loosely chosen term for druid," Drena says. "Portal jumper: Wave meaning riding the dimensional wave frequency."

"Got it." Rory puts up a thumb.

Redmae growls.

"Even in human form you sound like a wolf, you know that, sis?" Rory turns to look at her. "Wait when did you turn back to a wolf?"

"The Super Blue Blood Moons evidently descended, but my curse appears to be in good working order," she replies sarcastically.

"I don't think she's happy about it, Rory," I say.

"Something definitely has shifted," Cory says.

Cole grabs the hilt of his dagger as though Sarmira is about to appear. "If Redmae is back to a wolf, then the phase of the moon has ended. The curse hasn't lifted yet and Sarmira is still alive, which means we failed."

"Not necessarily," Drena argues. "Redmae's curse has something to do with her bloodline. The fact that all of us are improving in strength tells me that Maura's clone held the curse. She's been defeated."

"Yet Sarmira still sails through the ether terrorizing us all," Cole argues.

Redmae's growl grows louder. *"I hear many voices taunting me."* She takes off.

"Red, stop!" Rory looks at me. "Where is she going?"

"I fear we're no match for them all. Those Shadow Walkers we killed earlier have turned to wraiths. And they're back. I'm going back to the big area where we fought them earlier."

Casey transforms into his beastly self.

"Come. This battle isn't over." I look back at the twins.

"Right behind you," Cory says.

I CLOSE MY EYES AND LISTEN CLOSELY TO THE WAVES of energy. "Something is off." I open my eye still seeing darkness. Although the moon has descended the sun isn't up yet.

Rory looks at her arrows. "These arrow tips were made from Valiancium steel. Queen Sara had them specially made for me. I remember her warning, that the spirit world would arrive and when they did these arrows would come in handy." She pulls one from her quiver. "You're not going to try and project, are you?"

"No, the last time I did that I was sick for a few days."

"Wynter, duck!" An arrow whisks by my ear, almost nicking me.

"There!" Petra points. A wraith with glowing blue eyes, stares back.

"That looks like the same creepy robed creature that chased me in my dream." Ear piercing screeches echo within the walls of the catacomb, and it guns right for us. "Rory, shoot now!"

"I can't see anything!" Rory cries.

"Just shoot!"

Derek casts a spell, and I feel a tingle sensation flow through my veins.

Wailing discomfort shatter across the stone walls.

"I assume I hit it, and it's one down and twenty to go?" Rory asks.

I bring my head between my knees and pant. "Uh-huh." I take a few more breaths. "Derek, what was that?"

"Something that will help us see these apparitions better. It only lasts about fifteen minutes, so we better make the best of it. That spell takes a lot of my energy. I, too, am out of breath."

Redmae continues growling.

"They are good at hiding, I will give them that," Cole says.

"And fast," Petra says. "Guess you're right, Wynter. Our fight isn't over."

A scream calls out from the other end of the room. "Got another one, it sounds like." Rory grabs a third arrow.

"I can see many eyes staring at us, now." Cole pulls his dagger once again.

"I see them, too," Cory says. He clutches his hilt, ready to attack.

"One of these apparitions is Sarmira," Redmae says.

This time I grab my dagger. Something tells me I am going to need all the strength I can get. "We all need to focus if we're going to beat them."

The wraith—Sarmira—must be angry because she comes roaring, shoving both Cory and Cole. The force of her power sends them sailing a few feet, hitting a wall.

"No!" I yell.

Sarmira circles the room, howling, and sweeps by brushing against, Rory throwing off her game, and she jumps backward.

"I really don't like the feeling of this raging spirit flashing around," I say. "Something tells me we made her a bit angry."

"Ya think?" Rory glares my direction.

I try to keep up with Sarmira's speed, watching her glide back and forth around the crypt bouncing like a rubber ball.

Cole dances with a Shadow Walker as they mince weapons against each other. "Remember to use your daggers, they will protect you from their death touch."

"Death touch?" Rory shoots as fast as possible with each gaping breath. "Right, you mentioned that before. I didn't like the sound of it then, either."

Redmae's jaws clench, and she goes into full-on attack mode. Sarmira laughs as she whirls around, taunting us.

Another wraith comes to her aid.

Dad shouts. "She's bringing friends!"

A second wraith swooshes in to settle the score and pins

both Rory and me to the wall. Redmae charges at it, prompting it to release us, and we fall to the ground.

"Ow," I say, groaning.

It takes a minute for us to catch our breath.

Dad and Derek battle a third wraith to our left.

Drena casts a second spell forming a bubble around us as we gain our strength. "For protection."

Another wraith comes straight for Petra, and she blocks its movement with the flick of her wand. She moves her wrists in a circular motion and says something out loud I can't understand. In seconds the wraith turns into flecks of light which adds more depth into the dark room giving us an advantage to see clearer.

"Nice effect, Petra," I say.

She smiles and targets the next enemy.

Dad raises his sword and slashes through the ghostly being before him, where before he didn't see it.

I charge at the one that had Rory, and I pinned. Before I land a final blow, an arrow shoots through the apparition, and it disintegrates to ashes.

Two more wraiths appear in its place.

"Guys, incoming!" Rory takes out another arrow, and shoots, landing a direct hit.

Cory charges at the second wraith, and it disappears.

Four more appear.

"They're multiplying each time we kill one, like last time," Cole says.

"Just like a hydra dragon," Cory says.

Cole fights a ghostly creature. "Except fire doesn't seem to extinguish them. They come back double the wraiths."

Another apparition appears and smashes the wall behind Derek and Dad with bricks and mortar spilling everywhere, knocking them out.

"Well, that was unexpected," I say.

Redmae pounces the wraith. Cole takes another entity out with the swipe of his blade.

My anger rises, watching Dad and Derek lying on the ground, unconscious.

"Stay back. I think they are attempting to pick us off one by one," Cory says. "These aren't ordinary wraiths; these are dead, soulless necromancers."

"And a vindictive dark witch," I add.

A wraith manages to push Cory and Cole back.

Casey retaliates with one swipe of his claws, forcing the wraith back which allows Cory to collect his dagger and stab the wraith in the back turning it to ash. Two more replace it. "We're getting nowhere."

Cole picks up his blade and massages his neck. "They have unbelievable strength." He races forward and slices through the ghost before it reaches us.

The other wraith glides behind Cory but Cole thrusts a finishing blow. "Not your day," he says. "Better luck next time."

Rory readies another arrow. "This feels like a lost cause. They will keep coming at us."

Eight more wraiths appear.

"I've noticed the daggers are working, and they disappear, but with each kill more keep returning. How do we keep them away for good?" Cory asks.

"I think I know," Petra says. She pulls the Soul Catcher from her cloak and aims the mechanism at their faces, and one by one the entities get sucked into the Soul Catcher. "See, works like a charm."

I nod, saying, "Petra you might be onto something. I wish we would have thought of this before."

Another wraith comes swooping in, surprising us, and manages to pin Cory and Cole against a wall, kicking away their blades.

"A little help would be nice," Cole says as he finally is able to stab his opponent.

More apparitions take place of the undead ones that are defeated.

"Drena, use the Soul Catcher!" A wraith heads right for her, and I stop him with a fire ball.

Drena finishes him. "Thanks for the tip!"

"There are more of them hiding in the shadows." I nod in the corner.

Petra does a gliding sweep aiming her Soul Catcher right at them. Screeching moans confirm she got them.

A wicked laugh calls out. "I knew my instincts were right! My sweet girl. You are getting stronger. This will indeed rule in my favor."

Redmae growls.

"Sarmira!" I cry. "You never quit, do you. Don't you know, you're not going to win this family dispute?"

She steps out from the shadows.

We regroup as Sarmira hovers over us and hisses. "This is all too familiar. You all look exactly like your father did before I took his soul. He didn't see it coming..." She glides across the floor, circling the room.

We turn with her, trying to keep up with her quick pace. "What do you know about our father?" Cole sneers, holding out his blade at her.

Rory surprises us and knocks Sarmira with one of her Valiancium steel tip arrows, dissolving her wraith form into black smoke.

"That was too easy," Blair says.

"You're right, Blair. She is projecting like Maura," Rory answers.

"Which means she'll be back just as soon as she gains back the energy she just lost from Rory's arrow. I propose we find out where she is meditating," Petra says.

"I can hear you..." Sarmira calls out. A playful laugh follows.

My flaming hand lights the sides of the crypt, allowing us to see Dad and Derek huddled together in a heap, still unconscious. "It's up to the rest of us. We can't afford any mistakes. We're only going to get one shot at this."

Rory nods.

"Works for me. Let's find her," Casey growls.

She cackles louder, as if his remarks humor her.

Rory readies another arrow. Redmae growls and takes off at the other end of the crypt after Sarmira.

"Wait, Redmae, she's taunting us!" I call.

We follow Sarmira's lure knowing it's probably a trap. "I don't like this one single bit," Rory says.

Casey and Redmae lead the way.

My anger builds, and although I haven't mastered the ability to use my eyes I think outside the box and bring a ball of fire to my palm. "How's this for light?" I guide my flaming hand through the dark room, working on trying to cover a hundred-and-eighty-degree radius. Nothing peers back at us except endless walls of skulls. *"Can you sense her?"* I ask Redmae. A heavy rush of air passes in front of us, then circles behind. It's so fast I have a hard time focusing on its location.

"Yes. She's watching us."

"Why aren't Shadows attacking?"

"They're waiting for her cue, perhaps?" A swish of wind passes between us, knocking Redmae to the ground. She yelps in pain but recovers quickly and growls in anger. Casey growls, too.

"Red," Rory yells.

"No, Rory. Concentrate. It's trying to separate us. Focus on me. We stay together." I look at Red. *"You okay?"*

She grunts. Casey licks the top of her head. *"I'm fine."*

Movement in the corner prompts Cory to move. "Did you hear that?"

Blair turns a circle, cautiously inching forward with each step and Drena and Petra are close behind.

Sarmira peers at us at the other end of the crypt with glowing eyes. "I see her," Rory says, and she takes aim.

Both Casey and Redmae growl.

"Rory, get ready." I feel like we're in a duel to the death. "When I give the signal, I want you to shoot."

"Got it."

Redmae growls, doesn't wait, and she pounces towards the spectral demon.

Sarmira doesn't leave Rory time to prepare a shot and she charges at her in a high pitch scream that renders us helpless.

"Not this time, Sarmira!" Petra slaps Sarmira with a spell so powerful it binds her in place. This time it isn't ice that keeps her still, it's ethereal magic that looks like a wave of heat swimming in the air.

"Petra, I do say, you surprise me," Drena says.

Sarmira is angry and tries to wriggle out of her situation.

"You will never win this battle. I will see to it." Sarmira calms and her body goes completely limp. Her eye glaze over and then rolls into the back of her head.

"Not today, Sarmira!" Drena shouts "You will never hurt me or my family ever again!" She slowly pulls the eyes from Sarmira's sockets. They flow through the darkness and into Drena's palms. "Now I have eyes to see into your soul." Her tone sounding malevolent and not all like the Drena we have come to know. It's a source of magic I've never seen. She quickly covers the pair of eyes with a dark cloth and tucks them away in a coffer like the ones used for the hearts of our loved ones.

The sheer terror on Sarmira's face says it all. She knows she's about to be defeated.

"You're turn, Cory. Send her demons a message," Drena says.

The Blade of Hope comes up the front, gutting her. "This is for all the times you have stripped your victims of freedom," Cory says. "May hope live forever."

"Cole, you're next." Petra hold Sarmira's energy in place.

The Blade of Truth slides through Sarmira's back. "This is for the deceitful lies you have told. May the light now be free." Two bright beams of illumination, like wings, escape from her shoulder blades.

She screams once again. It isn't a scream of pain but a scream of anger. My instinct tells me she will attempt to seek revenge.

Petra nods at me. "Your time to shine."

"I have waited for this day." The silence is filled by the sound my blade makes as it is pulled from its sheath. "Finally, it's happening." The tip of the blade traces her cheek. Sweat beads down her face. The steel tip glides down her neck, over her collarbone, between her chest, landing slightly to the left breast. "This is for my mother." The weapon slides in slowly. "Unlike her fate, I have the magic of all three blades with me. I can feel your pain. Your confusion. Your rage." I smile, feeling satisfied we finally got her. "You will not win this battle today. You stole my mother's life, and now I'm stealing yours!" I finish with turning the blade as it reaches her heart and finally rips from her body. "This is for all the hearts you stole. And are now set free."

"*Thank you,*" a voice whispers. The blue swirl of smoke is back. It shimmers a little more than in previous times.

Sarmira falls to the floor dissolving into a pile of ash like all the other foes. For a brief moment we can relax. She's gone.

"I'm still confused how she could look like human flesh, yet, still have the elements of a spirit," Rory says, looking down at the fallen dust about our feet.

"That's easy," Drena explains. "She is a necromancer witch. Something tells me it isn't over though; I have a feeling she'll show her face again. She'll be back. She isn't going away that easy."

"Anything is possible, I agree," Petra argues, "but this time the three daggers were together and that is just as powerful as having the Sword of Valor. In any case, ashes to ashes and dust to dust."

"Looks like I was just in time," Drena says. She puts out her hand to help Blair who had been knocked down earlier.

"We should check on the others," Blair says. "Jeff and Derek will be bummed they missed all the fun."

We laugh.

The light movement from the piled heap of Storms in the corner notifies us that they're all alive.

Derek grabs the back of his head. "Ow."

Redmae lies down on the ground and continues to pant. *"I'm taking a break."*

"What did I miss?" Derek asks.

"Everything," I tease.

Dad is still out cold. His chests is moving, which is a good indication he is okay.

Blair's hands glow. "Nothing a little mending can't do." She glides over the injured area.

The blue smoke lingers above Dad's head. *"Look beyond the stone. That is where you will find me."*

Out of the corner of my eye, just behind Dad's head, I notice something flicker. It's not obvious, but it does grab my attention. Where's a pocketknife when you need one. *"Something is behind this wall, am I right?"* The swirl of smoke doesn't answer and instead fades into the stone before me.

"Wynter, what is it?" Rory asks.

"Do you see that?" I point to the hole.

"Yeah." She comes over and wipes the grout. "Guys, I think we found something."

Derek and Drena join us, along with Cory, Cole, and Blair.

We hear Dad stir.

"It's about time you woke up, Dad. You're missing all the fun."

Derek holds out his hand to help him up.

"What did I miss?"

We all chuckle.

"Everything," Derek says. "Don't worry, though, you're just in time for a new adventure. It appears there is another hidden room behind this wall."

37
A DISCOVERED PAST

Dad gets his bearings in order before investigating the crumbling grout. He glides his fingers across the stone. "Hang on a second. There's light coming through here."

"Yes, we know," Derek says.

He feels the wall. "This structure's new."

"What? Are you sure?" Cory asks.

"It's been years since I've stepped down into these catacombs, but I don't remember this wall. You're right. It's new," Blair says.

"But how would you know that unless you're the one who built it?" I ask.

"I didn't build it. Maura's—Sarmira's gang did. Before they strapped me to the chains at the manor they threw me in the cell block over there." She points to the chamber. "I peeked through the iron bars and watch as they piled it up brick by brick."

"So, what's behind it?" Drena asks.

"It was used as a storage room."

"Well, guess we should find out what's behind it."

Cole glides his fingers across the cracked grout and pulls

out his pocketknife to scrape the mortar and jabs at the stone. Debris falls. "This will take forever. We need something stronger."

"Will this work?" Cory asks, holding the sledgehammer he conjured.

Cole grins.

"Guess that's one way to do it," Rory says.

Cole swings, blasting the stones through to the other side.

My hands light up with flames to get a closer look inside the gaping hole.

"What do you see?" Rory asks.

"It's a hidden room, as we all suspected. I can't get a clear visual," I say.

"Well, keep going and bust it out," Rory says.

"Stand back." Cory takes another swing.

The mortar crumbles more easily with the second blow, and a few more bricks fall into the dark hole beyond the wall on the other side. He swipes away more mortar.

Rory's eyes veer over Cole's shoulder to the widened space. "Something is in there, for sure, but I can't see it clearly." She turns around to look at me. "Another glass coffin."

"We need to make the hole bigger," Cory says. He smashes another block of stone.

Redmae growls. *"Let us try."* She charges at the wall, and it cracks more, making it easier for the twins to chip away at more stone. *"One more ought to do it."*

Casey rams the wall on Redmae's cue.

The weight of both beasts plowing at the crumbling wall cracks the mortar more, leaving a larger hole. They're more powerful than I thought.

We watch in awe as dust flies, and more stones fall to the floor, making a dirty mess.

Cory smashes the last stone, and it leaves enough space for all of us to slip through.

Cole steps in. "Something doesn't feel right."

"Does anything ever feel right in a stale smelling crypt?" Rory pokes back.

"Brother, something tells me this isn't a room we were supposed to discover." Cory moves ahead of us into the dark room, lit with our glowing eyes.

What stands before us is something I cannot comprehend. *"Red, are you seeing what I'm seeing?"*

"Yeah, how is this possible?"

"I don't know."

In the center of the space is a dais, with two glass coffins. One is an open casket. I can't get a clear picture of the second body in the casket and move for a closer view. "Are they dead?"

"Only one way to find out." Casey steps up to investigate. "I sense a faint heartbeat." He puts an ear to the woman's chest. "She's still alive, but barely."

I step forward to investigate, gazing at her lying in the casket. Her features just as beautiful as when I first met her on Dragonscale Island. Her silky hair combed perfectly. She appears to be sleeping. I can see the slight rise and fall of her chest. "She isn't dead." My hands glow, and I place them onto her chest.

Eleena opens her eyes. A tear trails my cheek as I breathe a sigh of relief. "You're safe. We found you."

She smiles back. "I knew you would."

"Her wounds are deep." Blair hovers her hands over Eleena. "I'm going to need help with healing her."

We're going to get you out of here, Grandmother."

Cory looks over at the second body lying unconscious in the other closed casket, and his eyes widen.

"What?" I ask. I can see the fear in his eyes. Something I haven't seen Cory ever show.

Casey moves away to reveal their identity but I still can't see a clear picture of who it is.

"It can't be," Drena says, stunned.

"Indeed," Derek says. "We found her."

I fight back the well of tears, seeing my other grandmother, Maura Moyer. Rage consumes me, but I concentrate on keeping the emotions in check, just like I've been taught to do.

"You know what this means, don't you?" Drena has a worried look on her face.

"Someone must have lured them," Cole says.

"Let's get them out of here and back to the cottage." Dad scoops up his mother in his arms.

"What about the others in the catacombs?" Rory asks.

"We will get them all out," Dad says.

"Easier said than done, Jeff." Drena comes to his side. "To think she was here in this hollowed room the entire time."

Cory looks up at Drena. "Even if the Soul Catcher is the only way to get rid of Sarmira indefinitely, at least we have a few minutes to breathe."

"Let's hope you're right," Rory says. She readies her jumping rune.

"When this is over, we're throwing a huge party," I say.

"I'm up for that," Derek says. He lifts Eleena in his arms and carries her out of the crypt.

"Let me go with you back to the cottage," Blair says. "I may not be a good as Drena, but I can at least do some healing magic. Drena still needs to revive the other members."

Dad nods. "Good idea."

"Perhaps I should go as well," Derek says. "There is still a little magic left in me. If the cottage is weakened from protection, I can at least mirror an illusion hiding it from our enemies."

Drena smiles and squeezes his hand. "We won't be far behind, my love."

"Are we ready?" Rory asks. She casts her jump spell and in

seconds they all disappear except for Cole, Cory, Redmae, Petra, and me.

Cory and Cole come by my side, while Petra wanders in a new direction.

"Where are you going?" I ask.

"I still need to find the portal book, and we still need to help those poor souls trapped by that magical door Sarmira locked earlier. Something tells me that magic has been lifted." She stares at my neck. "And your necklace is glowing which leads me to believe I'm onto something."

I look down and smile. "I think you're right. Let's go."

Petra leads and we follow weaving in and out down the halls until we come to the very room where we slid down from the upper-level trapped door. "Wynter, try that key."

"Petra, you know you're brilliant, right?" I smile and insert the key until I hear a click. We all gasp.

The door opens and the overwhelming sensation of freedom unlocks.

We walk in to find the room empty.

"Geneviève. She had to have come and gotten them."

"I hope you're right." I look around, hoping someone might be in this room. "No one should be left behind."

A voice calls to us as we turn to walk away. "Tell me, is that really you, Cory, or is it just my imagination?"

We turn back around. "Aoes? I hear you but do not see you."

He appears before us.

"We have been looking for you everywhere. We knew people were trapped in this room. Boy, are we glad to see you alive and well."

He's the first to give Aoes a hug.

"I had to make sure," Aoes says.

"Make sure?" Cory looks confused.

Like the same skill Derek has, an illusion fades within the

room, revealing the missing children, servants, and our friends."

"I can't believe what I am seeing right now," Cole says.

"We thought we were going to rot in here. I can't believe my eyes, either." Aoes goes up to Petra. "And you, my dear, I have something for you. Something I never thought I would see the light of day to give you." Within his robe he pulls a book. "The Book of Secrets and Shadows, my dear. May the benevolent magic follow you wherever you go. It took a lot of energy to hide this from Sarmira."

"No need to worry anymore, Master Aoes. She is dead." Petra bows. "I don't know what to say."

"Does this mean you're leaving us?" I ask.

Petra's aura brightens.

"Her mission was to repair Earth's portal," Aoes begins. "She has found the door." He points the Hall of Secrets.

"It's another mirror to the Mirror of Souls?" I ask. The frame lights up like the portal doors of the

"Similar, yes," Aoes answers. "A mirror to many more, but that is for another day for us to tackle. This moment is a celebration of freedom."

I gaze into the mirror and see the other side. A familiar side. "The Hall of Secrets?"

"Indeed." Aoes bows. "And we are closer to completing the twelve portals."

The room shakes and debris falls. A couple of nervous voices cry from within the space.

"Not to worry, folks, they're just tremors. Nothing to fear." Aoes smiles. "We're all going home."

"Wait, Aoes, I have so many questions."

"Wynter, it can wait. Cory knows where to find me." He gathers the children, The faces of so many friends I've seen while attending the school at Storm River Manor, but one face in particular stands out. "Stella?"

She comes and gives me a hug. "I've missed you."

"Oh, Stella, I'm so happy to see you're alive and well."

"Come, children, we mustn't waste time. The portal will only be open another thirty seconds. Let's go."

"See you on the other side, Wynter." Stella waves before stepping through the mirror.

The portal closes seconds later.

"How many mirrors are there?" I ask.

"I think I can answer that. For each portal book, a mirror follows. And although the book is a gate on its own, the mirror is too. Both connect together. If you recall, the Hall of Secrets has a mirror within its hub, I will venture to guess, so does the cottage up in the loft and the mirror in the Crystal Cave has now been restored which will allow for much more travel for a travelling mage." She winks. "We now have access to connecting the sister planets, once more."

Above the frame a clock lights up timing down from 42,480 minutes. "What does that mean?" I ask.

"That the portal will not be available to open again until the next full moon," Petra says. She grins. "We did it, Wynter. We freed everyone from the curse. Not long after I lost Bryce. I was hoping this quest would bring me to him."

"Perhaps finding the mirror is the key to finding him?" Cory guesses.

"Perhaps, but my time here is up as well. Before I go, I must relay a message to you," Petra says. She pulls from her pocket an envelope similar to the one I gave Cole, and hands it to Casey. "I was instructed to give this to you once I found the portal book. It was given to me by a stranger. And no, this was not from The Raven. He called himself Sam."

Petra adjusts her cloak and in that split second, she vanishes.

"Well, what does the note say, brother?" Cole asks.

> *Casey,*
>
> *If you're reading this then you found the Mirror of Souls. I have the answers you and the others seek.*
>
> *To lift your curse and bring the three to be one, you must find Hannah. Wynter gave Sarmira the most valuable thing a magical being should never give. And now she is free. But first, you must find the Blue Oak Tree. There you will find an answer.*
>
> *Sam*

"Why was this letter different than ours, Cole?"

Cory shakes his head. "I don't know."

The letter ignites in flames. And Casey drops it to the floor. We all watch it burn.

"What did I give her?" Stunned, I turn to Cory. "I gave her nothing." He shrugs.

"I know," Cole replies. "Remember when you fell and hurt your knee back at the manor?"

"Wow, that seems so long ago. Thinking back, I remember passing out. I woke in a doctor's office."

"I witnessed Madame Moyer taking a sample of your blood," Cole confesses. "She couldn't figure out why—no matter the attempts—you could never be turned to a vampire. So, she took your blood instead by putting you in a dream stamp where you consented."

"I would never—" My eyes burn with fury.

Cory holds me back. "He's just confessing to what he knows, Wynter. Do not punish him for giving you answers."

I swing around at Cory. "Did you know about this?"

"Of course not!" He attempts to soothe me with his eyes.

"Ha! That isn't going to work with me this time."

Redmae enters my thoughts. *"They are both telling you the truth."*

More tremors occur only this time it feels much stronger than the last one. "Why is this still happening? Petra isn't here."

Forcible winds funnel through the catacombs. "She's back!" Venom spews through my veins.

We rush in the next room where we defeated Sarmira earlier and witness dark shadow-like figures flowing out of the ashes. All of us struggle to keep up with the gust of strong winds.

Sarmira's ashes swirl around turning into a funnel cloud. A large dark dragon forms. The beasts wings flap fiercely in the wind. Laughter calls within the chaos. "I'm free! You fools played right into my hands! I'm free at last!" She widens her jaw.

"Look out! Take cover!" A fireball forms in my hand.

"That isn't going to work on me, Wynter." She attempts to char me and misses. She narrows her gaze at Cory. "I shall leave you all with a parting gift, my sweet children."

"No!" I dive toward Cory.

"Wynter, stop. Trust me." Cory throws his dagger into the opened mouth of Sarmira with her flames spewing hot flares, before he himself is singed to ashes.

"Cory!" I attempt to go to him, but Cole holds me back. "Wynter no, you can't!" He holds onto me tight.

Sarmira roars in pain. Cory injured her. He did it. The ceiling cracks. Glass shatters onto our heads so, Cole quickly casts a shield to protect us.

She spreads her wings and busts through the charred half covered ceiling. A second crack ensues before the entire crown of the cave-like structure hollows out into the morning sky. Black wings form, smoke seeps through her nostrils. Her talons are much larger than mine, when I'm in this form.

I look at Cole with worry. "A dark dragon."

"This isn't over," I hear in my mind. The voice laughs

wickedly. Her missives strength creates powerful gusts that Cory's ashes scatter, leaving minimal remains behind.

Sarmira flies through the open roof and vanishes into the radiant sun that chases the descending Blood Moon in the sky. We lost our chance to defeat her forever.

I sink to my knees scooping what remains of Cory's ashes into my palms as his dust spills between my fingers. The pang in my chest is too much to bear. My heart bleeds. Cory is gone.

IT ISN'T OVER

We all gather at the cottage. By now it's full of many family members. Drena has been hard at work treating everyone with what magic she can muster. I stand in the loft overlooking our entire Storm family visiting and catching up on the past.

My mother Isalora still sleeps. Dad carried her out of the catacombs and through the woods to the cottage where she would be safer. Maura also still sleeps. Drena managed to reunite my mother's heart, as well Queen Sara and King Ailbert's. Now we wait for them to wake.

Cole stands next to me and leans forward, clasping his hands. "He's not dead, Wynter. You must know that."

I turn my head and scowl. "Yeah? Then why hasn't he transformed yet, huh? I mean, what about our theory?" My voice raises, drawing attention. I lower it. "You and Blair came out of the ashes and formed into a dragon within minutes, Cole. It's been three days." Tears well in my eyes. "I'm not as strong as you might think I am."

I walk away. The pain is too much. I need to go ground myself by the river, somewhere away from distractions.

Thoughts push in and out of my brain. None of this makes any sense. He's a vampire. I find myself downstairs and look down the hallway where his remains are still in an urn. Cory is dead.

I push the front door of the cottage wide open and sprint outside. I run as fast as my feet will take me. It feels good to have the fresh air fill my lungs and the cold air brush across my skin.

I stop and catch my breath, bring my knees down to the frozen ground and heave. I scream the loudest scream I have ever cried. Even the snowbirds scatter from my frightful outburst.

A hollow space in the pit of my stomach slowly comes to the surface and up my throat, blocking my airway. I can't breathe. My heart races, my blood pressure rises. And although I'm kneeling on the frozen ground flashes of heat covers my entire body. *What is happing to me?*

My body falls forward, my cheek hits the snow and my eyes are wide open. I can't move. I'm frozen. *Is this what it felt like when I froze Lira?*

The darkness continues to impale the cottage with dark magic, with each attempt failing, yet, I no longer have the strength to care.

"Wynter, get up!" Cole pulls at my arm. "Come inside. This is doing no one any good. You must be strong. There is still more work to do."

"I can't, Cole. He's gone."

"No, he isn't. Trust me." He pulls me up and cradles me in his arms. "I would know, wouldn't I? I am his twin after all." He walks us back to the cottage.

Cole kicks the door open and lays me down on the couch where family fuss over me.

"Okay, okay, I'm alright. I'm fine." I sit up.

Drena hands me a cup of coffee. "Here, this might help."

A roaring frustration follows outside. Any ordinary human

would think it's just strong winds kicking up. I smile inwardly knowing it's probably Sarmira. She's still trapped in this world. Even as a dark dragon, she can't leave Earth.

"How many times will she try before giving up?" Margaret, the woman that had been turned to stone by Daniel, asks. She nestles up against Uncle Chad. He arrived yesterday to help with the transition to Storm Castle.

Daniel, too, has been awakened, and I found his demeanor to be quite opposite to the man I previously met.

"You mean Sarmira? Never," Chad answers. "Now that all our family members have awakened it's going to be next to impossible for her magic alone to penetrate this house. I'm still worried about the state of our kingdom, but Aoes assures us that we are in good hands thanks to the help of Rory's grandmother Queen Laveena and her army."

Chad brought other news with him, too... that the war isn't over and that the fighting continues on both sister planets. Vothule took a great hit when the three daggers were returned to their rightful owners. What he didn't anticipate was his daughter Sarmira losing her power and transitioning to a dark dragon shifter. And she's trapped here for the time being. Part of me feels great satisfaction in knowing that.

"Okay, I think I finally have it!" Drena smiles with triumph. She looks at us for approval. "With any luck, this will unite your mother's soul and body once again. It took some strong meditation to connect with her, but I think she finally found her way from the other side. And you will finally be reunited with your mother." Drena smiles, cupping her hands in front of her.

"You will finally have the opportunity for a mother/daughter relationship," my Aunt Fran says, coming to sit next to me.

"I still can't believe you're here with me, *alive,* and not a ghost!" I lean in and hug her.

"Not the way I expected this to go, that's for sure." She hugs me back. "This is a time for us to all rest. The greatest battles are yet to come."

"Still not the same without Cory here." I take a sip of coffee.

"You haven't showed her yet have you, Cole?" Drena asks.

He shakes his head.

"Shown me what?" I set down my coffee cup.

"She isn't ready."

I tilt my head. "Cole?" I stand. "Gawd, I am so sick of everyone telling me what I can or cannot handle! I ripped *her* heart from her body! The least you could do is have a little faith in—" A loud gasp startles me. At first, I feel like my screams went a little too far when I hear my mother's voice.

"What have you done?" My mother sits up and looks around to see us all. "Oh no, what have you done?"

She looks at me with a worried smile and tears fall from her cheeks. She looks at Drena. "You must kill me. Kill me now. Take my heart out at once!"

"Mother!" I come by her side. "What are you talking about? Do you know what great lengths we have done to bring you back from this curse?"

She shakes her head and lets out a depressing sigh. "Do you know what great lengths I have done to keep you safe?"

"Mom, I am safe, and we defeated Sarmira." I pull from my waist the Blade of Peace. "All three of us have the blades. We figured out your riddle." The Blade of Hope lies still on the coffee table and I take a pause knowing its owner isn't here.

"You don't understand, my sweet girl. She hasn't been defeated. You have just set her free by resurrecting me."

A loud roar vibrates through the cottage.

"She's been trying to penetrate this house all afternoon," Cole says. "Collectively all our magic is stronger."

"Not for long," Isalora says. She looks at Geneviève. "You need to get everyone back to Ladorielle immediately."

"Mother, not yet. Queen Sara and King Ailbert haven't awakened." I point to the bedroom down the hallway.

"She will become stronger with every minute that passes. She will now be allowed to regenerate quickly. I had cast a binding spell sealing it upon my death. We haven't much time."

Another roar shakes the cabin.

"There is no time! All of us link hands now!" Geneviève screams. "Jeff, Derek, go grab the king and queen. We have no choice. We must leave before it's too late."

I run to grab Cory's urn.

Smoke fills the upper rooms and flames appear.

"Everyone, lock hands," Geneviève instructs. "Rory, grab the rune for Storm Castle."

"Yes, Mother."

"I'm thankful many have already been ported out previously," she says. "Rory, on the count of three we must cast at the same time. Before this entire cottage is engulfed in flames. The odds of us surviving are minimal, otherwise."

"We are Storms, Geneviève," I counter. "We will not burn."

"Not all of us are like you, Wynter," Geneviève says.

"Ouch." I tear up, realizing my words hurt.

"Grab hands and let's go." Geneviève grabs Redmae's collar. "On the count of three."

Each druid pulls a stone from their right hand.

"One," Rory says.

A protection bubble forms around everyone.

"Two," Geneviève says.

"I think I speak for everyone here, when I say, this battle isn't over. It's just the beginning," Cole says.

"Three," they say, together.

We disappear into the void of darkness leaving the once beautiful cottage in ashes.

MY ROOM AT STORM CASTLE REMINDS ME OF THE SET up at Ashengale except it's not big enough to fit Namari. And Charlie my stuffed rabbit isn't here. Ironic as it may sound strange but that stuffed toy gave me comfort in the past.

Rosie draws my bath, and I find myself drifting to sleep on my bed when a knock wakes me from my slumber.

"It's just me," Rosie says, bringing with her fresh garments.

"I didn't know you left."

"I didn't want to disturb you. I knew you needed rest and saw you had fallen asleep, so I stopped the bath and started on washing your clothes. The dirty ones are downstairs in the linen quarters. Your leather jacket, however, I'm not sure I can save, but the maids will do their best."

I huff, remembering the slip down the embankment.

"I'll lay these clean garments here across your bed."

"Thank you, Rosie." I can hear her fuss about my room as she swats the curtains and sweeps the floor. "Wait, Rosie, you said my leather jacket is getting cleaned? What about my medicine Nyta gave me?"

"You don't need that anymore, dear, remember?"

"Right, the whole transformation thing." I sigh.

"Shall I finish drawing your bath?"

I nod. "That sounds lovely."

Once I change into a more presentable attire, I ask Rosie, "Will you find Cole and the others for me, please?"

I look in the mirror, waiting. "Nyta, you have really outdone yourself this time," I murmur, remembering the first time I visited her secret armory below one of her many houses.

Rosie mentioned that the priestess required me to have an upgrade in clothes, but I had no idea the extent of it.

My outfit is all black leather with shoulder and wrist armor that matches the black, tight-fitting tunic, and snug pants. A belt firmly fits around my waist, accompanying a silver buckle, adding a touch of style.

I can feel magic tingle through my toes all the way up my shoulders. Black boots that go to my knees complete the attire. It brings a smile to my face, knowing this time when we confront Sarmira, we'll be more prepared.

A knock disrupts my assessment. It's Cole, Rory, Red in wolf form, and Casey.

"They stopped me on the way to see you," Rory says, pointing to the rest of the gang. "And they threatened me with bodily harm if I didn't allow them to tag along."

"Thought we might still find you here," Cole says. "We passed Rosie in the hall. Rory likes to exaggerate."

Rosie waves behind them.

Redmae grunts plopping on the floor.

"Well, hello, my friend. How's Nyta doing on making you a new antidote?"

"She's doing, I suppose. Said something about having it ferment for a few weeks. That the last dose was temporary, but if I wanted a longer lasting medicine, it would take longer to season. Whatever that means."

"We'll find the cure, Red. I won't stop until we do. I promise"

"Hey now, you're not allowed to make promises you don't like."

"Fine, I'll do my best. Is that a better answer for you?"

"No comment."

Rory's distracted by my attire. "Wynter, you look like—"

"An assassin?" I grin.

"No, a badass that's about to take on the world." She comes closer and has me twirl.

I giggle. "My thoughts, too. Although, it seems Nyta gave you all upgrades, as well."

Rory turns full circle, allowing me to see her red leather attire. "And look, a new quiver set. Same arrow tips, though."

I take in a deep breath. "Sarmira is still out there somewhere hunting us down as we speak."

Don't worry, Wynter," Cole says. "We'll find her."

I smile, looking at them all.

Rosie pokes her head in. "I have a little confession to make."

"What is it, Rosie?" I ask.

"The night your mother died..." she smiles. "When I came to Isalora's dead body, I was weeping with grief from what Moyer had done. I knelt by her side and that's when I felt the blade under her skirts. I picked it up. I'm well versed in about any language on Ladorielle. I read the blade, and that's when I knew how important the dagger really was." She comes closer. "I hid the blade until Isalora was laid to rest.

"You hid the dagger?" I ask, shocked.

"Well, I didn't see that coming," Cole says.

I give Rosie a hug. "Thank you."

She bows. "Like I said, I am thrilled everything worked out. Dinner is at five." She closes the door behind her as she exits.

"You know, your queen now, by right," Rory says. "The coronation makes it official, yes, but the people of Ladorielle need you. It's time to think of a strategy and strike back."

"I feel the rage build with every death that passes, Rory." I look into her worried eyes. "I'm afraid if something doesn't change, I will end up like her."

Cole stiffens. "Who, Sarmira? Impossible."

"But it's not. Sarmira comes from my bloodline."

Cole's eyes begin to glow blue. "Right, I did know that. It's how we have the magic we have."

I tilt my head, studying Cole. "How long have you known?"

"That Sarmira is our grandmother several generations removed? I learned of it while I was in Scarlet Hollow." He looks at all of us. "The rumors, of course, I knew of them, but then when I visited that place, I found out the truth."

"Are you saying Sarmira is possessed, too?"

He smiles. "No. Sarmira never was. But she was a practicing necromancer witch, who made sure her immortality reigned forever."

Worry etches across Cole's face, like he's avoiding telling me the whole story.

"You have more to say, so tell me. I can feel it."

"You know the story of the Sword of Valor, right?"

"Yes."

"When the sword melted and split into three daggers, it was to keep Sarmira from finding the sword. Only the sword can kill her."

"Yes, I know. Drena already said that. So why would Sarmira want it back?"

"To keep it close to her so it wouldn't be put in her enemy's hands?" Rory suggests, theorizing.

"That would be the logical choice, yes. But it's much more complicated than that," Cole goes on.

"Come on, what is it? What do you know?" Rory demands.

He breathes in deep. "I was given a glimpse of the future. But you know dream stamps. They are not always true." He places both hands on my shoulders. "It's all in her plans. Sarmira wants your power, she wants the blades to come together as one. She wants all our magic for her own."

"Hang on a second...Are you saying Sarmira is waiting for the right time before possessing me? That once I absorb all the magical powers, then she will take over my body?"

"Your grandfather knew this and now you hold some of his power. Queen Sara has some of the same powers. We managed to thwart that, as you know, by finding them in the catacombs."

"It's all beginning to make sense. That's what the Soul Jars were for. If she could keep the soul separated from the body, it would be easier for her to take possession."

"Yes."

"What if I'm not strong enough to defeat her? Then what? And Cory he's..." I stiffen pushing back the harsh memories. "Not here." I turn and pace the floor. "This was her strategy all along." I stare back at the others. "Before I was even born, this was to be the prophecy foretold, and we're watching it unfold in real time." My eyes grow wide, thinking back to when Cory turned to ashes. The rage in me builds even more than before. "She will not capture my soul."

"Wynter, if the future told is to come true, you'll go willingly," Cole adds.

I take a step backwards, facing him. "What? I would never go willingly." I swallow hard, dissecting this devastating information, pausing to take it all in. "There has to be another way." I shake my head in defiance of his words. "Dragonscale is our only hope in restoring magic. He's still missing."

"Wynter, you have his magic," Cole says.

The thought of Sarmira wanting my body as her vessel for eternity churns my stomach. "We have to find another way to stop her. Something is off, I feel it."

My mind takes on a whiplash of emotions, and I breathe deep. "I need air, and this castle is getting too stuffy." A knock at the door distracts our thoughts. "Come in."

A servant bursts forth, out of breath, as though she ran clear from the courtyard. There is a hopeful gleam in her eyes. She smiles wide with shock as well as joy. "Your Majesty, he's back!"

STORM BLOODLINE SAGA

Book 1: Eyes of Wynter
Book 2: Different Shade
of Wynter
Book 3: Wynter Reign
Book 4: Wynter Eclipse
Prequel: Eye of the Raven

House Trilogies
Vol 1: House of Shadow Raven
Part of the Storm Bloodline Saga

Mirror of Fate
Mirror of Souls (coming soon)
Mirror of Darkness (coming soon)

Other Books

The Fairy Mermaid and the Crystal Key

THE STORMS

Ailbert Storm: (AKA Charlie and the name of Wynter's stuffed rabbit.) The middle sibling of the three Storm brothers, Gavin and Bram. His wife is Sara Deagon. Their son is Ian. Great-grandfather to Wynter Storm.

Arik Storm: Son of Gavin Storm and Isobel Deagon. Storm Wife: Maura Moyer.

Aoes: Grand Master Wizard. He is a master of time.

Blair Storm: Mother is Drena (Vampire). Father is unknown, but she knows she's a Storm. Adoptive Mother: Madame Moyer. Her sons: Casey, Cole, and Cory. Born a vampire.

Bram Storm: The youngest son of Bryce and Petra Storm. His wife is Clarice. Their sons are Derek and Daniel.

Bryce Storm: The knight that killed Sarmira's original body, causing her to exile her remaining years as a wraith. Bryce is married to Petra. They have three sons: Gavin, Ailbert, and Bram.

Casey Storm: Son of Blair. Born deformed. Redmae's best friend. Father unknown at this time. Cory and Cole's older brother.

Chad Storm: He is the son of Madame Maura Moyer-Storm and Arik Storm. Jeoffrey's younger brother. Wynter Storm's uncle.

Clarice Storm: Married to Bram Storm. Died in childbirth.

Cole Storm: Son of Blair and twin brother to Cory. Born a vampire. Father unknown at this time.

Cory Storm: Son of Blair and twin brother to Cole. Born a vampire. Father unknown at this time.

Daniel Storm: The son of Bram and Clarice Storm and Derek's older brother.

Derek Storm: He is the son of Bram and Clarice Storm. Daniel's younger brother.

Eleena Storm: Married to Ian. Mother to Isalora and Francesca Storm. Grandmother to Wynter Storm.

Francesca Deagon-Storm (Fran): Older sister to Isalora and daughter to Eleena and Ian. Sara Deagon Storm is her grandmother. Wynter Storm's aunt. Her formal name is Drelanda.

Gavin Storm: Oldest brother to Ailbert and Bram. Parents are Bryce and Petra Storm. Son is Arik.

Ian Storm: Son of Ailbert and Sara Storm. Husband to Eleena. Their daughters are Francesca and Isalora. Wynter Storm's grandfather.

Isalora Deagon-Storm: Mother to Wynter Storm and wife to Jeoffrey Storm. Her parents are Ian and Eleena Storm. Her grandmother is Sara Deagon-Storm. Younger sister to Fran.

Isobel Deagon-Storm: Sara's younger sister. Wife of Gavin Storm and mother to Arik Storm. She's the grandmother to Jeoffrey and Chad Storm. Both sisters married Storms in secret, causing a great scandal among the Houses.

Jeoffrey Storm: Son of Madame Maura Moyer-Storm and

Arik Storm. Husband of Isalora Deagon-Storm. Chad's brother. Wynter Storm's father.

Madame Maura Moyer: Married to Arik. Mother to Jeoffrey and Chad. Adopted mother to Blair. Grandmother to Wynter Storm. Possessed by Sarmira.

Petra Storm: Wife to Bryce. Mother to Gavin, Ailbert, and Bram. A traveling Mage.

Sara Deagon-Storm: Married to Ailbert Storm. Mother to Ian Storm. Grandmother to Isalora and Fran and great-grandmother to Wynter Storm. Oldest sister to Isobel. Her father is the slain king of Ashengale. Her father was killed during the great battle.

Wynter Storm: Daughter of Jeoffrey Storm and Isalora Deagon-Storm.

First cousins: Arik, Ian, Derek, and Daniel.

LADORIELLE COMMUNITY

Angelica: Sage's sister. Drena's aunt.

Drena: Elvin daughter to Gage who was turned to a vampire. Blair's mother.

Eve: Drena's sister.

Gage: Elvin. Drena's father.

Garrick: Head commander of Ashengale City.

Geneviève Fernshadow: The Royal Storm's porter. Her father is Gage and mother is Laveena (Dryads).

Gretta: A Dryad.

Huntress Arryn & Akira: Queen Sara's Royal Guards.

Jasmine: Light witch. Sage's sister. Drena's aunt.

Kyla: Gretta's sister, also a Dryad.

Laveena: Geneviève's mother.

Lira: A dark witch and Eleena's sister.

Nora: Iknes Shaw. Wynter's Lady's Maid and a Shadow Walker.

Nyta: (Nigh-ta) One of the last of Sara's court. The medical doctor for the Storm Castle and its surrounding people. High Priestess to the castle. A Diviner of magic.

Nytemire: (Night-my-er) A cross hybrid of a necromancer and vampire.

Redmae: A wolf. Rory's sister.

Rory: Wynter Storm's best friend.

Sage: Drena's mother.

Stella: Wynter's friend from Storm River Manor.

Thom & Dom: Dwarf twins and warriors.

The Raven: Thermyah in bird form

Zak: Nora's brother. Also an Iknes Shaw

UNDERWORLD

House of Bloodbane: Home of the vampires and the place where the academy of assassins learn the trade of combat. This community resides on Elleirodal, the sister plant of Ladorielle.

Iknes Shaw: Snake-like creatures that are of a humanoid form. They have the head and arms of a human and a body of a snake. They have the ability to look like a human.

Sabretail Prowlers: Invisible demon dogs that work for Vothule, the Underworld King. They have the body of a dog and a tail like a sabre.

Sarmira: A powerful necromancer sorceress. Ultimate power of evil. Has the ability to raise the dead, create poisons, read minds of anyone. Often places memory stamps on her victims. Necromancers see the undead and can possess the bodies of others. As long as they breathe the essence of life, they can live forever. Weakness is Labradorite.

Trek: Ogre-like creatures that can have skin shades from green to a pale white. They have the innate ability to shift into anything.

Vothule: King of the underworld. Sarmira's superior.

LADORIELLE AND ELLEIRODAL
THE SISTER PLANETS

Ashengale: City of dragons

Ashville Rock: A community that resides within the Underground city.

Crimson Moors: The physical dimension on Elleirodal and the only path that leads to The House of Bloodbane.

Elleirodal: (Elle- ir o dal) Elleirodal and home of Zhir and the twin planet to Ladorielle.

Giant Country: A heavy mountainous terrain where giants and Iknes Shaw live among each other.

Hannah: A Tora'Nari and Arryn's sister.

House of Dhalri: Nyta's people of Nuknir, who were overthrown on Elleirodal and sought refuge in the Underground City. Their queen rules under the umbrella of Dragonscale.

Geneviève's Ranch: An Elvin city where Geneviève, Redmae, and Rory are from.

Grengore Mines: Area where minerals are located and the tunnel to the Lake of No Return.

Ladorielle Territory: An area that is at war with the underworld that's trying to overtake the land.

Ladorielle: (La- door - ē – elle) Twin planet to Elleirodal. Ladorielle is divided into three continents. Ladorielle Territories, Storm Castle Realm, and Dragonscale Island. The Storms once ruled all of Ladorielle, with Dragonscale Island coexisting on the same planet. Elleirodal's realm and the house of Zhir plan to take over both realms.

Pine Willow Valley: The place where Geneviève's ranch is located.

Scale Rock: The crevasse cavern where the Iknes Shaw live.

Scarlet Hollow: A place where the supernatural go after they die.

Scarlet Hollow's Veil: The space between where the subconscious—and sometimes conscious—meet the dead.

Shadow Vine Forest: The home of the Dryads and haven for fairies.

Songbird Meadow: The meadow where the killer birds sing their prey to sleep.

Storm Castle: Where the Storm family resides.

Thermyah: (There- my- a) A Sea witch.

Underground City: A hidden place beneath the Dragonscale Island. It's like a world within a world; the city is as large as a continent with many communities.

Wisteria Keep: The city where Fae, live. They welcome shadow elves, and those of dark blood. You must be morally grey to enter. However, neutrality is acceptable. They are enemies with The House of Zhir.

THE HOUSES

Dragonscale: Ruler of the universe and the balance of power with good vs. evil.

The Council: the circle of balance. The ruler of each realm seats at the table of balance. They are the high courts of the universe. Each house has their own set of rules and leaders. If a decision cannot be made, it is brought up to the council for a vote.

- House of Storm ~ Nytemires (hybrid Vampire/Necromancer)
- House of Deagon ~ Dragons
- House of Fernshadow ~ Elves
- House of Fae 'Oria ~ Dryads
- House of Grengore ~ Trek (aka ogres and goblins)
- House of Zhir ~ Vothule's underworld and Sarmira's home. (necromancer)
- House of Silverback ~ The wolves
- House of Bloodbane ~ Vampires
- House of Ashburn ~ Light Witches Coven
- House of Shaw ~ Iknes Shaw snake people.

- House of Dhor ~ Giants
- House of Odewyn ~ Wizards
- House of Ironstone ~ Dwarves
- House of Dhalri ~ Dark Elves
- House of Shadow Raven ~ Dark Witch Coven

About the Author

Emmy R. Bennett lives in the Pacific Northwest and grew up in Washington State in a Lutheran household. Although she's strong in her faith, she believes everyone has the right of free will, in their beliefs.

When she isn't at her desk writing, she's spending time with her family, gardening, crafting, or reading.

She loves to study genealogy and her family line has been traced back to the Vikings. It's one of the many inspirations from which she's drawn to write.